UNSTAKE MY HEART

SUE JAMES

Dedication

To Lauren, thank you for always being the kind of best friend I could share my limbo winnings with.

Chapter One
BRITTANY

Blood smelled like a 7-Eleven.

I guess it was probably different for every vampire, but as I stepped into the attic and the intoxicating sweetness curled its way through the stale air, I couldn't help but think of that ice cold slushie machine creating hypnotizing swirls of brightly colored frozen goodness. My mouth watered as a delightful pain shot through my gum line and an exhilaration bubbled within me.

A metallic beeping sound pierced through the dark room as I struggled to focus past the smell of blood making my throat clench. The piercing sound that had tracked my tiny friends life, came to a long drawn out pulse before silence took over the space.

"You killed him!"

Soryn snarled at me, "I have extinguished many souls in my years, Brittany." Her words rolled past her teeth— a deep accent from a bygone era coating every syllable. "This one means nothing."

My words hitched in my throat as a black silhouette crossed my vision. If my heart still beat, it would have leaped in my chest as the ghost of my small friend flickered in and out, "He meant something to me!"

"I will never understand you mortals." She let out a puff of air before snatching Jazz from my hands and tossing him into a far corner of the dark and mold scented room. "Can we focus on why I summoned you, please?"

"Twelve years, Soryn. I've never kept anything alive for that long."

"Twelve days." She corrected with an annoyed lilt.

"You could show a little sympathy."

"It's not my fault. I have no experience with your little tommygotchum. If it was that important to you, you shouldn't have put the troublesome creature in my care."

"It's a Tamagotchi." I stared at the little egg while a fresh wave of musical beeps sounded a hopeful cheer. My claw tipped fingers itched to pluck it from the corner.

"Can we be done sulking over your magic egg now?" She made her way across the room, following a patch of the dark wooden plank floor. The flickering candle light illuminated her path, showing traces where something large had been dragged, pushing the decades of dust aside. Her long fingers closed around the bronze handle of a door, the rust leaving dark speckles on her pale hands. An ear splitting squeal rent through the air as she opened the small closet with one quick swing. A hard thump shook the rickety floor as a body, its front covered in a mixture of old and fresh blood, crashed at her feet. "You will not yell at me for this one too, will you?"

My eyes stayed fixed on the bright blue bowling shirt. Patches of dried blood left sections of the material crumpled and stiff on the chest of the lifeless body in front of me.

"What did you do?" A tingle shuddered through my gum line and into my canines as I inhaled the sickly sweet smell and my mind whirled with hunger. "Did you have to make such a mess?"

"Believe it or not, the blood isn't my fault this time." A deep chuckle left her lips while the soft moonlight faded through the cracked window.

"Alright, let's get him out of here before the smell makes it downstairs."

If you would have told me a few months ago that I would be throwing the dead body of my ex down a well, I would have laughed. Not only at the fact that I had a boyfriend to dispose of, but an ex one at that. As we tipped Keith over the moss coated stone circle, the sound of Soryn's heart beat was a steady drum in my ears. She giggled at my side when the distant sound of flesh hitting the watery tomb below made it back to her ears.

I leveled a stern expression on her, and her soft laughter trilled away.

She took my hand and we walked back toward the old farmhouse. "I'm sorry. Would you feel better if I got you a new magic Tomagotchu thingy."

My new fangs poked my lip as I smiled.

Chapter Two
BRITTANY

"Hey, Brit! I got the drop off from the Ellis estate here!"
Keith's voice was hard to hear over the mix of crooning
from Henry Hall on the old record player, and Savage Garden
from my headphones.

"Coming." My hands moved quickly to wrap the long black
chord around the broken CD player, as it skipped and sputtered
out *Crash and Burn*.

The bright sun filled the antique shop with a cozy warmth as I
quickly made my way through row upon row of old antiques and
knickknacks. At Day's End was the pride and joy of my Grandma
Winnie. And it was just as quirky as she was. The shop was filled
with aging belongings that had outlived their previous owners.
Most people would have just thrown them in the heap pile. Not my
grandmother. She turned our family's generations old antique and
artifact business into a strange hodgepodge of hobbies that
refused to expire with the hands that had once created and

cherished them. I loved this place. The only thing that could make it any better was standing at the doorway.

My heart skipped along with the record as I fidgeted and fussed to stop its rotation. "I really appreciate you going out of your way to do this for us. It's really nice." My cheeks flushed as I jerked at the needled arm, heat flooding my chest and face as *Here Comes The Bogeyman* finally came to a staccato-ed ending.

"Yeah, no sweat." Keith's eyes wandered, taking in the surroundings, his tall frame blocking the doorway. His dark frost tipped hair made my heart beat a little faster, and bright smile flooded my face as my excitement fluttered in my stomach. What would it be like to twirl my fingers through those unruly locks while he smiled down at me? His usual ti-dyed shirt was covered with a black plaid button up that really brought out the deep brown of his eyes. He clung to a heavy-looking box, his long fingers gripping the firm cardboard. I imagined his hands being rough. Fingers covered in calluses from hours of strumming soulful tunes on his guitar.

"Um, Brittany?" I jumped as his soft voice broke through my day dream. My eyes went wide as I realized I had stopped moving to stare at him.

A knot stuck in my throat as I struggled to recover from my stupor and my legs pushed forward awkwardly through the maze like set up of the store. Instead of straight rows of aisles, Grandma Winnie had turned the place into a switchback of winding oddities. Keith smiled at me again as my feet traversed the trove of death treasures. I made my way past an old wooden puppet that hung from its strings off of a large brightly painted armoire. I tossed him back a red faced grin as I skirted around the thin suit of armor which held purses from its propped arms.

"Are there many boxes?" I puffed as I spoke, half out of breath from my hurry and half from the anticipation of spending time with him.

His eyes looked back toward the parking lot where his faded yellow car was parked. "There's probably eight or so more in the back seat." He lifted the cardboard flap and pulled what looked to be a shadow box containing a skeletal fairy posed in dance. "This isn't even the weirdest one."

Meanwhile, my knee tangled with the row of rocking chairs to my left, sending them nodding back and forth in an angry wave while I fell to the floor.

A sharp intake of air came right before the sound of glass being jostled. My body froze in embarrassment. Maybe if I laid completely still, I would blend in to the dark red carpet under me. Unfortunately, my bright blue cropped sweater would still give me away.

The surrounding air shifted as he came to stand beside me and offered his hand down. They were much softer that I imagined they would be. Heat rushed through every inch of my skin as he pulled me from the floor.

"First day with your new legs?" He smirked, proud of his jest.

"Apparently."

His smile was a gorgeous and brilliant white. Years of braces throughout high school and my teeth still didn't compare. *Stop staring at his mouth, Brittany!* My head spun as I took a step back, aching at the space I left between us.

As if reading my mind, Keith moved to fill it again.

A nervous sputtering of syllables flowed from my mouth before a final, "What's in the box?" came out in an over dramatic yell.

He put the distance back between us before tucking his hands in his pockets. "Uh, yeah. Here." He picked up the cardboard box and placed it on a sticker covered steamer trunk, pushing the flaps aside to reveal a collection that would rival anything else in the shop. We pulled several glass boxes from inside, each one haphazardly covered in newspaper, and each one stranger than the last.

Mr. Ellis had been a self proclaimed entomologist in his life, so I had expected at least a few cases of butterflies with their wings stretched and pinned for display, but this was something else all together. Each insect had been posed and pinned into a scene. Just from this box there was a family of spiders sunbathing at the beach, beetles wielding what looked to be lances in an Arthurian arena, and a butterfly winged fairy dancing with a moth winged death. Of all the strange things that came through the shop, this was quickly becoming one of my favorites.

"This old dude was a freak." Keith said.

A momentary panic surged through me before I spoke. "Yeah. Totally grody." I lied.

The next half hour was filled with the jostle of boxes and the creak of wood as we moved each of Mr. Ellis' masterpieces down to the basement for later inventorying.

The small subterranean space was brightly lit and overflowing from the stone floor to the dark wooden ceiling with items that even Grandma Winnie didn't think would fare well in the shop above us.

"Whoa," Keith's fingers brushed over an ornamental scabbard resting on the powder pink work desk that held the shop's inventory and shipping logs. The gold sheath of the dagger was covered in onyx jewels of various shapes and sizes as swirls of stamped metal flowed down to where the blade curved slightly.

"This thing is wicked." His voice was low as he unsheathed it, obviously in awe of the weapon.

"My grandma uses it to open boxes." I let out a tiny laugh as his face fell, his find turning out to be no more than a weird old lady's office equipment.

"So it's like a fake?" The metal gave a gentle tinking sound as he flipped it end over end several times, each time catching it by the pommel before tossing it up again.

Worried that he may break her favorite letter opener, I reached for the blade. "Gah!"

The weighty dagger and sheath let out a sharp metal clank as they fell to the floor, followed quickly by silent drops of scarlet. A pinging sound made its way toward the far wall of the basement.

"Oh, my god. Are you alright?" Keith stared at the blood now puddled in the palm of my hand.

"I'm sorry. I shouldn't have grabbed it like that. I'm okay. I just need a band aide."

His own blood drained from his face as he brought a fist to his mouth.

"Can we cover it up?" Keith had panic in his voice as his eyes searched the room. He grabbed a roll of silk fabric from the nearby shelf and tossed it to me. My heart sank as I instinctively caught it before it hit my face. I stared down at the bloodstained silk tapestry and mishandled blade.

"That wasn't a fake either." I said under my breath, a sour feeling sinking deeper into my stomach as I watched the antique cloth seep up more of my blood.

Keith let out an annoyed puff of air before pacing around the small area. "So, is the other side filled with more of this weird stuff or what?" He gestured with a nod of his head toward the wall, where several large paintings hung. Grandma Winnie's style had taken over the basement office. It was most apparent in the large portraits. Each one had some type of addition to make what would have been a scene of stoic faces into whimsical art.

"Oh, that's my Grandma's work." I smiled as I walked to my favorite of the canvases. The floor to ceiling work of collaboration was once a portrait of a handsome young Colonial man painted to be wearing the style of clothing of the French Revolution. The young man looked to be no older than Keith, and was perched against an enormous tree trunk. Grandma had added large blooms to the branches of the tree as well as rose-colored glasses, feathered boa and a few other bright pops of color, all made from felt and fabric. Nothing permanent that would completely ruin the painting, but it was altered none the less.

"It's just what you see here." I smiled hopefully at Keith. He hadn't liked Mr. Ellis' fun bug boxes, but a hope bubbled in me that he would enjoy these.

"No, not the weird pictures." He knocked against the low, arching wall, "The other side of this wall."

"There's nothing on the other side. This is the entire basement."

"I don't think so. My grandma had the same root cellar conversion setup in her house. It was hella creepy, too. Here, come take a listen." He gestured me over before knocking on the space between two of the paintings. My ear chilled against the canary yellow paint as the hollow knocking gave off a strange echo. "This wall is definitely separating the space."

He shrugged, as I folded my make shift bandage on the chair. The cut hadn't been all too deep. "The med kit is upstairs. I should really cover this before I handle anything else. He nodded and headed back toward the steps.

The usual warmth from the upstairs shop seemed absent as the cold air from below leeched on to my clammy skin. Bone rattling chills raced down my spine and a haunting shadow seemed to follow my every move.

"Hey, I gotta bounce, but when you're done working, would you want to come hang out? A couple of us are headed to The Rink, if you wanna tag along."

The Rink was the place to be on most nights. Although I usually avoided large social gatherings, I had, on several occasions, tried my hand at bowling. Mostly just during the daytime hours when most of the usual Rink goers were in class at the University. My heart sputtered out a beat that would have rivaled the Beastie Boys as I answered, "Totally." My neck strained as I struggled to tamp down my shaking nerves.

Keith pushed his hair out of his eyes and arced a brow in my direction. "Cool."

My body froze as a montage of us played through my mind. His quick hands tying the laces of my skates before pulling me around the floor. All the while, *As Long As You Love Me* played in the background. After that, he would stand behind me, placing his hands on mine while showing me how to properly roll a bowling ball down the slick lane. Everyone around us would jump and cheer as the ball collided with the pins in a strike just as his lips collided with mine...

"Earth to Brittany." All at once I was back in the shop, and Keith was giving me a knowing look from the open doorway.

"The Rink. Yeah!" My hands tugged on the bottom of my sweater. "Sure. I could probably make it."

"Sweet." He dipped his head low. "I'll see you there."

My knees were goo. Keith, my crush all throughout high school, just asked me to hang with him. At The Rink. With him. I had thought all hope for a happily ever after with him had faded after graduation. Almost everyone went to Sedgemoore University. Most of my graduating class was now half way to their forever, or whatever awaited them after college life. That dream for me was delayed when Grandma Winnie's health went south. My schedule quickly dropped from full attendance to a few night classes before freshman year even started.

Now that I knew that hope wasn't shattered and tossed to the wind, nothing was going to ruin this perfect day.

"Hey Honey Bear! We got an emergency." If my eyes could have gotten any larger, they would have popped right out of my face. Keith let a small chuckle escape as my mom bounded across the parking lot in quick strides.

Leave it to my mother to make a liar out of me.

Chapter Three
BRITTANY

"I'm so sorry, sweetie. If I had known you were...busy."

"Mom, please don't." My cheeks burned as I stared out the window. I sighed as Keith's yellow hatchback faded down the old cobbled road that led away from the antique shop. "And, it's alright. You need me."

She let out a soft but pained sound, "I need you too much. But I promise. I'm going to get some help for the shop this year." She placed a large stack of papers on the counter. "So that means, you should get yourself over to the university and enroll in some more classes." A bright smile bloomed over her face.

"For real?"

"For real." The smile faded as she got back to business sorting through the teetering stacks of papers.

"So, you said there was an emergency?" I asked.

"I found another stack of orders that never got sent out." She rounded the glass counter full of quirky, aging trinkets and tossed me an apologetic smile. "We've got a decent bit of shipments to pack, but we can knock it out in a few hours."

I flipped through the stack of papers. "Let's get started then." She was back from the basement with the supplies we needed by the time I was done looking through the stack. She wasn't wrong. It was going to take a few hours to get through this mess. The papers hit the desk with a thud as I stared out the window toward the direction of The Rink. Maybe, if we moved quick, I could still make it.

I grabbed a big stack of folded boxes and the familiar stamp seal that marked most of the shop's outgoing shipments. The mark of the Dorsetty Company- a trade business out of New York that pulled items for rich collectors. If it weren't for them, this place would have tanked decades ago. Almost the entire inventory we were pulling was going to them with a few choice pieces heading to the University.

"Have you talked to them yet?" The smooth metal handle of the stamp was at home in my hand. It was an oddly satisfying feeling to squeeze the manifest paper between the circular clamp. My fingers traced over the now bumpy seal. Pressed into the paper was a tree with branches curling to sharp points that held hanging fruit. "Are they going to cancel the contract?"

"I don't know, Brit." Her head hung low. "But would that really be the worst thing?"

It was as if a bucket of ice cold water had been lobbed at my head. "What do you mean, mom?"

"Don't get me wrong, I have some great memories in this old place but..." She paused, collecting her words while sealing another box with the brown packing tape, the sound punctuating her silence.

"But?"

"But this place was never my dream. I'm so glad that you and your grandma connected to this place in a way that I never did, but I'm just not sure that I want to continue with it once she's gone."

It was a knife to the heart. "I put my life on hold after graduation to help keep this place going."

"And you shouldn't have had to." She was quick to interject, as if the words had been readied on the tip of her tongue for some time.

She had always held a little resentment for the store, but I never thought that she would throw all the hard work we had put into it aside so easily. "I was happy to do it." I said. It wasn't a complete lie.

"Well, you might not need to for much longer." Her eyes pulled away from mine as she realized what she said. Though regret was pasted across her face, I didn't give her a chance to apologize.

A storm of fire surged through my veins as I stared at her in shocked betrayal. "Is that why you want to sign me up for classes at the university? Because I'm not going to have a job soon, anyway? Grandma Winnie is still here! You shouldn't talk like that."

"You've already had to put your life on hold. Your twenty years old, Brittany. You deserve to be out there living, not babysitting junk left behind by the dead. I spent way too many of my days and nights here and every day I think of what my life would have been like if I hadn't."

"Well, if you would like to mourn you not having a life when you were younger, then that's on you." My heart twisted in my chest at the words spilling out of me.

I hadn't felt this kind of rage toward my mom since I was fourteen and she had accidentally donated my entire collection of Babysitters Club books. This was infinitely worse.

"Look. Nothing is settled yet." She ran her hands over my shoulders. "Mr. Dorsetty said he wouldn't even consider having any kind of contract written until…" She paused, obviously not wanting to say the words.

"How kind of him." Disdain oozed from my every syllable. My anger churned into an uneasy pit in the bottom of my stomach. Even if he was trying to take the store, talking badly about Mr. Dorsetty wasn't right. His family had long run their own business and had, throughout the years, always taken care of shops like ours. Without his connections, At Day's End would have long been turned in to some cheesy themed restaurant or bougie boutique. Several interested parties had tried to purchase the space over the years. Thankfully, Grandma Winnie had never been interested in selling.

"I know. It's not the easiest thing in the world, but I think it might be what's best for us." She gave me a sad smile. "You can't go explore the history of the world if you never leave this town."

"So what happens now?" My voice sounded far away, my mind disconnected from me.

"For now, I keep taking care of Grandma Winnie. Our insurance is going to cover the live in nurse for at least the next few months." The unspoken words were there. She would only need a few months. Her eyes held a sheen to them when she turned them back to me. "And you, go pump some ancient history into that big brain of yours." I nodded, the motion making me slightly sea sick.

My stomach was in knots by the time I grabbed for another piece of the thick brown packing paper, wadding it up into a ball before shoving it in between two wooden figures that had been nestled together at the bottom of the cardboard box. "Who are you going to hire to help with the store?"

"Mr. Dorsetty is actually helping with that." She gave another apologetic smile. "We thought it would make things easier with the transition, when and if we sold At Day's End to them."

Nausea roiled in my belly, as the blood drained from my face. Easier transition? Nothing about losing the only place that had been constant in my childhood felt easy.

"Great. Let me guess. You're going to want me to train said help to take my job. Am I right?"

"Yes. But it shouldn't be too hard, since he's already pretty familiar with how things go around here." She smiled, "Remember Ben?"

I did, in fact, remember Ben. I had spoken with him on several occasions, each one more irritating than the last. Mr. Dorsetty's assistant was the last person I wanted running our shop.

Instead of letting out the scream that was building from every fiber of my being, my fingers curled around the bronze lever that opened the antique cash register to my right. The drawer punched out to reveal our till as well as my stash of treats. The scream I had been trying to avoid was replaced with a small yelp as I ripped into a Milky Way and chomped down hard on my tongue.

My mom was quick to act on it. "When was the last time you actually ate something?"

The half empty wrapper crinkled as I waved it in the air.

She shook her head before taking the candy from my hand to finish it herself. "How about I go get us a pizza?"

I nodded while my stomach growled in agreement. It was enough to break the tension. My mom gave a soft chuckle, slinging her heavy carpet bag over her shoulder. For someone who seemed to hate this place, she sure had an affinity with out-of-date pieces herself. "I'll be back in an hour." She wove her way in and out toward the door. "Oh, and if, by chance, you finish packing shipments before I'm back, would you mind doing me a favor and trying to find the stone that's missing from that letter opener in the office? It looks like it fell off the desk or something and broke." She shrugged, "It's silly, but your Grandma would be devastated if she saw it like that."

"Oh yeah, mom I need to tell you about..." She closed the door before I could ask her about the basement wall. It would just have to wait until she got back.

My eyes narrowed on the large stack of items that still needed to be wrapped and packed. A large assortment of nesting dolls stared back at me. "Actually, you can wait a little longer."

Chapter Four
BRITTANY

The stairs creaked as I made my way back down into the office. A heady cloud of dread hung in the air around the arching, yellow painted, brick room. The basement seemed…ominous? The strange sensation was out of place here. When I was smaller and Grandma sent me down for a quick errand, I had that same feeling of being too small for the space. It gripped me like icy claws.

A broken creak spread through the all too quiet basement as I stepped down and waited on the bottom step. A small alarm sounded in my head and my ear twitched. It was fascinating how humans still possessed such a strong fight-or-flight response. We had long since been prey and yet evolution hadn't disposed of it yet. If it had, I probably would have a much easier time not being a total weirdo in front of Keith. A warm sensation worked its way through me as I thought of meeting up later.

The ornate scabbard was placed back in its sheath on the desk, and the tapestry that Keith had tossed on the chair was still there. Still ruined. I would deal with that later. The ancient blade was heavy as I rolled it in my hands, the smooth crystals sliding along my palm. The spot my mom had mentioned was, in fact, missing a dime sized onyx stone.

The lingering dread had disappeared as I moved around the familiar space on my hands and knees. Cobwebs clung to my long blond hair as I pulled myself from beneath the desk. Nothing had been under there but crumbs from my breakfast and several pieces of broken stone that had worked themselves out of the earth packed floor. There was no denying, if I held on to the shop, it would need some serious renovations. Sooner rather than later.

The thought plunged me further into my hunt.

My fingers traced their way around the floor, searching for the stone between boxes and shelves. The room wasn't especially large, but the bronze clock on the desk seemed to tick out an eternity of seconds as I searched. Disappointment coated my skin thicker that the cobwebs that stuck to me. Mom was right. Grandma Winnie would be heartbroken if she saw one of her favorite treasures broken.

With an exasperated grunt, I sat myself down on the cold floor with the pommel of the ornate blade resting on my knee. I stared at the wall. More specifically, I stared at the space in between the shelves and portraits. Something seemed off about it. How had I never noticed it before? Of the four walls that made up the space, this was the only one not made of beams and stone. The rocks that lined the floor and walls seemed to continue on underneath it, cut off by more modern materials. A cloudy image pulled at my mind. The smell of cut drywall and sawdust. Something from when I was little, perhaps. A faint memory of another remodel when I was much, much younger.

Unstake My Heart

My eyes roved over the wall as a memory pecked at my brain of bricks once standing in its place. A glint off of the smooth black surface of an onyx stone signaled an end to my search. I crawled over and plucked the stone from its resting place. A chill ran down my spine as the fear that had hung in the air when I first descended into the basement seeped into my skin again. Goosebumps raced down my arms as I slowly tilted my chin forward and glanced up.

The portrait of the colonial gentleman smirked down at me as I knelt at the bottom of the gilded frame. Another bit of gold peeked from beneath one of Grandma Winnie's artistic additions. The bright pink splotch left an abstract puddle around the gentleman's waist, no doubt to mimic some kind of skirt or tutu. Part of the felt had rolled up on itself, revealing the man's belt.

The felt was scratchy under my fingers as I tugged it away from the painting. I stared at the object in my hand, then back at the canvas. There, painted forever to the man's hip, dangled an ornate gold dagger, the exact match to the one that now rested in my hand.

There was absolutely no way that this was the same blade. It couldn't possibly be. If it was, it would belong in a museum. Although, to be honest, so did this painting. I peeled another piece of felt aside, this one a cerulean blue bubble that was covering a portion of the tree trunk with a carving that read SH + CC wrapped in an uneven heart. The blue fabric joined the pink splotch on the floor as my hands wandered over the work of art.

My heart pounded faster as another blue bubble peeled away. Another burst of gold was underneath, but this one was substantially different. This one was made of metal, not paint. The strange object, set into the canvas, looked like an odd keyhole made to match the dagger. The same onyx stones were fitted around its edges.

My hand seemed to move on its own as I placed the pointed tip of the blade in the keyhole and pushed. A clicking sound made my ears prick up just before the knife moved, plunging itself further into the painting before starting a slow spin. A mechanical whirring came from behind the wall and echoed into the space.

Blood rushed through my ears. My pulse let out an uneven beat until, all at once, everything stilled. Seconds were like an eternity as I held by breath, the sound of my heartbeat was deafening in the haunting silence.

The painting gave a soft creak as one side slowly swung away from the wall. My eyes struggled to adjust to the dark space beyond, although a gentle glow seemed to emanate from the far side of the room. I took a deep breath, expecting the aroma of mold and dust to flood my nostrils, but found none. Instead, I was met with a soft vanilla and woodsy scent. Incense, possibly?

The light from the office seemed to be swallowed up by the room. The space where I now stood was a stark contrast to the one on the other side of the fake wall. The walls that had been painted yellow on my side were left to age in peace there. Its once white mortar was slightly stained by time. It reminded me of the buildings that made up downtowns historical district except for one obvious difference. Besides the funeral home, none of the buildings downtown had coffins.

My body froze. What was in the coffin? Did I really want to find out? Of course I did.

My feet sounded like anvils crashing on stone as I closed the empty distance. The only thing between myself and the mysterious box being strange divots in the space's floor. An invisible hand seemed to pull me in closer and closer; the warm scent getting stronger and stronger with each step forward.

A surge of adrenaline flooded the highway of my veins at top speed, making my body act faster than my brain. My fingers closed around the edge of the lid and before I could rethink or back out, I pulled.

Nothing happened.

The lid, whether locked from key or time, wouldn't budge. I took a deep, steadying breath and tried again. My face was feverish from exertion by the time I finally took a step back and huffed my frustration into the air. This wasn't working. Although brute force should never be the first method of exploration, sometimes it's needed. Like when there is a mysterious casket sitting in a dark, hidden room in your grandma's basement.

Cardio wouldn't be something I would have to worry about for a while. Not even the winding inventory upstairs slowed my hunt as I gathered lamps and extension chords from around At Day's End to aid my task. The tunnel like room was bathed in light in a matter of minutes, chords strung out through the doorway and branching out over the bumpy floor.

The bumps created another mystery. A vast array of shapes, and symbols had been etched into the cobblestone floor.

The heavy rusted metal toolbox that had come from last month's estate sale haul jostled and crashed as I lugged it to the front of the casket. Now, in the light, I saw that several of the symbols on the floor were also carved into the intricate and ornate resting place.

A cloud of frantic energy engulfed me. I had to get this opened. Whatever was inside needed to be found. I sensed it. The bitterness of rusted iron sat heavy in my mouth as I struggled with the latches that held the tool box shut. A puff of dark orange grime coated my hands, but the latch finally gave way. Yes! I held the claw hammer I took from the pile and pried at the wooden lid. What was this thing sealed with? Cement? No matter how hard I tried, the coffin lid wouldn't budge. My desperation steadily climbed as I dropped the hammer and began clawing at the seam with my fingers.

"Brittany!" Mom's voice sent a shock wave through my body as her voice floated down from the shop above. "Brittany?"

"Coming." I yelled up to her, scrambling to cover up my mess. I quickly pulled at the chords that connected the lamps and darkness engulfed the hidden room again. The bloody tapestry that had rested on the office chair now brushed the floor as I draped it over the unopened casket.

The all consuming determination that had coated my mind began to slowly pull back until a burst of air left my lungs and the heavy panic that had weighed on me was suddenly gone.

"What the..." My head spun in an uneasy wave. "That was weird." I muttered under my breath while making my way back upstairs. An overpowering need to tell someone what happened sped my steps upstairs. "Hey! You're not going to believe—"

"I'm sorry, honey, but I'm going to have to drop the pizza and run. The new nurse just got called back to the hospital, so I've got to get back to your grandma's house before he can leave."

"Is everything alright?"

"I'm sure everything will be fine, but I have to run now." She gave me a quick hug and a peck on the cheek before heading back out the door. "I just wanted to make sure you got some food first. Love you!" The door gave a cheerful chime as it closed behind her. The sun was barely visible behind the tree covered horizon as she walked across the darkening parking lot.

The white and red checkered pizza box was still hot as I sat it on the glass counter. Canadian bacon and mushroom should have been an inviting enough aroma to have my stomach raging with hunger. Instead, my thoughts strayed back to the basement. "What just happened?"

Movement came from behind me. A quick sound of something brushing against fabric left my hairs standing on edge.

"Mom?" *Don't be stupid Brittany. You just saw her go out the front door.*

"You are an adult, idiot." I pursed my lips and made my way back downstairs, but once again found myself frozen on the bottom step; no more than a statue as my eyes adjusted again to the darkness.

Something moved.. There, in the inky recesses of the chamber, was the casket; its lid opened and, standing in front of it, a shadow. The darkened figure with glowing red eyes held the blood stained tapestry in its clawed hands.

It inhaled the fabric before letting out an otherworldly hiss that sent an electrical current skittering over my skin. My body didn't move — wouldn't move, as the figure walked, no — glided across the distance between us.

I stuttered out, "Who...." I choked down my fear. "I'll give you whatever you want. Just please. Don't hurt me."

A faint laugh pierced the electrified air as a thick accent rolled from the creature's lips, "Dear girl. You have already given me what I wanted. But..." It stepped into the soft light of the office, "that doesn't mean I will not still hurt you." She smiled, showing two dangerously sharp fangs.

Fangs! And her pale skin and dark curls only accentuated the horror of her fiery eyes. Eyes that seemed to cut through me like hot knives, leaving me exposed. My mind reeled with thoughts of whatever terror this monster might inflict upon me.

The deep jewel green of her flowing gossamer dress was an ethereal contrast to her sharp features. In an instant, she was at my side, raising her dagger like finger nails to my cheek.

"Now. Be a darling and tell me where I can find..." She paused, raking her gaze up and down my figure at an achingly slow pace. A snarl pulled at her blood-red lips. "How long have I been in slumber?"

My mouth was dry as cracked desert earth as I struggled to scratch out incomprehensible sounds.

"I am quite famished. So, unless you can be of use to me in some other way, I would suggest you try your very hardest to say something that I can understand." She smiled again. It wasn't a friendly smile. It was the smile of someone who took pleasure in others' fear. And I was petrified. My body had forgone its statue like state and instead shook uncontrollably.

"What year is it and where is the owner of this home?"

A sharp pain shot through me as she drug her nail along my cheek. A warm trickle of blood burned at my skin as she wiped the drop away, bringing the bright red liquid to her lips. A low growl resonated from her chest.

"19 — 1999."

The growl intensified at my answer. Her voice held a deadly fury back as she spoke again in my ear, "And the owner?"

"Cordain. My grandma Winnie Cordain." Despite my frightened gasps, she understood me.

"Cordain." She spit my family's name out like a curse. As if it was rotten in her mouth. She pushed past me. The train of her dress cascaded up the steps as the many gold chains and trim around her waist left tiny tinkling sounds echoing through the room and a set of keys gently clanked on her golden belt.

The chime of the door continued to ring in my head long after it had stopped. She left me behind in the dark office with nothing but an empty casket and a mind full of questions.

With my feet no longer stuck in mental quicksand, I paced the space, quickly but cautiously making my way to the empty resting place. I stared inside, hoping that I had imagined every terrifying detail of what had just happened. I have never hoped to be staring at a rotting corpse before, but there was nothing I wanted more at that moment. Unfortunately, nothing but an almost empty box stood in front of me. In the middle of the rich purple satin lining of the coffin rested a small golden pouch.

Unstake My Heart

My voice was strained as I tried to piece together what had just happened, hoping that it would make more sense if I said it all out loud. It didn't.

"There's a vampire; in a coffin, behind a hidden door, that opens with a dagger, in the basement of my grandma's shop. My grandma's shop. My grandma's dagger. My grandma's hidden vampire?" A sharp intake of breath sent a clear thought through my head. "I gave a blood sucking monster my grandma's name!" I willed my legs to go faster as I made for my blue Toyota. "Damn it, Brittany!"

A cloud of dust streaked behind my car as I planted my foot on the gas petal. The gold pouch was still clasped tightly in my right hand.

Chapter Five
SORYN

The dark woods hadn't changed. The ancient trees leafy, weighted bows held skeletal branches that created a natural cover for the ghosts that walked below them, their dim blue light casting shadows along the root covered earth.

1999. My body had succumbed to sleep for two hundred and nineteen years. The hunger weakness pulled at my limbs. I should have drained the girl dry, but the pull of her blood fueled my centuries old rage.

Shame.

A bright glow of lantern light swung through the trees as I made my way through the forest. Its power was greater than any fire I had ever seen. My throat stung with the need to eat. If there were lanterns, then there were people, and I was in desperate need of a hot meal.

The lights moved at devilish speeds. What kind of witchcraft was this?

The blanket of overgrown nature thinned as I reached what I thought was the town's edge. My eyes peered for a great distance. The town had outgrown my memory of it. What should have been a small sleepy haven was now a brightly lit and noisy metropolis. Carriages moved rapidly while lights of many colors peppered my sight.

"Where are you?" As soon as I breathed the question into the chaotic night air, I caught a familiar scent. Cordain blood. The girl was traveling. What were the chances she would lead me straight to grandmother's house? My fangs itched to follow. And so I did.

Chapter Six
BRITTANY

My tires crunched and kicked up rocks along the winding road before skidding to a stop just behind my moms car. The nurses truck was already gone leaving my usual parking space wide open for me.

Good. Maybe that would mean that he was safe.

"Brittany? Why aren't you at the shop?" Mom must have heard me pull up the drive. "Is everything alright?" She rushed down the steps of the Georgian style home.

I stared at her. Did I tell her? Would she think I was losing it? Was I losing it? Her eyes were shining above her red cheeks as she sniffled down at me.

She had been crying.

Again.

"Is grandma okay?" I held my breath, waiting in the chilly night air for an answer I didn't want.

She wiped her cheek with the sleeve of her coat. "Oh. Yes." She smiled through her sniffles. "She's having a tough day. Is that why you…"

"Yeah." Something had upset her and if it wasn't already a blood sucking member of the undead, I wasn't about to add to her troubles. A breeze looped through the early August air, bringing the smell of leaves and earth with it. Goosebumps peppered my skin as I scanned the tree line that surrounded the two story brick house.

The next hour crept by as I sat in the chair next to my grandmother's reading nook, staring out the window into the darkness below, the pouch I had taken from the casket in my hands. The fabric was lined with beads and matching thread that wove scrolling patterns across it. It reminded me of some of the costume pieces I had seen in the university's theatre productions. The smooth metal of the clasp came away easily as I slowly opened the mysterious bag. Inside was a small scroll. My finders traced the soft, slightly waxy paper. It was unlike any animal skin parchment I had ever encountered. The soft roll wanted to stay curled as I stretched it to its length. Long scrolling handwriting was written with thick charcoal colored ink. The parchment seemed to take on the light as I leaned in closer to the small lamp and read the text.

> *Ichor of the dead, shadowed by time and veils unsung,*
> *Give to me the breath of life, purchased by kindred tongue*
> *Twist what has been stolen to carve away the heart*
> *Until the moon bleeds malice born, and curse is rent apart.*
> *By blood sealed and bargain struck.*

I let out a small shriek when something small and brown hit the floor several feet away from me. A hard candy rolled across the well-worn wood before stopping at my feet.

"What's got you so jumpy, girl?" Grandma Winnie had been fast asleep when I came in and after convincing mom to take a much needed rest as well, I had been running through what I had to have imagined at the shop.

"Hey Grandma Winnie." My bare feet padded to the large ornate bed that I had climbed into on so many nights as a little girl. Sleep overs had been my favorite past times with her. That was before. When we had our own house. Before we had to sell it to help with this one. My mind went back to At Day's End. I hadn't thought to ask earlier, but if mom wanted to sell the shop, did that mean that she would want to sell Grandma Winnie's house as well?

The mattress sank where I crawled in, careful not to pull on any of the tubes or wires that helped keep one of my favorite people here. At least for a little while longer.

"Mom said you had a tough day." I smiled sadly at her.

"Better than you, apparently." She popped a shiny brown candy into her mouth, throwing the gold Werther's wrapper onto the growing pile in her lap. "Now, answer my question."

She had always been blunt. I loved that about her. It was something that I could never be.

"I just had a weird day at the shop. That's all."

"Mm-hmm," she rolled the candy in her mouth, the sound of it clicking on her teeth punctuating the sound. "And?"

"And. I'm just happy to be here. Spending time with you."

"You spend time with me every single day. That doesn't explain why you are looking through that window like you're trying to find the bogeyman." A slight tremor registered in her voice, and before I could ask on it, she was going again. "How is my shop? Are you taking care of it?" She stared into my eyes, searching for something.

"The shop is fine." I said, "Why? Should I be worried about the shop?"

"Are you worried about the shop?" She probed.

I narrowed my eyes at her. She may have been blunt, but bluffing had never been her strong suit. She had to have known about the room. She was the one that covered the painting. Even if I imagined the five foot four vampire princess, there was no way I imagined the hidden door to a crypt in the basement. On the other hand, she was sick. She had already had a hard day. I didn't want to push it. But, then again, I might not have much time left to ask. I shuddered at the thought. A gesture that she didn't miss.

"Brittany. I'm going to ask you something and you are going to be very honest with me. No matter how silly or strange you think it may sound."

My heart clambered as she reached for something buried in her side table. Her wrinkled and worn hands came back into view clutching a small leather journal. Her fingers shook, old age and a life full of hard work had taken its toll.

"I had always hoped to show this to your mother." She ran her hand over the pages. "I thought there would be more time." She laughed. "But time makes its own plan and we just have to roll with it." She pinched my chin before flipping through and stopping on a page. I studied the detailed sketch of the ornate dagger there as she studied me. She let out a breath. "Did you open the door?"

I swallowed hard. It was as if that same blade was sliding down my throat. "Yes."

She took a solid breath. More steady than I had seen her take since she had gotten sick. "Is she free?"

My heart dropped like a lead weight and lodged into the pit of my stomach. "Is who free, Grandma?"

At that moment, her face fell, all color draining from it as she stared off past my gaze. "Grandma. Is who free?"

Her hand rose. She stretched her long finger out in front of me. My eyes followed and locked onto the frightening face that hovered outside the two-story window.

"Her."

Panic gripped my entire body again as the machine at grandmas bedside started beeping angrily.

The old glass window did little to muffle the voice I had desperately hoped had belonged to a hallucination. "Hello, Winnie." She gave another wicked grin, just before her hands flew out grasping at thin air, her rich accent still coming through the glass pane. "No. No. No. No." Her body bobbed for a moment more before completely falling out of view. A muted thud was all that followed.

Chapter Seven
SORYN

*I*f I didn't eat soon, I was going to wither away. Well, if it was possible for me to die, at all, then I would wither away. But, as I was immortal even by vampires standards, it would still be quite troublesome. A slashing pain encased my heart punctuating my thoughts. Very troublesome indeed.

The woods provided a cover of darkness again as I waited to gain a bit more strength. To my great displeasure, my arrival had been less than agreeable.

However, from the terrified look on the girls face as well as the bob of her head as she tried to peek over the bottom of the window, I knew that I had brought an air of fear to the house. A house that was closed to me.

The Cordain's had done very well for themselves. Much better than their previous residence, or what they had made of it now.

The junk that had littered the place where their timber shack used to be reeked of dead people. And not in a good way.

The blond one was still trying her best to stay hidden. The top of her wispy hair and dull blue eyes were all to be seen as she moved to various placed around the window, trying to peer into the night.

The air smelled of leaves beginning to darken and return to the earth beneath the bark and bows that had once held them. Despite the years of progress and change, the woods were unchanged. The same darkness coated the mossy ground as I walked closer to the house.

Three hearts beat behind the brick walls. Two of them raced like horses galloping across a snake covered meadow. The beautiful sound of it made my own heart want to pulse within my chest again. It had been so long, I had long since stopped wondering what that might feel like.

My lips pulled up in a grin as the owner of the third heart beat began to stir from their slumber. My fangs brushed against my bottom lip and a low vibration hung in my throat.

I followed the mossy stone path that led out of sight around the house as the sound of water pouring made it to my ears.

A shaft of light played on the ground outside the old home. It was more lovely than I had even imagined it would be. The large windows and polished columns near the entrance, though showing signs of age, were a sign of wealth and prosperity of the Cordain clan. A traitor did not deserve such a life.

A shadow moved across the window as I placed a gentle knock on the door. A woman pulled the curtains aside before opening it. Yet another Cordain stood with the door barely ajar.

"Good evening, I am here for Winnie Cordain. Would you be so kind to let me in?"

Unstake My Heart

The woman's eyes were a lovely shade of brown that sparkled as she succumbed to my powers. "Please, come in. Make yourself at home."

"Oh darling. I am home." The sharp burn of hunger raged down my throat as I fought the urge to drain her veins. Her wrist was warm in my hand as I breathed her in before letting it go.

"Now," Her hand dropped like a weight to her side as she stared off into empty space, "Where might I find Winnie for I wish to speak with her."

A promise I had made centuries before warred against the painful hunger clawing at my insides. For the first time in two hundred and nineteen years I was awake. The blood called to me and I would have my fill before the night pulled back its veil.

Chapter Eight

BRITTANY

"**I** don't see her down there." I turned back to the bed, adrenaline shooting through my body like bolts of lighting.

"She's there. Which means we have a lot to talk about and not a lot of time to do it." She pointed to a beautifully stained roll-top desk that sat next to her little library of books. "There is a false front beneath the bottom right drawer. Just tug on it and it will come loose."

I ran to the window first, squeezing my body against the wall, I moved my neck just enough to get one eye peering down to the drive way below. Still no sign of the vampire. Oh, god. How was that a thought in my head? How was any of this even happening?

I slid to the desk and did as she asked, pulling on the sides of cherry stained wood. The shallow hidden drawer slid easily from its spot. Tucked inside was what looked to be a ornately designed handkerchief wrapped around a faded indigo journal. The silky fabric slid beneath my palm as I pulled it away from the small book.

"Come. Quickly." Grandma Winnie held her hand out to me.

"What is this?"

"Something I wanted to hand down to your mother." She looked at me through watery eyes, "I'm so sorry that it has come to this. Your mother was never prepared but you are."

"I don't understand what's going on. Grandma, who was that in the window?"

"That, my love, was Soryn Floaire. A vampire that tried to destroy our family but because of your ancestor, never got the chance. Two hundred and nineteen years ago, our family trapped her in our root cellar."

"Excuse me?" The papers rustled and threatened to slide out of the tattered binding.

"You know what I'm talking about, Brittany." She said, adjusting herself to sit up on her stack of pillows. "You saw the it once. When you were little."

The wisp of a memory circled my mind. The memory showed a cloud of dust where an aging brick wall had crumbled. The image tugged at the corners of my thoughts as if it were willing itself not to fade. Clear in my mind was a familiar painting, completely unmoved.

My fingers caught at the aging edges of paper as I flipped through the book. Between its pages were tucked old deeds, contracts, and several yellow tinged and faded photos that she handed to me. Several were of portraits, paintings, as well as one picture of the room I had just left, the carvings fresh in the floor.

The dark boards of the old floor creaked as I paced in a circle, making sure to stay just out of sight of anyone peering up from the driveway. A spackeling of wilting paper and dust coated my fingers as I sifted through the stack of historical documents. Notes were scrawled in each margin. Each bit of writing changing to new hands as the pages continued on.

"What is this?"

"That is our family's' legacy. You must protect this book with your life. Do not let her have it."

"Legacy? Grandma, we aren't some kind of knights on a quest. It's almost the twenty-first century. Things like this don't happen." I scoffed.

Her normally caring eyes were void of all warmth as she narrowed them on me, "Did you or did you not just wake up a blood sucking evil from the basement of my antique shop?"

A chill raked its icy fingers down the flesh of my neck and rushed down my arms. My spine straightened where I stood and my eyes darted back to the window. Only my own reflection peered back at me as I stared.

A dark voice crept its way out from the shadow clad hallway. "Oh, Winnie. Such lovely words. I'll make sure I live up to them."

My brain shouted at me to bolt for my grandma but my body was still partially frozen in fear. When the pounding in my heart finally pushed the adrenaline through my veins, I tucked the book in the back of my pants and sputtered forward. My foot caught the carpet sending me spilling over the floor.

My knees ached as I pulled myself up just enough to peek over the fluffy duvet.

A pale face hovered in the hallway, its dark smile piercing through the darkness.

"How did you enter my home?" Grandma Winnie's voice was bold as she stared in the face of the monster.

"The very nice lady downstairs was kind enough to let me in." She slowly wiped her chin accenting the horrible and unspoken words that dripped with it.

My eyes went wide. "You bit my mom!"

The machine at her bedside beeped a steady rhythm as she spoke, "If you touched my daughter, the next sleep you are cursed with will not be so peaceful."

"Curse?" I breathed out.

The creatures' face contorted into a mask of pain and hatred for just a moment before the wicked smile fell back into place. "You are not a very accommodating host. In my day, we welcomed our guests to enjoy any food left out in our kitchen." The fact that she was calling my mom food was terrifying and made all the worse by her deadpan words.

She stepped fully from the shadows, her green dress and golden chains still flowing unnaturally behind her as they did in the shop. Something was missing from her belt. I glanced back to the golden purse that still rested on the reading chair. Of course. The poem must be the curse. I just needed to get to it. Her eyes locked on mine as I inched away from the edge of the bed.

"Don't you worry little pet." The vampire matched my movement. "I won't forget about you." Her focus fell back on Grandma, "Now. You will tell me where I can find Renard and the book."

"I don't know what you're talking about." She had always been a bad liar. It was something that I usually loved about her. Usually.

"I will kill you this night if I have to." A rage built in the woman's tone as she crept closer to the bed, "Your ancestors were a stubborn lot, but I do not believe such knowledge has been allowed to be lost with time."

Grandma tilted her chin toward the stranger. A sob caught in my throat at the sight of her defiance as I scooted myself further back and away from the bed.

"You will tell me this night, all that I seek, Winnie Cordain. You will tell me or—"

"No." Grandma's voice was firm. I swallowed down the tears bubbling to the surface as my back finally hit the chair.

"Very well." An exasperated sigh left the woman's lips. "Good night, Winnie." She took a deep breath and blew it out over the top of the bedside lamp.

Nothing happened.

She tried again, harder the second time. Her cheeks puffed up as she grasped the lamp with both hands, a torrent of air flowing from between her lips. "What is wrong with this lantern?" She pulled it, the tasseled shade teetering back and forth rapidly before she accidentally yanked it from the plug, casting the room in semi darkness. "Better."

I reached for the scroll.

The sound of shuffling came from the bed just before another click and a hiss. Grandma had shifted to the other side and switched on the matching lamp. The light shone on the vampire crouched next to her, a horrid snarl pasted to her face as she barred her sharp fangs.

The two stared at each other for a long time, both women squinting their eyes and assessing the other.

"You do not fear death?"

"Death and I have become pretty close lately. I believe we're on good terms."

A look of admiration flashed across the beautiful woman's pale face. Admiration and, something else. Longing, maybe? It passed as quickly as it came just before she turned her eyes on me. "You may be ready for the reapers scythe but I doubt your lovely granddaughter is."

In an instant, her claws were digging into my skin as she held me out at the end of the bed, my feet helplessly kicking at air.

"Stop! Don't hurt her! She doesn't know anything." Grandma's voice cracked.

"But you do. Tell me where I may find Renard and the book. Tell me this or she dies."

Grandma's voice was strong as she spoke. "My family has protected this world since 1780 and I will not be the one to fail them." The betrayal sunk deep into my skin as she hissed out a name, "But I will end it, Soryn." Soryn.

Grandmas movements were painfully slow as she fought to grab something from the side table drawer.

Soryn the vampire ran her nose up my neck, inhaling the scent deeply as she did. A wicked laugh punctuated the end of the creepy motion.

As I turned my terrified eyes back to the bed, a small shaft of hope bloomed in my chest. Resting on Grandma Winnie's shaky arms was a small wooden cross bow. She slowly knocked an arrow and pointed it toward us. A click sound had barely made it to my ears before a whoosh of air tousled my hair—the arrow burying itself into the large dresser behind us.

"Holy hell, Grandma!"

Soryn laughed. "I see." The room shifted in an instant and we were next to my grandmother as she fidgeted with another arrow. With a swipe of Soryn's hand, the crossbow went flying, as if a huge gust of wind had blown it away.

She leaned forward, pulling me awkwardly with her. "You are so ready to give up your life and even your kin's, but tell me, Winnie Cordain, will you be so tight with your secrets when you see her blood flow? Or should I turn her into that which you so desperately hate?"

"No, no, no, no, no, no, no, no…" I twisted in her arms until I faced her, my shoulders pushed up to my ears to guard my neck as best as I could. "I would make the worst vampire. I would probably forget and just stroll out into the sun. Or, garlic. I love garlic. I just know I'd accidentally take a bite and, POOF, you know. Everyone would know. Jig is up for all vampire kind and, you don't want that. Nobody wants that. So this really wouldn't be in your best interest." I looked back and forth between the two. My ramblings bouncing off of them as my panic grew to a crescendo.

"You would never."

"In my centuries on this earth, I have done things you would not fathom in your worst nightmares. I have destroyed towns. I have drank them dry and found no sorrow in their passing. I will kill her, and I will bask in the pain her passing brings." A rage festered behind the bright emerald green of her eyes.

A plea hung on my voice, "Grandma, please."

The vampire growled, "Your family betrayed me. Now tell me what you have done with Renard and the book. Give me what I want."

Grandma Winnie sat silent as the grave that she was about to put me in.

"So be it." She pulled the golden dagger from the chains at her side. I hadn't even seen her take it when she left the shop. I stared forward in horror as she twisted me to face the bed before dragging the sharp blade down the side of her own neck. I tried to squirm away from the sharp point as she brought it back around to aim at my throat. The black stones seemed to swallow any light that dared touch them as her dark blood spread across the metal and dripped down my arm. Panic laced my thoughts as I squeezed the scroll in my hand tight, the words within it etched into my mind suddenly coming out in rivulets of petrified noise.

"Ichor of the dead, shadowed by time and veils unsung, give to me the breath of life, purchased by kindred tongue..."

"What are you—"

I kept going, not waiting for her question. "...twist what has been stolen and carve away the heart" I spit the words out rapid fire as the vampire laughed. "until the moon bleeds malice born, and curse is rent apart."

My body flew across the room. A white hot pain lanced through me as I crashed into the dresser– the arrow that had lodged in the door protruded from my shoulder, sticking me into place.

"You stupid mortals. Did you think you could use my own curse against me? I have kept it for years! And you teach it to your progeny." She leaned down and snarled in Grandma Winnie's ear. "You are truly the evil one if you would wish such a thing."

Grandmas eyes were wide and full of horror as she stared at me, the beeping of her medical device growing as fast as the throbbing pain in my shoulder. "We don't know how to take your curse." Her eyes trailed down to the parchment. "Brittany don't say another word."

Something in me snapped as I managed to grit out the final words through pained breaths. "By blood sealed and bargain struck."

"Then how could she?" She stared down, eyes wide, searching for something that was meant for her belt. "Where is the scroll?"

A unison of horror came from both women, "No! You can't—" and "Brittany, no!"

A deep red glow emanated from within the rolled paper. The house seemed to be shaking as windows were thrown open giving way to a torrent of wind that ripped through the old house. Another searing pain racked my body as I caught a glimpse of the moon outside. It seemed to pulse in the night sky as both Soryn and I were thrown to the ground, my chest was ablaze where it felt like my heart was being ripped out just like the arrow had been.

I rolled to look at the vampire as a red tint bloomed across her cheeks. Another hard burst shot through my chest.

Grandmas voice was strained in the chaos of the room, "Brittany! Get out of the house!"

"Grandma?" My body was shaking from the searingly hot and intense pain, and she was kicking me out! I couldn't breathe. Air. I needed air.

Soryn groaned on the floor beside me, "What have you done, you stupid girl!" She brought the dagger up to her face and where there had been several onyx stones, there were now rubies, their glow rivaling that of the moon outside.

Outside.

I ran to the hallway, the staggered pounding tearing at my chest as if my heart was fighting to escape. Thump. My hands pushed at the floor as I took a deep and searing breath before climbing to my feet and picking up speed, the hallway carpet shifting and bunching under my strides. Thump. I made it to the top stair before another internal crash sent me tumbling down the heavy wooden steps. Thump. The time between each new thud became more and more distant as I pulled what should have been my broken body from the entry way floor. Thump. The door swung wide with a horrible cracking sound as I flung my body out into the cold night air and waited for the next, earth shattering thump.

I waited.

And waited.

And it never came.

The moon gave off a dim red glow as it gazed down at me through the canopy of branches and turning leaves. Dread coated my soul.

"Do you have the slightest idea of what you have done! Do you have any idea what I have sacrificed– the years I have suffered and tormented to make sure what you just did never would come to be!" Soryn was flushed red and out of breath as she raged at me through the broken doorway. Splinters of darkly stained wood jutted out like monstrous teeth as the paneled door hung from a single bent hinge.

"What I've done!" I tried to scream but the pain in my chest turned my words to breathy gasps.

A shadow moved from the second-story room as the window opened. My grandmother's voice was low and shaky in the darkness. It must have taken all her energy to make it across the room. She called down to Soryn. "Can you undo it?"

Soryn didn't turn to face her. "Why should I." She snarled though it didn't hold the same gravel like sound as before. "Your family is full of nothing but traitors and cheats. This was just another trick, yes?"

"My granddaughter knew nothing of the curse. She's innocent."

Soryn's eyes flinched in pain as she brought a hand to her head and stared at the red spots that smeared on her small hands. "She is hardly innocent." She curled her fingers open and closed around the streaks of blood. "Tell me how to find him, and I will break this curse your progeny has brought upon herself."

"Renard died."

Soryn straightened, "and the book?"

"Everything that was his was donated." Grandma remained in shadow above us but the warm caramel scent of the candies she loved caught my nose. Along with another even sweeter scent.

A mask of anger fell over Soryns' face before she turned on Grandma Winnie. "I don't believe you! Where is it crone!"

I sped across the gravel and up the steps, the wind whipping past my skin and slammed, face first, into an invisible barrier. The pain of it sent tremors through my entire body as I writhed, body half hanging off of the few steps of the small porch. I groaned as Soryn let out a disgusted grunt.

"The University." Her voice sounded more than exhausted. She sounded defeated — and ashamed. "Everything was given to them for safe keeping." I sensed her eyes on me as my own sight began to shift, the moonlight growing to fill every dark space.

Soryn kicked past me, determination in her stride before stopping beside my car. She didn't say another word — just waited, a deep scowl set on her face.

"Grandma?" I stood and took several cautious steps toward the entryway.

"No. Brit. You can't come in." Tears streamed down her face. "My girl, you have no idea what you've done."

"Why? What's happening."

"You have to stay with her." She narrowed her old eyes on Soryn. "Keep her safe. She is your only hope now."

"But I…"

"Keep her alive, Brittany. I will take care of your mom. We'll be fine."

That smell circled the air again, and I breathed in deeply reveling in the sweet scent of it. A shaky growl rumbled through my chest as I tried to pinpoint the source.

She took a step back from the window, "You need to go with her right now."

"Go with the blood-sucking vampire psychopath that tried to kill us all?"

Her head hung low, "No, my sweet girl. Go with the human so that you don't kill us all."

A heavy silence hung in the air between us. Her words rattled in my head but made no sense. Soryn cleared her throat from behind me.

"Is somebody going to come open this carriage door for me or do I have to stand here all night. Seeing as I'm no longer immortal, I would rather use the time I have left doing more thrilling things."

I tried to speak but nothing would come out.

"Also, if we are still standing here come daylight, you are going to be quite upset with yourself." She turned, arms crossed in front of her body as she glowered at me. "Actually, that could be fun for me." She leaned against the car. "Let's just do that."

My body was unnaturally weightless as I stumbled to the car. I eyed Soryn. What had been stone like skin was now dewy with tiny beads of sweat. Her eyes were a mossy green, and no longer held the other worldly glow from before. And a bounce at her neck marked the pulse of blood being pumped through her veins.

She stared at her reflection in the window, studying her features as she spoke. "If you try to drink my blood, you will find yourself tormented by the excruciating pain like that of being impaled by a thousand burning hot stakes." Her knowing eyes shifted to me, "Now, open my door so that we may take leave of this place." She glared back toward the house. "If we are to reverse your stupidity, I will need to get home. If home still stands."

The engine roared as I started down the road, leaving my family and everything I knew of my mortal life behind.

Chapter Nine
SORYN

My eyes burned. The carriage wasn't as fast as my immortal form and yet, it jarred my newly human body. The memory of a boat ride with my young brother came to mind. His laugh, like the snorting of an old donkey, rang clear in my ears as my stomach turned in torturous knots. That day, the rolling of the water pushing at the sides of the small wooden vessel had pulled my morning meal up with it. An internal quaking set my body tensing again while a pathetic moan escaped me. Had I really wanted this back?

"Are you alright?" The thing in the front of the carriage stared at me through a small mirror as other brightly lit carriages shot past us in a dizzying whir.

"Oh yes." I seethed, "I'm doing quite well, thank you. And you?"

Her brown eyes pulled from mine and her fingers bit into the wheel — the shiny black material cracking under her new strength. She let out the most irritating sound; like a pig choking on a dying mouse.

Her torment brought a smile to my lips. "That well? Good for you."

Quiet yips and whines were the only sound that came from her as she struggled to rein in the ride. The back and forth obviously bothering the other travelers. I turned to stare at the one behind us. It had to have been carrying a musician, though not a very good one. The sound of their instrument was obnoxious and out of tune. Or perhaps that was the preferred style of music in 1999. Brittany remained silent.

"Oh, no no. I'm in the mood for conversation now." I leaned forward, my body rebelling against the quick motion. My cheeks puffed as I fought to hold whatever may have been waiting in my insides, inside. It had been centuries since sickness had touched my body and in second,s the actions of one stupid mortal had it all catching up to me.

"Do you find enjoyment in this carriage?"

"Carriage?" Her voice was still dipped with high-pitched fear as she held, awkwardly to the broken wheel.

The spinning in my head had begun to war with my stomach. I squeezed my eyes shut tightly and spoke through clenched teeth. "This, moving metal lump."

"Car." She flustered, "It's a car."

"Well, I'm about to redecorate your car."

Various items bombarded me as the carriage let out an ear splitting squeal and my face met the scratchy gray fabric of the floor. The car-carriage had come to an abrupt stop. If only my insides had as well.

"Don't die alright. I need help and..." Brittany's words were muffled by the opening and closing of a door. Her talking reminded me of a sailor I had once held under water until he expired.

The hollow muffled sound continued until a rush of cold night air hit my face. Her voice became clear although, what she said was lost as a torrent of brilliant green bile splattered on the bumpy black ground.

The darkness had been overtaken by a glow of brightly changing lanterns. Burst of blue, green, and purple flashed in my vision as I looked up from my place among the refuse.

"Oh no. No no no no no no no. It's everywhere." Her 'no,' chant continued on before she began to speak more nonsense. "Why does it look like Surge?"

"Yes. Poor you. Now, if you don't mind helping me up."

"I'm sorry. Let me just.." She held her hands out for me to take as I bunched my dress neatly with one arm.

Brittany pulled. I flew.

"I'm sorry. I'm so so sorry." She was by my side in an instant. Her insistent blathering scratching like a bug trapped in my ear. If I would have just eaten her when I had the chance I—my thoughts trailed as a the scent of something, more delightful than any blood I had savored in centuries, curled through the air.

Brittany seemed to be locked in hunger as well. Her eyes glowed a deep crimson; her gaze set upon the flashing lantern covered building that loomed in front of us. The snarl that vibrated from her chest shook me. Fear hadn't been a known enemy of mine in so long, I almost didn't recognize its frigid claws as they raced down my spine.

In this moment, the true horror of what had happened coursed through my now pumping heart. It quivered, a small animal finally cornered by the hounds of hell.

The girl in front of me had my hunger; my immortality; my curse. The day I had fought to avoid had come to pass, and I had to do everything in my now mortal power to reverse it.

Unstake My Heart

But first, food.

My new companion had already left my side, darting into the noisy building in search of something to satiate her own hunger.

An excited chattering came from the doorway as I inched closer, gazing again upon the lanterns, the words The Rink, spelled out with the magical candle light.

Chapter Ten
BRITTANY

The thrumming base of music rushed past my ears. A warm glow pulsed around the familiar space, the strobing lights casting the abstract shapes splattered around the walls in vibrant shades of green, pink, and blue. The busy carpet made a colorful trail toward the large circular customer service desk that split the area between the roller rink and bowling alley. The crashing of pins to my right battled the clattering of plastic wheels on wood to my left; the ping and whirl of arcade games and food court accented the warring chaos.

My teeth itched as a painful stabbing radiated from my chest. What was that delicious smell? I closed my eyes and savored the delectable aroma. Something of a mix between spiced dark coffee and Dunk-A-Roos flooded my nostrils and left a fluttering panic circling my insides. It continued to build and build with the music that bumped like the beating of a heart.

Warm bodies jostled around me as I stood, frozen to the dark blue speckled carpet.

"Brittany, you made it." Keith's voice was in my ear.

My body revolted against me as I took a labored step back from him. "Keith. Hi. Uh, what are you doing here?"

"What do you mean? Aren't you here for me?"

"Right. Yeah, no I mean, like…what are you doing over here, with me, instead of like bowling or whatever." Vampirism had obviously not enhanced my speaking skills. A burst of outside air pushed into the room as someone opened the door. The shifting of air swirled Keith's glorious scent to my nostrils. An instant later, I was on him. My nose trailed against the collar of his shirt as I breathed in deeply.

"How did you…"

"You smell amazing." His eyes seemed to burn into my skull as my nose smashed against his chest. My head was screaming at me how weird I was being but something even deeper inside of me refused to let me pull myself from him.

"It's, uh, Burberry Men." His hands were light on my shoulders as he pushed at me. "I'm going to get a slush from the food court. You don't want to come, do you?"

He started to leave before I answered. The cloud in my head was hard to focus through as I closely followed his quick strides.

The long wooded counter was already covered in bright red baskets full of some of my favorite foods but the place reeked like spilled ketchup left out in the humid summer air. I took a step back. "Did the fridge clunk out or something?"

The loud music and raised voices smothered my own. I pulled away from Keith and the food counter. The rancid stench of rotting food overpowered my senses and sent a roll of nausea through the pit of my stomach. I needed to get out of this place but first I had to find —

"Disgusting isn't it." The slightly garbled rolling accent caressed my burning ears. Soryn sat at a table; stacks of the red baskets overflowing with fries, tater tots, mozzarella sticks and more teetered in front of her.

"We need to get out of here, like now."

"We can leave after I've eaten." She stared up at me and shoved a handful of fried food in her mouth while simultaneously reaching for a plate of Frito pie.

"Stop, Soryn. It's gone bad." I slapped it out of her hand. It flew across the room leaving a chili splattered wake across several tables. The last thing I needed was her dying from salmonella or something and leaving me like this forever.

"Can we please leave now?"

She let out an exasperated sign. "Come here, girl. Sit."

A rumbling of irritated people sounded from behind me. Embarrassment should have reddened my face, but it remained cold and pale as stone as I took my seat. The offending scents coming from the junk food had me pinching my nose while I spoke. "You can't eat that. It's going to make you sick."

"It hasn't spoiled. Your body doesn't want it anymore."

I swallowed a huge lump that was fighting to close my throat. There was no way of telling whether it was caused by the smell or the thought of never having another hamburger. "But I love junk food." I thought of the pizza still sitting on the counter at the shop.

"Love it all you want, but if you eat it," She bit a mozzarella stick, the cheese oozing over her fingers, "you will be sorry." She finished it and immediately began scarfing down a small personal pizza. "You can still enjoy some beverages." She smiled and stared off into the ceiling, licking some of the ketchup from her mouth as she went on, "I found the mixture of a Sangiovese paired with this lovely middle-aged farmer from Modena Italy to be the most delightful pairing." She took a deep breath, lost in thought, before diving back into her plates.

I couldn't eat food. My head spun as the room began to pulse like heartbeats pounding to the pop music. I focused in on the sound. A fluttering of awe and fear rushed over me as I realized, the sound wasn't like heartbeats. The sound was heartbeats. Each vein carrying blood like some kind of morbid bendy straw waiting to be tapped. Strands of hair caught in my mouth as I shook my head, trying to dislodge the very messed up thought from my brain.

"What happens if I don't." I gulped trying to force down the thorn like pain clawing at my throat and whispered, "What if I don't feed."

Disgust coated her every word, "Feed?" She sneered around the ketchup covering her mouth and left cheek. "We are not some kind of feral animals."

A flutter of napkins landed on the table between us. A straight haired blond with full angry red cheeks glared down at us. "Could have fooled me." She plopped down a bucket of soapy water by our table before tossing the rag down. "Clean up the mess and pay for your food or your gonna get kicked out. I don't get paid enough for this."

I spoke first, "Of course. We're so sorry for the mess." I grabbed the rag and began wringing the water from it.

Soryn caught my hand and slowly turned her head to the girl, "I believe I misheard you for I do not think you would…"

"Would what? Call you out for being a couple of total freaks?" She made a show of chomping her gum as she entered into a showdown with Soryn, neither breaking eye contact.

"Please can we just…"

"Did you insult us again?"

"Soryn, please."

She stood slowly, "We will go when you have taught this peasant a lesson."

"Whatever, loser. Just clean the mess." The Rink worker turned her back on us and began to leave.

"Wait. Stop moving." The girl turned back, the look of anger she held before now a piercing stare of pure malice at Soryn's demand. "Tell her to clean it, Brittany."

"What?" and "Excuse me?" sounded from myself and the woman, respectively.

"I'm not going to…"

"Do it, and we will leave."

Guilt tugged and contorted my face with each syllable, "Can you clean this up — please."

"Not like that." Soryn continued, "Look her in the eyes, picture her doing the task, and command her to do it."

"That's it. Both of you need to get out. Now." She started to wave at someone near the service desk up front.

"Yes, I think that would be a great idea. Soryn, let's go."

Soryn sat, arms crossed and unmoving. "Do as I say or I stay like this forever. Your choice, girl."

"Wait! Just wait, please." I glared at Soryn before staring into the bright blue eyes in front of me. Everything around me sharpened. I heard everything. The vein on her neck pulsed in time with the beat of the music, both now happening in slow motion. The blue of her eyes dulled; all light draining from them. The stabbing pain throbbed in my chest again as I spoke. "Clean it up." Her body straightened. "Please."

The entire room seemed to catch back up for the lost time as she wet the rag and began scrubbing at the basket of ketchup and fries Soryn had just tossed to the black-and-white checkered floor.

"Hungry yet?" Soryn purred.

I shook my head as an invisible knife seemed to stab at my heart for the lie.

She gave a knowing smile. "The more power you use, the hungrier you will get so," She took a huge gulp of her slushie drink, "take a look at the menu and we can take something with us." She stood and brushed crumbs from her flowing emerald gown, licking the extra bits from her fingers. "This was fun but we do really need to get home."

My eyes darted back and forth. "Could you be a bit more discreet, please? Especially when you're talking about people like happy meals." A veil of confusion fell over her still stunning features.

I tried to fumble out a few syllables before Keith's distinctly sweet smell collided with the surrounding air.

"Are you and your new friend coming over?" His eyes lingered on Soryn while he grabbed my hand in his. He was touching me. He wanted me to come over with him. He invited me out and now he was holding my hand. And I wanted to eat him.

"Brittany?" His lips moved in slow motion as he said my name, "Are you alright?"

"Yes, Brittany. Are you alright? You should eat something? A happy meal, perhaps?" Soryn's smile was focused on me, but my eyes were locked on Keith. I took another deep breath, and then another, and another before suddenly, his lips crushed against mine. Or more like, my lips were crushed against his. I pulled him in closer and he didn't resist as the two of us stayed locked together. His breathing was erratic and intoxicating. My fangs stung as they pierced his bottom lip.

Soryn laughed.

"You bit me." Keith placed a finger to his lip before smirking down at me.

The hunger was growing as the small drop of blood swirled on my tongue.

"Keith would you like to take a ride with us?"

His gaze locked on mine. I inched forward, an internal voice demanded for me to drain his blood.

Soryn gave another loud slurp of her drink. "Unless society has become much more accepting of our diet, it would be best if we took your meal of happiness to go."

I fought back the urge to follow her direction as the hunger continued to build. I stared into Keith's eyes and spoke through gritted teeth, "You should go bowl. You love to bowl."

"I do love to bowl." His eyes went dull as the need to bite him grew.

"But don't you want to make Brittany happy?" Soryn purred.

He smiled. Soryn laughed. I growled.

Holy hell! I was growling now! "Go bowl, Keith. Now!" Without another word, he turned and sprinted toward the far lanes. I grabbed Soryn's hand and fled in the opposite direction just as a crowd of people flooded the front doors.

This time, it was Soryn who pulled me away as another even deeper sound began to swirl in my chest. " I need you to eat but a massacre will be no good for any of us right now. Is there another way out?" My whole body ached as I pointed toward the arcade room..

The ping and chime of video games bombarded me as I made for the bright red glow of the emergency exit sign. If I could just get out the door, I could make it to the parking lot and get in the car and just drive. I could figure this out, I just needed more time. I just needed to be away from all of this blood so I could think straight. My hand was on the bar of the door when the pain locked me in place leaving a guttural moan shaking my entire body.

"Do you mind, freak?"

My head shot up as I stared dead on in the eyes of a twenty something man playing a flashing video game, in a metal box. The words GAME OVER pulsed on the screen in front of him.

"Thanks a lot, skank. You got me killed."

He didn't have the chance to blink before I was on him. A spray of red burst in front of my eyes as deliciously warm liquid soothed the pain in my chest and throat. Vividly bright colors swirled around as my body felt like it was floating on air. I continued to gulp, unable to stop even if I had wanted to as a presence loomed behind me.

"I'm not intruding am I?"

I growled.

"Don't you growl at me, girl. I'm on your side. But unless you want the whole town chasing you down with pitchforks, we should really be taking your meal and our leave."

I looked down in horror. The man that had called me a freak had gone pale, the sound of his failing heartbeat barely audible.

Soryn stood at the door, holding it open for me. "Well, come on."

My body felt surprisingly alive as I stared at her. Every car, every creature and every conversation made it to my ears. The wafting smells were a mixture of pungent and sweet as the cold air from outside mingled with the Rinks'. My body tingled all over.

"Soryn."

"Yes. Yes. I know. It's wonderful. Now if you don't mind grabbing him so we can go."

My heart sank. The man was moments away from deaths door as I scooped him up and we crossed the parking lot in the dark. He gave an almost inaudible whimper as I lowered him into the trunk of my car. Soryn and I stood side by side, staring down at what would be my dinner.

"I was supposed to be having pizza." My eyes watered along with my mouth. I gripped the trunk, readying myself to trap the poor man inside.

"Wait." Soryn placed her hand on mine and gave a gentle nod. It was the first kind look she had given me. She lowered the slushie still grasped in her other hand to the open wound at the mans throat. The quickly cooling crimson blood combined with the icy cherry treat.

She handed it to me with a smile.

Chapter Eleven
BRITTANY

With every bump of the old dirt road that Soryn had me turn the car down, the body in the trunk was tossed. I had tried to turn on the radio to cover the horrible sound, but Soryn had already yelled at me for it. Apparently, she was not a fan of pop. But, I probably should have guessed that.

The winding road that led to the top of Harrow Hill was pocked with pot holes. We had already had to stop twice to move rotting branched and trees that had fallen on the path.

Well, I had cleared the obstacles while Soryn told me what to do.

"What's up here?" I asked.

"Rest. You need to be in darkness before the sun come up."

My foot inched further down on the gas pedal, "Am I going to fry if we don't find a coffin by daytime?" The lights below marked the buildings and paths that wound around the University, all just barely visible through the trees. "Can't we just go back to the shop and get yours?"

"That box was not mine." She stared far off in the distance overlooking the town. "But if you want to risk being trapped in there for a few decades, go ahead."

"No—no, thank you." We drove the rest of the way up in silence until finally, the trees began to thin, but only enough to show a large timber house tucked in the woods.

"What is this place?" Just as I said it, the path stopped abruptly marking the end of the road.

Soryn let out a sigh, climbed out of the car, and began to walk to the house. I tucked the keys in my pocket and followed.

A kind of electricity hung faintly on the darkness engulfing the home, as if a small spark might set the air around it crackling with energy. "What is that?"

"You will have to be more specific, girl. I have no idea the depth of your understanding, though I must say, from the events of this night, I could no more that wade through it." Her eyes were piercing as she glared through me. Whatever sympathy this monster may have felt for me before, was already dead.

My words fought to stay trapped in my throat as I croaked out, "Um, the air. It's like, pop rocks." I shrugged as her eyes widened. Her head tilted slightly as her eyes continued to burn into me. "I mean, it's like, sharp? I don't know, like, there is something…"

"It is charged?"

"Yes!" The too loud cheer echoed against the heavy woods and crashed like symbols against my ears.

"You are sensing a spell that was put on my home."

"What kind of spell?"

"How would I know that? I'm not the one who placed it there." Her green dress trailed along the ground, picking up traces of the foliage as I followed behind.

She turned, her arms crossed and her foot tapping on the uneven ground. The crunch of leaves and twigs accented each annoyed thump. "Forgetting something?"

My brows pinched. Forgetting something? Oh! "I can't come in, like, without an invitation or whatever. Is that it?"

"Usually yes, but this home was owned by me, while I was a vampire, so you may enter without invitation."

A hesitant smile pulled at my lips as I stared at the withering house. The dark timber beams were stacked one on top of the other, the material used to pack in between them crumbled in places where vines had burrowed and reclaimed the natural wood. A path of overgrown stones led to a large set of doors; each one being held up by rusted hammer marked hinges.

The gabled roof was covered in more large branches that rested on the heavy wooden shingles. A large stone chimney stack peeked out over them. The house deserved to be on the towns historical landmark list. And being so close to the university, I was surprised they hadn't already bought up this land to preserve it.

I couldn't wait to get inside and see what other treasure might be waiting there. My mind raced at the thought of what undiscovered history might be on the other side of the large, vine covered door. My excitement hit a wall as Soryn's arm shot out to stop me from taking another giddy step forward.

"Not so fast, girl."

"I thought I could go inside?"

"Yes. You can." She turned to the car. "But it might be good to get rid of the body in your car-carriage-thing first."

"Oh, my god! He's still in there." I rushed back to the trunk. The light blue paint scratched beneath my nails as I pulled up on it. The car had seen its fair share of dirty boxes, muddy shoes, and spilled fast food to last a lifetime but what I had put it through tonight was off the charts bad.

My eyes searched the road we had driven up to make sure no one was there to see what we had done. The trunk let out a metallic whine as I pulled it open in one quick motion. The ride up the bumpy road had tossed the body into a pretzel. Surprisingly enough, the only visible blood was on his neck and shirt. Any blood the poor guy had left after I got a hold of him had been emptied into my drink. I closed the trunk just enough to peer into the car at the empty slushie cup still sitting in the holder. That would need to be disposed of as well.

"Come on then." Soryn rushed, "Grab it."

I froze.

"What. He's not going to bite." She snorted at her joke. "Pick it up and follow me."

The thought of carrying the body made my stomach churn, so I opted for dragging instead. I stayed close behind Soryn as we skirted the main house and tracked into the large backyard.

A peppering of, "Sorry. Sorry. Sorry." filtered into the night air with each rock and branch the mans head plopped over.

"I do not forgive you." Soryn said firmly.

"Not you. Him."

"He's dead. He does not forgive you either."

Before I could give a retort, the body snagged on something in the tall grass. I pulled. A loud crunch went through the air as fast as I did. With my body laid out flat against the damp earth, I stared up at the star speckled sky and let out a guttural moan into the heavens. "Why is this happening to me?"

"Because your family line is full of traitors and fools." Soryn's head peered down from the high waving grass. "Now, come."

The pull had dislodged the body from whatever it had been stuck on, though now his right arm drug behind at a strange angle. I did my best to keep my eyes cast over my shoulder and on Soryn.

The wave of the plants was the only sign of Soryn as she went through the overgrown maze.

A dilapidated stone fence weaved through patched of the tall grass and vines. I followed through a broken section of it before making my way to an open area. My mouth dropped in amazement again.

An old barn loomed in front of me. The doors stood wide open to a gaping dark space. I could see the outline of Soryn's silhouette searching for something inside. A circle of large moss-covered stones caught my eye just a short distance from the large out building. I slumped the cold body on the ground and peered into the black hole of the well.

"Hello." My voice echoed back to me as a shuffling came from the barn. Soryn emerged with several burlap bags and rope.

Her hands moved quickly as she laid the man out on the bags and went to work tying the rope and knotting it. Before long, she stood — a feline grin curling up her face as if she were a feral cat presenting its new friend with a macabre gift.

"Thank you?"

"You're welcome. Now," She pointed to the well, "toss it in and we can go get comfortable inside."

"Toss it…in." I peered down the dark hole, "In there?"

"All is well. It's not like he will be all alone." She curled her fingers over the stone rim and hoisted herself up to look inside.

"There are more people down there?"

"Oh, at least two or three." She said, "If I remember correctly, I think Samuel might in this one." She looked up and squinted her eyes toward a far away line of trees, "Or maybe he was in that one."

"There's more than one?"

"Don't be silly. Of course there is. You can only put so many bodies in a well." She let off a short whistle and twisted her finger toward the bottom.

Taking my cue, I picked up the body and rested it beside her on the stone ledge.

She gave an annoyed grunt and pushed it over. My eyes followed its decent until darkness engulfed it.

My ex-vampire companion was already making her way back to the main house as I slowly trekked behind her. The hairs stood on my arms as a strange blue glow was cast on the ground beside me. I turned slowly to see two frighteningly hollow eyes peering at me from the edge of the well. The blue light seemed to pulse from several places around the yard and tree line as panic overtook me. I darted to the door Soryn had just entered and crouched, throwing my weight against the wooden blockade.

"There's something out there."

"Most likely many things."

"No. You don't understand. I think," I turned my face toward the door as if I could see the things stalking me through the solid wood. "I think they might be…"

"Ghosts."

"I'm not out of it. I swear I saw them."

"Yeah, probably." She went about the room collecting wood and placing it on the large stone hearth and fire place.

I moved to the shuttered window. The crack between the board was just big enough to see through. Several of the glowing blue forms hovered a distance away in the heavily wooded area behind the barn. The eyes from the well, were thankfully gone. The sound of stone striking stone scratched at my ears as Soryn worked at starting a fire in the old fireplace. I turned back to the yard. Immediately I flew backwards scrambling to push my self as far away from the malice ridden eyes that stared back at me.

"Go away!" My hands fluttered around me in an abysmal attempt to shoo the floating figure away. The dead man didn't flinch. "Can I get rid of it?"

Her head swiveled back and forth between the window and me. "You can't kill them again, if that's what your asking." She stood and walked toward the window. "They just float there and watch and silently judge while you go about your day, or change, or eat." Soryn opened the window, poking her head straight through the Colonial dressed ghost before taking a step back.

"What does it look like?"

"You can't see it?"

"Apparently when you decided to be foolish and take my curse from me, you took my sight as well." She was irate. "Well?"

The floor creaked as I stood. "Well, he's wearing a collarless jacket with a lot of buttons, it looks to be Colonial. Maybe late 1600s to early 1700s." Another creak filled the house as I took another step toward Soryn and the ghost. "Tricorn hat, fluffy cravat. And, oh, it looks like he has some kind of pin on his coat."

"An arrow pin?"

"Yes!"

She turned, grabbing the window sill meaning to yell into the yard, and instead released her words right into the ghosts face. "Hey! I didn't kill you. Okay, Stan! You can move on now!" She went to close the shutters. A puff of dust clouded the air as the hinges gave way, the entire thing crumbling into a pile of wood on the ground just outside the window. She shrugged, "To be fair, I did kill his brother Samuel but, he doesn't know that." She crossed back to the fire as I stared at Stan, his mouth open in shock.

Soryn went back to work on the fire as a shudder went up my spine. "What's going to happen to me?"

The smell of burning twigs and dried leaves was my only answer.

"Will he haunt me too?" I stared out the broken window toward the well, fully expecting to see another pair of ghostly eyes staring at me.

"We will need to start repairs tomorrow." Her shoes click clacked across the room where several trunks were tucked in the alcove of the staircase. Another coat of age slid off of it in a plume of dust; hinges screamed as she raised the lid of the largest one. She groaned.

A snap of fabric sent the musty smell of rot through the space. What looked to have once been an intricately decorated quilt had become a nest for some small animal; apparent by the large hole chewed through the middle. The same hole that Soryn was glaring at me through. She gave a grand huff as she wrapped the tattered shroud around her.

"Your place is upstairs. Go, now. Don't touch the windows. They are boarded to shut out the light."

"Are you sure it's safe? What if someone messed with it?" The dark space at the top of the stairs felt ominous from below. "And don't you think we should figure all of this out first? I just killed someone! Shouldn't we…"

"Tomorrow we will need to find either a witch or a farmer. There's the plan. Now leave me to freeze in peace."

She crouched beside the flames, the crackling and popping livening the dead space. The stairs were surprisingly sturdy under my weight as I made my way up into the dark room that would be my new home for now.

A burst of blue hit my eyes. Another ghost, this one a female, sat with her head down on a small but comfortable looking bed. Her eyes followed my steps as I searched around the room. The journal Grandma Winnie gave me needed a better hiding spot than the back of my jeans. A pile of moth eaten cloth tucked in the back of the heavy wooden dresser would have to do for now.

A heavy cough raged through the floor below followed by a loud moan, topped to the brim with absolute annoyance. I glanced back down the stairs while Soryn popped in and out of view. Furniture shuffled, cabinets slammed, and glass chimed as she created a teetering stack of objects on the large round table by the hearth. My eyes cut through the cloud of soot and dust she had stirred up in the process.

Unstake My Heart

"I can help you."

Her back straightened, but she remained facing the table. "You have done more than enough already."

Her sharp words were the final twist of the knife. The door had barely latched before I let out the first cry of the night. The first of many. My sleeve smeared red where I had wiped away the tears.

Chapter Twelve
SORYN

" **W**hy is it blood?" Brittany's guttural sobs rolled down the staircase and pounded in my ears. "That's so unnecessary!" Another sob followed.

I thumbed through the stack of books knowing the one that I needed would not be amongst them. The spun glass bottle tinked in my hand, as the glass rod inside twirled with nothing to stop it, the liquid inside long since evaporated. Time had tried to consume my home while I was gone. It had failed. The rich brown of the hand carved mantle still held under the coat of dust. The heavy river rock of the kitchen still held its warmth, though the fire in the stove had long been extinguished. I stared around the room. Everything was just as I had last seen it last. The candelabras sat bare, their candles burned and extinguished, the wax still puddled at their bases. Several chairs still lined the walls of the long space some still with glasses perched on the floor beside them. Remnants of a night of revelry. The night I had been tricked into sleep.

I sniffed at the inside of the glass bottle, the hope that the familiar vanilla and woodsy scent would linger there quickly snuffed out.

I pushed my thoughts back further.

"I can help you." Those words still taunted me. Though spoken from different lips, they still cut at my soul.

My eyes stung as I stared through the fire, thinking about the one who had uttered those words. My mind had been tricked by her false tongue. Every syllable a carefully planned rouse. A trap for a prey who bartered blindly thinking they had already been caught.

The revelry of the evening left far behind me as a darkness tried to swallow my soul. She had asked for me to listen. She asked for me to follow. So I did.

"Clarette. Where are you?" I could hear her heartbeat galloping wildly from the earth below my feet. Pots and plants were strewn across the cold room showing were they had been pulled from their place against a far wall. In their stead, a linen was draped over something large — the coffin she would put me in.

Her words echoed over and over again, "I can help you." She pleaded, "Give me the curse and I will help you!"

The one I had loved above all others. The only true friend I had ever known, and she was wishing for my death. I had wished for it too, but not like this. Not her.

"I would no sooner kill Renard that let this evil wither your heart as well."

Shouting sounded from above us as Clarette stared at me with panicked eyes. "I'm sorry Soryn. I'm so very sorry." Her words flowed in clipped syllables as she held her hands over the stone floor. Etched into the surface were all too familiar runes.

Soryn

"How did you— Clarette, why would you..." My eyes became heavy, *blurring the words and the world around me just as a familiar shadow loomed behind her. His arms wrapped around her waist before black night engulfed everything.*

The house I had loved became my tomb that night.

She had not taken my curse that night but she found a way to make sure someone else could. The curse was mine and I would have it back. I whispered into the flames, "Renard. Please let what I saw be wrong."

A soft creak came from the bed upstairs. She wouldn't sleep for a long time. This I knew. I didn't sleep after my first kill either. Though, one well would not have held the carnage my own hunger had demanded. The orange glow of the flames on charred stone mirrored my memory.

The night fell heavy on my lids, exhaustion pulling at my now human body. The moth-eaten couch I had dragged closer to the warmth of the flames had taken the last of my strength and as I collapsed on to its aging cushions, the sour smell of time barely had time to settle on my senses before sleep over took me.

Chapter Thirteen
BRITTANY

Soryn's snoring had just begun to taper off as I creaked my way downstairs. It must have been a human ailment because if she sounded like that in her coffin, I would have found her much sooner.

She had been right about the upstairs bedroom being dark. After she had gone to sleep, I spent several hours flipping through pages of the journal by ghost light. The eerie blue glow that poured off of the girl in strange curling wisps became steadily more unwelcome as I tried to make sense of what was happening.

We had sat in uncomfortable silence as she seemed to read over my shoulder, her hollow eyes occasionally piercing mine until she finally dissipated.

When morning came, I was more than happy to leave the room behind.

The creaking door brought a bright shaft of sunlight with it. It pierced through the air, stinging my eyes and creating a wall of floating dust particles that blocked my way down the stairs.

A mess of dark brown curls popped over the edge of the couch. Soryn's sleepy face tipped up with an exaggerated grimace.

"Morning does not seem to agree with you." She snarled. A cloud of dust puffed into the air where she dropped back down to the couch, followed by a breathy cough and moan. "You should refrain from weeping in the future."

I found a clear spot on my sleeve and rubbed at my cheeks—the dull blood caked to my face came away in rust-colored speckles.

"The wash room is that way." Her hand stuck up in the air and pointed toward another space on the other side of the stairs. She plopped it back down before continuing, "It is well water though." I could hear the smile in her voice.

The house had to be early to mid 1700s Colonial. Of course it was well water. Why would she...oh. Oh no. "Gag me with a spoon, Soryn!"

"If you wish."

"Uh," I planted myself on the stairs, avoiding the light coming in through the dusty windows . "Do you have something I can use to get this off of me?"

"I was going to go fetch myself some water from the stream if it is still running." She looked me up and down while I inched closer to the dark space at the top of the stairs. "Are you quite set on lurking up there all day?"

"What else am I supposed to do? I don't want to burn to a crisp."

Her brows furrowed as she gave me a questioning look, "I suppose we do need to speak on a few things. First, you have taken my curse from me."

"Obviously." I gestured to my very pointy new fangs.

Soryn sighed, her hand cupping her forehead as she spoke. "No. Being a vampire is not a curse. No, you can not eat food. And like any other creature of the night, sunlight is unbearable to your sight, but a mortal death can not touch you. You can live however you like but it is truly for eternity."

"So being a vampire isn't the curse, but not being able to die — like really really die, is?"

She stared at me, a look of contempt so strong in her eyes that my knees began to shake.

"So, sunlight is fine." I hesitantly moved down the stairs, no longer being able to stay still.

"No. Do you not listen? I just said, sunlight is unbearable for your sight. Just because you can not die does not mean you can not feel great pain."

I clasped my hands over my eyes, "What if I just do this?" I took a breath and ran the rest of the way down, feeling the heat of the sunlight as I passed through it.

My body landed in a puddle of warmth as I flung myself off of the staircase. "I did it!" My excitement was quickly pushed aside.

"At this moment, you should be very glad that you can not die." Soryn's words were muffled by my shirt.

I had ran full speed into her. "If you want to be rid of this curse, you should be very careful to keep me alive." A sadness clouded her words.

She pushed at my shoulders with a rage filled grunt. It must be hard to have so much power only to lose it so quickly. I covered my eyes and moved to where I thought the couch was, my knee colliding with the sturdy wood of the table. The things she had stacked last night toppled to the floor with heavy thuds as the table slid.

I squinted as she collected the items, stacking them back on the table before holding a glass bottle that was surprisingly unbroken, to her chest. The sorrow that brushed her face was almost imperceptible. I was more than certain that she wanted nothing more than to hide it from me. And, for good enough reason.

"My family cursed you?"

She laughed, the sound barely coating the air before falling away. "The curse was formed thousands of years before the a Cordain trapped me in slumber." I kept my distance as she moved to stare at me over the high backed couch.

"Please, tell me. I promise, I didn't know anything about you or your curse. All I want is to go back to normal." My eyes pulled to the window, "If it's possible after what..." the words fell, unspoken.

Her footsteps were soft as she moved to the hearth. She drew a sun and a moon into the ash. *"A fost odată ca niciodată, că de n-ar fi, nu s-ar mai povesti,"* She took a breath that shook as she expelled it back again.

"It was once upon a time, that if it wasn't, it wouldn't be told anymore, that orphaned at birth, two sisters loved each other greater than any power of the earth. Seeing their love, the Sun and Moon grew fond of them and each took one as their own. The Suns child grew to be beautiful and graceful while playing in fields with the lele, while the Moons child practiced magic under the bows of trees with the Strigoaică. But as the Sun and Moon changed many times in the sky, so too did the world change.

The girls grew to share their great love. The Moons child shared her love and bore fruits to the land while the Suns child worshiped her mother alone.

One day the sky grew dark and cold, the Suns child grew bitter and angry at the Moon and when the Moon swallowed her mother Sun, the girl became murderous with rage.

The blood of her sister glistened like stars as it painted the forest floor in bright red jewels, the Moons daughter called out to the sky in pain, and when there was no answer, the words of the Strigoaica fell from her dying lips."

"What did she say?" I whispered to Soryn.

Her eyes were unfocused and far away, as if pulling the story from the very air she was breathing. "You have already spoken the accursed words."

My head spun as she went on.

"When the Sun and Moon finished their dance in the sky, they looked down upon their daughters. The Moon burned red. The Wind sang the dying words while the Sun scorched them into both daughters flesh. The Sun's daughter cried out for forgiveness but only her sister reached for her. And as the beating of their hearts slowed together, a curse was sealed."

A red sheen blurred my vision as more tears threatened to fall.

"Soryn, that's a heartbreaking story, but I don't understand…"

"The Suns daughter was cursed to live forever with the blood she had spilled." Soryn pinned me with a dark stare.

My eyes went wide as I stared back, unable to speak above a breathy whisper, "You're the daughter of the Sun?"

Her face scrunched in disbelief, "I am old, girl, but I am not so old as that."

"Then how did you…"

"Enough," She cut me off, crossing to a small closet nestled by the door, "we have much work to get done before the next blood moon, whenever that may be. We also need to obtain some help to make this place livable for mortals again." She tossed a hooded cloak toward me. "If you are to move around in the daylight, this will help. Keep it pulled low over your eyes. It will draw less attention to you that way."

I held the heavy purple material up in front of me. "Thanks, but, I think I have a better way to blend in, If you don't mind."

Soryn slammed the car door as my sunnies fell from my visor. I quickly popped them on. Stray rays leaked through the sides of the circular pink plastic and made the drive to At Days End a bit more perilous that usual. Soryn clambered out of the car as soon as it stopped, slamming the door again behind her. I pulled my fuzzy black bucket hat further down on my head and starred at her over the roof of the car. Beads of sweat were resting on her brow as she glared at me.

"I'm usually a great driver." The lie was surprisingly convincing. It must have been a vampire thing.

"This block of moving metal is a death trap with you at the reins." Her gaze wandered across the open and empty parking lot. "When we compel workers for my home, you can add someone to drive us around as well."

"Compel?" I grimaced.

"We have important work to be done and my home is in shambles." She pulled open the unlocked door, the chime inside waking up with the rising sun outside. "Compulsion insures that whoever lays eyes on my home, will do my bidding and not remember it." She weaved in and out of the antiques to the counter as I watched from a distance. "It makes getting things done much easier."

"Is that how you got in my grandmother's house?" I waited at the shop door.

"What are you doing?"

"What do you mean?" I stared at the threshold of the store wondering what the invisible barrier might feel like. "I haven't been invited in."

"You do not have to be invited into a shop." Her annoyed tone made it seem like this was information that I should have already known. "Shops are welcome to all who seek to be their patronage. The invitation is implied."

I thought about that for a moment, "What about welcome mats?"

My eyes squeezed shut as I stuck one foot on the shop floor, when I didn't feel any kind of pain, I zigzagged the rest of the way to the counter where Soryn was already digging into the cold pizza from yesterday.

"What is a welcome mat?" She mumbled out, her cheeks already stuffed with two slices.

"It's a mat that people put at their front doors. Sometimes there are pictures but a lot of the time it just has the word 'WELCOME' written on it."

She let out a laugh as she went for another, "How incredibly foolish! And quite helpful for us." She began tearing into another piece before grabbing the box and moving to an old yellow floral settee in the corner. "You shall take me to one of these homes later to test this."

We both jumped when the phone began to ring. "At Days End, where every end gets a new beginning. This is Brittany, how can I help you?"

"Hey, Honey Bear." Moms voice was shaky through the land line. "I wanted to let you know that we are all okay, but there was an incident at the house last night."

"Are you hurt?" I stared at Soryn who had already polished off almost the entire pizza and was now lounging like a cat, licking her fingers without a care in the world.

"I'm fine. I was already asleep when everything happened but apparently a bear tried to break in the house. It knocked the front door down before something spooked it and it ran back off into the woods."

"A bear, mom? Really?"

"Really. And your grandma and I both agree that it would be best for you not to come to the house until we get everything a bit more bear proofed."

"Grandma doesn't want me to come home?" A fresh wave of sadness swept through me as I willed the bright red drops not to fall again. "But mom, where…"

"I know. Where are you gonna stay? Well, here's some happy news. I pulled some strings with the university this morning and we got you set up in a dorm! They said you can move in today." Her excitement was contagious. "Just stop by the registrars office and adjust your class load, okay."

"And the shop?"

"Your grandma called Mr. Dorsetty before I called the university. He's going to be sending someone early, they should be here by the end of the week."

My heart had been still since last night but at her words, it gave a phantom pulse. The thought of someone else owning the shop broke my heart. I didn't risk speaking, knowing the crack in my voice would ruin her good mood.

"Gotta go. The carpenter is here to fix the door. I love you so much, Honey Bear!"

"You, too."

The line went dead as I stared out of the front shop windows, trying my best to keep the tears from my voice. "How did this happen?"

"You cut yourself on a blade that you shouldn't have touched, read a spell you shouldn't have been able to read, and stole a curse that should never have been yours." She smiled at me through the middle of two pillars of books, stacked high to the ceiling, twisting herself around when then the angles of the spines changed to swirl toward the rafters. "This is the most foolish library I have ever encountered."

"What are you even looking for?" The lightness of my feet was still a shock to me as I all but glided to her side like a leaf floating on the top of a calm stream. Inside my thoughts battered against my skull like waves crashing against a sandy shore, taking more and more of it with them with every pass. I needed to figure this out and get back to what was really important. I couldn't lose At Days End. "If you're looking for a book, you won't find it in that."

She had pulled a white garden pedestal over to perch on top, holding her arms out to her sides like she walking a tight rope. She teetered back and forth slightly while trying to see the books further toward the top. "There are many here. It may be here, as well."

"Seeing as how that is a sculpture. Probably not."

Soryn reached out. Her fingers unable to pry apart the carved stone books. Her face went from hard like the artwork in front of her, to soft and full of warmth like the facade of paint that had been used to create the illusion that had tricked her eyes.

"It's been in the shop for as long as I can remember. It's too heavy to move. Grandma spruces it up now and then when the paint starts to chip or fade."

Soryn gave it an appreciative nod before continuing her search. "Where does your establishment keep its books?"

I glanced around, "We don't keep anything super valuable here at the shop— at least not for very long. This is pretty much just knick-knacks and bobbles that Grandma Winnie liked." I ran my hand along an intricately twisted coat rack made to look like a withered and dying tree.

"How could you possibly provide for your family with any of this?"

"We have people from the university come in here all the time to buy stuff. Not only that but the University itself has bought a lot of our inventory. In fact, before Grandma Winnie took over the shop, we used to have a ton of actual antiques and artifacts. Grandma said it was more of a mini museum." I glanced to Soryn.

She had stopped rummaging through the brightly painted armoire and was staring intently. Her eyes fixed on me like she could see the words as they left my mouth. "And?"

"And?"

She huffed, "And now where is this mini museum?"

"Oh, well, some of it went to the history department at the University."

"Let's make haste." She turned, leaving piles of cloth that she had pulled from the dresser in her wake.

"Can we just hold on a sec?" She continued toward the front of the shop. "Soryn?" She pulled the door open. "Soryn, stop and talk to me!" The words felt heavy on my tongue as I tried to imagine her stopping and explaining everything.

Her body went rigid as she turned, the gap in the door not even big enough to set off the bell. Her face was a torrent of red lines as she stared daggers in my direction.

"Did you just try to compel me, girl?" She began to move slowly through the path towards me, like a venomous snake, its head the only thing not hidden by the tall grass it stalked its prey through.

"Um. I just…You're not telling me anything and…I can't help you if you don't and…I don't want to be stuck like this either and… I get that you're mad at me but I'm just scared and I just…whatever… ya know?"

She leaned over the glass counter, her face a stone mask but her eyes piercing through me.

My feet were frozen in place but the top half of my body instinctively leaned away and out of striking distance. "Sorry. I won't do that again. Promise."

"Be very careful who you use that on. The wrong person could spell disaster for us both. I must keep this mortal body alive, and you must keep my immortal form a secret."

"Okay." I whispered as she turned to leave again. "But, please, just tell me what I'm supposed to do."

Her feet stopped and her shoulders slumped before she turned around again. "Fine."

I leaned forward and furrowed my brows ready to learn.

She sighed and went on, "The blood moon will reverse what you have done but we must be prepared. We have several things to uncover before then."

"Okay!" Excitement bubbled up as I grabbed for a notepad and put a column of square boxes along the side. "Shoot."

Her head tilted ever so slightly, "What?"

"I'll make a checklist." I smiled weakly, "A list of all the things we need to do."

"I need my book."

"B-O-O-K. Got it." She looked less than amused as I wrote out each letter, distracting myself from the fact that there was an indigo journal hidden away back at Soryn's house. One that Grandma Winnie told me to keep hidden from her. "What kind of book are we looking for?"

Her lips seemed to twitch. She eyed me before giving another glance around the shop. "It's a wide leather tome. It is a journal of sorts." She leveled her eyes on me again seeming to search for something in my wide gaze, "It is marked only by a blackthorn tree tipped in drops of blood."

Whew. Not the same book. "I don't think I remember ever seeing something like that before."

"You wouldn't. It is spelled to be forgotten by anyone not touched by its maker."

"Am I..."

"Yes. You will know it now should you see it."

"And you..."

"Yes. I will still be able to know it."

"How do you..."

"I just know." She cut me off—the sharpness of it telling me not to pry, so I didn't.

Soryn shook her head but went along reciting her list, "I will need at least a dozen men to prepare my home."

"Prepare?"

"Yes, Brittany. It is hardly suitable for my return to civilization. If I intend on regaining my status, I need a place to host parties and find good graces again. This town was once under my domain and it shall be so again." The intensity that shone through her dark green eyes lit something within me. It was a mixture of fear and awe.

"About that, one, how are you gonna pay for repairs…"

"You will compel them for me."

"Um, no, but thanks for asking."

"I wasn't asking."

"Oh—kaaaaay, let's move on to two. The world has changed quite a bit since you were…sleeping. You want this whole thing to stay a secret? Then you have to work on yourself a bit too." I took another step backward, worried that she may strike if I pushed my boundaries too far. "This is definitely a look, but not if you're trying to blend in."

She glanced down at her clothes. "Fine. What do you suggest?"

"Follow me."

The office was just as we had left it. The painting that had hidden the coffin was still hanging wide open, although the darkness that had seemed to swallow the small space was less suffocating.— as if something had lifted it away.

"Come here." I said.

She took slow, deliberate steps to avoid the door. Her eyes met mine in challenge before I continued on, "Most of my clothes are going to swallow you but I think I have something that might work for now. At least until we can go get you something better." The small metal rack that lived a few feet from the stairs held several pairs of jeans and tops. Working through estate boxes wasn't always pretty and having a change of clothes on hand was lifesaving at times.

The jeans I handed her were way too long but a few cuffs at the bottom were all that was needed. Her wider hips held the top without the need of a belt. My favorite shirt rested low on her thighs and just off her shoulder. She snarled at the baggy top and jeans.

"What is…" She twisted the shirt on her body and tilted her head, trying to read the bright splashes of colored letters there, "…In Living Color?"

"Life." I smiled. "I'll make sure to catch you up on all things amazing. I promise."

Her gaze shifted to the room where she had been trapped in sleep. "Shut that."

It wasn't a request.

The painting swung back with a sharp creak and rested against the wall, though there was no click to signify it was locked again.

"How did you get trapped in there in the first place?" I turned, expecting Soryn to brush off my question like she had so many others. She held on to her secrets like a vice. Instead, there was a shine to her eyes that I hadn't seen before. She stared past me, her chest raised as she fought a catch in her breathing.

A whisper, barely audible to human ears, resounded in mine. The pain that cut at her insides shone through the cracking facade she had been holding on to and wound itself around the single name. "Renard." Her fingers moved lightly over the portrait, brushing aside the whimsical additions of color to reveal the painting in its original form.

"Who was he? My grandma…" I moved closer to Soryn, her pain seeming to pull me in, "back at the house, you asked my grandma about a Renard. She said he was…gone."

"No, Brittany. She said that he was dead."

"Right. Sorry. I just didn't want to upset you. Dead is just; its ugly. I didn't want to make you more sad."

"Death is not ugly, She is not a villain. She does not take what is not hers. We all belong to her, and when it is time, she denies no one her embrace." She gently caressed the cold cheek of the man in the portrait. "Unless, you betray her." She turned back to me. "Like if you were to make a deal with a creature of the undead, to trade what belonged to her. To give them the death they should have been fated to and in turn absorb their curse. Then, no matter the number of sunrises, fires, or steaks to the heart, she would not greet you. No matter the decades or centuries of seeing life, even immortal life grow and fade, she would not welcome you to that peace. No matter how many wishes and prayers you whispered to her in the dark, she would not come." The light that had puddled down the wooden stairs began to darken as if the sky outside could hear her and willed the world to be silent as she spoke.

Her eyes bore into mine. "This curse that you have stolen, you will restore it to me."

"But if we can't; if I'm stuck like this—I won't...can't die?" I didn't want to be a vampire, but if I were doomed to be one forever, not ever dying seemed like a good thing. "Do we have time?"

"Time is more foe than friend." She made for the stairs, her words trailing behind her. "Time is ugly, and he punishes at will."

Chapter Fourteen

SORYN

"This university— would it have a scholar who could tell us the cycle of the moon?"

"Yeah, probably. But I could tell you that."

Finally, some good tidings. "Then tell me, how long do we have before the next blood moon?"

"Blood moon?"

"Yes. Blood moon. You asked if we had time. We have until the next blood moon. We must have all preparations completed before then." I tugged at the blouse, relishing the feel of the unconstrained billowy fabric. Centuries of clothing and this was quickly becoming my favorite.

Brittany's fingers tapped rapidly at the long white rectangle that rested on the glass desk. The clickity-click of her fingertips creating a calming rhythm as she stared at the strange window box in front of her. My brows furrowed as I studied the whirring box just as a horrible sound emitted from the contraption.

"What is this instrument?" I covered my ears, "Why does all of your music seem to carve at my ears."

She looked up with a quizzical smile, "It's just a dial tone. It's what you hear whenever you go online." She smiled in earnest, "I'm just gonna Ask Jeeves about the next blood moon."

"Is this Jeeves person a scholar at the University?"

She laughed.

I twisted the black vines that grew from the white box while trying to think of any way to respond. Her words bounced in my head with no meaning or place to land. I stared at her instead.

"Here!" She said, "The blood moon is a kind of eclipse." She gave a slight chuckle. "A total eclipse of the sun." She sang her words before smiling at me again. "As long as we don't plan on buying any plants we should be good."

The curses of the blood moon were abundant. It made sense that there would be more since I slumbered. "Alright. We shall buy no plants."

She bit her lip and continued, "The next one is on November 1st. That gives us a little less than three months." Her eyes grew large, "I'm gonna be like this for three months!"

"You'll be like this forever if we don't hurry. Renard and I searched for that book for a century before we finally found it the first time. Let's hope Winnie was telling the truth and that this university has held on to it.

Chapter Fifteen
BRITTANY

A ring sounded from the front of the shop joined by cheerful chatter. One very familiar voice called out, "Britt? You open yet?" Keith's voice left a fluttering in my chest and a desert-like dryness in my mouth.

Soryn stared at me with a knowing grin, "I will not fault you for a quick bite."

"Why do my gums itch?"

"You smell something you want. The more you eat, the stronger your powers will be. So, if you smell something you like, just indulge."

"We're not talking about a cake here. That's the boy I've had a crush on since as long as I can remember."

"Even better."

I ignored her. "Hey, Keith. Yeah, we're open." A feminine laugh flittered its way to my ears and ground at my already sensitive nerves. The fruity perfume that hung in the air made my nose itch as well. My eyes locked on to a tall brunette linked on his arm as he escorted her through the shop.

"Oh my god, you were so right, Keith. This junk is gonna be great."

"Um, can I help you?" A very Soryn like snarl crept into my voice and didn't go unnoticed by either of them.

"Are you getting sick? Is that why you left so quick last night?" Keith's hand was warm as he ran in down mine. The gesture obviously not going over well with the brown-haired siren beside him. She took no time at all to pull him toward the line of rocking chairs. "Keith is being an absolute doll and helping with our Halloween show this year." She batted her long lashes in his direction, biting her lip as Keith cleared his throat.

"I thought, maybe your shop could donate some stuff for some free advertising in the programs."

A warmth was pulling at my gut as the pulse in his neck quickened. I licked my lips instinctively. A move that he didn't miss.

He pulled at the collar of his shirt, "Um, Britt?"

His eyes were glossy as he stared at my mouth and took another step toward me.

"I've never seen you on campus before." The girls voice was grating on my ears.

"No, you wouldn't have. I take—"

"I guess higher education just isn't for everyone." She smiled— a gesture that didn't reach her eyes.

My sharp fangs stung as they grazed my lip.

Soryn's voice was a gentle thrum behind me, "Actually, we will be venturing to the school today to register for classes. Both of us will. In fact, Brittany was just saying how nice it would be to have someone show us around. So it is fortunate you made your way to us."

"Why do you talk like that?" She scoffed at Soryn, who was holding on to a calm composure with a gentle grace that only she could muster in the face of someone so insufferably annoying. "Anyway, we can't." She pushed her body against Keith, who didn't move but continued to stare at me. "We have plans." Her tone was more than suggestive enough to read.

"Oh, no, I really must insist." Soryn gave me a pressing look. "Brittany, don't you agree this..." She turned to the girl, "What's your name, darling girl?"

"Ashlie."

"You're quite accommodating." She patted my hand, "Brittany, tell Ashlie how much you would appreciate her helping us to become accustomed to the University."

My throat burned as something deep within me growled at the sight of the girls hands on my Keith. My eyes slid slowly to hers. I could smell the quick shot of fear and adrenaline that pulsed through her. The scent was intoxicating. "Ashlie, why don't you go ahead a do whatever Soryn says."

She twirled her hair around her finger before turning and shooting a dazzling smile at Soryn. "Yeah, totally. Whatever you want, I'm here for it."

Soryn shot me a smirk before walking her new friend to the front door, the bell barely registered in my mind as I stared at Keith, his heart was beating rapidly in his chest; its rhythm a more inviting song than any other I had ever heard in my life.

"Brittany, I promise she's not...we're not...," He brought his lips so close to mine as his heavy breath stirred my hair. The sweet smell of blood that pumped through his every vein seemed to call to me. Fire ran through my body, igniting every part of mine where his fingertips now touched. Before I could stop myself, I kissed him, pressing every inch of my body to his as he pushed himself against mine. His breathing quickened as we bumped into the book sculpture. The rough stone would have scratched at the bare human skin on my legs but my new immortal skin only registered where Keith's lips touched mine. My fangs tingled with anticipation.

The memory of blood from last night made my stomach twist as Keith fought to breathe through each deeper kiss. Something shook at my back. The large sculpture had begun to sway back and forth and was dangerously close to toppling on both of us. I steadied the teetering tower with one hand and tossed him to the side with the other. A sickening crack came from below me as his arm smashed against a concrete turtle that sat at the books base. It didn't do a thing to slow his advances as he reached to pull me down to him, his right arm bending at an unnerving angle.

Images of the man from last night flashed in my mind.

It was as if someone had poured an ice cold bucket of water over me. Immediately, a wave of embarrassment flooded my body.

"Keith, I'm so sorry. So, so sorry."

"It's okay. I'm fine. Really fine." His sluggish movements almost make him seem drunk as he went to pull me in again. I darted away, needing to make space between us and quick.

"Tell Ashlie she can come back later and pick out whatever she needs." I shouted from the top of the steps to the basement office, hoping he wouldn't try to follow me. "I really have a lot of work to do right now though so you should probably leave. Right now. Bye!" I closed the door to the top of the steps before his footsteps could approach the glass counter.

"Can I please see you later?" A pained grunt filled the air. He must have hit his arm on something again, or tripped. Even with my new hearing it was hard to tell.

I couldn't stop the smile that spread across my face at his question. "I would really like that."

"Okay. Very cool. Um. Okay, well, just come find me on campus. I'm in Oakley Hall." The sound of something small and plastic hit the glass counter. "I can't wait."

After what felt like an eternity of silence the bell to the front door finally chimed and he was gone. I could smell his absence but my eyes still roamed the store just to make sure. Soryn had finally come back from her talk with Ashlie when I saw what Keith had left on the counter. There, coiled on the glass, was the chain necklace that I had never seen him without, and resting on the end, was his bright yellow guitar pick.

Soryn looked at me with a devious glint in her eye. "Did you have fun?"

"I almost ate him and I'm pretty sure I broke his arm," My head spun as I held up the chain, "but I'm pretty sure he just asked me to be his girlfriend."

"We shall work on something called standards." She touched the necklace as if it were dripping with toxic sludge before brushing off her hands. "But for now, we have an escort to the university waiting in your car. Hopefully she can drive better than you."

Chapter Sixteen

SORYN

Brittany was singing to the invisible minstrel that flowed through the car, the music making her face alight with joy. Pain lanced through my heart at the sight. I would not let this happen again.

After her almost snack in the shop, it was clear to see that she did possess much more restraint than I expected. Much more than I had as a newly transformed vampire. However, the circumstance were oceans apart in likeness. The trees passed by quickly through the glass windows, their trunks hundreds of years old, held memories of a different time. A time when their bark was young. My mind raced even further back, to a time before the great oaks that blossomed these trees were young saplings.

An ocean away, another tree carved into my memory. The Blackthorn twisted its branches around my now beating heart. It raced as fast as it had the day I had stood beneath it, staring into red eyes that held promises of a life free of shackles and torment. Free of a dowry that should have never been offered and blood that would never be shed.

I had often thought of the day I accepted the curse.

"*Hit me baby, one more time!*" Brittany and our compelled chaperon's raucous duet pulled me back through time as we continued to weave around the black stone road. Thankfully, she was a much better driver that Brittany.

Large metal lanterns stood free of their internal flames and marked the distance as we approached the school. My eyes feasted on the Gothic architecture that loomed before me. It was beautiful, stunning amidst the orange leaves that gathered around its steepled towers and arched entries. It reminded me of something I had once painted, long ago in France.

The beautiful scene was overshadowed by the flurry of cars and people rushing about like mole rats.

"Where to first?" Ashlie's asked in a cheerful tone.

"What do you think, Soryn? Should we go straight for the History Department and see what they've held on to?" Brittany's eyes shone. Her adoration of the school was impossible to miss in her face or the wonder that seeped into her voice.

"Do you know the way?" I asked.

She nodded and began down the wide path that led to a yawning archway and overlooked the schools center.

The compelled one linked her arm in mine as I began to follow after Brittany. "This is going to be such a good year with the two of you here. We're gonna be like best friends."

The taste of bile hit the back of my throat. I had been savoring so many of the sensations I had missed of being human. This, was not one of them. "Take your leave of us." I thought of her addressing Brittany earlier; my lips curled with a delicious thought. "Go find a bench somewhere and stay."

"Yeah, totally. When should I find you again?"

A warmth hinted at my cheeks as I stared at her, "I'll find you."

◆ ᐧ ◆

The halls of the history department were riddled with moments of my past. What were presented as time relished artifacts were cutting-edge inventions when my eyes had last laid upon them. Only a few items seemed to surpass even my years across the sea. Another place where my heart thrummed as it did now.

The sound of merriment flowed in through the many open windows though the halls here were thankfully empty, only a few souls wandered about sharing exuberant greetings.

"I see nothing here of use to us."

Brittany answered from in front of another glass case down the hall. "No magical, glowy, tree books here either."

My footsteps clacked across the slippery floors as a short gust of wind came through the window. Along with it, came a round disc. Glass shards peppered a neatly folded blanket that was nestled in a display box.

"Are you okay?"

A door opened between us cutting off Brittany's words.

"What's going on?" Deep cerulean eyes met mine. The man in the doorway scowled down at the broken glass and picked up the circular projectile before brushing it off. "I'm gonna take a stab in the dark and assume this isn't yours. Am I right?"

"If you try to stab me, dark or not, It will not go well for you."

His brows pulled in for a moment as he looked me over. He pulled at the cuffs of his light blue button up before straightening the brown vest that rested over it. If it weren't for the jeans that everyone seemed to favor, he would have almost seemed to belong in another time as well. When my gaze traveled back up, a single brow lifted on his slightly amused face.

He gave a light chuckle, "Well, now that we have the rules of combat settled," He took the disc and extended it to me. Words stuck in my throat as I gave a quick shake of my head. He looked out the second-story window, before heading back to the opened door, "I keep telling them that if they insist on having antiquities displayed around college kids, they should at least store them under acrylic instead of glass." He vanished into the office for only a moment before returning with a leather cross-body bag and empty box. "But hey, what do I know. I'm just the expert." He tossed a light-hearted smile my way as he dug for something in his bag. The door made a click as he turned the key to lock it. His hand pulled down his jaw, smoothing out the short beard there before reaching into the case, shaking off the bits of glass and placing the blanket that had rested there, in the box.

"So are you looking for someone in particular, or just wandering through time?" His scruffy voice echoed in my head.

"What do you know of me?" My heart slammed in my chest, "Do you know Renard?"

"Sorry?" He straightened the strap of his bag before tucking the box under his arm. "I... am I supposed to?"

Brittany was beside me before I had time to answer. "Hi. I'm Brittany and this is Soryn. I've taken a few classes, intro mostly, just getting the basics out of the way, but I'm about to start…"

"We will be attending classes here." I cut off her rambling.

She took a step back and continued at a more agreeable pace, "History majors, in fact. So we were just, you know, taking in the sights and trying to get a lay of the land in the daytime before classes start."

"Great. Love to see it." He gestured to the box and continued, "I have to get this to preservation and archive but Welcome to Sedgemoore University."

"Excuse me, what did you say, Mr. …" I read the metal plate next to the door, "Jaxson Harwell- Adjunct Professor of Historical

Preservation." My thoughts still clung to what he had said while my words had sent Brittany into some kind of stupor or trance. Her face beamed with childlike glee and she looked as if she could float into the sky with matching wonder.

She tripped over her words yet again as she spoke, "Professor Harwell I am so excited that your going to be a part of the history program here. I've heard so much about some of the artifacts that you personally gathered while you were on your last dig. Is it true that you are the youngest person to be accepted into the Thorne Archaeological Society? And that they offered you a position while you were attending school here at Sedgemoore? I would just die if that happened to me, like in the best way."

Maybe not the best choice of words, I thought.

"It's nice to meet someone as enthused by history as I am. Yes, that's all true but I can't really take all the credit for that." He leaned down and covered his mouth in mock secret, "Nepotism is a hell of a thing." He chuckled, "It's easier to be an expert when you grew up around it. My uncle is a part of the society as well."

Brittany and the man continued to speak as a wispy fog crept over the room.

My skin crawled as unmoving eyes pressed down on me. The portraits that covered the white walls around me seemed to know my secret, and sat in silent judgment. The air grew heavy, a crushing sensation halted my breath and white spots hovered in my vision.

Brittany's voice continued on ahead while my footsteps slowed. "My great-great-grandfather donated a lot of our stores collection to the university when it first opened. I would love to see some of it."

Jaxson, answered, "Well, the archives aren't usually accessible to first year students. Maybe Spring term, if you're really dedicated."

Their voices began to blur, as if I was listening from the bottom of a muddy pond; my lungs burned as if I was being held beneath that same water. Someone called my name from a world away as I was pulled further under. Bright doey eyes hovered above the surface right before I was swallowed up by the abyss.

❖

A cold trickle ran across my face as my vision shifted to focus. "Do you need me to get someone?" Harwell's face hovered next to Brittany's blocking my view from the floor of the hallway.

"Soryn, what's happening?" Her eyes darted quickly to Harwell and back before drawing her words out slowly. "Is this a…" Her eyes shot to him again, then back to me, "Symptom or something?"

"What's wrong with your eyes?" My voice seemed loud in the empty space around us. Looking around, we were the only souls here.

Brittany gave a pointed look as Harwell opened his mouth to speak. A loud growl tore through the room and cut off his words. The sound accompanied a tightening of my stomach and a wave of light-headedness.

"I think I know the problem here." Harwell's voice held a hefty amount of humor as he reached for his bag, pulling several items out and handing them to me. The brown paper crinkled in my hand as I took it from him. The delicious smell of meats, cheese, and mustard captured all of my senses. A large bite was rolling around in my mouth before I knew it, the exquisite tastes combining to create an ethereal sensation on my tongue. The taste of blood was delectable but sandwiches; oh, sandwiches were eternal.

A piece of cheese fell from my lips when I jerked my head to the side as a sharp pop and hiss ripped me from my reverie.

Harwell gave a strained smile as he handed another item to my ravenous hands. My fingers wrapped hesitantly around the cold tube–the bright green reminding me of a poisonous snake as I brought the drink to my nose before taking a hesitant sip. The liquid gave a pleasant burn as it swirled down my throat in a current of fizz and citrus.

"Late night?" Harwell asked.

Brittany leaned back and nodded her head exuberantly just out of his line of sight.

I mirrored her nod as I brought another bite of the delicacy to my mouth.

"Alright." Harwell stood, "It's probably best if you take her home."

Brittany snapped to action, "Yeah, for sure. Thank you for all your help, Professor Harwell." She tugged at my arms, "I'll get her taken care of."

"It might be best not to party too hard once classes start next week. Sedgemoore has a pretty strict code of conduct." He nodded his chin toward me before turning and disappearing down another hall, Brittany's eyes remained fixed until even the sound of his footsteps were gone.

"What's going on? Are you alright? Do you need…" She glanced around, waiting to catch anyone who might be lurking in the shadows before continuing, "do you need blood or something?"

"Did you forget the part where you are the blood-sucking vampire and I am the helpless mortal?" I moved to the window for its warmth but also to put distance between myself and the eyes that seemed to follow from every frame. "The University is called Sedgemoore?"

"Yeah, it's named after the town."

"Cordain."

"What?"

"The name of the town is Cordain. This town bears your family name. Sedgemoore is well, it is somewhere else." Sharp tears sliced through me as I fought to swallow.

Brittany shook her head, "Sedgemoore was established in the early 1700s long before the university was even founded."

"Where you there?" I narrowed my eyes on the people wandering around the large courtyard below. The archway we had passed through stood as a stone portal to the landscaped green space that welcomed all to this great lie.

Brittany's voice was soft behind me, almost a whisper. "You created the town?"

"Don't be a fool. There was already a settlement here." I couldn't help but smile at the memory of the dumb oaf that had been put in charge. He had gladly knelt before me before I rid the town of him and his name putting the Cordain's in his place. "It seems, someone has followed my work."

"So, what happens now?"

"Now. We make ourselves comfortable. The answers I seek are in these walls. I can feel it." A shiver ran down my spine as a cool breeze brushed through the hallway.

"Great." Brittany's eyes widened slightly as her back straightened. "They're coming back"

My eyes searched for Jaxson Harwell, while she tilted her head toward mine and whispered, "They were all over you when we were walking. I thought that was why you fainted for a second."

"Who?"

"The ghosts."

A sinking feeling of dread wracked my body with icy shivers like fingers raking over my rod straight spine. I placed my hand on her shoulder, "We should take our leave of this place for now."

The musty smell that coated the trinkets of time seemed to follow us as we made our exit, Brittany's body finally relaxing once we were over the threshold.

"Something strange is happening here."

She adjusted her glasses pulling the rim of her bright pink hat further down on her furrowed brow. "You mean something stranger than trading places with a 300-year-old vampire, seeing ghosts floating around literally everywhere you look, and almost eating your brand new boyfriend?"

"500 and yes, more strange than that." The warm sun above heated the stones of the cobbled courtyard but a foreboding weight kept the warmth from seeping into my skin. "We should retire to somewhere more private before we speak any further."

Chapter Seventeen
BRITTANY

The registrars office was quick, the old stone building, though aging and showing signs of recent repairs, was thankfully ghost free. Mom had already done a great job of setting up my classes. I only had to change one that conflicted with my schedule at the shop. I still wanted to make sure that, despite the chaos, I didn't let it slip away from my family. Besides, with everything happening, it may be more important than we ever even realized.

Soryn's class list was as similar to mine as possible. The lady behind the desk was kind and helpful, which made compelling her all the more awful. Three months. Three months and I would never have to do it again.

The girls dorm was covered in ivy; one section had been cut away to reveal a row of crumbling corbels. Two workers donned in bright yellow hats teetered on top of a tall metal scaffolding to make the repairs; their conversation making it to my new vampire ears.

"The bathroom's on the other side of the hall. But, if you're here at the right time, they just wander the halls like that." A snicker left both men as they continued to work, oblivious to my eavesdropping.

"Why do you growl at me?" Soryn looked like something out of a magazine as she placed her hands on her hips, staring me down from her place half way up the white concrete steps that led to the dorm.

"Nothing. I didn't even realize I was doing it."

Her eyes followed mine as I glowered at the men who were pointing out something of interest through one of the many high windows. Another snarl resonated in my chest.

"Come. We have much work to do."

I forced my mind on our task and followed Soryn up the steps. Hopefully our dorm room was one of the windows the Toms were peeking in. If I had to eat, at least I would have a couple of deserving meals. I tried my best to physically shake the thought.

Soryn was first through the large glass doors. They looked off to the rest of the architecture and were obviously a somewhat recent addition to the building.

I had taken field trips to the University when I was in grade school. I remembered stepping down from the bright yellow bus and breathing in deeply as if just the air here could impart some kind of wisdom. I knew the map of the campus and had dreamed of this day from the first time I set foot on its hallowed ground. The feeling of awe still held even now. Maybe even more so now since this was the first time I had been back in years.

My heart had broken when Grandma Winnie got sick and I was charged with taking care of At Days End. I loved the shop. I didn't love putting my life on pause right when it was beginning. And now, here I am. Finally starting after it had already ended.

Soryn cleared her throat, holding the glass door open and tapping her foot impatiently.

"You look like you're about to cry. Stop it. You're going to scare the living." Holding the door with her hip, she shot me a sad face and ran her fingers down her face to mimic tears.

A small panic ran through me, and just like that, the urge to cry was sucked back into my body. The last thing I needed was a face full of bloody tears.

A small group laughed and gave quick hellos as they shuffled past Soryn in the doorway. I waved quickly and moved toward the entry, head down just in case a stray tear got away from me. I barreled forward, eyes already sore from the bright sun and hoping the dark interior of the dorm would be more welcoming. The aroma being carried through the open doorway carried a cornucopia of enticing smells. I felt like a cartoon cat smelling a pie resting on a window seal, the smell propelling me forward until, WHAM! My head collided with the door.

I looked up from the ground, the laughter from the group of girls that had only made it down the steps was ringing in my ears. "What the heck, Soryn." My eyes shot to her, standing in the still open doorway, a look of defeat on her face.

"You should be able to enter." She took a step into the dorms foyer while I pulled myself from the ground. On a normal Brittany day, embarrassment would be flushing my cheeks, ears, and chest a bright crimson red. The girls laughter made me want to crawl under a rock and die. I guess to do that, I would have to solve this mystery first.

Soryn disappeared into the building without another word.

After about ten minutes of sulking on the top step, I walked to the open green lawn of the quad. People ran around playing disc golf, while others laid out on blankets, reading excerpts of poetry books that sounded like something that would make Soryn grimace. Familiar faces from school peppered the space occasionally, and I made my quick hello's before moving to a more secluded area.

A familiar whisper floated to my ear, "Hey beautiful."

A smile spread across my face as I clasped the guitar pick in my hand and turned but Keith was no where to be seen. I was sure it had been his voice. My eyes searched the large quad before the voice came again, this time from a dark corner tucked in between the history courtyard and the science wing. The shaded seating area had several wrought iron and wooden slat benches. Each bench held a name plaque belonging to a benefactor; the ones that didn't make enough to warrant having their name on a building. In the farthest corner, several familiar things marked my favorite of these benches; My families name, Keith, and Ashlie with an I.

"Hey guys!" I waved over one of the waist high shrubs that obscured this part of the quad. Keith's eyes looked concerned as I quickly made my way over to them. Ashlie looked up with a dizzy gaze as she stared, searching for something past me. "Is Soryn with you?"

"Um, no. She's touring the dorm right now. You know," I wondered if I looked as awkward as I felt, "just exploring. So I just thought I would go for a walk." A fluttering started in my throat and flowed out through my hands and feet. My nerves felt itchy as I stared around instead of looking at either of them head on. The awkward energy I was unwittingly putting out into the air had reached an unbearable level. I finally tried to release some of it by giving a small kick to the ground but the patch of grass there tore from the earth and showered both of them in dirt.

"Gah!" Keith spit the pieces of grass that had made it into his mouth while Ashlie continued to smile with clumps of the earth sticking out of her hair and plastered to her tanned her cheek.

"I'm so sorry. I didn't mean to do that." I brushed the dirt out of her hair, "They must have just laid sod here or something. Let's go get you cleaned up." I tried to help her from the bench but she refused to budge.

"No, thanks. I'll just wait here for Soryn." She smiled again and looked toward the open quad.

I looked to Keith for help but he had already moved away from the bench and was brushing off the last bit of dirt from his pants. "You don't have anything to be worried about."

His words caught me a bit off guard, "What do…"

"We were just talking about some of the classes were going to have this semester." Keith grabbed my hands and pulled me further away from where Ashlie still sat. He brushed his hand over the guitar pick at my neck before bringing his fingers to my face. "So do you want to see my dorm?"

My eyes traced his where his hands trailed down my arms. Wait. His arm. "Keith," I took his hurt arm gently, moving it back and forth to get a better look. "Did you go to the hospital already? Your arm looked bad back at the store." A flood of butterflies created chaos in my chest at the mention of At Day's End.

He smiled, knowing where my thoughts had been pulled to as I tried to take a cautious step back. "It's safe to say, I'm more than fine."

I hadn't hurt him, this time. We might not be so lucky next time.

"Actually, I should probably wait for Soryn, too." That familiar tingling feeling was already coursing through me.

"I just, would really like to pick up that conversation we were having at the shop." His nose nuzzled into my neck as his arms clasped around my back, pulling me closer to him.

I crushed my lips into my teeth with my closed fist, willing the fangs to stay away as I backed away and out of his arms. His face pinched in frustration for a split second before a softer expression settled over him.

"Britt. I'm sorry. I guess I just though, you know, with the shop and since your wearing my necklace and everything — I thought we were like a thing now."

"We are. I mean, yes, that's what I totally want, too."

His hand raked through his long hair before gripping at his neck in frustration. "I mean, I like never want to make you uncomfortable or ruin what we have."

My heart sank, "No. I don't want to hurt you." The words came out before I could think of anything better. Before I could think of anything else to say, Keith had closed the distance again.

"You could never hurt me." He whispered before gently placing his lips on mine. The kiss was quick and left my head swimming. "But you need to find your friend. I get it." He tucked a lock of hair behind my ear before saying his goodbyes. He said something about seeing Ashlie in class before saying goodbye to her as well and crossing the large green space toward another old building. A cloud of butterflies pounded at my stomach as I watched him leave.

"Soryn!" Ashlie all but screamed as she frantically flailed her hands back and forth. Across the quad, Soryn was making her way toward us, a string of what I could only assume were curse words falling from her quickly moving lips.

"Not one of these mortals are helpful." Her chest rose and fell quickly, her breath coming in quick bursts. She swatted at Ashlie, "Remove yourself." Soryn laid out on the bench while Ashlie and I stared on.

"Did you do something to her?"

Her chest rose and fell quickly as one hand went to her forehead and the other she held aloft for me to wait. Ashlie leaned forward, all but buzzing to have Soryn's attention again.

"I'm focusing on breathing right now. This whole forsaken place is step after step after step. How is one to get anything done when you are constantly climbing?"

"Remind me to tell you about elevators. But seriously, Soryn. What did you do to her?"

"You are the one that compelled her, not me. I just asked her to find a bench somewhere." She pursed her lips and gave a small clap for Ashlie, "and look how well she did."

"What if I hadn't found her?"

"Did you know your name is on this bench?"

"Yes. And don't change the subject."

"She's fine, see. She's smiling, she's happy, she's fine." She sat up, "Now. Let's talk about us. Since the 'RA' person was absolutely no help, I think you should go eat them."

My hands closed around Ashlie's ears as I angrily whispered, "I'm not eating anyone else. Now, stop that."

"Disappointing. Well, then we will have to make do with my home." We both looked toward the mountainous copse of trees that spread out over the hills above the university as if we could see through it to the aging farm house. "But if I am to survive dwelling there in this form, it will need some updating."

"We only have three months to fix this. How are we supposed to renovate your house too?"

"I am certain you will come up with a solution. You are a very clever girl. A naïve fool, but a clever one."

"Excuse me?" My fangs were still on the edge of making themselves known as Soryn's words caught on a nerve. "I'm not a fool."

She smiled, "Just naïve then?"

The wind had begun to circle as a low hum sounded in my ears. "If I'm naïve about anything, it's only because you aren't telling me anything."

She ignored me again, turning instead to Ashlie, who continued to look at her with a child like adoration. "Would you mind fetching…"

"No, Soryn! We aren't puppets for you to boss around." The sound of chatter began to course through my ears while a burning sensation clawed at my neck and continued down.

Soryn gave a knowing smile but said nothing.

"You haven't really told me anything. You keep acting like you are the only one that matters in all of this, but you're not. You've put my family and now my friends in danger and I've still went along with all of it." The skin on my hands stung as I clenched them into fists, my nails digging into my palms.

"Your family?" She let out a sad laugh, "Your friends? You think this creature is your friend? Or that the man you should have already drained is your friend? And yet, you balk when I rightly call you a naïve fool." She stepped into my space, leaving only and a few inches between us. I looked down at her and suddenly felt like a bug about to be squished under someones boot. She didn't turn her emerald green eyes from mine as she spoke, "Ashlie, what are your intentions with Brittany's male companion, Keith?"

"Keith is absolutely obsessed with me." Her words flowed freely, "He even said that…"

"Enough. Ashlie," I finally broke Soryn's cold stare to focus on the girl trying to break my heart, "you don't have to follow anymore directions from Soryn unless you really want to. You don't have to listen to anyone you don't want to."

The ground began to tilt as I broke from the compulsion. Ashlie's words blurred into a strange hum. By the time I pulled my body upright she was gone.

"I wish to take my leave of this place now. It has been nothing but a disappointment. We will try again once I have rested."

We walked, in tense silence, through the quad. The pounding sound of work being done hammering at my already frayed sanity.

"We will return to search for my book another day. In the meantime, we at least need a way to get running water to my home since we can not stay here."

Another round of banging rent through the university grounds.

"Alright. We can go get some jugs of water on the way back." The anger in my voice was strange to my ears.

"Good. You will have something to wash your face after you spend the night weeping again."

My anger was reaching a tipping point. So much so that it took a second before I realized the whistling I was hearing was coming from the dorms instead of my own head. My eyes burned as they shot to the source. Several girls were scurrying away from where the two men were lurking.

Bells rang in my head. I wrestled with my conscience for an alarmingly short time before a wicked grin pulled at my lips. "Scratch that. I've got a better idea." If I was going to have this power for three months, I could use it for some good. I stared across to the girls dorm where the men donned in yellow were now perched at the bottom step of the dorms, wolfish grins on their faces as anyone in a skirt passed.

Soryn remained tight-lipped as we made our way to the car with our new helpers in tow. I had been more than patient enough considering just a little over 24 hours ago I was normal and now, two grown men packed up all their tools and left a paying job just because I told them to. My life had done a full Prince of Belair, but not in a good way.

Both of us slid in to the back seat of my car, doors slamming in unison.

"Can I please know what's happening now!" The rage grew until I could no longer hold back the bile that I felt consuming my insides. "I'm stuck in this mess too, ya know."

"Because of you." Soryn's anger matched my own as her shouts filled the small backseat. "What kind of imbecile finds a scroll and thinks to themselves, hmm, let me recite this ancient curse instead of running for my life from the evil blood-sucking vampire."

"Who carries something like that around on their hip?" I balked, "Don't you think something like this could have been avoided if you just, I don't know, maybe left it at home."

Her voice shook as she fought to latch the seat belt, "I wasn't planning on taking a two hundred year nap in your family's cellar!" The click of the belt seemed to be just the thing to punctuate her argument and ignite the last of her fire. "Centuries of looking after you lot and you manage to ruin it in one night." She huffed at me, "That is truly an accomplishment. I'm sure your ancestors would be very proud."

All I could manage was a gruff, "UH!" before turning to the window. Silence filled the space as the car weaved back and forth through the trees and climbed up the road toward home.

"I'm here if either of you need to talk." Our new driver flinched as, "Shut up!" and "Silence, peasant!" bombarded him from the back seat.

The sky had begun to fade and with it so did my need for the dark shades. The hat and glasses rested gently in my lap as I stared at my reflection in the glass. I gave a small chuckle.

"What?" Soryn snapped, but in a much softer tone than before.

"I can still see myself." I smiled at the woman staring back at me. Her skin was paler than mine and her eyes gave an almost ethereal glow around the honey brown edges. She was beautiful. I had never thought badly of the way I looked, a bit self conscience at times, but looking at this face, a glow latched on deep within me.

"There are many rumors and myths about our kind that are untrue." She laughed, "In truth, most of them were created by vampires themselves."

The anger from moments ago wasn't gone, but a sense of calm clicked between us in that moment. I stared past my reflections to the eery blue blobs that passed by the window, hovering just at the edge of the woods.

"What makes these ghosts blue?" I gestured to the woods, "The ones back at the university, they didn't glow like this."

The car rolled to a stop, the house in view. The white work truck driven by the other peeping Tom pulled up next to us only moments after.

Soryn shooed at them, "Go fix something." An urgent tone clung to her words, but the men didn't budge.

"Do what she says." They began to grab various tools and boxes before heading toward the house.

She continued toward an overgrown path alongside of the house away from the hammering and banging of the two men already starting their work.

"These ghosts back at the university; did they seem to be latched to something? As if something were drawing them in?"

"Yeah. You." I said.

A look of worry dropped over her face as the sky above darkened even more. She gave a sad sigh before speaking again. "Someone has trapped them. Put a spell so they cannot pass on until they find an object sought by the caster. They have no blue light because their souls have been separated from them. They are a husk. Nothing more than an alarm bell to warn someone of my presence."

"That's horrible. Who would do something like that?"

"Someone who has been following my tricks very closely." She turned to me, a realization dawning, "And most likely, the same person who helped your ancestor trap me in sleep."

Chapter Eighteen
SORYN

The hammering left a muffled beat pounding in my head. Too much. This was all too much. My thoughts whirled to a familiar face. "Renard."

"You keep on saying that. Who is it?" She took my hand. Having my powers was making her bold...or she was just incredibly naïve. "Please. I'm trying really hard to just shut up and follow your lead, but..." she paused, biting her lip and deep in thought for only a moment, "something really weird is happening. I know I should be scared to death right now—no pun intended," she gave a soft laugh at her own joke, "but this. All of this doesn't feel...wrong. And that does scare me."

My eyes went to hers, a worry working its way into them. She quickly balked, like a child who has just been caught pick pocketing, her face pinched with guilt. "No, like— the killing and the mind control stuff doesn't feel great, I don't mean that." She let out a frustrated huff. "I mean," she gestured to her body, "when do I start to feel scared about the thought of this. Forever."

My human heart beat a dissonant tune that fought with the memories that screamed in my head. "Soon."

"Soryn, please. You say this is a curse but your not telling me how to break it or why it's so important to."

I steadied my breath, preparing myself, "The woman that gave me this curse." Her brilliant azure eyes flashed in my mind as they did the first time I had laid my own on her. She was the most beautiful woman I had ever seen. "She was a demon. She lured me in with a promise of freedom."

"Freedom?"

"A life of my own. One that would not be chained to the whims of a cruel man."

"You were married?"

"Destined to be so. My dowry already secured, it was only a matter of time when she came to me." The rage I had felt on the night before my wedding, knowing what was to be traded away. I could feel the blood rushing through my veins. Same as it had been on that night. Even the sky seemed to hold the same stars, and they looked down on me now, already knowing the atrocities I had rained down on that fateful night. "She had told me, she was giving me a gift and all that I needed to do, was embrace it. I had to want a life that was not mine. That all I needed to do was to take the years that she offered me, and in exchange, I would never know the pain of death. She was a liar."

Brittany was still beside me taking in every word without interruption. I could still see her pale face, though youthful, twisted with dark hope.

"I went that night to the house that bore my new betrothed's' name." The screams replayed in my head, their shrill calls to death as clear in my mind as the day I cut them down. "My anger fueled the hunger, sparing none that crossed me save one." Her cries still haunted me. I had been too late in realizing the wickedness of the woman's deceit. "I went back to the place where we had made our bargain, the moonlight shone down on the gnarled branches of the tree where we had made our pact. She was no longer there. In her stead, was the dagger and the book. The same tree marked its leather and inside its pages were the words of all who had been bestowed with the curse."

A breeze swirled through the air, bringing with it the smell of wildflowers and mossy wood. I breathed in deeply, appreciating the beauty that had escaped me for so many years. "I tried to end the curse that night. With blood still on my hands, I made a blaze of my horrors and when the flames did not take me, I realized the true power of the curse."

I stared out into the darkness, imaging how bright the forest beyond us glowed through Brittany's eyes. "The curse isn't just about betraying death." I looked to her, feeling the cracks that were breaking open on my heart. The promise I had given to the life I had spared. Knowing that one thing that kept me through the abyss of time, was broken. It was as if her eyes shone through Brittany's. "The true curse is knowing, that some day, when your soul is weak, when you have lived through so much grief and given it to so many, you will sacrifice another to take your place."

When Brittany finally spoke it was barely above a whisper, the sound of the wind shuffling the leaves and the workers clanking inside making it nearly imperceptible. "But you didn't."

"I wanted to. I dreamed about it. I do not regret much. Most lives I took were worthy of their fate." I stared up into the sky through the canopy of twisting branches, "The night I came to the curse, I wanted to make them all suffer. Instead I gave them all a quick death, as well as the innocents that had already suffered too much."

Brittany whispered, "And the one you saved? Was that Renard?"

I couldn't bring myself to look at her. "Renard was someone I spared." My face scrunched as I thought about my words, piecing each sentence together thoughtfully before speaking again. "There was a battle many decades later. Renard wasn't a soldier and yet he was mortally wounded in a battle." His face had been a shroud of death twisted in pain when I had first come upon him, the smell of blood luring me in from my search for another who had already escaped. "He had pleaded for me to help him. He saw what I was and begged me to stay. Until last night, he was the only mortal that was ever turned at my hand." When I finally looked up at her, a bright red smear coated her right cheek. "He should have been the last. I left him soon after. The thought of what I had done to him weighed heavy on my heart until one day, a few years later, he found me again. We were travel companions from that day forward. We traveled all over Europe as I sought to discover the root of my curse and after many years, fell in love."

"So what made you come to America then?"

I remembered the smell of the saltwater that battered the ship that carried us across the undulating waves. My shame had never felt so great as it did on that trip. If not for my mission, I would have wished for the waters to swallow me down into the farthest trench where no light or life could reach me.

"A promise forged in fire."

We sat in silence, staring in the darkness for a great while before anything disturbed our calm.

"Let me tell her." A whiny voice pierced through the darkness to where we sat.

"Why should you get to talk to her first?" Another voice argued.

"What is that?" I asked.

The two men teetered into view, stumbling over themselves to get to us.

One long discussion later, the two men had given an explanation of repairs that needed to be done along with a list of what was needed to do the work. They were happy to offer the materials that were already purchased for the university. After another few words from Brittany, they left, promising to tell no one and to come back tomorrow with supplies.

I fought a yawn as they pulled away down the winding drive.

"Let's get you to bed. Tomorrow, we find that man of yours." She smiled as we went inside and she helped me get comfortable on the couch. Her gentleness reminded me of happier times. I stared into the crackling fire, remembering days where Renard and I would sit, silently taking in each others company. The only man who had ever held my heart within his own. Brittany was right. I could feel his presence. Somewhere in this new world, he still held on to life. And come tomorrow, we would work to find him.

Perhaps she did not hold the wickedness of her ancestors. A pain that had been buried deep in my chest long ago began to swell again at the thought. At the end of it all, I knew, no one could escape blood.

Chapter Nineteen
BRITTANY

The parking lot outside of At Day's End felt like graveyard. Over the past few days, Soryn and I had turned the entire shop over. We had searched every nook and cranny where a book could possibly be hidden. There wasn't much that pointed to any book, cursed or not. My heart ached to talk to my mom and Grandma Winnie. Mom was still blissfully unaware while Grandma all but refused to talk to either of us. One thing we had agreed upon, over the phone of course, was that it would be best to close the shop for a few days. Mom thought it was so I could get settled at school while we waited for Mr. Dorsetty's assistant to make the trip. His lackey was already three days late.

The car had barely came to a stop in the familiar parking lot before Soryn started dolling out her orders. "You go in. I need food." Soryn shooed me away before turning to one of the Toms.

Our new chauffeur slash handyman was smiling from ear to ear as she instructed him on what she wanted for breakfast.

My key turned, the familiar click and chime soothed the mental madness that still circled my head like a hurricane. I breathed in deeply of the dusty smell that embraced the shop. The familiar aromas that had always lingered were so much stronger. Leather, earth, and violets; I had never thought about time having a scent before, but this was irrevocably it. I scanned the room as memories of adding each age worn piece with Grandma Winnie and even some with my mom came to mind.

A knot seized in my chest and I worked it with my palm. I focused on a set of Russian nesting dolls someone had painted to look like the Greek pantheon. Mom and I had laughed when we found it resting in the bottom of a rat eaten cardboard box. Chronos felt smooth in my hand as I rolled the doll back and forth and thought of the women who had raised me. I hadn't gone this long without seeing them since I went to camp the summer before I started 7th grade. Jesse Pollard had dared me to eat some berries on our first nature hike and I had gotten so sick that I had to go home on day two. I spent that summer helping my grandma in the shop and watching historical documentaries with my parents. Long weird hours at the hospital meant that both of them were often preoccupied. I didn't mind. I loved the shop.

It had been a little punch to the gut when we sold our home and moved in with Grandma Winnie though. It made sense. Her house was paid off and big enough for everyone. I still wondered about our house on Brandymill though. I drove by it now and then and remembered what life was like when it was me and mom and dad. He called often, but I hadn't talked to him in weeks and I cringed at the idea of getting on a plane to go see him. The thought of being trapped in a flying lunch box threw me in a small panic. I took another steadying breath and focused on the shop.

Unstake My Heart

My ears twitched. The sound of metal hitting concrete pinged around the old antiques and tickled my ears. Someone was here. My chin tilted upward as I smelled the air, a faint unfamiliar scent trailed through the shop. I followed it, silently moving through the store as if I were April O'Neill stalking a lead. I took off my hat and sunglasses, placing them on the glass counter as I tip-toed closer to the basement door. A creak and a click came from below followed by the sound of footsteps on the wooden stairs. I counted each one. One-two-three. I readied my hand on the brass knob. Seven-eight-nine. Only a few more to go. I tightened my grip as the stranger got closer and closer. Thirteen-fourteen-fifteen. I swung open the door. "What are you doing in there?"

Wide eyes met mine just before a fluttering of hands. A look of shock fell on the strangers face as his heels teetered on the top step. Panic struck me as I realized he was about to fall. My fist clenched into his shirt, the black material silky between my fingers. A single lock of his disheveled black hair fell over his panicked eyes.

"Don't let go."

I pulled. A ripping sound filled the air as he flew forward, rolling on the floor and slamming into the counter. The rattle of trinkets inside the case he hit punctuated the collision.

"Who are you and what are you doing here?"

"I was sent by Mr. Dorsetty." He straightened and looked at his torn shirt, the woven necklace and coin that rested there stood out from the rest of his sleek clothes.

"Oh. I'm so sorry." I glanced back at the open door. "Here. Let me help you." He moved quickly out of my reach to stand on his own, his eyes never leaving mine as he slowly rounded the counter and added more distance between us.

"Brittany?" He gave a gentle smile as he thumbed through several of the papers laid out on the work space.

"Yeah." I crossed my arms, back on guard as he picked through several items. "And you are?"

"Trying not to get lost in this mess." He raised an eyebrow while a smile hinted at his lips. It was gone as quick as it came as his face fell into a bored stare.

"Just a guess, but judging from the crumby attitude, you must be Dorsetty's assistant."

He didn't look up from the trinkets he was shuffling through, instead he just gave a short huff while a smirk tugged at his face.

"I think I liked you better on the phone." I said

He finally looked up from his rummaging with a bright smile, staring intently in my eyes before a dark shift took him over again.

"Yes, well. You seem to be quiet different in person as well."

"What does your boss want with At Day's End?" Paper crinkled in my hand as I shuffled everything he gathered into a pile in front of me. "He can't possibly make that much money off of it. It's pretty much just old knick knacks now. Nothing of true historical significance has come through here in years."

His hand reached through my sloppy arm fortress and snatched a small notebook from the pile. "Oh, I wouldn't say that." His teeth gleamed, a quick gesture before his finger traced a page. "You have some pretty strange interests, huh?"

"What?" I could feel the glare I leveled on him creasing the lines on my brow. Something about him grated at me even more in person. "Don't act like you know me. Just because you've annoyed me on the phone a couple times a year doesn't mean you can assume anything about me."

"Oh, really?"

"Really."

He smirked as he thumbed through my notebook, his smooth voice held a hint of humor as he read from the pages, "Blood Moon. Dozen Men." He tilted his eyes up to stare at me, "Wardrobe Montage?"

He had flipped to the checklist I had made the day after I took the curse from Soryn. I tried to act as cool as I could while changing the subject. The last thing I needed was some hoity-toity stranger poking around in to mine and Soryn's business.

"Can I like, help you or something?"

"Or something."

I sucked on my teeth before continuing, "Did you find anything downstairs?"

He leaned forward, holding on to my notebook like a bargaining chip, "Is there something of interest downstairs?"

"Not at all." I reached for my book. He was quick, but not quicker than me. The book was tucked neatly in my bag before he could pull his hand back.

His face changed. In an instant a coldness fell over his playful features while a sharp toothed anger whispered behind his words. "Alright well, I think I'm good here. I've already been caught up on what needs to be done so I don't think I will need your assistance."

"What needs to be done?"

"Mr. Dorsetty just needed a few documents before he and Ms. Cordain can proceed with the sale." He reached into the back pocket of his sleek black dress pants and held up a roll of papers.

"What?" I grabbed the phone, the dial tone buzzing in the air before I pushed each number to call home. "She wouldn't sign anything without talking to me first."

A click cut off the first ring. The long spiral chord led straight back to where Ben's finger rested on the phone.

"I'm going to need you to remove your hand before you lose it."

A shadow crossed his face as he leaned in. "Ms. Cordain, have you spoken with Mr. Dorsetty lately?"

"Why does that matter?"

"Well, I was under the impression that you were on good, even pleasant terms." The knot at his throat bobbed. I could hear his heart quicken as he avoided my eyes. "He's even spoken about offering you a position in his acquisition department once you graduate."

I could feel by brow dip in confusion as a small flutter of excitement began to swarm my stomach. It wasn't quite my dream of going on historical digs all over the world, but it was definitely closer than working in an antique shop.

Ben flipped through another stack of papers, jotting notes down on them while he spoke, "He's been so impressed with the work that you've sent us that he personally set up your way to go to school." He looked up and locked eyes with me, reading the confusion that had to have been pasted there. "Didn't you know?"

"My mom didn't tell me anything about that." The bell to the front door chimed and Soryn's voice rose above the large pieces of furniture that blocked her short frame from our view. A myriad of bygone expletives made it to us before she did.

"Soryn, we have company." I shouted as she bobbed around the large armoire with a box of donuts that were looking a bit worse for wear.

She stopped and stared, her eyes going back and forth to each of us several times before she continued. "It seems that you have already found your breakfast."

"You're right. I already ate earlier." My eyes widened, begging her to take the hint and change the subject. She seemed to understand and nodded with a wink.

"So who might this…" She stopped after only a few steps, her gaze locking on Ben's chest.

He reached a hand to her, "I'm Ben. Mr. Dorsetty's assistant."

Soryn faked a cough before continuing, never taking her eyes off of whatever had caught her attention. "I'm sorry, I really shouldn't shake your hand." Her eyes finally met his but the fire that usually consumed them was replaced by a wall of stone. "I would hate for you to catch whatever ailment has befallen me."

She moved to my side, pulling me in and smiling. She was already strange, but this was odd, even by her standards.

"Well. It does seem that the two of you might have some work to get done so I won't keep you." He gathered several papers into a briefcase before turning back to me. "Brittany, it was so nice to put a face to the voice on the phone." He smiled, a gesture that didn't make it to his eyes. "You are certainly not what I expected."

I remembered all the calls we had before; none of which were particularly pleasant. I had almost forgotten that this was the same person. He certainly seemed like a different man, too—though the voice was unmistakably his. Of all the people Mr. Dorsetty could have sent, why did he choose him. And for that matter, "Ben, wait." I peeled Soryn's hand from my arm and made my way to the front door where the chime had just sounded. Ben stood, a terse look on his face as he waited for me to catch up. "Why does Mr. Dorsetty care about my school?"

The cold seeped back in. The changes in his demeanor set off alarms in my head. "Mr. Dorsetty is great at spotting talent. He takes great pride in training new blood."

The shop was eerily silent as I watched him cross the parking lot to his very expensive looking car and drive away. I couldn't help but think about his strange choice of words.

I fully expected Soryn to be half way through her giant box of sprinkle coated confectioneries by the time I walked back to the counter. Instead she stood there, chewing on her long nails instead. Her voice was a low whisper as she waved me closer to her.

"Is he gone?" A hint of fear nestled into her words.

"Yeah. He drove off already. What's going on?"

"Whoever that man says he is, he is lying. Otherwise, your benefactor has hunters in his employment."

"Hunters? Like vampire hunters?" From the look on Soryn's face, whatever that meant couldn't be a good thing.

"Vampire, Ghoul, Fae, anything that is not human, they destroy it. Without thought or remorse."

"How do you know…"

"The coin he wears around his neck is a mark of the Hunters. He bares the insignia of the Order of Rosewood."

A nervous laugh trickled down my throat, "It's a good thing I can't die then, right?"

Soryn's eyes wandered toward the basement door. I could hear her heart beating frantically, the sound of it sending my own nerves on edge with worry.

"Do not be fooled into thinking that death is the only way to make one suffer."

Chapter Twenty
BRITTANY

"**H**ey, could you help me find room 203?" The buzz of students coursing through the halls was deafening. Every conversation bounced through my brain as I tried to work my way through the building. A week full of making a plan and learning how to blend had ended too quickly, and the days were ticking by to find Soryn's book and boyfriend so we could swap back when the blood moon came back around. Not to mention the man that had been sulking around and making a mess of At Day's End may very well be vampire hunter sent to make me suffer unimaginable, though not deadly, horrors. Soryn was still pretty tight-lipped on what exactly these hunters had done and it made my head spin trying to keep it all together, but no big deal. Right?

"Hey. How you doin'?" The guy blocking my path took his time to commit me to memory as his eyes tracked up and down my body. His baggy clothes and facial hair looked like it was copied straight from MTV.

"Fine. Do you know where I can find room 203?" I held the canary yellow paper up, "Professor Harwell, intro to history."

"Yeah, I know where that is." He bit his lip and raised a brow in my direction. He was about as helpful as my Grandma Winnie had been when we called her from the shop this weekend. My stomach lurched at the thought of her. Although she had answered our questions as best as she knew how, she had seemed cold and distant.

A throat clearing brought me back to the present. "I said I could show you." He rubbed his hands together, before playing with the small patch of hair below his lip. "But I'd rather help you spice up those day dreams, girl."

"Ew, gag me with a spoon." He had stolen AJ McLean's look but none of his charm.

"Whatever." He walked away, quickly locking on to another girl wandering around with a matching yellow paper.

The torrent of conversations were blaring in my head. Soryn had warned that being around so many people at once might be too overwhelming. Flashbacks of the skating rink pounded in my brain.

Somewhere down the hall, pop music blasted through someones headphones. I sucked in the air, meaning for the familiar feeling to bring a sense of calm. Instead the smell of blood, pumping though veins had my fangs itching to snap out. I focused on the chipping taupe colored paint as I quickly moved through the hallway. I was no longer worried about finding room 203, but instead searched for somewhere to escape the pulse of life coating the halls. I focused all my efforts on the posters that I passed. They boasted images of campus life, Greek sororities and fraternities, as well as signs for ways to donate and help the school. A pained yelp left my lips as my fangs shot out. A flier for the start of semester blood drive had the last of my restraint ebbing away faster than I could catch it. Soryn had been right. I wasn't ready for this. Not yet. I needed to get away from the throng of people and only one place came to mind.

I rained in my speed as best as I could as I made a mad dash for the safety of my car. My hands gripped the duck taped wheel as I counted the leaves that fell from the giant oak in front of me. Five hundred thirty-two, five hundred thirty-three, five hundred thirty — tap tap tap.

The world seemed to slow. There was absolutely no way this Backstreet Boys wanna be followed me down to my car. And yet — tap tap tap.

I cracked the window. The smell of his adrenaline spiked my already aching hunger. "What do you want?"

He ran a hand through his hair before resting an arm above my window. "I feel like we really had a connection back there, and I ruined it. Ya know? I would love to make it up to you."

A practiced sincerity coated his words. I had the distinct feeling that if I checked where he touched my car, it would be coated with slime. "I have a boyfriend."

"Lucky guy."

"Yep."

"So, where is he right now?" His voice was low as he slowly leaned down, his eyes level with the small opening between us.

His eyes went dead as I stared into them and compelled the truth from his mouth. "Tell me what you're doing here."

"I followed you when I saw that you were walking to the parking lot alone. I figured I could trap…"

"That's enough." The anger building deep within me wasn't unfamiliar, but it was begging to be let out. Another word from this scum bag, and I didn't know if I could hold back.

I focused on the thought of him walking back to the campus and attending all of his classes. I focused on the thought of him never acting like a creep again. And I focused on the thought of him treating every person he met from here on out with decency and respect. My vision blurred as I told him as much, compelling him to heed my words. I couldn't help the people that he had no doubt already treated like trash, but it felt good knowing he would be a better person moving forward.

A sharp pain lanced through my neck. Soryn said that the more I used my new powers of persuasion, the sooner I would need to eat again. The thought left a warring feeling soaring through me. I pulled at the crank on the door, rolling my window down all the way before shouting. "Hey!"

The leaves crunched, their orange and brown pieces as dry as the inside of my mouth as I tracked his footsteps back toward me. He stared blankly ahead, waiting for whatever direction I might bestow on him next.

The voice that left me was deep and guttural and nothing like the woman I had stared at in the mirror my whole life. "On second thought."

My sharp nails clawed into his shirt. A puff of white dust where his feet had left the ground was the only sign of where he had been as I hauled him over me and into the front seat.

Regular Brittany was appalled by the thought of taking another life, but vampire Brittany purred at the idea as his blood soothed the anger that had been building to a crest. As the hunger subsided, a stab of panic shot through me.

The university grew smaller and smaller in my rear-view mirror as I set my now very clear mind on At Day's End. There was just one stop to make first. I needed to see a man about a well.

◆•◆

The windows of the shop were already reflecting bright shards of daylight on the almost empty parking lot when I pulled into my usual spot, the expensive-looking car only two spots away.

Unstake My Heart

Several loose bits of pavement skittered as I kicked at the ground. Was it really too much to hope that I could get here first to prepare for a day full of lies and sabotage? As I unlocked the door, only the sound of slurping hit my ears as I took another big drink of the ice cold slushie like mixture. A quick pit stop at he gas station had been necessary before popping over to the well. I stared down at the chunks of red mixed in to the frozen treat. They could be mistaken for bits of strawberries if anybody asked.

A deep sigh left my body as I steadied myself and reached for the door. Soryn might be scared of this guy, but I knew him. I knew what made him mad. Well, I knew what had made Mr. Dorsetty's assistant mad. Unless this guy was actually a hunter like Soryn thought, and then I didn't know. Hunter or not, if I could get under his skin, maybe I could get him to slip up. Pester would be the name of the game today. And I was very good at that game.

The familiar chime I had grown so accustomed to didn't greet me with its usual ding-ding. The white box that had perched above the door for as long as I could remember was gone and in its place, was a mismatched square of blank wall. The bell wasn't where the changes ended.

Apparently, he was no stranger to the game.

Annoyance pecked at my brain like a ravenous vulture, tearing more and more of the calm I had tried to muster away piece by piece. Every bit of the shop had been rearranged, creating a clear path to the far office door. Even the counter had been moved and cleared and a chunky buffet style cabinet served as the new counter for the aging register.

The carpet was a maze of discolor and divots; A map of how the shop should be.

"Do you like it?" A deep voice flowed up from the open office door. He leaned against the dark wooden frame, his white sleeves were rolled up his forearms, and a book was open in his hands. The smug look on his stupid face made it seem as if he had been waiting there for me this whole time. I took a long pull of my drink, as the anger in me began to rear its head again. It was followed by my an immense urge to push him back down the stairs.

"I don't know how you got anything done before." The book in his hands gave off a puff of dust as he closed it with a snap.

"We did just fine." Something was off about him. He didn't smell like a regular human and though the urge to pummel him with a garden statue was strong, I also found myself not wanting to drain an artery. Although, that could be because I was still pretty full from breakfast. I gave my drink a heavy slurp before speaking again.

"When will you be leaving Mr…"

"Benjamin Somers. I'll be here until you are fully cataloged and Mr. Dorsetty is satisfied with my work." His eyes remained on me as he moved to the new counter.

My body mirrored his as I moved to the opposite corner of the room to sit on the couch, its white fabric still stained red in places thanks to Soryn and her new love of pizza. I tried to look intimidating despite the dried sauce surrounding me. "And how long have you worked for Mr. Dorsetty, Benjamin Somers?"

"Why do you need to know, Brittany Cordain?"

"I want to know the credentials of the man helping to steam roll over everything my family made."

A challenge seemed to hang on the air as our eyes locked, neither looking away.

"Four years."

"How did you start?"

"College intern."

"Where did you go to school?"

"Moorington University."

"What was your degree in?"

"Archaeological studies."

"Who was your favorite professor?"

137

"Doctor Knightly."

"What's was your first dogs name."

"Geral...What?" He took a beat to shake his head. "What exactly does that have to do with my credentials?"

"It's important to know. Having a dog growing up says a lot about a person."

"Like what?"

"If you're a cold-blooded monster or not." The irony of me calling him a cold-blooded monster was not lost on me.

He leaned forward, his face as hard as uncarved stone. "Have you met Mr. Dorsetty?"

"Not in person yet, no."

My eyes caught a flit of movement as his shifted quickly to the door and back.

"Then you don't know cold-blooded."

"He can't be that bad if he's paying my way through university?"

Without another word, he began working at the files he had stacked on the counter, boredom written all over his face. I had to admit, if he was a hunter, I was impressed. He was really good at this whole hiding a secret identity, thing. If he didn't probably want to kill me and I didn't definitely want to flip that heavy counter over on him, I would've asked him for tips.

"So, you never said why you were late getting here, Ben."

He was silent as he worked, no longer seeming to want to add to the conversation. His eyes barely shifted to me as I spoke, his cool demeanor really selling the whole thing. Maybe Soryn had been wrong. Maybe he really was just Dorsetty's assistant.

"Unfortunately my train was held up." He shrugged, "Mechanical issues."

The air became thicker as I moved toward his spot at the counter. "You scared of flying?" I stopped, suddenly not wanting to be any closer to him.

He gave me a knowing look. "I have work to do and I believe you have classes to attend."

"Nope. I'm all yours for today." I smiled, my mouth stained red from what he may or may not believe was my cherry slush. "So what can I help you with, Bennie boy?"

He didn't look amused at the nickname. "Why don't you go get some breakfast. I'm sure you're starving and probably nursing some kind of hang over, right? I hear college girls are notorious for partying."

I shook my drink at him. "I'm on a liquid diet."

He reached for my cup. Thankfully most of the cherry-flavored frat boy drink was already happily swirling in my belly. "Go get your own." I pulled it out of his reach and made a point of looking him up and down.

"What's in it? I can smell it from here."

My words formed around the straw as I quickly made to finish my meal. "Vodka." I slurped, "Lots of it. And not the fancy kind either." I finished it off with a flourish. "The cheap kind that comes in the plastic bottle. So, yea, it's probably not up to your standards."

"That seems to be the case with most things in this town."

He eyed my cup as I huffed around the shop and got busy undoing his mess. It was a struggle to remember to pretend to struggle while moving things back to normal. After the first few hours of forced grunting and pretending to need help to move everything, and a rather spirited argument about whether our collection of uranium glass was authentic or not, both of us were throughly annoyed with the others company.

I needed to get some air that didn't have the smell of Benjamin Somers in it.

"I'm going to get something to eat." I stormed out of the shop without another word. I had marched only a few steps into the light before spots took over my vision and my eyes burned. The sun was doing a great job of ruining my exit. I stumbled back inside the shop only a few moments later. The couch was a blur as I picked my denim purse off of it, pulling out my sunnies and hat and readying myself to storm out again.

"Just so you know—" I glared at the tall dark blob behind the counter for a second too long before it reshaped into a coat rack. I stilled, looking and listening for signs of him.

Benjamin's voice came in rushed whispers from downstairs. "Well she wasn't before…not a single conversation I've had with her in the past few years would have led me to believe that she was."

Silence.

"Yeah. Ninety-nine percent sure." He scoffed, the sound of it grating at my ears. "She spent the last three hours pretending to struggle at rearranging furniture while drinking blood from a Seven-Eleven cup." He laughed, "It's pretty obvious."

He was on the phone downstairs. An electric buzzing whirred in my ears as panic began to claw inside my chest. I was silent as I made my way behind the buffet cabinet. The counter was clean except for a single bag tucked into one of the many cubbyholes hidden from front view. Several wicked looking stakes along with bottles of what I assumed were holy water were stashed inside. Well, I guess my question was answered. Benjamin Somers was a vampire hunter. "But I'm the obvious one." I whispered.

My fingers shook as I held the dial down on the counter phone, bringing it gently to my head before releasing it.

A rusty and rough female voice came through the line. "We can wait until the book is uncovered to take further action."

Ben replied, "Yes maam."

"Have you found any sign of it?"

"Nothing yet. I'm not sure they would leave it here, anyway."

"Fine." The voice seemed genuinely disappointed at that. "Then follow the girl. She's your new priority just in case we need some insurance."

There was a click just before I put the receiver back but no movement from the basement office. Too many ideas pummeled through my head. Did I confront him about what I heard or did I run. The creak of wood started up as I shouted in my head, "*Make a decision, Brittany.*" Creak—Creak—Creak. The coat rack went crashing to the floor as I started for the door and my fingers blurred as I sent a message from my pager for Soryn to meet me at The Rink. Creak. Creak. Creak. Creak. He must have skipped several steps this time.

"Hey, Brittany."

"What? Sorry. I just came back for my purse really quick. So, yeah, bye." The words were loud in my ears as I realized I was almost shouting though my nerves.

"I could use some food, too." He grabbed something from behind the counter before putting on his blue tinted metal trimmed glasses. Wow. This guy had watched one too many vampire films. If that look didn't scream Bram Stokers Dracula, I didn't know what did.

He pushed passed me, holding the door for me to exit before following me to my car and climbing into the passenger seat. "I think we should get to know each other a bit better."

Spice Girls blared from the speakers as I steered the car toward The Rink. Whatever he was planning on doing, he would have a crowd for it. Hopefully Soryn would get there soon. And fingers crossed, she was having a better day than I was.

Chapter Twenty-One

SORYN

My stomach twisted and growled again as I made my way to another one of my classes. If not for the excitement bubbling under my skin and propelling me forward, I would have slowed to nab the pastry from the sloppily dressed boy half asleep at the bottom of the stairs. Last night I had devoured the books Brittany had handed me for my Intro to Health Science course. The advances in knowledge of the body were astonishing. It was a beautiful thing to know the names and functions of the organs I had often held in my hands.

The white-haired woman who taught the class made an ear scratching noise as she moved around the front of the room, her clothing constantly brushing against itself in an irritating rhythm. But as soon as she began to speak, the sound faded from my mind and instead, I was caught up thinking about the beauty and power of the woman standing before me. A woman held the attention of all who sat before her, men and women alike. Her strong voice demanded respect. How many bodies were left behind and rotting for her to hold such a place of power? I couldn't help but be in awe of her.

My hands gripped the front edge of the desk as I hung on her every word. Unfortunately, my second class passed without so much fervor. It held little exuberance as the one before it and by the time the teacher up front had finished speaking, I had already forgotten what the class was about.

My mind and gaze wandered to the window. The midday sun poured out pools of buttery light onto the faded cream colored flooring. I breathed in and out slowly, relishing the feeling of warm air filling my chest where my beating heart pulsed with life.

Life.

A sickness clawed at my insides, the sinking feeling dragging all the warmth around me down with it. I stared down at a tree in the courtyard below and imagined a pair of other worldly eyes staring into the depths of my soul. They seemed to taunt me as they had in my nightmares. They had tricked me into a world of death and decay. I would not let Brittany face the same torment. *Focus.* A tremor had begun to grow in my arms as I looked out on the university's library. All else would have to wait for now. I needed to find my book. The library was large, though not as grand as the ones Renard and I had searched across Europe. Countless hours were spent searching for my book in years before and as much as I wanted to indulge in the ways of mortals, I couldn't. I would not leave Brittany with my curse.

The demon did not stay to teach me the ways of my immortal life. She did not halt to aid in my transition. She left only the book placed under the blackthorn tree where our pact had been sealed along with both of our fates. The only trace of her left, besides the book; was the dagger, her cloak, and a wind blown pile of ash. In the last pages of the book was a short letter. She told me of the curse and of her fate. I had stared down at the pile of ash and mourned. Though not for her. In anger I had rid myself of the book not knowing its importance then. And yet again, I was searching for the accursed thing.

I made my way to campus library with a sinking feeling building in my heart.

A harsh-looking crone was slumped behind a tall stack of books, her fingers scratching through a block filled with slips of paper. She used a bony finger to push up the large spectacles that were falling down her nose. As I approached, a bright smile crested over her face, dispelling the unease her original form had held.

"Hello dear, are you needing help?" The woman's voice was warm but shook with age as she spoke.

"Yes." I looked around the large open space. "I may need quite a lot of help, I fear."

The Gray-haired matron smiled, the light reaching her eyes, though nothing seemed to click beneath the warm expression. "What kind of book are you looking for?" Her words sounded automatic, like she had said them so much they had lost their meaning through the years.

The deep earthy tones of the shelves and tables contrasted heavily with the cold metal and tile floor. They had tried to pull the space into another era by plastering it with newer, shinier things; its aging beauty would not be covered, though. I stared down at the clothes Brittany had put me in this morning. The bright lavender color of the silk top left me suddenly feeling bare. Even the soft material of the form fitting jeans, though they covered my skin, had apprehension gnawing at my chest. Hen flesh peppered the skin on my arms as I suddenly felt entirely out of place. I hadn't noticed that the Crone had continued to speak while my thoughts worked themselves into a maelstrom.

"...and downstairs is where you would find the uncirculated books. The university has several rare and historical records in its archives." She leaned forward, her chair inching out from beneath her in a slow glide as she stood.

"Archives. Yes, I will go there." My feet seemed to be bewitched to trek forward as I hastily moved for the heavy black metal stairs that wound to the back shadows of the large library space.

"Miss, you aren't allowed down there on your own."

"It's all right, Gertie." A deep voice said. "I can help her." I turned to see Jaxson Harwell leaning against the counter, a flaky pastry in his outstretched hand.

"No chocolate today." The elderly woman crossed her arms to stare at Jaxson. "Don't pout at me Gert, take it up with the Never Bean." The warmth she had just moments before held, quickly faded as she went back to her work of shuffling through papers while small bits of baked goods stuck to the corners of her mouth and sprinkled the counter.

Jaxson narrowed in on me as he took a long chug of whatever was steaming from the paper cup he held. I could smell whatever delicacy was in the bag that held the same logo.

"So?" He asked. I stared at him for a long moment, not sure if him being here was yet another strange custom of this time that I had to learn, so I repeated.

"So."

"What class are you needing to search the archives for?" He brushed by me, his feet heading directly for the stairs, while what smelled suspiciously like warm chocolate trailed behind him.

Hands already full, he clumsily pulled a leather square from his back pocket. Opening it, he pulled out a small rectangle. This one, he slid along a black box attached to the metal cage that blocked the way down to the archives. A metallic beep and green light went off before a gentle click came from the diamond grated door. He continued downward.

"Yes. I have a class that I must have access to the archives for."

"Right...which one?"

My mind frantically sorted through the list of classes Brittany had given me before deciding on the one that would make the most sense.

"Intro to European History." The metallic clip-clop of Jaxson's footsteps on the stairs stopped just shy of the bottom. I stared out over the expansive room. The bright light was harsh at eye level with the stair that I was on and left me looking out straight across the low ceiling, where row upon row of shelves were lined as far as I could see. My heart gave a hopeful flutter.

"Is that so?"

"Hmm." I said, just remembering his presence.

"I said. Is that so?" I could feel the challenge in his voice as I twisted down the stairs until my feet rested only a few above him.

"Yes. So if you would be so accommodating as to escort me to the rare books I've heard about." I smiled. "I'm in need to search for one for my," I paused, unable to grasp the right words.

He answered for me. "Research paper?"

"Yes, research paper." He didn't budge. "Do you mind?"

He leaned against the rail, still blocking my only way down.

"Who's your professor again?" I ignored him as my eyes began searching the rows of books where my book might be found.

"I do not yet remember the name of every person I meet."

He chuckled and took another slow gulp of his drink, "I see. Well, do you remember my name?"

I narrowed my eyes on him thinking of how to answer. "I'm sure you've said it. It's..."

"Jaxson Harwell."

"Oh, yes. That's it."

"Uh-huh."

"And?"

"As in Professor Harwell of the history department. I teach intro to European history and I'm fairly certain I haven't assigned any research papers yet."

A bright flush rose to my cheeks as he stared me down, a smile slowly growing on his lips. "Maybe you were thinking of another class?"

"You're right. I was." I moved to close the few steps between us, hoping to move him further down the stairs. He didn't budge.

"What book did you need?" He asked.

My brain was starting to feel foggy as frustration and hunger warred over my body. "I need an anatomy book for Health Science." I smiled at the quick and clever response. He wouldn't be able to thwart me now.

He held both the white bag and his drink cup in one hand to scratch at his short trimmed beard. "Then you definitely don't need to be down here."

"What?"

"All the material you might need for Health Science is going to be back upstairs." He held out his full hand in a gesture to guide me back the way we had come. I couldn't help but glare at him as he did. The still warm pastries taunted my stomach, and I didn't wait for it to growl before I snatched the bag from him. He chuckled..

Harwell led me to a long group of square topped tables, each holding one of the loud buzzing boxes like Brittany used in the shop. "Start here."

I stared at him in obvious confusion. He chuckled at me again. "Really? I thought everyone your age new how to use a computer by now."

"And what age is that?"

He took a step back to pull another chair toward the one in front of me. "I believe that might be a trick question."

A laugh trickled from me as I took a bite of the warm chocolate croissant I had stolen from him. "Yes. I suppose it is."

A shiver struck my body as soon as I sat in the cold hard chair.

Jaxson took quick note of it. "Here, this should help." Although I had already eaten both of his treats, he offered up his drink as well. The hot liquid warmed my hands and chest as I held it tight to my body. "Thank you." I paused to look at him. "What age are you, Professor Harwell?"

"Anyway…" He ignored my question and pushed my chair toward the "computer", as he called it. He pointed to several places on the box, showing me how to search and explaining the ways of the technology in front of me.

I was enthralled and fully versed in the ways of the webs by the time he checked his leather watch. "Gah. I've got to run. I have a class starting in ten minutes." He slung his satchel over his shoulder before giving me an expectant look.

"Yes. You may leave." I said, still focused on the screen.

"It's Intro to European History."

"That sounds lovely for you. Thank you for your help."

He gave a heavy sigh before leaving back out of the front doors.

My eyes were heavy by the time I left out of the same doors. I couldn't help wondering if I might run into him again. The thought left a strange warmth coating my stomach.

Posters hung at intervals on the glass doors, several accompanied by images of large red drops of blood. Requests for blood donations filled their pages. A brilliant thought bloomed in my head as I left the library in search of Brittany.

"Soryn!" Ashlie and a group of friends shouted from across the crowded green space in front of the library. "Hey, come eat with us."

The idea of sitting with them grated at my insides like the spikes of a pitchfork, which, unfortunately I became very accustomed to in the 1600s because of a mishap with a Moldavian wheat farmer. I wanted to be in their company about as much. However, perhaps they could be of use.

"Have you seen my Brittany anywhere?"

"No, but I did see Keith." A few of her friends giggled before she lightly slapped at their arms, the coy smirk she held on her face never budging. "He should be — Oh, over there." She pointed across the quad to a long, white ship on wheels. The same red drop was painted on the side as was on the posters I had spotted around campus. Keith was perched against it, cookie in hand as I approached.

"Where is Brittany?"

"Hi, Soryn. Good to see you too."

My stomach turned as I forced myself to hold in the snarl I wanted so badly to give him.

"I'm sure it is. Where is Brittany?"

He gave a breathy laugh before closing the distance between us and hoisting his arm over my shoulder, his fingers brushing my hair off my neck. I couldn't hold back the gag that rolled through me.

"Wow. Whatever." He popped the cookie in his mouth and started to head back toward the group I had just left.

"You misunderstand me. I'm not feeling well at all. I need Brittany because of my illness."

"Oh, damn." He brushed off where his arm had touched me, "Are you both contagious or something?"

"Both?"

"Yeah. I saw Brittany leaving campus earlier this morning. She looked disgusting."

I didn't hide my snarl this time. "Disgusting?"

"No, like, she looked like she was feeling super gnarly."

I closed the distance that he had made, "You can not catch what ails us."

Unstake My Heart

"Oh." It was his turn to snarl. "You're synced up then?"

I nodded, not sure of what he was trying to say as I held out the little box that would summon my ride home. "I need your assistance with this thing." No matter how many times Brittany had explained it, the 'pager' made little sense to me.

Keith took his time, but finally placed the small thing back in my palm with a smirk. Days of tortuously having to watch this charlatan with Brittany was enough to make me ill. She was foolish. She was naive. She was dreadfully clumsy. But she deserved better.

The long wait for my ride left me mourning the power to compel men to their death.

"You should really try to get to know me better, Soryn. I would love to get to know you better." Keith's hand rested on my backside for only a moment before I slapped it away, slipping out of reach and into the large metal safe haven before he could breathe another foul word.

"You can go away now."

A small grain of mirth slipped back into my soul as I turned to a man that would listen. The Tom in the drivers seat beamed at me as the metal carriage roared back to life.

"You are very skilled at procuring items for my home. Let's see what else you are skilled at stealing."

I jumped as something rustled at my side, the vibration like that of a swarm of bees. The little egg Brittany had given me knocked against the small black rectangle it was attached to. I had already banged and pushed every button to silence the small creature and yet it still moved. Never had I had so much trouble killing something before.

The small box buzzed again. An even tinier scroll flashed at me from one end, with the words — The Rink.

Chapter Twenty-Two

BRITTANY

My hands gripped the hard plastic of the steering wheel as Ben's eyes continued to stare through me. I half expected the cork sole of my right shoe to be flattened by the time I skidded into a spot in The Rink parking lot. If Ben was worried about the speed, his stoic face didn't show a hint of a worry line.

The deep blue of the university parking passes peppered the windows of the cars that crowded the full lot, though the bright neon of The Rink sign hadn't yet been switched on. "So how's the food here?"

"Great." I squeezed my eyes shut, hoping that the fast food I had this morning would help stave off the difficulty of being around so many people.

"What's your favorite…" Ben's words were cut off by the car door slamming shut. The need to get my distance from him was overpowering. Whatever Ben was — whatever that phone call was about—one thing was for sure, he wasn't safe. Whoever he had been talking to certainly wasn't Mr. Dorsetty.

The steady thump of his pulse stalked behind me like some strange telltale heart. The only difference was the dead body I was trying to hide was my own. Well, mine and the two others that were rotting in the bottom of a well. As the thought swept across my panicked mind, two more heartbeats joined in the haunt.

"Why did you do it?" I paused at his question.

"I'm not sure what you're talking about." The footsteps behind me became heavier as Ben closed the distance.

"What?" He asked.

"I said, I'm not sure what you're talking about."

Ben looked confused. "Are we talking about the food here? Did I miss something?"

A hopeful flutter started up in my chest as the voice I had confused for Ben's came into focus again.

"Because if I play along, I'm gonna get a lot more out of it then just cash, man." The all too familiar voice was coming from the far end of the parking lot. The music thrummed and coursed through the afternoon air as groups of people entered and exited through the double glass doors.

"Are we going in or what?" Ben asked. "I wasn't kidding about being hungry."

"Give me just a minute," I said as I slowly backed away across the parking lot," My boyfriend is actually waiting for me right over here. I let him know that we were coming, so I hope you don't mind."

I kept a watchful eye on Ben as I listened for Keith again. With any hope, he would get the hint and go inside and Keith would be there to help me. Not that he could really help me, an immortal creature of the night, against a hunter sworn to take me down, but at least I wouldn't have to be alone with him. Ben gave a gentle nod and joined a group that was entering the building.

"Yeah, but that whole family is crazy, dude." A jarring laugh joined in with Keith's.

"She's a freak in more ways than one." The tone of my boyfriends voice left an unease in my gut as their laughter continued to fill the air that hung heavy around me. Was he talking about me?

"And besides, what this guy offered me just to keep an eye on her…" he gave a low whistle, "And all the weird shit I'm finding out about is priceless. Brittany Cordain is my ticket to finally getting what I deserve out of this town."

The leaves seemed to crackle and pop as a warm gust of air shook the trees skirting the black pavement.

Though my blood ran cold, my skin itched from the burning anger bubbling just below the surface. For the second time in not even an hour, I stumbled upon a conversation not meant for my ears.

Keith had been using me. The cold metal of the necklace made my skin crawl where it touched. The toxic yellow of the pick added to the sickly feeling creeping its way through my every vein. The chain broke with barely a pull as I backed myself away from where the two men were still huddled near Keith's car.

Before I could get far, something hard stopped me.

The little pink bunny symbol hanging from the rear-view mirror swung in protest, its little black bow tie waving angrily back and forth from inside the red corvette.

My ears twitched as they picked up the sound of the click-click-click the swinging charm made as it rubbed against the dark gray of the mirror.

The thin metal of the door panel made popping noises as I straightened my back and leaned away from it. I hadn't thought I had been going that fast and yet there was a sizable dent where I had collided with it. Hopefully it hadn't made enough noise to…

"Brittany?"

"Keith. Hi. I didn't know you were here." I lied. My hands grazed against the divot behind me wanting nothing more than to melt my anger away and into it. As his fingers traced down my arm, the words *don't kill him* became my silent mantra.

"You don't have to lie, babe. You can just say that you missed me." He leaned in as a breathy laugh passed us. Keith didn't say another word as his buddy crossed toward the entrance. "Besides, I'm always glad to see you." One hand landed on my hip as the other grazed along my cheek. The new ring he wore was warm as it traced a slow path along my jaw.

A rage boiled inside of me. He may have been lucky enough that I had already eaten today, but that didn't mean he wouldn't answer for a few things. When his lips met mine, I bit down. The taste of blood coated my tongue as he pulled back with a hiss.

"What's wrong, Keith. I thought you liked that I was weird. Or, how did you put it? A freak in more ways than one."

"Brittany, are you alright?"

"Oh I'm great. I just found out that my boyfriend is being paid to date me, but, yeah, I'm just peachy."

"Babe, I don't know what you think you heard, but I can promise you that you misheard that." His eyes were soft as he reached for my hands. "I've been head over heels for you since high school. You think I'm about to mess that up?" He dipped his head to look in my eyes, his finger cupping my chin at the same time. A flutter in my stomach began to beat down the anger I had felt toward him just moments before.

"But I heard you say that someone…"

"Were you eavesdropping on me?" The hurt in his voice made my throat tighten. The guilt twisted inside of me.

The sticky static of a car pulling up and parking just a spot away from where we stood caught his attention.

"It's fine." His fingers sent chills down my spine as he pushed his hand into my hair. "I'm not mad."

The feeling in my gut soured again as another voice I was never meant to hear made it to my ears. The woman's sharp words melted in with the hum of her still running engine.

"I give it a week."

"A week? I saw him sneaking out of the girls dorm just last night."

Keith took another step back, whatever words he had to say were lost as I tuned in to our audience.

"Poor thing. But, I mean, if she's dumb enough to fall for a guy like Keith, that's on her." The other girl gave a sad, "Hm."

The necklace I had been gripping in my fist hit Keith's chest with a satisfying thump. He rubbed the place where it made contact.

"What the hell, Brittany?"

"Were done. So whatever bet or deal you had going on to 'date the freak girl' is over."

The sky had finally begun to give off its amber glow of evening as I made an effort to storm away at a human pace. I may have been naive—I'll admit to that, but I refused to be used by some cheating jerk.

The cheating jerk grabbed my arm and pulled. "Stop. What do you think you're doing?"

My nails dug in as I peeled his hand off of me and clawed into his skin. A small yelp of pain left his lips as he went down to one knee in my tight grasp.

"Let me break this down for you very slowly so you'll understand." The girls I had overheard were laughing a short distance away. "If you ever even think about laying a single finger on me again, I will break all ten."

My body was shaking by the time I finally entered The Rink and saw Ben, already sitting at a table with a basket of fries. Whatever rage had possessed my body only moments before had me feeling shaken, if not a bit reckless.

"Have you been sent here to kill me?" The words spilled out of me like word vomit. "Or did you hire my boyfriend to do it?"

His hard stare softened as he tilted his head and stared but said nothing.

I needed to get it all out before regular Brittany took back over my body. "You can try to lie to me but I just talked to Keith and I heard your little phone call back at the shop."

A puzzled scowl wrinkled his brow before he chuckled, "You know, if you're going to listen in on other people's conversations, you should probably make sure to eavesdrop on the entire thing."

I glared at him over the giant pile of fries that neither of us would end up touching. "Then would you care to explain — vampire hunter?"

"Vampire hunter?" His smile grew wide, "I'm just Mr. Dorsetty's assistant."

"Oh really?"

"Really."

I reached out to pluck the round talisman tied around his neck, "Then why are you wearing this."

"It was a gift," he slowly pulled the necklace through my fingers before buttoning his shirt to hide the trinket, "from Mr. Dorsetty. And as for, Keith was it? Well, I am very happy to say that I have never spoken a word to that idiot."

"But you know about him, right?"

"After days of being in that shop with your non stop gushing about your boyfriend, yeah, I know far more than I would like to about him." Something twitched at his brow before his gaze lifted from mine. "Speak of the imbecile."

"Brittany!" Keith's voice cut through the sounds of acoustic guitar coming from the speakers and the rink. "What's going on?"

"Not that it's your business or anything but I'm hanging out with a friend."

Ben tucked his hands in his tailored suit pockets, a coy smirk planted on his lips.

"I want to talk to you."

I breathed an annoyed sigh in his direction. "We've talked. Now were done talking."

"Why? Is this guy the reason why you dumped me?"

Ben smiled in earnest, "You dumped him?"

"Yes. I mean no. I mean, Keith, I dumped you because I don't want to be with someone that I can't trust."

"You can't trust me?" His eyes bore in to mine, "What about you. I knew you were hiding something from me. But I cared about you enough to wait and see if you would just tell me." His confident demeanor faded as he spoke again, "Please. I just want to talk to you. Alone."

A cloud of guilt fogged up my brain as I looked him over. His slumped shoulders were a strange look for him. My eyes trailed down his arm to where he clung to the necklace I had thrown.

"Fine. We can talk."

His hand gripped mine as he led me toward a far door. Ben kept his eyes on me as I mouthed, "Be right back."

The room where the pins fell and reset was loud. Even more so to my ears.

He raised his voice above the clatter, as he rubbed his hand down my arm and took my hand, "It's alright. I don't blame you for getting jealous. I did too when I saw you with that guy." He took a step closer, "If that guy isn't the problem, then let's just forget about everything you did out there."

"Oh, yeah." I smiled sweetly, "That's so big of you. But what about Ashlie?"

"What about her, babe?"

I sucked on my teeth, urging my fangs to stay where they were. "Unbelievable. I'm done, Keith. We are done."

I spun on my heel and reached for the door to my back. Keith's fingers wrapped around my arm before my hand made it to the handle.

"You think I don't know what's going on?" He leaned in to whisper in my ear. "I know what you and your new BFF are."

I scoffed, "The only thing you know, Keith, is how to get on my nerves. So if you don't mind," I pushed back as he fumble for me. A pain hissed through my teeth as something sharp caught my arm amid the cacophony of struck pins and flashing neon lights. I twisted away from whatever it was, reaching for the door and slamming it shut behind me. The need to get as far away from Keith as I could was strong. I needed to get to Soryn, and fast. She should have been at the Rink by now but I couldn't wait. I needed to get out of there.

"Britt." Ben's eyes flashed from casual to concerned as he took me in. "What's wrong?" His gaze went from me to searching the crowd. His body went alert like he had practiced the stance a thousand times until it had become second nature. He was definitely a hunter.

The door to the pin room opened again and Keith stepped out, while adjusting something on his hand. When his eyes met mine, internal alarm bells went off. Something about him was off. The brown of his eyes looked darker for a beat before he took a deep breath and locked them back on me. The crashing of pins seemed to highlight each moment that he stood staring at me from the doorway, unmoving. I was trapped between a vampire hunter and my psycho ex — and right now, looking at Keith's face, I preferred my odds with the trained killer.

Ben held out his hand, resting it gently on my back. "All right let's…" He grabbed my wrist just as gently and turned my arm.

"Did he do this to you?"

"What?" I looked down at my arm where a deep cut formed a slithering red path from my forearm to my hand. Several dots of bright red blood dotted the carpet and left a trail snaking back to where Keith still stood. Ben was quick to follow it, closing the distance between himself and the still glaring Keith before I could register what was happening.

"Back off, man. She's not even…" I didn't find out what I *wasn't even* as Ben's fist put a stopper on whatever Keith was about to say. Without another word he turned and walked back to me. By now all eyes were on us as he placed his hand on my shoulder and I let him lead me towards the door. I didn't look back.

I could feel Keith's eyes following me, tracking my every movement. A strange tingle began to creep under my skin until it solidified into a feeling of dread and formed a hollow pit in my stomach. As we began to drive away, I could almost sense Keith pacing behind the faded brick wall that was shrinking in the distance.

The verbal silence in the car cut through the cool fall air that rushed in through the open windows. The quick pace of Ben's heartbeat betrayed his relaxed demeanor. A faint blue glow highlighted the passing trees in a blur of ghostly light as I tried to focus on the dead eyes following my car. It was better than thinking of the rage filled ones of the man who had been a dream of mine.

"I'll drop you off at the shop. I need to find my friend." My nails trailed where the yellow pick had rested since the day Keith had given it to me. "She can't drive."

He nodded. A pained but pensive expression took over his features. "Your neck looks better without it."

A deep furrow set on my brows as a very different silence began to invade the front seat while Ben began to give me side-long glances. "What I mean is that, he could have at least bought you actual jewelry."

I nodded slowly, choosing to focus on anything but Ben's rapidly growing heartbeat.

"I'm trying to say that he's not worth being sad over. Anyone that would hurt you, isn't worth crying over."

"Mmm, hmm." I bite my lip. Seeing him fumble over his words was too good to risk ruining and I needed anything to take my mind off of the mess that had just happened.

A long, exasperated sigh left his lips, "I'm not any good at this whole, consoling thing." He shrugged.

"No, you're not." I couldn't stop the smile that was creeping up my face, "But you did give Keith one hell of a nose bleed so that's one thing you got going for you."

Chapter Twenty-Three
SORYN

"The little box said she would be here! The whole reason I was given the infernal technology was to keep track of her." I spoke to the angry air that whipped in through the open glass doors of The Rink. Heat built in my reddening cheeks as I stared out over the overcrowded space, already sure that the tall lanky blond was nowhere in sight but searching all the same. The strobing lights and thrumming music wore further on my nerves.

As if to purposely push me to the cliff of my rage, a chirping came, not from the pager device but from the troublesome little egg that Brittany had attached to it. *"It's for little kids but something about taking care of it is kind of soothing to me. Maybe it will soothe you too."* Her words writhed in my ears. They could be nothing but lies spoken to drive me further to the point of insanity in this new age. The chirping sounded again, this time more incessant than before. A heavy groan dripped from my lips as my fingers stabbed at the little buttons. "Shut up. Shut up. Shut up." I ground out as every jab elicited another command to the little monster.

The sounds of heavy bowling balls crashing onto the thin wooden slats left my ever retreating patience even more frayed.

An image stabbed at my mind as I watched a pearlescent red ball roll along the glistening wax coated floor. A hot line seemed to radiate from my neck as the memory of a dirty cobblestone street tumbling by flashed into mind. My whole body vibrated as I tried to shake off the feeling of the blade to my neck. Not even a thousand lifetimes could dull the memory of such pain. As I stared ahead, the ball continued its journey until it had finished its destruction and rolled just out of sight.

And there, in the maelstrom of my torment, was a putrid glob of a man. Keith seemed to lay his eyes upon me at the same moment.

"Soryn."

"Bedswerver."

His head dipped as he started at me. "Keith." A coat of frustration coated his name as he spoke it.

"I am aware." My own annoyance grew the longer I stayed in the presence of the blubbering buffoon. "Where is your only good half?"

"Really cute, Soryn." He made a show of looking around, "As you can see, I'm all by myself." He took a step forward looming over me like a starving rat ready to devour a bit of food that had fallen from a high table.

With an exasperated breath, I took a step back and held the little black box out to him. "This said that she would be here."

He wrapped his fingers around the message box and my skin crawled and pebbled were he touched me. My hand felt the wind as I snatched it back with such speed and shook the feeling of him off of my fingers.

He chuckled before looking at the box, while the little egg attached to it let out a high-pitched echo. He jabbed at the buttons as it continued, "I never understood why someone would like something so useless."

I snatched the egg and message box back from him, "Strange that we should agree on that." The daft creature laughed.

"Well, you actually just missed Brittany. But, she did tell me that if you finally showed up here, that I should help you get home." A dark glimmer rested in his gaze as he looked me over.

"That won't be necessary. I may find my own way home."

He grabbed at my trinkets again, holding them away from me when I tried to recapture them. "I really have to insist." He smiled, "What kind of boyfriend would I be if I didn't give Brittany's best friend a ride home."

A small voice in my head was screaming at me. Something was very wrong. Brittany knew the rules. Never would she suggest that someone go to our home.

"No. She said she would be here."

His hand bunched at the back of my blouse as something cold and wet stuck to my arm. I looked down to see a streak of blood were his shirt had grazed against me.

"Really. I don't mind taking you to her."

My chest felt like it was being crushed under a pile of stones as we crossed the crowded room, his hand still grasping tightly and creating a vice of my shirt.

I was not fond of the feeling of fear. It rushed through my veins like water over jagged rocks as we made it to Keith's car and he slammed the door behind me.

Keith sped through the streets in the direction of home while music blared and pounded from inside his car. The musicians voice was angry and Keith mimicked it well.

I cursed under my breath and hoped that this mortal body was not going to betray me. Keith took another turn at full speed, bringing us even closer to the end of our journey. I could only guess if that would be my home or the grave.

"How do you know where you're going?"

"I don't really. You're going to have to tell me where to go soon." He smirked and placed his hand on my knee. "Up ahead is as far as I saw her go."

I slapped at his hand, "Well, you can let me out at the store of convenience just up ahead and I will walk from there."

His arm slithered across the back of my seat and my body collapsed further down on instinct. Years of being the hunter and yet the urge to protect myself rose to the surface so quickly. The bright red sign ahead meant that the car would soon stop. Perhaps if I could catch him off guard, I could be lost in the trees before he could catch up. My heart pounded as my chest tightened again. The rushing in my ears was a staggering symphony of my blood and breath quickening with each second we came closer to the red sign.

The car began to slow as I risked a side glance at Keith. There was something about him that was screaming at me to open the door and run. To put as much distance as was possible between him and I. He had been weak. A vermin among men. What had changed?

He continued to stare ahead as the car began to roll to a stop, the click-click-clicking sound that punctuated another vitriol fueled song counted down the seconds to my escape.

The wheels stopped. My hand crept to the smooth gray lever. My lungs filled with a wavering breath. My fingers tensed. I let out a silent plea for help just before Keith's arm shot out in front of me. His fingers slammed down on a small peg that locked the door to my escape.

"You can never be too safe." His eyes narrowed on mine before he slowly pulled his hand back, not missing the opportunity to drag his fingers over my shoulder before curling them back around the wheel.

He continued to stare at me. "Where to next?"

By now, he could no doubt see that he had fear gripping my insides. I hated him all the more for that. But in this form, I needed to outsmart him if I could not overpower him. Lucky for me, that shouldn't take much. I stared at the almost completely faded light that was setting below the tree line. After a brief moment, I led Keith to my home, knowing that there would be two people there compelled to protect my well being.

...they were gone.

The large white truck that so often accompanied the sight of the Toms trudging away and making repairs had not yet returned. Keith pulled slowly into the place where I had hoped they would be.

"Wow." He turned his venom filled mouth toward me, "This place really suits you." He reached across me again and pulled at the handle, the little stick popped back out as he pushed the door to swing wide. My heart sank at the realization that I hadn't actually been trapped.

He didn't wait for me. His footsteps fell heavy along the freshly cleaned stone walk way that led to the front door. "So, were you here for the build?"

His words buzzed in my head, "The repairs are mostly done while Brittany and I are at the shop or class."

He disappeared into the house before I finished my sentence. He was picking through the kitchen wares when I caught up to him. His usual condescending tone was replaced by a hollow drone when he spoke again, "I'm not talking about your renovations." He looked back to me, a hard glare pinching his features. "I know what you are, Soryn." He trailed his hand over the long wooden table that sat in the middle of the kitchen before slamming it back down with his fist. "This whole town, I know what's going on. What all the things like you are keeping from the rest of us. From me."

"I don't know what you're…"

"Shut up!" He turned, his feet moving at unnatural speed to the wooden block that held several large kitchen knives. He clawed at one before pointing it back toward me and froze. His face seemed to bulge. His rodent like eyes scanned from me, across the space toward the open doorway.

"Who the hell is that?"

I turned, seeing nothing but the large open space beyond, where we once held parties. Nothing but air filled the room.

A chill ran up my spine just before he scurried back, pushing his back to the counter and carving the knife through the air in front of him. I didn't wait to see what had caused him such a fright. I ran. My feet clambered on the runner that lined the stairs. Keith's shouts from below continued to quicken my blood as I made for the much more narrow stairs that led to the undisturbed attic.

Dust twisted in the air as I opened the age warped door and bolted inside. I let out a tiny curse as I willed my woefully weak body not to cough. The lock that used to accompany the knob had fallen out and been lost to time. Now there was just a hole in the door where it had once been.

Keith's curses were becoming louder in my ears as doors slammed from the floor below me. Blood iced in my veins as he called out my name.

"Soryn!"

My eyes searched in the darkness for a place to hide.

"Soryn."

My nose wrinkled at the stench of death that rolled into my lungs with each fear laced breath as I threw myself under a long table covered with moth-eaten fabric.

"I'm going to make your little friend pay if you don't come out."

My ears twitched as the scratching of blade on wooden walls carried through the night air.

Bile rose in my throat. He was going to hurt Brittany. That must have been who he saw downstairs. But why hadn't she stopped him?

The creaking of aging wood sent adrenaline riddled shocks down my spine before the silence hit.

He had stopped.

His breathing became erratic as he waited just outside the attic door. The chirp and caw of night time creatures became more and more present as I strained to make out his movements. Another chirp seemed to screech through the silence. I didn't dare move as the little egg betrayed me.

Keith threw wide the door, running straight for my hiding spot with murderous rage in his blackened eyes. A dust cloud formed as he flipped the table shielding me through the air. It landed several feet away, its legs sticking out from the angle where it had crashed into an old— now broken— dresser.

"Brittany will never forgive you if you do this."

He bent down, inching closer to my face, "I don't have to care what Brittany thinks anymore. That dumb skank tried to ruin everything for me." He straightened again. "But that doesn't matter. I have all the evidence that I need to take what I deserve."

His eyes flared with excitement as he continued to stare me down, "And if I have you,they will give me whatever I want."

"Who will — what are you saying?"

"Show me where you keep that book, and we can be on our way." He grabbed my arm. A sharp pain radiated out from my shoulder as he pulled me to his side. "But if you and your creepy little friend keep trying to pull these stupid tricks, I'll kill you both and cut my loses."

"Brittany!" I called out.

He held the knife to my chin. "I don't know if you know this about yourself, but the sound of your voice is extremely irritating." He squeezed the spot where he had undoubtedly rent my bone from its rightful place. My knees quivered and gave as he pushed me back to the ground. "Tell her to come out."

"Brittany, please!"

"Brittany's not here!" He snarled in my face. "And if you're not careful…" The door to the attic creaked open slowly as his head whipped to the side. "You think this is some kind of game?" He straightened, staring in the wide open but empty doorway.

"I did not do anything." I said, my body moving further back and away from him as I did.

"Oh, god. You're not…" A sharp intake of breath was my only warning before Keith launched himself backwards. His feet tangled in the rotting fabric that was strewn across the aging wooden floor as he continued his fearful retreat of what I could not see. The only other sound for what felt like an eternity was the sickening squelch that followed his head colliding with one of the skyward facing table legs.

I waited in the darkness. Waited for a breath — a word — a movement that would never come. After years of watching death work, I knew he would not make another sound until his body began to decay.

A pained moan left my own lips as I struggled to drag his body to the far closet. I wasn't sure where Brittany was or when she would be home. The last thing I wanted was for my home to smell like rotting Keith when I could barely stand his stench when he was alive.

A shiver skittered up my spine as I latched shut the closet door on the corpse. Invisible eyes seemed to be studying my every movement as I slowly walked closer to the door. Lantern light flashed in a sweeping motion through the uncovered window that faced the front of the house as the sound of crunching rock popped in my ears.

"Soryn!" For the second time tonight, someone was searching for me. My heart was grateful that this time it was my friend. I shouted down to Brittany, her frantic calling pulled at my heart as she sped up the stairs, all the while her pet egg sang a sad death march.

Chapter Twenty-Four
BRITTANY

"**G**ood morning, Sunshine." Ben tipped his dark glasses low, settling them further down the bridge of his nose as he made no effort to hide the fact that he was taking stock of how I looked this morning. His eyes trailed up and down my frame from the top of my over-sized newsy cap to the bottom of my brown Doc Martin's.

"It was." I said, sarcastically. Well, part of it had been a good morning. Better than last night. At least this morning I hadn't disposed of yet another body.

"It's beautiful outside. How about we go for a walk?" His vice was tense as his eyes moved almost imperceptibly to the spot on my arm where Keith had cut me. Not even a trace of the wound remained. I pulled at my long sleeve, though the green lace did little to stop his gaze.

"How about no?" My stomach did a flip-flop as I pushed past him and through the already unlocked door. The strange smell that always lingered around him caught my attention as I forced myself to keep walking forward. He followed through the maze and got straight to work. I admired the dedication but refused to give in to his side long glances though the urge look grew the closer he got to me.

"So are we going to talk about that phone call or are we both pretending it never happened?" I turned, not expecting him to be so close. His eyes widened for only a moment before he took a small step back. Tension coiled in his arms though his stance seemed to give off an air of ease.

His whole demeanor threw me off. His words said he wanted to be friends while he seemed to be forcing his body to be in the same room as me.

"You seem jumpy, Ben." I smiled and inched forward. He didn't move a muscle this time.

"And why would I be jumpy, Brittany?" He smiled back. The challenge set on his glowing face. "If I can be around Mr. Dorsetty, I can be around you."

My eyes knit in confusion. A gesture that Ben pounced on. "You can't be serious right now. You really don't know anything about Mr. Dorsetty, do you?"

"I've never even met him."

"Well, lucky for you, he's waiting for me to bring him these." He held a manila folder packed to overflowing with age stained documents. "You can ride with me."

"No thanks." I said.

"Alright. So, I'll just tell Grandma Winnie hi for you then?"

His smile reached all parts of his handsome face as I grabbed my things and pushed past him. "Fine. Let's go."

The car ride went by quick as he sped through the quiet streets never once needing to ask for directions. It was a far cry from the feel of last night as the unease that had been a staple for us settled back over the ride.

"You look a little young to be working so close with someone like Mr. Dorsetty." If not for the anger bubbling below the surface, the sounds of the road and heavily tinted windows would have sent a calm feeling flowing through me. Instead I sat sideways in the passenger seat, one leg folded under me, as I stared daggers at him. Just because he punched someone in the face for me, didn't mean that we were good.

"You should really buckle. Even in the daytime, these winding roads can be unsafe."

"Trust me, I'll be fine."

He cocked an eyebrow up as he continued to focus his eyes on the road, "Hmm."

"What? What does 'hmm' mean?"

"Nothing."

"Good."

"Good."

The awkward silence hung heavy like a thick smoke in the dark interior.

"Your car is like a freaking cave." I pouted, not wanting to sit in silence.

"Would you like the window down?" His finger rested on the door before a small stream of wind began to rush through the car.

"No." He was toying with me. Although I had gotten used to wearing my sunnies and hat constantly, it felt nice to be without them. Even if it was only for a few more moments as we started to turn on the road that led home. A tightness squeezed in my gut. Was I taking a risk getting so close to them. I had been so angry at the thought of Dorsetty and his assistant upturning everything that I hadn't stopped to consider if what I was doing was safe.

"Brittany?" Lost in worry and thought, I hadn't noticed that the car had stopped at the end of the very long drive way.

"What?" I looked around. "You gonna take me home or what?"

His brow arched again. "Regrettably, I have other places to be." He held the papers he had taken from the shop for me to take. "If you would please make sure Mr. Dorsetty gets these."

"Isn't that your job?"

"Hm. I suppose it is." He held the papers out until, with a more than exaggerated huff, I grabbed them from his waiting hand. "Thank you for your help, Brittany."

"You're not welcome…"

He smiled. "Thank you anyway."

Papers in hand, I slammed the car door and began the walk up the drive. It wasn't that long of a walk, the house was just out of sight along the tree line, but it was still annoying. What would have usually taken me five minutes took ten. Vampire speed was amazing…if you knew how to use it. After hitting the first three trees at full speed, I decided it would be better to take the open path to the house instead. Not wanting to tip anyone off on my very unhuman like traits, I opted for a slow trek. And on the way, I took a peek at the papers that Ben had given to me. It was a stack of old inventory logs from before grandma had even taken over the shop from my great grandpa. Black ink had smudged my finger where I had rubbed an unfamiliar sketch beside several of the items. An image of a rose; its thorny vines wrapped around an equally sharp point.

The canopy of trees around our house usually gave a blanket of shade, but the overcast sky left no room for sunshine to squeeze through. Despite the slight chill, Grandma Winnie was sat at the large concrete table in our dying garden tucked at the side of the house. My eyes wandered to the patches of lighter wood on the door where it had been patched. Had mom really believed a bear had done that? I looked back to my grandma. Was she just an exceptionally good liar?

She waved when she caught sight of me, a bright smile planted on her tired face. "Brittany! Over here, sweetie. There's someone I want you to meet. This is Mr. Dorsetty."

The second tall dark and handsome man of the day stared at me. Although this man couldn't have been much older than his assistant, his face was hard with lines branching out from his furrowed brow. A gentle smile calmed his stern features as he stood and crossed to open the garden gate for me to pass through.

"I've so looked forward to meeting Winnie's brilliant granddaughter." He shook my hand as an electric buzz seemed to coil around my chest and made my head foggy. "Although, from all the correspondence you've sent our way, I feel like I already know you." His warm voice soothed over my frayed nerves as he went on, "The in-depth research and descriptions were truly impeccable. I would venture to say you've had several people on my staff afraid for their jobs." He chuckled, the deep timbre of his laugh falling softly around me.

"Um, yeah, I…." My stomach growled. I stared wide eyed at him as another more boisterous laugh escaped him.

"We'll make our introduction quick so we can all go eat." He grinned at grandma before gesturing back to the table for me to follow. I did, sitting just to his left, and away from her. "I'm sure it comes as a bit of a shock that I'm here." He said.

I shook my head, focusing on keeping my hunger tamped down. Soryn's advice to eat was becoming more and more pressing though, at least according to what she had said, I should have more time in between. I didn't want to eat some strangers, but I wanted to take a bite out of my grandma even less.

I swallowed the lump in my throat, "Yeah. It is, but your assistant didn't really make it easy either."

He looked down the long drive way. "Is that who dropped you off?"

"He kind of insisted." Annoyance crept into my face as I thought of the awkward meeting.

"I will be sure to speak with him about his manners. Did you…"

I passed the papers to him, "He said to give you these."

He slowly shuffled through the papers, his face unreadable as the feeling of calm seemed to leach out of my body.

The crunch of tires on gravel made its way up the drive. The dirty white of the work truck held a very angry-looking Soryn perched in the passengers seat.

"We need to come up with a better way of communicating." She slammed the door as Tom gave me a happy nod. Soryn marched toward us still going on non-stop, "You said you would be at the shop and after last night I…" She stopped at the gate. Soryn had told me several times over the past week that she couldn't see ghosts, but from the way her skinned had paled, I would have thought otherwise.

"Soryn." The gruff voice behind me wove through the air as if her name held some sort of magic within it.

Soryn didn't move besides her chest rising and falling, her chin jut out as if she were waiting for battle. "Renard." Her voice was strong, though I caught the glimmer of a single tear. "Brittany, it would be best for you to take these two inside."

I didn't hesitate. If something was about to go down, I wanted my grandma and Tom as far away from it as possible.

"Come on Grandma Winnie. I want to introduce you to someone now. Maybe you can bake some of your famous cookies and get to know each other." I waved toward our compelled friend, who happily made his way to us, taking Grandma Winnie's elbow and helping her up.

We walked Grandma Winnie to the back door, the wooden ramp leading up let out small creaks as our movements got slower. "Can you make it inside on your own? Was this too much today?"

She patted my hand as I continued to stare at the unmoving Soryn. "Oh, I'm fine, sweetheart. Your mother will be so sad that she missed him." I stopped at the opened door while she and Tom went inside.

"Grandma do you know who that is?"

She turned in the kitchen to look back at me. "Of course. That's Mr. Dorsetty." She smiled as she went to work grabbing several items. I looked on while perched in the door frame.

She asked, "Can you help—"

"Who is Renard, Grandma?"

She seemed like she was coming out of a daze as she stared at the bag of flour in her hands. "Renard? He was my grandfathers best friend." A confusion rested on her face as she began and her body slumped a bit.

The brain fog I had felt before was completely washed away. A week of combing through documents and trying to pry information from her, and now here it was. The answers we had needed spilled freely from her.

She began to look weak again as I directed Tom to the wheelchair parked at the bottom of the stairs. The straight shot from the back to front door showed the destruction I had been capable of on that first night of my transformation.

"Tom, you need to stay here. Protect my mom and grandma at all costs. Whatever they need, you help them. Alright?"

His eyes were dull as his head bobbed to agree.

An angry churning took hold of my gut as I watched Grandma Winnie try to gain the strength to open the container in front of her. A twisting burn moved up my throat as my eyes locked with hers.

"You've had a good day today, grandma. A quiet day alone, but a good one. Come close the door and don't open it for anyone but mom, Tom,..." I paused for a moment, considering my next words, "or Soryn."

"Soryn?"

"She's a friend. She'll protect you. I promise." She gave me a hollow smile as she closed the door in front of me.

Chapter Twenty-Five
SORYN

"Hello love." Renard's expression was painted in elation and pain as he rushed toward me, arms out, his hair twirling around him like the fields of wheat that had waved on the first day our eyes had met.

My hands went out but his body crushed into mine and I fought to twist from his arms. My breaths came in painful bursts as I took a step back. "Hello, Love?" I punched at his chest; his hard skin jamming my mortal fingers. I tried my best to disguise the pain, but my traitorous eyes began to water.

"Soryn?"

The taste of dirt lingered on my tongue as the wind began to pick up and swirl. My already tired eyed watered even more, as his fingers brushed my face.

"My Love." He whispered with a grin. "I have missed you, too." He leaned forward to place his lips on mine. I breathed in his familiar scent, still the same through all these years. I fought the urge to kiss him back as his hands roamed down my spine. My lips stayed tight until he finally pulled away, his eyes locking with my own.

"I know it has been two-hundred years for you, but for me; it was only yesterday." I took a step toward him, my head down and ready to fight, "Sleep has not addled my memory, my love." I hissed. His words from the night I was trapped had plagued my mind worse than one of Brittany's songs.

"What are you talking about Soryn?" The clothing he wore seemed too dull for him but he carried it well. Even his voice was different, the beautiful Welsh accent he had once sung to me in was now covered by his disguise. "I've done nothing but try to find a way to get you out since that awful night. I've kept this town safe from those who did this to you." His hand went to my hair, his fingers twisting through my dark waves in an all too familiar way.

My hand stung as I slapped his away, the memory of that night still clear in my mind.

———————— ◆◆ ————————

The silver moonlight reflected off of the glass windows and added to the candelabras glow. Their milky white drippings already creating pools of wax along the wooden floors. Several of the long dresses that swept through, guided by the musicians revelry had already left short smears of wax behind them.

The smell of vanilla and sandalwood met my nose just before an arm wrapped around my waist. "I'm surprised the moon even dared to come out tonight."

I turned in Renard's arms, and he pulled me in closer, raising our joined hands to follow the dance that was twirling around us. I smiled up at him, already knowing what his next words would be but loving to hear them spoken all the same.

"For how could she think to shine when someone as radiant as you walks the earth beneath her."

"Sweet words will get you everything." I laid my head against his chest as the music continued its morose melody.

"Mistress Floaire, there's a messenger here for you." Clarette's voice barely rose above the music that floated on the night air, but I didn't miss the gentle tremor that laced it.

I smiled at Renard, "Do not give all of your dances away whilst I am gone."

His lips feathered the palm of my hand, "How could I when they all belong to you, my love."

Clarette gave a small cough beside me as we weaved in and out of the dancers, many stopping to greet us as we passed. "Soryn, come." Clarette hurried us along until the night air brushed against my face and whipped at my dress, the green fabric swirling like ghosts about my feet. The golden chains at my waist gave a gentle tink-tink to add to the music that bled into the darkness. The giggle of lovers hiding somewhere in the trees tickled my ears as invisible eyes cast their silhouettes in a soft blue glow.

"The spirits are enjoying the revelries of this night as well." My laughter was not joined by Clarette. Instead she walked further away from the lantern light puddled outside of my hilltop home. "Where is this messenger, my friend?"

"Yes. Friend. I am your friend, Soryn." For centuries I had stayed in the shadows in my work to keep them, but this human had worked her charms and made her way through. Of all I had known, she was my most cherished friend. And with that, she knew of my curse.

"Yes, Clarette. You are my dearest one."

"Which is why I hope that you believe me when I tell you this." Her hands closed around mine. "Renard's past is not what he says. In the years that you have been here, you have done such great things for my family. And now, I wish

nothing more than to repay that kindness. I only wish it did not come with such pain."

I spoke to her gently, "We have lived many years. There is much that you do not know. But please, do not fret. If there are indeed shadows in my loves past, he has already shown them to me."

"Do you know of the Order of Rosewood? What has Renard spoken of them?"

The name wasn't foreign to my ears though I thought of them as no more than a fear dreamed up by too much mead. "Clarette. I love you as I love myself." I laughed as I gently rubbed her shoulder, the soft white material ruffling under my fingers. "There is nothing to fear."

A violin lent its staccato trills to the sounds of boisterous cheers coming from the back of the house. I began to make my way there, not wanting to miss whatever had moved the party outdoors. She grabbed at my arm.

"If you do not fear for yourself, then remember your promise." She cast her eyes down, knowing the words would plunge straight for my unmoving heart. "My family is not safe where he roams."

Something glowed a gentle orange down the path; a carriage nestled just beyond the moonlights reach had opened its door.

"Please, Soryn, go speak with them. And be careful." She wrapped her arms around my shoulders, squeezing me in the tightest hug she could muster. "Come to me at my family's home before you return to Sedgemoore."

"Sedgemoore?" Why would I go back to that place. Images of Renard flooded my head. His war torn body weak and pale as the life drained from him. Dark blood stained the earth beneath his broken limbs and turned his soft wheat hair into tendrils of crimson. I had caused such suffering like this before but his pleas had struck me. They had matched another that haunted me for all time. I saved him that night, and like once before, I wished to never lay eyes upon the place where such suffering clung to its history.

"Speak to them and all will be understood." Clarette's hands squeezed mine. She lifted her dark cloak to cover her hair before unhitching a horse from its post. My name carried on the wind as she rode off and out of sight.

Unstake My Heart

"Mademoiselle Floaire, if you please." A faceless voice called to me from the orange glow of the low carriage light. It shifted slightly under my weight as I pulled at my skirts and climbed inside. Two men sat across from me, both covered in what would make any other vampire quake. Wooden stakes were tucked into leather straps at their sides, bottles of holy water sloshed from the sway of the carriage being jostled by the wind. The smell of rosewood and garlic gently wafted in the air.

"The Order of Rosewood, I presume." I smiled, making a show of my sharp fangs. Neither stranger balked nor seemed surprised. They simply nodded their heads.

The shouting outside had grown louder as we sat, and my impatience grew with it. "Do you know who I am?"

One smiled while the other pulled out a large leather folder filled with several heavily scrawled upon papers. "Soryn Floaire. Born in Romania sometime in the early 1400s. Traveled around the Middle East and Europe for most of the following centuries for, until recently, unknown reasons. Sired Renard Dorset at the Battle of Sedgemoore in 1685." He flipped past the bulk of pages, several sketched with variations of my face. "Reunited in the year 1700 and have been traveling together since."

"Is that all?" I leaned forward, barring my teeth further.

"I'm afraid not." The man beside him spoke. "You have been staked at least twice as well as burned. And on at least one occasion, you have even been beheaded."

"Well then you know I have no reason to suffer through this conversation. Speak freely before you outstay your already strained welcome."

"We wish only to bring something to your attention. Throughout your long life, we can only find a small amount of bloodshed on your hands."

At that, a dark laugh vibrated through me. "You should find better historians."

"We have pieced together your beginnings. We know that you feed."

I hissed at the word. I was no animal. I was unsure about these men, however.

"When you do, you very rarely kill. In fact," he turned to his companion, *"it would seem that you do a fair amount protecting humans."*

My hands balled into fists. This must have been what Clarette had meant. *"If you lay harm to any of those under my protection, I will give you a bloody and painful end."* The snarl that ripped from my throat echoed in the small carriage. The sweat that rolled down each mans face and neck pricked at my sensitive nose. Fear, no matter how well a face was trained, always found a way to escape the body. These men were not so foolish as to not fear me.

"Please," the man with glasses held sketches of my face out for me to take, *"look at these before you decide to strike us down."*

My fingers clasped the rough pages.

"We are not here for you, Madam Floaire." A sad pang gripped at his tone, *"We are here because of them."* Each sketch, held the face of a woman with dark hair and green eyes. None of them, my own.

"What is this?"

"This is Renard's work before 1700. Each a flower, cut down in the time before he found you."

A knot worked at my neck as liquid ice coursed through my skin. The wind outside shook the unlit lanterns that hung outside the carriage door. Somewhere in the distance, the owls were making their presence known. At least a hundred faces, all baring some similarity to my own, stared back at me.

"We know we can not harm you, but we also know that there is something that keeps your evil at bay." He held out another page. A list of names. Names that I cherished and knew all too well.

His companion spoke up, *"Make no mistake, we are not here to help you. If someday we find a way to end your curse and you with it, we will. But we do fear for them and any that are in the path of Renard Dorset."*

"And why do you come forward now?"

"You have both stayed hidden well. But in his search to gain power, he has given you both away."

"What power?"

The man who spoke had sharp lines that criss-crossed his cheek. It added to his foreboding words. *"Yours. Soon, no one will be able to stop him."*

"He does not bare my curse. It can only be taken by a willing mortal."

"We think he has found a way. Which is why we must ask you to run. You must go where he will not think to find you."

The shouting had grown to a thunderous roar. If there had been any music still being played, there would be no way to hear it over whatever chaos was raining down.

"What is happening?" I leaned over to move the fabric at the window and a hand came down on mine.

"We are giving you the chance to run." The man with glasses held on to me, a plea set deep within his bright eyes as both men exited the carriage. He gave me one final nod, *"No harm will come to the Cordain's while we watch over them."* He called for the driver to pull away while I stared at the token he had placed in my hand. A wooden coin, carved with the crest of the hunters. A holly stake strangled in rose thorns. *"We will protect them but you must return to a place where he won't follow. Our men will be waiting for you in Sedgemoore."*

"Soryn." Renard's voice broke me from my memory. "As soon as Winnie called and told me you were awake, I knew I had to come back." The look of longing he held in his eyes was tempting. He had always been tempting. Perhaps that was why I had turned him so many years ago. And why I wanted so badly to not believe the things the Order had said.

"The Hunters; they came to me. They showed me what you had done. All those women?"

"That is why you were running the night I lost you? They will say anything to wipe us off the face of the Earth. They are no more than an order of extreme zealots and hypocrites. How many have they killed in their mission?"

He straightened his jacket, "They tried to kill both myself and Clarette that night but I kept her safe despite her betrayal. And I have protected you and the Cordain's from them ever since. I know how important they are to you, and I kept them afloat because I knew, one day, you would come back to me." He inched forward lowering his voice and letting the Welsh lilt I had grown to love slip back in his words. "We've both done terrible things alone, but together," He spread his fingers through mine, "we dull even the moons glow." He twisted my hand in his, feathering kisses in my palm. His breath on my skin sent the hairs on my arm standing up.

"I saw you. That night, at the Cordain's, I saw you with Clarette. Just before I…" The words stuck like pins in my throat.

His hand trailed through my hair, pulling at something within me. "What Clarette did to you was my fault and I have lived with that heartache ever since." His eyes locked on mine, "I was trying to find a way to be with you forever. You have to believe me, my love. These decades without you have been torture."

I wanted to believe him. Every fiber of my mortal heart seemed to beat for him as it never could before and a warmth settled deep in my stomach as I looked into the face I had thought I would love for all eternity. Perhaps I was wrong about what I had seen.

A door closed from around the house, the sound setting a stern look on his face.

"I have to ask." A hint of anger ticked at his jaw before disappearing just as quick. "Why did you choose this now?" He placed his hand to my beating heart, the sound loudly whooshing in my ears.

"You know more that anyone that I would never choose this." I smiled, a realization dawning on me, "but if anyone is going to help me end this curse, it will be her."

"Please be careful, love." He looked back toward the house. "I would hate for you to have to flee just as you have returned home. And at the hands of another Cordain."

"Clarette told me…"

Unstake My Heart

"Clarette truly believed that you had become evil and was willing to do whatever it took to stop you. Including joining forces with the hunters. They all plotted against us. I just wish I could have seen it and gotten to you sooner."

"Brittany is not like that. She is extremely level-headed. She is calm and controls herself far more than any fledgling that I have ever known."

I looked up to see Brittany, determination on her face as her feet crushed through the dry and dying garden under her feet.

"Hey asshole! Mind telling me what the hell you did to my grandma?" Her words were punctuated by the crashing of a pot slamming into Renard's perfectly serene head.

Chapter Twenty-Six
BRITTANY

"I don't like him." I repeated for the thousandth time as we settled in at home.

The new flooring and cabinets had done wonders for Soryn's old house. The smell of sawdust and fresh paint permeated the air with a welcoming and clean fragrance. I almost felt bad for all the work that the Toms were doing. But if they were working for us, that meant they weren't peeping on girls at the university.

"And if hearing you say that on repeat for three hours was enough to sway me, then I would agree."

"Mr. Dorsetty is Renard?" I shot up, the bubble chair I borrowed from the shop squeaking with annoyance as I did, "Okay, and can I just ask— and don't go all ragey on me, but how did you not figure that out? Renard Dorset. He literally just added a ty on the end of his name."

Soryn stared off in to the fireplace, "In my defense, your accent is atrocious. You could have been butchering any name for all I knew. And I thought that if Grandma Winnie knew him, she would have said so by now."

"He compelled my grandma. He could have killed her!"

"I could have killed her too, but here we are." Soryn opened the fridge as the large generator whirred outside. She plopped back on the old couch, an armful of cold fruit already staring to dwindle as she spoke around a fresh bite of apple, "And just so you are aware, I may love him but that does not mean that I trust him."

"Uh." I moaned as another set of eyes glowed from the top of the stairs. I had grown accustomed to most of the ghostly figures around the house but it still caught me off guard. The floor creaked as I walked to sit beside Soryn. "So what does tall, dark, and shady have to say for himself?"

"Well, maybe if you hadn't launched a topiary at him, he would have stayed long enough to tell us." She picked at the apple skin stuck in her teeth before starting on the multiple oranges, dipping the pieces in a bowl of yogurt and chocolate chips before moving on to the Dunk-a-Roos she had stuffed in the pocket of her pink and yellow tie-dye hoodie.

I slumped further into the couch, my stomach growling for something even more satisfying.

"You're grumpy when you're hungry."

"No, I'm grumpy when I find out your blood sucking ex is running around town messing with my family while there's a group of Buffy's out there gunning for our heads?"

Soryn stared at me, frosting still caking her mouth. She placed the rest of her stash on the table before silently moving around behind me. The fridge door opened and closed before the beep beep beep of the microwave sounded.

"You know, it would be really nice if you could focus on the problem instead of your stomach for just a few minutes." I huffed as a delicious smell began to swirl around the house and a few seconds later a piping hot F.R.I.E.N.D. S mug was waved in front of my salivating face. My heart sank as I took the mug, "Sorry."

"I get it. Don't be sorry."

I took a gulp. My head swirled before snapping back into focus. My body vibrated as if every nerve ending were firing all at the same time. "Soryn. Where did you get this?"

"One of those giant carriages…" She corrected herself, "cars, were taking peoples blood in exchange for baked goods." She pulled a plastic baggie half full of chocolate chip cookies from her hoodie.

"Soryn." I stared in horror at the steaming coffee cup, "Is this…your…"

"What? No. Of course not." She eyed me for just a second before smiling. "I had Tom procure most of it for us and bring it back to the house." She plopped back on to the couch and a small drop of hot blood fell from my cup as she adjusted to glare at me. "And if we are going to be talking about untrustworthy lovers…"

"Ew. It sounds grody when you call it that."

"Your record is not the best. Renard might kill someone but at least he's not some charlatan Casanova. Next thing we know, you will be falling for that hunter pretending to be Renard's assistant."

My eyes narrowed on her as I caught myself wondering what Ben would think if heard her say that.

She patted my leg, guilt written on her face as she scooted closer, "I know you have qualms about taking life, so say the word and I will kill this one for you as well."

Laughter erupted as neither of us could hold back.

Soryn's laughter abruptly stopped as she stared into my eyes from only inches away, "I will kill him."

I patted her hand, "No. No. That's really not necessary. Thank you though." I let out a slow puff of air. "The past two days really didn't go as planned."

"Tomorrow. We will have a better plan."

"I can't go back school." I sighed, "It was too much. All of those people. I'll be putting them all in danger." I put the empty cup on the floor and rested my heavy head in my hands. "I'm going to flunk out of college before I even start."

"No." Soryn was resolute. "You will have a normal human life after all of this is done. And I will not allow it to be ruined right when its begun. So, tomorrow, I will start going to your classes in your stead. It can't be that hard."

"Okay?"

"Besides, I have to get into that archive place anyway."

"How? Didn't you say Harwell already stopped you."

"I have a plan for that." She smiled and we both nodded our heads.

"What plan?"

She leaned in close like she was about to tell me greatest secret of all time. Her lips curled in a triumphant grin as she opened her mouth, "I'm going to steal his little card thingy."

Her enthusiasm, though possibly misplaced, was contagious as she stood and paced in front of the crackling fireplace. "And you," She pointed at me like a general passing out orders to her troops, "will go to the shop and get cozy with our hunter friend."

I stood, "And I will…wait you want me to get close to the vampire hunter? You just said that you wanted to kill him."

"True. I would enjoy ending him but we need to know what the hunters are up to. If what Renard says is true, they were responsible for my slumber."

"Couldn't he really be Renard's assistant?"

"Renard said he sent someone to look after the shop and he shows up three days late." She stared at me with wide eyes, urging me to put the pieces together. "Brittany! Oh you sweet naive thing. The hunters sent someone to dispose of him and take his place to spy on us."

My head felt like it was about to explode in a confetti storm of information.

My words were slow as I went through everything aloud, Soryn nodding her head in time with my revelations. "So the actual Ben that I've been talking to for years is dead, and the Ben that has been in the shop with us for over a week now is actually a vampire hunter who killed the real Ben so that he could spy on us while doing Dorsetty's paperwork?"

"Close enough." She grabbed her bowl of fruit, popping several pieces in her mouth before laying back down and shoving at me to move. "Now go away so I can sleep. I've got class tomorrow and a heist to perform."

Chapter Twenty-Seven
SORYN

Hello, Love. The words had flowed through my dreams and into my waking hours as well. The rough lilt of his Welsh accent was heavy on each word that hit my ear. I had heard those words for such a long time it had never occurred to me that they may not have been true.

The faces of the women the hunters had shown me created a sickening carousel through my mind. "Lies." The word flew like poison from my mouth. No matter what had happened, how long I had been held in sleep, or whatever his part in it may be, Renard would never truly hurt me.

"The moon is still shining."

"What did you say?" My heart skipped a beat as I stared up into the early morning sky to see the bright reminder of his words.

"It's still really early, Soryn." Brittany pointed out her open window as the cool morning air nipped at the bare skin on my arms. "See. The moon hasn't even gone down yet."

Something sparked inside of me. A sense of determination overflowed the cracks that had broken into fissures about my mind.

"Drive faster. I have much to do today."

The morning air seemed to hold a tremor to it as Brittany delivered me to the school.

"What is that?" She stared at the giant brown rectangle that had been resting on the floor of her car.

I smiled, "I commanded one of the Toms to procure it for me." I unrolled the brown welcome mat, and all but glowed with excitement. "I'm going to see if I can convince the RA monster to put it at the door."

Her smile grew bright as she stared at me. The bustle of other arrivals began to persist around the space and for one small instant, I could see as her smile fade as she glowered through the open window at the warm bodies that passed by.

"Go. You need to spy on the hunter."

A sad nod was all she gave before pulling away. Her little blue carriage moved slowly out of sight before I dared move my feet. An aching grew in my chest for her.

"Poor, desperate creature." I whispered to myself before moving in the morning air, the light finally beginning to peak through the spaces between the large, ornate buildings.

Music and chatter had already begun to twist into the sea of breakfast aromas and the heady scent of coffee hung in the air.

Brittany had been right. It was early. My eyes shot to the right of the campus where a small winding path led through the trees and just beyond to a small outcropping of shops. The tantalizing scent that billowed through the crisp air was no doubt spilling out from their doors.

Unstake My Heart

The orange and red glow of the morning had finally crested over the history building by the time I made my way up the stone steps with breakfast in hand. The plain white bag was full of delicious crumbs by the time I tested the door of Jaxson Harwell's locked office.

"Du-te Dracu!" The familiar curse felt at home on my lips, the words soothing some part of me.

"And here I was thinking you were working on your manners." Jaxon's words still held sleep in them as he narrowed his eyes first on me, then to my hand, still resting on the metal door handle. "A little early for office hours, I'm afraid. Maybe come back after I've had my coffee." He shuffled me to the side and unlocked the door.

"Coffee. Yes." My hand bumped into his shoulder as I hurried to bring the large brown paper cup to his attention. "For your assistance in the library."

He eyed me wearily before taking the cup. A small pang of frustration rolled through me as the absence of the drinks clammy warmth left a cold wet feeling clinging to my hand.

"Thanks." He began to close the door.

"Actually." My mind rummaged for any reason I could think of to get into his office. If he wouldn't escort me to the archives, then I needed a way to access them on my own. And his key card would be mine on this day. Unfortunately, Harwell was holding the one thing that I had come to need to function and form coherent thoughts. So instead, I continued to stare at him, wordlessly.

He smiled and sniffed the steaming cup before bringing the warm drink to his sleepy mouth. "What? It's not poisoned or something, right?" He took a slow sip, a gruff noise came from his throat as he took delight in its warmth.

"I have always found poison to be overdone. If you are to kill someone, you should be more creative in their demise. Besides, poison makes the blood taste sour."

The sipping sound stopped as he stared at me over the paper white rim, his brows pulled together in puzzlement and concern. "Come again?"

"Uh." The constant back and forth of words was starting to become more troublesome. No one in this century knew how to live and it showed on their stupid human faces.

"Ah ha ha." I tried my best 'just joking' laugh that Brittany had taught me to use if people looked at me weird for something that I said. "Gotcha!"

He gave a bright smile and continued on and into his office. I squeezed in before he shut the door.

"Thank you for the coffee but I really was being serious about office hours. I'm not…"

"I know. You are probably so busy with all of your discoveries and artifacts." I shifted toward his desk where he had swung his brown satchel. Peeking out of a side pocket was the brown square I needed. This was going to be easier than I had imagined. Even more than the time I had seduced a Sheikh into giving up four of his young wives. Of course, I had killed him after the negotiations were finished. It had just been a treat to know that I could do it. Jaxson Harwell just needed to be distracted.

My fingers closed around a small figurine that was nestled between the mess on his desk. "Is this something that you found on one of your explorations?" I twisted the small image of a woman in my hand, feeling the smooth texture give way in places to more rough areas.

He crossed his arms and stared at my hands, resigned to the fact that I was still in his office. I locked my eyes on his, refusing to blink as he peered deeply into mine.

"No. That's just something I found at a yard sale and thought was neat." His words were slow and deliberate as he reached for the item and as his hand closed on it. This was my chance to make him do whatever I wanted. I grabbed him to pull in for a kiss.

Instead, we both went flying. Jaxson pulled away fast, as I held to him. The flutter of papers billowing down over his office covered the decent of the small stone woman that had been sent into the air and was now careening down straight for his quite handsome face. Without my vampire speed, I merely managed to swat my hands wildly in the air in hopes of knocking the thing off course. It collided with his forehead all the same. All the while, my wild parries had only managed to knock the still, very hot coffee out of his hand and on to the front of my blouse.

"What have you done?" My annoyance seethed and bubbled. My fingers and chest felt like hot coals as I peeled the thin silk material from my skin and over my head.

"What have I done? You're not even..." His words stopped abruptly. The wet and stained shirt lay in a pile over his cracked leather couch as I rummaged through my bag for something else to wear. "I'll, um...I mean, why don't...I'll wait outside." He was gone before I had a need to answer.

The feeling of triumph was slightly muted by the sinking flutter of disappointment circling deep within me. Though not something I had often felt, it was hard to shake. I took what I came for before throwing another shirt over myself.

The hallway was empty when I emerged. Another heavy weight pulled at my chest before I turned and left.

The library was beginning to fill as I made my way toward the archives with my prize in hand. It hadn't exactly been how I had planned to get my hands on Harwell's key but it worked. The small blue and white rectangle rested firmly in my grasp as I approached the looming gate that led down.

It had to be here. After all of this time, I could still sense that it hadn't left the town. My fingers trembled with anticipation as I held the card to the square black box that would grant me entry. I slid it through and waited for the same metallic beep that my ears had heard before.

Nothing. The small light still pulsed red as I tried to slide it again. Nothing. I stared at the small bit of plastic. "What kind of witchery is this?" I puffed out as my triumph quickly came to an end. The card must only work for its master.

My heart gave a angry thud as I pocketed the card back into my waistband. It was time to come up with another plan. But first, I needed to make it to Brittany's classes on time.

Chapter Twenty-Eight
BRITTANY

The shop felt hollow, the only warmth came from the man standing behind the counter and even he was luke-warm at best. My mind warred at the thought of categorizing any more inventory today. Besides, if I was going to catch the hunter Ben off guard, I needed to get him out of his comfort zone.

"You wanna play hooky?"

His eyes didn't budge from the computer screen as he spoke, the gentle click click click of the keys punctuating his words. "What exactly is *hooky*?"

"It's where we go find something more fun to do instead of arguing back and forth over inventory logs. Besides, you owe me."

"For what, exactly?"

"First off, you didn't even warn me that Mr. Dorsetty was a vampire."

"It's not my fault that you are woefully unaware of the people you work with. Besides, you never warned me that you were a vampire either."

"Well, you made me walk all the way to my house."

"Hmm, I distinctly remember being in a car with you for most of that trip." My jaw clenched tightly when a flicker of amusement flit over his face.

"You're really enjoying yourself, aren't you?" I chewed at my lip —grasping at anything I could think of, "Let's go to the Rink."

He remained silent except for the tapping of keys while I spoke. "You punched my boyfriend in the face before I had a chance to enjoy myself."

Ben's face glowed as he peeked his head over the whirring computer. "I did do that didn't I." A smile crested over his lips before he collected his long coat from the rack behind him. "I'd hate to think I robbed you of a fun evening. And I think you meant to say ex-boyfriend."

Since becoming a vampire I had lost my family, my shop, any chance of going to school and to top it off, I had become a murderer too— but damn, could I skate now. The first twenty minutes at The Rink where a blur of the brightly colored walls as I made circles around the chestnut colored floor. The gentle thud of the music was hypnotic as Ben and I passed each other, the only sign of another soul in the early morning hours was the occasional crash of pins at the far side of the large building.

Ben's smile seemed genuine as he took my hand. I couldn't help but wonder how cold they must feel on his skin. Had Keith noticed it? My eyes narrowed on where we touched as my thoughts continued to bubble to a breaking point. Someone had hired Keith to get close to me. Was it the same person that Ben had been talking to on the phone? My thoughts coiled and coated with venom as every smile- every touch- every kiss played on a dizzying reel in my memory.

Two could play at this game and after Keith, I knew what to look for.

Ben's hand seemed to burn in mine but I didn't let go, "How did you learn to skate so well?"

"My parents loved it. We would spend whole weekends just skating around our neighborhood."

"And how do they feel about you working for a member of the undead?" I forced a gentle laugh into my voice before watching the easy expression he had fall from his face.

"Let's just get this out of the way then." He pulled us both to a stop. "I work for Dorsetty because of my parents. They had a run in with some vampires and they didn't make it. Dorsetty helped me after when I really needed it. End of story."

"So how long have you known that Dorsetty was a vampire?" The question felt odd on my tongue but Ben answered without hesitation.

"Since I first met him."

"So you really aren't a hunter?"

"No, I'm really just his assistant. Yes, that may also include protection detail, if the occasion calls for it. Sometimes that does involve some hunter like activities. I know about the Order of Rosewood, but I'm not one of them. I'm paying my dues to Dorsetty and getting as far away from every single one of those blood-sucking leeches as I possibly can."

My stomach dropped along with his hand. "Good to know." I stared out across the way as another bowling ball shuffled across the far floor, the pins crashing in a whirl of plastic on wood. I hadn't realized until now how much I had needed to talk to someone besides Soryn about what was happening to me. And the one person in on the secret probably wanted me dead. My eyes betrayed my brain as I looked back at him, hoping to see some kind of kindness there. Instead, there was only the stone wall I had grown to expect from him.

The rattle of the plastic wheels helped fill my head as I made several silent circles around the floor. Ben stayed where he was, watching me intently from the sidelines until I finally made my way back around.

"Why tell me any of this? I'm one of those blood-sucking leeches, right?" His eyes fixed on mine as the dizzy feeling that often accompanied his closeness began to swirl in my head.

"You're not one of them, Brittany."

I flashed my pearly white fangs at him, "I beg to differ."

"You won't stay like this though." His fingers brushed against my hand again as his eyes remained fixed on my lips. Was he about to kiss me? Anticipation circled around my heart as a heat flooded my stomach. The invisible string pulled taught as the distance between us became almost non-existent. His mood quickly changed and his voice held a subtle crack in it, "Just find the book and you're free."

My knees locked. There it was. The book. That's what he was really after. The voice on the phone had said as much.

"Right. The book." I said, "Soryn and Mr. Dorsetty are pretty sure they know where it might be so that shouldn't be a problem."

I saw the light flicker in his eye as doubt shadowed his brow. "Really. That's great. Did they say where they thought it might be?"

"Why don't you ask Mr. Dorsetty?"

He nodded his head slowly. "What do you know about Clarette Cordain?"

I thought of the journal stashed safely away under the moldy brown mattress at my new home. I hadn't told Soryn about it yet. My gut twisted at keeping it from her but it wasn't the book she was looking for and giving it up felt like betraying my family. I couldn't do that. Clarette's journal was full of entries on art and dreams for the future. Pages about daily life as well as the appearance of mysterious strangers with strange accents. My nights were often spent reading through page after page of her twisting notes by ghost light. I knew that she was supposed to marry and that something happened to him. I knew that her father wanted her to go away to live with her Aunt after. I knew that she was a talented artist and that she had started dabbling into spell work. But more than anything else, I knew that she had felt like she needed to stop Renard and Soryn. More than anything else, that was clear. And the notes that continued by more of my ancestors after her last entry only added to that certainty. The authors of that journal wanted to make sure Soryn paid.

"She's mentioned her. Why?"

The music swirled as he inched closer while a strange surge of energy seemed to be drawing me in.

"She is the reason…"

Another monstrous crash of pins ricocheted through the space while several extra pairs of skates began to thunder across the wooden floor.

The Rink had begun to fill with the lunchtime rush before I had even thought of checking the clock.

Bursts of sunlight flashed like lightning across the busy carpet as more and more warm bodies filed into The Rink, most clad in brightly colored league shirts. My eyes lingered on a group of familiar faces with bright blue shirts. One was missing.

Chapter Twenty-Nine
SORYN

"Alright class, settle." Harwell announced to the room. I had found a place in the back corner of the large lecture hall fully anticipating being one of the few women there. Instead, as more and more students had filed in behind me, I was a glow with the number of them that went straight for the front of the class. Ready to be seen and educated. No wonder Brittany wanted so badly to be a part of this school.

Jaxson Harwell talked for over an hour. His voice was warm. The passion with which he spoke about the wonders of history made my head swim with a myriad of fond memories of another time. His words weaved a brilliant tapestry as if he himself had walked through the ages of which he spoke.

"Alright, guys, I know that was a lot so if anyone has any questions — now would be the time to ask them."

A brunette in the front row giggled as she raised her hand and asked the first question. "Is it true that Sedgemoore is haunted?"

Harwell leaned against his desk with legs out and arms crossed. "No. I don't believe there are ghosts haunting the town or the University. The only things from the past stuck here, are the artifacts that we've uncovered. So if you're expecting ghost stories, you still have time to sign up for a creative writing class."

I couldn't stop the laugh that rolled from my lips. Even the most brilliant of humans were dreadfully wrong at times. And Jaxson Harwell was most dreadfully wrong.

"I knew I was funny but — ah, it's you again."

I pressed a hand to my mouth before waving him on.

Another hand shot up, this one belonged to a tall boy with a mop of curly brown hair. "Professor Harwell, is it true that you were the one to discover the original boundary marker for the town while you were working with the Thorne Archaeological Society?"

"Yes. I discovered it while doing a dig of an old storage house about five miles west of the university…"

Another laugh. Whatever discovery he was so proud of, it wasn't a boundary stone. All had been destroyed when I renamed the town. I had made sure of it.

Dozens of eyes locked on to me, the silence of their voices overshadowed only by the shuffling of chairs on the hard floor. Several gentle snickers and heated whispers began to fill the room as Harwell leaned against the lectern, arms crossed and focus pinned solely on me. "I'm happy to see you are awake for class. I can't say I'm not surprised, miss…?"

"Cordain." Using the name as my own felt strange, almost like a betrayal to the life I had lost when I was turned.

He gave a deep sigh as he lifted a letter from his desk, tracing his finger along the page until he found what he was looking for.

"It would be, wouldn't it?" He tossed the letter to the overflowing desk.

"Well, Ms. Cordain; since you obviously have so much to say, perhaps you can stay after class and chat? He glanced down at his watch and addressed the rest of the room. "That's it for today. Make sure to have the next three chapters read before our next class."

Voices chattered excitedly as they passed, each set of eyes either glaring or alight with humor as I crossed them on my way to the front of the lecture hall.

"Care to enlighten me as to how you managed this?" I glanced at the page he had held up. It was a letter from the dean of the university stating that Brittany Cordain needed to have supervised access to both the preservation archives as well as the library's uncirculated texts.

My lips curled gently into as innocent of a smile as I could fain. "What's the problem?" I repeated a phrase I had heard Brittany say one too many times in the last week as I picked at the items on the desk, "It's not like I'm going to set fire to the place or something. I know how to handle antiques… and stuff."

He re-stacked the papers I had been browsing. "That stuff is older than you can image."

I chuckled, "Oh, I can imagine."

A gentle grin peeked through his freshly trimmed beard, "You seem to have grown a sense of humor since the last time we met." He stuffed the papers in a drawer before grabbing his things, "Follow me." His strides were long, and I struggled to keep the pace. "Where is your friend that was with you before? I thought I would have seen her in class by now. She seemed genuinely interested in history."

"She, um, had a family emergency."

"Hey! Harwell!" A man rushed to his side, before engaging in a strange handshake that at times involved both hands. "How are you liking being back?"

Harwell smiled while readjusting his shoulder strap. "It feels great." He leaned toward the man, "Still a little strange being on this side of higher education."

"I hear that. Well, hey. Stop by the house later and we can grab a cold one." He started to disappear into the throng of students rushing by, his hand raised in farewell, "I wanna hear all about your trip."

"Sounds good." He waved back. "See you later, Brant."

By the time we passed his office, the hall had almost cleared. We skipped his door and continued on and around the corner, our footsteps echoing through the empty hallway.

"What's a cold one?" I asked.

He cast a side-long glance my way before turning down another hall. "I'm pretty sure, just from our first meeting, that you know exactly what a cold one is."

Ah. Spirits. Of course. He continued on, "I can't condone underage drinking."

"Am I not old enough?" Times had changed, and so apparently had the rules of drinking.

"In this country, the legal age to drink is twenty-one."

"I am very much old enough, then." I laughed.

The corner of his mouth tilted up in a half smile as he waited for me to stop laughing and explain.

Taking another page from Brittany's language, I went on, "I waited a few years to further my higher education."

He shook his head, the movement full of mirth, but if he held a question behind his smile, he didn't voice it.

We stopped in front of a large set of double oak doors. The key he pulled from his bag to unlock them seemed as out of place and time as I did. It was a reminder that this building held history, even if it was not as old as I.

The rooms high ceilings were completely dark, the only light coming from lamps on the many tall wooden tables. Their blue glow had my eyes wandering and wondering how many souls haunted the aging relics held there, and thankful that whatever spell had latched them to me was no longer in place. No feeling of unease held to my bones like before. Instead, a deep sorrow washed over me as I stared at the shelves of antiquity. At least a few were certainly older than myself, but many paled in comparison to my years.

I had awoken in a strange world and this would be my connection to it. After so many years of wanting nothing more than to end my immortality, I found my self looking around and mourning the years I had lost.

I do not know how long I stood silent before Jaxson spoke again. "Brittany?" I turned, grateful for the presence of my companion. I took a few steps, looking in the places where the rooms dull glow reached, but did not see her. Jaxson stood, staring at me from the end of a large bookshelf.

"You mean Soryn?"

"Who's Soryn?" he smiled.

"I'm Soryn."

"I thought you were Brittany?" He pulled out the letter. "I'm supposed to grant access to the archives to Brittany Cordain."

A rush of adrenaline shot through me like fireworks. Lying was so much easier when you were a vampire. "Yes, it's Brittany, but it's also Soryn. It's a family name. It goes way back."

Suspicion clouded his eyes, "And where is the family from, exactly?"

"Here. We go all the way back to the founding of the town."

"Strange, because I could have sworn that was a Romanian accent."

What was that thing that Brittany had said to me again? I tapped my fingers on the long desk as I tried to remember the story. "Foreign exchange program. I spent so long there that I must have picked it up." I shrugged before taking a seat on the table.

A shuffling sound came from a back corner. The dim lamp light stood no chance against the darkness that swelled behind the shelves and in the corners of the large room. Harwell gave an annoyed moan before running the palm of his hand down his face. "Just hold on a sec. Okay." He started toward the source of the sound before turning and pointing a finger at me. "Don't move and don't touch anything." I put my hands in my pockets. It was such a wonderful thing to have pockets. My fingers brushed against the candy hiding there. He didn't say I couldn't have a treat while he was gone. The plastic came away easily as I twisted the top from the container of powder and dipped the bottle shaped sweet inside. I closed my eyes enjoying the blue flavor. How strange it was that color had a flavor.

I could hear the professor as he started to scold someone out of sight.

"Alright. That's enough. Find somewhere else to have your alone time." His footsteps continued as his voice became more stern. "Hey! I said you need to get out of here. This isn't the place for that."

I was half way through my sweet before I noticed the silence. "Harwell?" There was no answer. "Jaxson?" The table gave a slight protest as I scooted off of it and planted my feet firmly on the ground. Perhaps he had stopped complaining and decided to join in whatever merriment had caused him ire. The heavy silence weighing down the room would suggest otherwise though.

I crept around the large shelves, making sure to stay low. My heart pounded in my chest as I thought of the fact that I could now die. My eyes strained to focus in the low light as another shuffling sound pricked at my ears. Hairs stood up over my arms as a shiver ran down my spine freezing my feet in place. I took another lick of my candy to busy my hands. A rustling sound from behind me had me straightening my spine, not sure if it was best to turn around or run. The air seemed to escape the room as something loomed behind me. I could feel its weight mere inches from my scalp. I gulped painfully slow, hoping that whatever monster laid in wait to finally end my life would be quick with its scythe.

I looked down at my hands as a fire began to course through my veins melting at the ice that had held me in fears grip. No. My time as a human would be short but it wouldn't be this short. I would not leave Brittany to anguish for centuries as I had. And if I did come to my end today, it would not be without a fight.

The scream that rent from my chest was a battle cry in my ears as the blue powder I wielded as my weapon created a puff of cerulean poison in the air around my attacker. The deadly sweet strangled the air from around him as he let out a chain of horrible coughs and gasps.

Jaxson went to his knee, struggling to breathe through the blue powder that coated his shiny black hair and short beard. He spoke apologetically through wheezing coughs. "I shouldn't have crept up on you. I'm sorry." Another round of coughs came as he brushed off his clothes. "That's on me."

I tried to hide the shaking in my voice as I spoke, "You owe me another sweet."

He smiled up at me, "Let's call it even for you eating my lunch the first time we met. And my breakfast the second."

"Fine." I huffed and moved toward the shelves, "Let's just find my book. All this talk of meals is making me hungry."

He gave a soft chuckle before narrowing his gaze on me, his face pinched with a laugh he was desperately trying to keep contained. "Is the book you're looking for by Tolkien because there are some characters in it who might share your view on food." His teeth shone bright white in contrast with the sweet covering his face. He looked to me for an answer, his eyes alight with a spark that seemed to grow with each new meeting.

"I have not heard of this author." A smile stretched across my cheeks as a cloud of blue sugar dusted the front of his shirt from his smirk. The powder fell away as I reached for his face, trying my best to knock what I could off of his short beard. The smile he held faded slowly as he looked down and a strange sort of fluttering rolled through me.

"You're not what I expected." He said.

A flush coated my cheeks. "What am I, then?"

A deep thought swept the spark from his face.

I looked back toward the shelves where the sound he had checked on had come from, "Was there a cause for alarm?" I pointed toward the dark space where he had went searching.

"No. just a couple of kids having some fun in the wrong place. They got scared as soon as I rounded the corner and took off." He looked toward the closed oak doors behind us. "I figured you would have seen them run out." He shrugged. "Alright, well, Brittany Soryn," He eyed me again, "Obviously you have a pretty important reason for needing to be in here if one of the biggest donors to the University is asking on your behalf. So, what exactly are you looking for?" He stared at his dark leather watch before continuing to brush at the blue still clinging to his hair. "I've got about an hour before my next class and I'm going to need time to get this off of me."

"A book." I walked further toward the area that held several bookshelves and began running my fingers over the spines, doing anything I could to erase the feeling of running my hand over his face.

"Ah, yes, I know just the one." He didn't move, his voice holding a sharpness that it hadn't just moments before.

"It's very old."

"Thank you. That really narrows down the list of possibilities."

He walked to the opposite side of the shelf and began checking and rearranging books moving back down the row as he went. The smell of old leather and dusty parchment whispered a light scent into the air as we pulled tome after tome from its place on the dark wood of the shelves. Only the sound of books sliding across wood and the flipping of pages filled the calm dark space.

An uncomfortable tension lingered between us. More than a few times during our search, a chill fluttered across my neck before I caught him staring in my direction with a puzzled pull to his face.

"What?" The sound was harsh to my ears after what felt like hours of silent searching and glancing back and forth.

His lips parted to speak, a softness returning to his face just before his eyes went wide. The sharp line of his jaw went taught as his spine straightened. His footsteps were deliberate as he closed the distance between us, never taking his eyes from the darkness behind me. Was he truly trying to frighten me again?

"Very funny." I sneered, "But I won't be falling for your trickery this time." My head had moved merely inches before his hands rested on my face, holding it so I could look nowhere but in his eyes which never left whatever had caught their attention. His hands moved slowly to my shoulders as he pulled me toward him. My heart raced as he continued to walk backwards, pulling us further toward the darkness and away from whatever threat his eyes were still locked on.

A harsh voice landed on my ears like a vulture stealing the last bit of life that had clung to the silent room. "Have you found it?"

My feet clumsily tangled in his with as a burst of adrenaline and fear propelled me forward. Jaxson stared at me for one shocked moment as we fell to the hard floor. He quickly rolled to the side and placed his arm out in front of me.

Even in the dull light it was easy to see the sharpness of the blade that was pointing at us from where I had just stood. "Where is it?" The man brandishing the wicked looking weapon was just as frightening in appearance. Scars cast his face in deep shadows as he glowered down, inching ever closer with deadly intention.

My eyes went wide as Harwell's arm locked around my waist, pulling me slowly upward, his body twisted to hold the stare with the man while keeping my body blocked from his sight. My hands gripped around his arm while his other went to his pocket. He tossed a small leather square toward the scrappy looking man that held the knife. "Take what ever you want and go." One of Harwell's hands came back to entrap me up against his body. I could feel my heartbeat warring against the warmth of his back as he slowly moved us further from the man. "No one needs to get hurt. Alright? Just let us go."

Another voice whispered from the shadows at our back and sent my skin crawling, "Wrong."

Before I could shout, Harwell had turned and wrapped both arms around me, taking us both even lower to the ground as chaos erupted behind him. The man with the blade screamed as sharp fangs sunk into his throat, a spray of blood arching over the bookshelf and painting it in a dark crimson splatter. Harwell's hands cupped my face, "Run."

I did, making it to the first table before I realized he wasn't with me. I went back to grab his hand, pulling him from whatever foolish thing he was about to do.

"What are you doing, Soryn?"

The sound of utter pain rent through the air as the mans life was quickly being snuffed out. I knew that sound. I had reveled in it many time before. But right then, it wasn't my doing. Something inside me began to quiver as I grabbed for Jaxson's arm.

The thing that was tearing the man apart was a vampire, and Jaxson was completely unprepared to fight it off once it was done filleting what was left of the man with the knife.

"Run, damn it!" He yelled, a plead clinging to his every syllable as I pulled his arm.

"Not without you!"

A gruff resignation sounded from Jaxson. He took only a second to look at the dying man before clasping my hand in his and taking off toward the doors. My arm throbbed where we ran into the heavy door on our escape.

"Pull pull, it's a pull!"

"What?"

He didn't answer, just pulled me and the far door inward toward the room before racing out into the hall. Our feet slid on the slick tile floor as we bolted down open hallway.

"Go to my office and lock the door!"

"But what about..."

"Go!"

This time, I listened, turning back for only a moment to see him pulling at a bright red handle on the wall before running back toward the room we had just escaped.

Horns wailed through the building as I slammed the office door behind me and locking it. A surge of panic ran through me as I paced back and forth in the small office. Being in this breakable body was starting to be more than just a nuisance. The loud sounds continued for an eternity as I warred with the idea of going back to help Harwell. But in doing so, I would be putting Brittany at risk of being trapped under the curse for all eternity. A click sounded at the door just before Harwell twisted inside, locking it back. He didn't say a word as he went to the voice box on his desk. "This is Jaxson Harwell at Sedgemoore University. We need officers here immediately. There's been a murder."

Unstake My Heart

Somehow, I had dragged him into a world of death and this new beating heart wouldn't let me keep him in the dark. As soon as the talking box was resting back in its place, I steadied myself and began. I had revealed my existence to few mortals and even fewer of them lived long enough to betray that knowledge. If I wanted him to live, he would have to be told. And for some even stranger reason, I needed to know he would live.

If Jaxson had a chance of making it out of this with his life, I would need to make him aware of several things very quickly.

Chapter Thirty
BRITTANY

Ben was enjoying a large basket of extra salty fries while I continued to stare at Keith's bowling league friends. I couldn't help but wonder where they thought he was. Did they assume he had to stay after class to talk with a professor about his latest failed test. Maybe they thought that pos yellow hatchback died again. Or, more likely, that he was playing with some brunette half way across town. I'm sure the thought of him rotting at the bottom of a well was pretty far down on his list of usual hangouts.

Ben's face snapped back into focus. If he was a hunter, did he know what Soryn and I had done?

The smell of burgers and deep fried cheese was making my stomach turn; the putrid stink of chili cheese dogs being dropped off to hungry lunchtime patrons was enough to make my head spin as well.

"Soryn is gonna be getting out of class soon so I should probably go."

He mirrored my move to leave and threw several bills on the table. "Alright, let's go."

"No, you stay and finish eating."

"You drove me here."

"Right."

I stared around the crowded food court before catching a pair of unfamiliar eyes locked on me. The man staring gave a mega watt smile before turning back to his table. On his chest was a hard to miss button; the large black pin read, *Lordy Lordy Look Who's 40!*

I tried to hide the juvenile smirk from my face as I leaned back over to Ben. "I'm gonna see if I can get you a doggie bag. I'll be right back."

He didn't say a word, but watched me as I bobbed and weaved to the server across the way.

"Hey, I know you are super busy but," I glanced back over to Ben and waved. He gave a half-hearted wave back before sitting back down. "My boyfriends birthday is today. Is there anyway you all could sing for him?"

She smiled. "I'd be more than happy to." A minute later she and several other servers made their way over, singing and waving napkins above their heads as I darted for the door. When I glanced back, Ben was barely visible through the well wishers singing for him, including the actual birthday boy and his table as well. Both were getting an exuberant birthday performance.

Ben caught my eye just as a full belly laugh barreled out of me. My fingers wiggled in the air as I waved and bolted through the door. My engine revved as I pulled the car in reverse, taking only a moment to glance back before driving the car straight for the university; my laughter only stopping when cut off by the blare of sirens.

"Soryn."

The car squealed in protest as I slammed down on the gas petal. Horrible images flashed through my head like a preview of my worst nightmares as I pulled up to the large green space in front of the university. The herd of students wandering around the quad was innumerable as I shouted Soryn's name over the chatter of voices.

"Brittany!" Ashlie waved at me from the steps outside of the boys dorm "Hey, Brittany! Over here." I scurried into a larger group that was huddled under one of the trees. I had just tucked myself behind a tall goth girl with platform shoes as an announcement boomed over the PA. The raspy tones of the announcer echoed uncomfortably off the old buildings but the chaos of the large crowd was too much to pick out what anyone was saying.

"...malfunction in the alarm." "Classes in the history building are canceled for today." "Fire department is figuring out what's up with them." The group began to disperse as the RA's made their rounds relaying the message to others around the quad.

My sights were set on the History building where several officers and firefighters stood sentry at the archway out front. False alarms didn't need this much police presence. Hopefully, I could have better luck if I took the long way all the way around the back of the squared in buildings. I needed to find my friend.

Hat pulled down to block from the sun's harsh rays, I made my way behind the dorms, following the bumpy concrete pathway that weaved through the trees. The deep green and brown weeds that popped up in the cracks showed its years of disuse.

My thoughts were so deeply trained on finding Soryn that I almost missed the click-clack of steps echoing my own. Someone had the same idea as I did. I darted from the path and my head gave a slight bounce back as it thunked into the trunk of a tall tree. "Ouch!" It didn't actually hurt but the autopilot outburst was enough to make the footsteps that I had been hearing stop.

Bark pulled at my bright blue sweater as I tried to become one with the tree by wrapping my arms around it. I really needed to start dressing for the part if this was what my days were going to consist of now.

A cautious peek around the trunk left a low groan falling from my lips as an annoyingly familiar face made its way far down the path. Despite my new, super sensitive vampire hearing, there was no way his could have been the footsteps I heard. Whoever I had been hearing was gone.

The high weeds at my feet gave little extra cover as I knelt further down to watch Ben pass by; angry mumbles escaping him with every step. I couldn't help but smirk at his words of annoyance since most were about little 'ol me.

With my head low, I crept through the foliage that bordered the broken pathway. It reminded me of a nature documentary we had watched in class. I had been immediately excited when the giant black TV was wheeled into the classroom but quickly lost interest when the animals we were supposed to be watching started attacking each other. At the time, it seemed barbaric to watch, but now, as I stalked my own prey I couldn't help but appreciate the feeling. The earthy smell that lingered in his wake seemed to pull me forward while his steady heart pulsed like a drum. My lips quivered as I imagined his warm blood flowing over them as that drum slowed and stopped its beating. My nails dug into cool dirt and tangled in the roots as I readied myself to spring.

The caw of dozens of agitated birds flooded the trees behind me as some other animal hunted deep in the wooded copse behind me.

I shook my head and stood straight. What the heck was I thinking. Stalking my prey! I forced a full shake through my body.

"Huh-uh. Nope. Not doing this." I watched from a distance as Ben entered the back door of the administration office.

His smell was fading quickly as I approached the building with a much clearer head. Why did I always feel this unnatural pull to him? The door was silent as I made my way inside; my footsteps light against the aging parquet flooring. This part of the building had yet to be touched by renovations and it showed through various stages of disrepair. I leaned into the darkness and waited. I didn't take long.

Hurried voices echoed off the yellowing walls. My ears pricked toward the sound of Ben's voice trickling down the stairs to my right.

"What's with the red and blue all over? Did one of your buddy's over-snack on some freshman?" Ben's voice held an air of ease as he spoke.

A deep female voice flowed down the stairs to me next. "Not one of mine, though, with the last blood drive stolen, that might be the case net time." My eyes went wide as I took off my hat in some strange hope that I could hear even better. Was this the woman from Ben's phone call? My body went completely still as I listened intently to the phantom voice. "It seems that both Renard Dorsetty and The Order are becoming restless waiting for the book to be found. Unfortunately, that restlessness has made a mess of the history archives."

Ben let out a puff of air but didn't say a word as she continued. "You need to do your job, Ben. The Cordain's must find that book before anyone else does."

"I know that, but I can't make them go any faster." His hushed voice seemed to reverberate with annoyance.

"You're in a position to make up for a good many things. I know that your feelings are tangled but…"

"Stop."

"Ben, I have always tried to do what was best for you. We are so close to the end." A silence fell so heavy between the two voices from above that I wondered if they had left. The only tell that they were there was the beating of Ben's heart and the seemingly inescapable pull towards him.

My hands shook as I moved deftly toward the stairs and upward. A trickle of light spilled over onto the top step but no shadows or movement of any kind touched it. I could almost place my hand in the small puddle of light by the time the voices finally came again.

"I know I'm asking much from you, but just know, your parents would be so proud. We're going to make him pay."

"And The Order?" Ben asked.

"Brick by brick. We take them all down one step at a time."

An uneasy cloud swirled in my chest at the implications that conversation left hanging in the air. Who the hell was Ben Sommers?

A beeping shot from my pocket and up, filling the once empty space with a tension that threatened to tear me apart. I didn't have long to wait to see if anyone else heard my pager alert.

"Go." The woman said is whispered tones, "Report back later when you know anything more."

My body shot down the stairs and out the back door at full speed. I was several buildings away before I took the risk to stop and look back. No one was there, but the feeling of eyes watching me set my every nerve on fire. What ever was happening with Ben would have to wait. I needed to get to Soryn and I had already wasted too much time.

◆◦◆

I made it to the back of the history building which was just as guarded as the front. Several cop cars were parked in the small parking area behind it though none of them seemed to be in a rush to go anywhere. I knew that Soryn was in there, though I wasn't sure how.

What kind of false alarm left cops guarding the front and back door? As I sat in the shadows of the trees, an idea popped into my mind and thankfully, a short search around revealed exactly what I was looking for. A small rectangular window was propped open on the first floor.

The woods surrounding the university had put forth a valiant effort of reclaiming the space. Roots pierced through the concrete path leaving small piles of rubble scattered about. The bit of broken walkway felt light in my hand as I bounced it up and down before launching it toward the opposite side of the building where it collided into the stacked brick and shattered. A sharp hiss burst past my teeth. It was a bit more destructive that I had planned but had done the job and gotten the cops attention somewhere else. Maybe a little too well, as another cop who was waiting in one of the parked cars made their way over to investigate.

With an extra pair of eyes being distracted, I didn't waste time getting to the window. My feet scraped against the stone building. Tiny bits of wood lodged under my nails as I gripped the window frame, hoisting myself up and into the rectangular opening. A moment of shock yanked at my nerves as I stared into a set of menacing dark brown eyes surrounded by a mess of long blond hair.

The sudden jolt of surprise left me at an awkward angle, feet dangling and unable to free my top half which was still wedged in place. I had grossly overestimated the size of the window. I glared at the woman in the bathroom mirror. Weeks had passed, and I didn't recognize my own reflection.

I stared down at the toilet just below me; my fingers stretched out for the porcelain anchor. Maybe if I could get a hold of it, I could pull myself in. I willed my arms to stretch but they wouldn't budge as I kicked my legs behind me. Nothing. Several short bursts of pulling and pushing later, and I remained firmly stuck. The thought of destroying university property made my stomach turn, especially when the people who would usually fix it were busy being compelled to fix up Soryn's house. However; hanging half way out of a building I wasn't supposed to be in made me even more apprehensive.

I dug my nails into the wood around the frame again, preparing myself to rip the now broken window even further apart, when something grabbed onto my backside and gave one big pull.

My body flailed as hands gripped onto my waist and I fell backwards. A short shriek was cut off as a hand slapped not so gently over my mouth and my body was pushed up against the wall. Ben put a finger to his own mouth before slowly pulling only inches away from me.

My thoughts whirled in a panic. If he was in league with someone here at the University, then would he turn me in for breaking in? My words came out in a breathy rush, "I thought I heard something coming from inside."

He tilted his head up to look at the window. There was a smile on his mouth when his eyes fell back to mine, "That's a bathroom, Brittany."

"Someone may have needed help."

"I can't imagine what you thought you would be helping them with."

"Shut up," I pushed at him, making a conscious effort not to send him flying into the woods behind us.

"Come on. There's a better way to get inside."

He didn't wait for me as he put his hands in his pockets and walked away. I followed, a good distance behind as Ben approached the still guard free door. The cops still hadn't returned.

"Ladies first." He opened the door and waited for me to enter.

"Was that unlocked?" I asked.

He raised an eyebrow and nodded.

I huffed past him, but he cut off my escape again by pulling me into an open room to our left. Footsteps echoed off the empty halls as someone paced just outside.

The click of a radio met my ears just as the door to the outside opened again, "Any update on the source of the disturbance?"

A voice came through, "Looks like part of the roof fell or something. No threat."

"Alright. Go ahead and come back then." Her voice began to trail back down the hall as she ended her radio conversation. "They're almost done with the alarms and we can get back to actually doing some police work."

I whispered, "Shouldn't you be back at the diner with your birthday buddy?"

He whispered back, "Dave had to get to a doctors appointment but he was kind enough to drop me off first."

"Why are you here?" I wanted to ask about the woman he had been talking to before but thought it best to keep some things up my sleeve, just in case.

"We can get in to all the questions later, alright. Right now," He moved to the door, sweeping the hall for signs of movement, "we need to get to your friend."

All thoughts of playing the calm and collected vampire went out of my head. "Why? Is she alright?" I rushed to his side, accidentally bumping him into the door frame to get to the hall. "Even the cops said it was just an alarm, right?" I wanted it to just be an alarm but somehow, deep down, I could sense that something was wrong with Soryn.

"You seem awfully worried about her well being," He said with a prying stare.

"I'm not a psychopath, Ben. I don't like it when bad things happen to people."

"I know you don't."

Who was this man? Dorsetty's assistant? Vampire hunter? Order member? Or just some poor slob that got pulled into something way over his head. His face was a hard mask as he turned, keeping his body low as he led me through the building and up the stairs and onto the landing that would lead to the archives.

"Ben." He stopped, though his eyes wouldn't meet mine. My brain tumbled through the mountain of questions I wanted to ask him. Who was he actually working with? What did they want with a book that only Soryn and I could read? Why had it felt like he wanted to kiss me at The Rink? But none of that came out. Instead, a flurry of voices as well as a very familiar accent made it to my ears. "I know where she is!" I whispered frantically.

We crept forward, and with each step, I could sense Soryn's frustration and fear growing stronger. I dipped my head around the artifact strewn wall to see a group of very serious looking people outside of Dr. Harwell's office.

I breathed in the scent that had been lingering in the air around the university. The same smell that had clung to Mr. Dorsetty. I finally knew what it was. Vampires smelled like the air before a rain storm and rust. The group huddled down the hall were vampires. Whatever was going on was definitely more serious than some joker pulling a fire alarm and somehow, Soryn was involved.

I grabbed a handful of Ben's shirt in my fist and pulled him a short distance away and into another dark room.

"What's going on!" I angrily whispered, my head exhausted from being left in the dark.

He stared down at me with an anger that didn't fully touch his eyes, "Your family has guarded Soryn for a century and you're really going to try to make me believe that you don't know anything?"

"I don't know anything! I'm completely lost in all of this mess and I certainly didn't ask for any of it." I scratched at my neck, mouth opened but unable of what else to say.

The anger on his face settled just slightly as he spoke, "Look. You help me and I'll help you."

"Help you do what, Ben. I don't understand what's going on or why I should even trust you."

"You probably shouldn't."

"Then why are you trying to help me?"

His anger melted away and was replaced by a far off stare. He let out a long stream of air before narrowing his focus back to me. "Because sometimes, revenge is more important than the greater good."

We stared at each other in silence as he gazed deeply in my eyes, waiting for the weight of his words to sink in.

My lips narrowed to a straight white line as I took a deep breath and whispered, "Am I supposed to know what that means?"

He rolled his eyes, before putting his fist to his mouth.

He huffed over to the door and peeked outside while I looked around the room. His words felt itchy in my head. Like there was a wall there that they were trying to scratch at. An echo of something I couldn't quite grasp before they settled back into no more than words again.

"We are going to need a distraction."

My eyes darted around the room before landing on a bright orange disc. I toyed with the weight of it as I tossed it up and down.

"As much as I would love to play a round with you, we really don't have time to play right now."

"I beg to differ." My heart sank a little as I eyed the long hallway filled with priceless antiques.

Chapter Thirty-One

SORYN

"Are you alright?"

He stared at me with thoughtful eyes. "Are you?"

I let out an exasperated breath. "I am not crazy. You just saw what that woman did, did you not?"

"I'm not saying you're crazy, Soryn. I'm really asking if you're alright. Were you hurt at all?"

"I'm fine, now please listen." I took his hands, needing to make certain his focus was entirely mine. "I'm trying to tell you that there are vampires in Sedgemoore and one of them just killed that man that was holding the very sharp, very scary knife at my back"

He let out a slow, deliberate breath. "I believe you."

"You do? Just like that?"

"I've lived here almost my entire life. Everyone whispers about otherworldly things and I'm not blind to them. This isn't the first time I've come across something like this in my research of the town either."

"And you believe that I was…"

The door swung wide and a stocky man barged inside the office. He didn't say a word to either of us but instead went straight for Harwell's talking box. He disconnected the long black chord that ran from it to the wall before making his way to leave again.

Jaxson placed himself between him and the exit. "I'm finding it very difficult to understand what exactly it is you think you're doing? There's no reason for that or to keep us here." Jaxson stood a full six inches taller than the officer, his voice unwavering as he glared down at the uniformed man only inches from him.

"Mr. Harwell, please take a seat. I've already told you, we need to have a grief counselor talk to the both of you before we can allow you to access the rest of the campus— by any means." Neither of the men budged.

"Can you at least let her wait in her dorm or something?" He glanced at me, "There's absolutely no reason she should have to stay here in this building after witnessing…" he paused obviously collecting his thoughts, but didn't voice where those thoughts had led. How sweet. He was trying to protect me. My heart strings gave a gentle tug as the officer closed the door, leaving us alone in Jaxson's office once more.

Jaxson raked his hands through his dark hair. "This can't be happening right now." The small couch gave way slightly as I lowered myself, my eyes tracking his slow pacing around the office space.

"If you understand that I am—or at least, I used to be one of them, why are you still trying to get me to leave this place. It would seem that I would be your best hope of understanding what is happening? Why do you not want that?"

"Whatever you may be, right now you are as vulnerable as I am. My only focus should be to keep you safe."

He continued to mumble for several minutes before he focused back on me. My heart sank to my stomach at the repulsion written in the lines of his face.

"What?" I tried to keep the shake from my voice as my heart continued to beat rapidly.

"Your face is a mess."

"Well, you aren't a portrait of perfection yourself right now." My hands balled into fists as I barked my lie at him.

"No. No, that's not what I meant," he snatched up a paper box of fabric from his desk pulling at the thin white sheets before holding them toward my face. Our hands collided in a strange fluttering as he tried to swipe the fabric along my cheek while I worked at swatting him away.

"Have I not been tormented enough for one day?"

"I'm not trying to— you have—" He pointed to my face.

My hands brushed against something slick, the cold liquid smearing tiny red trails across my fingertips. Until then, I hadn't noticed the peppering of blood that had cooled in small dots across my flushed skin. Jaxson's face held a soft apology as he held the thin handkerchiefs back to me.

"I've had worse." I laughed. Surprisingly, so did he, the warmth of it only growing when he replied.

"Yeah. Me too."

With sirens still wailing in the background, we sat together in soft laughter. My heart gave a warm pulse even when the sound of it faded from the small office. My mind reeled with the wonder of him. Never had I met a man with such a warm whit. He treated me as an equal even before the knowledge that, normally, I could rip him limb from limb. He was an exhilarating mystery.

"Would you like me to—" He reached out a hand and began to clean the blood from my face again. A delightful tingle ran through me where his fingertips brushed my skin. My arm seemed to lift of its own volition to brush at the blue powder that dusted the front of his shirt. His breath hitched as my hand rested on his chest.

He leaned closer, his fingertips sliding from my face, brushing the space behind my ear and curling gently into my hair. He paused. His eyes closed while he took several long dragging breaths. "I'm sorry." He didn't move away but my body rebelled at his halted advance. "I'm sorry. This isn't right. I shouldn't— I can't be this way with you." When his eyes finally met mine, a storm warred beneath their beautiful cerulean depths.

He was so close still. As I breathed deeply, I could smell the subtle scent of him. It's warmth left my chest tight with thoughts of leather clad books and cinnamon. Warmth swirled through me in a way that I had never felt. Love for me had always been cold. As cold as I had been and would be again. I forced myself to focus on the man in front of me instead of the one that left me to sleep. I would forgive Renard. He was my past and my future, always. As constant as the moon.

But in the present, while I was still alive, I would live. I would enjoy the fire that was growing until the night extinguished it again. His shirt bunched in my hand as I stopped his retreat, pulling him toward the kiss he had tried to deny. Electricity raced through my veins seeming to replace the blood that flowed from my ever warring heart.

His smile brushed against my lips as he spoke, sending another wave of shivers across my skin. "The cops are going to be back soon. I'm not sure if this makes us look guilty, but it surely would raise some questions."

"Maybe they found another crime to keep them busy for a while."

Hope fluttered in my lungs as he brushed his lips against mine again. "Is it horrible of me to hope you're right?"

Bam

We both shot to our feet as a chorus of shattered glass and yelling came from the hallway.

Jaxson narrowed his eyes on me, puzzlement written over his flushed features.

"What?" I said, "I was with you the whole time."

"We can't stay here. Whoever killed that man could still be in the building. I should be getting you to safety and instead…"

"You're keeping me distracted?" I smiled.

"That wasn't part of the plan."

"Oh, so you planned all of this?"

He grabbed my hand, pulling me closer to the door. It opened without a sound as we peered into the hallway. The officer that had been guarding our door was at the far end of the long window filled hallway holding a vibrant orange plate. A small group of men ambled around him. Shards of broken glass lay spread across the tile floor, the scratch and crunch of shattered bits being crushed under the groups feet echoed back to our ears.

The sunlight that bathed shafts of light into the history buildings halls did little to veil our escape, however it did provide some interesting insight. As Jaxson pulled us further away from his office, I stared at the group that hovered at the opposite end of the hallway growing further and further from us. Four of them donned dark glasses and hats while their pale skin gave off a sickly pallor that could be observed even from a distance. There was no mistaking what they were. Vampires.

"I don't care what you thought! This is my school and I will run it however I see fit!"

The harsh voice rasped its way up the empty stairway that led to the floors below us. Jaxson's finger went to his mouth though I needed no reminder to remain silent. Our bodies knocked against each other as we crouched toward the floor and just out of sight.

The owner of the voice made light steps on the stair case before heavier footfalls followed. "I gave the Order permission to help with the search on the University grounds." Jaxson's arms tensed as he moved one around my waist, readying us both to run if the voices made it to our line of sight.

"And we are grateful for that, however seeing as how one of ours was attacked, I think there is need for an adjustment to our agreement." The mans voice was so very familiar. It scratched at the base of my skull.

"I know that man." My thoughts swirled as I tried to sift through the countless number of voices that had met my ears.

"We let you set the alarm. We let you post several men within our walls. We have been open with you about everything and yet one of your own openly threatens a student at knife point while another…"

"We have to go now." Jaxson interrupted and the footsteps quickened. He didn't wait for my answer this time. Instead the arm that rested around my waist tightened as we moved toward an open room on the other side of the stairwell.

"We have no choice but to remain vigilant." The mans voice boomed where before it had barely made it up corridor. "With your acceptable supply of blood gone, our responsibility is to the humans that you are putting at risk."

The lighter steps halted and clipped anger resounded in her voice. "Do not insult my intelligence, Mr. Harken. You are searching for the same thing that we are. And now that she is awake, we will find it."

My breath stuck in my lungs unable to escape just as I could not escape.

The mans voice came again, "And do not insult mine by pretending that you will not relinquish both to Renard Dorsetty."

"Mr. Dorsetty is a patron of the University. Without his contributions, we would not exist."

The man laughed. "Yes, I am aware of all of his contributions to your existence and for what reason." My breath stirred like a storm fed by the warring of my heart against my chest. It wasn't difficult to grasp what he was suggesting. Whatever was happening was because of me and Renard. And here was Jaxson, plunged right in the middle of it. If there was a chance that he was anywhere near, I needed to get Jaxson away from here. If he had any idea what had just transpired between us, he would take no qualms in ending him. He had killed many others for far less in the quest for my heart.

"Keep your man away from her. You may observe, you may protect if called for, but if you meddle anymore in our search for the book, we will have no other choice but to take more immediate measures." The rasp of the woman's voice held a sinister note as it flowed back toward us. "You are well aware of what kind of things a human body can be subjected to before it fails. The Order will heed my warning on this."

Jaxson remained silent as he held me close, refusing to widen the space between us until the voices were well away. He didn't realize how important his silence had been. The woman that searched for myself and the book had been sired by Renard. A tremor ran through me as I came to an unsettling realization. There were far more undead in the city of Sedgemoore than there had been in the township of Cordain.

"I need to find Brittany."

"What about your book?"

"Brittany first."

A determined smirk bloomed across his face as he took my hand in his. "Let's go find your girl."

"You talking about me?" Brittany's head popped around the door frame.

My heart was pounding a tumultuous rhythm as I threw my arms around her, pulling her to me before taking her arms and pushing her away again. "Where were you!" I angrily whispered.

"I got here as fast as I could." She peered around door frame to wave someone else inside. Ben quickly scurried into the room before closing the door. "We saw you leave Professor Harwell's office. What's going on? Why were you being guarded by..." Her voice trailed as her eyes roved over Jaxson. "Um, there were a lot of really old, pale people— like, unnaturally so, ya know."

My head hung for a moment as I listened to her. "Brittany, he knows."

"He knows?"

"Yes. He knows. Everything."

"All of it?"

"Yes. That's why I said everything."

She eyed Jaxson for a long moment, seemingly weighing his worth before a wide smile brushed over her face, "Alright. Welcome to the craziness, Professor."

"It's been a hell of an initiation." His voice was strong, though unease clung to the single breathy laugh he used to punctuate his words.

"Not to be that guy, but can we bond some other time. There is a building full of vampires and at least one dead body here so I would really rather not be here."

"You are that guy." I said, "And no one said you had to be here. What are you doing here by the way?"

"I'm here because you all seem to be fumbling through this. You're not the only ones that are going to be screwed if you don't find that spell book."

"What does your Order want with it." I asked

Ben let out a heavy sigh and went on, "Where else have you not looked?"

Footsteps tapped down the hallway while the four of us froze. The conversation held by at least two people muffled by the closed door. Their voices rose and fell in heated debate and the sound of their decent quickly stopped.

Silence fell on the building while our breath held. Our heavy heartbeats would betray our hiding spot. I looked to Brittany, her face pulled in confusion as she seemed to peer through the door.

Several moments passed until Brittany finally spoke. "They're gone." Her hands held me back as Jaxson and Ben led the way out of the building.

"What did you hear?" I asked.

"The Order is at the shop searching it." Brittany stared at Ben, her brows dipped in thought.

The sound of students going about their day had returned to the outside air as we made our was to the line of trees. "There is one more place for us to search here at the University and since we now have the aide of the esteemed professor—" I presented the key card, "maybe you could show us how this works."

All eyes looked to me in confusion.

"I'm not sure how my Blockbuster card is going to help." Said Jaxson while Brittany held back a snicker and Ben shook his head in disbelief.

Brittany took my arm, "I'll explain it later but right now, we need to get to the library."

Chapter Thirty-Two
BRITTANY

"How could it not be there." Soryn said, as she tore into a warm chocolate croissant.

The low lit coffee shop would have to serve as our makeshift hide out since At Days' End was out of the question for now. My heart gave a gentle dip at the thought of some evil force having control of the place.

"So, what's the next step then?" I whispered.

The Never Bean Cafe was packed with faces from the university. Men and women dressed in all black, tipped back dark green mugs full of frothy steaming goodness. Others hunched over thick books, feverishly scrawling notes in spiral bound pages.

The table where we sat was covered in black and white newspapers, saved from years of brown rings by the acrylic top that held them down. The mellow music accented by the occasional drum made Ben's finger tapping on the table all the more irritating. Dr. Harwell clutched his bag against his chest as he stared at the newspapers. His poor academic brain was no doubt having an existential crisis as he sat next to a new vampire, a used to be vampire, and a vampire hunter.

Soryn gave him a stout pat on the back before licking the morsel of chocolate that was stuck to her finger. "We searched the many shelves in the history building and found nothing but dust and blood." Her eyes pulled to Dr. Harwell, inspecting him up and down while he furrowed his brow in deep thought.

She picked up another croissant, dipping it into her cup before eating half of it in one bite, her words rolling around the flaky pastry. "If it's here, it's not to be found in that place."

"Of course it's here." Ben leaned back in his chair, arms crossed as he glowered down at my friend. "Dorsetty wouldn't put such a huge stake in this place without reason."

"What exactly is the vermin doing here. Does he have a purpose?" She gave a pointed look to Ben before smiling, "Dinner perhaps?"

"I'm not hungry." He said.

I glowered at Soryn, "That's not what she meant." As if on cue, my stomach gave a lurch.

Dr. Harwell's head snapped to my face and Ben's hand went, almost imperceptibly, to his waist before his words whispered a defiant syllable. "I'm aware."

"You're fine." My voice was weaker that I would have liked. Soryn reached into my bag, pulling out a white Lisa Frank thermos with a bright pink cup lid. A small smear of red had leaked out and was adding another colorful streak of hair to the unicorn. Harwell's eyes went big as Soryn took the untouched coffee in front of him and poured half of it into her own almost empty cup followed by the dark red liquid. A giant clot of blood splashed into the steaming coffee and sloshed a swirl of crimson and black liquid onto the table.

"So you're the culprits." Dr. Harwell said, "How many did you get away with?"

Ben eyed Soryn, "From what I've been told, Ms. Floaire is quiet skilled in taking what isn't hers."

"I took enough to get us through." Soryn's voice held a note of venom in it. She leaned forward as Ben took a long swig of his coffee. "Again, why do we find ourselves graced with your unwanted presence if it's not for Brittany's pleasure?"

Ben's usually steady hands fumbled as he sat the mug on the table, adding to the mess already there. If my cheeks could glow red, they would have been lighting up the entire coffee shop. "Soryn, that didn't come out the way you think it did."

A bright voice bubbled from behind me, "Let me help you with that." A short brunette popped in between Harwell and Ben, swirling at the mess that we had made of our table. She sniffled, her focus landing on Soryn. "Are you alright? Do you need a band-aid or something?"

I looked down at the red spots that marked Soryn's white sleeve. I hadn't realize she had been splattered, the smell of blood already in my nose from the second we walked in the cafe.

"Yes. Parchment cut…"

"Paper."

"Paper cut."

The barista gave Soryn a sad look, "Those are the worst. I'll be right back with that bandage."

Soryn's voice was quick and low, "You see? You are messy and draw too many wandering eyes. No purpose."

"Oh really?"

"Really."

Ben leaned closer to me as she spoke, both he and Soryn seemingly trying to see who could take up more of my vision.

"Then tell us, oh great and mighty vampire, how many blood suckers are in this room right now." She began to speak, but he cut her off, "Brittany doesn't count."

Something in my chest swirled at his words for just a moment before I shoved him out of my space and answered for Soryn, "None."

"Wrong."

Dr. Harwell leaned in, looking around the room slowly as he moved in closer to Soryn. Ben scooted his chair even closer to mine before whispering, "The guy on the stage with the drum. Don't everybody look at once." His face went in his hands as the three of us went from a quick glance to a slow gaze up and down the man with the barrette and dark red glasses.

I bunched up to the table, "Alright. It makes sense that there would be more than one vampire in a town pretty much created by vampires."

Soryn's eyebrows pinched as a pale wash fell over her face, "There were more in the history building as well. We swore that we never sire anyone. None should be here."

"Well, Mr. Dorsetty isn't always the best at keeping his promises." A darkness shifted over Ben's face before he nodded his head toward the baristas. "He chooses them carefully, but don't let that fool you in to thinking that he only turns a few." The three women were huddled in a corner behind the counter, laughing quietly as they sipped on heavily marked cups. The one who had helped us waved, "I'll be right there with that band-aid."

Ben smiled and winked, "No rush, were fine hun."

The three of them giggled. I glared.

"Dorsetty owns this place. Do you think it's a coincidence that there is a student blood drive every couple of months?" He paused for only a moment to read our expressions, "Why do you think this school out of all the others has such a treasure trove of historical artifacts?" He stared, lines forming on his forehead, "He's created a place for vampires to thrive. And, Soryn, your curse is the key to making sure that they do."

"You're an infant." Soryn spoke softly but the bite in her words wasn't lost, "You know nothing of what Renard and I have had to suffer through the ages. You know nothing of what must be done to...."

"Survive." I whispered. "If you know you'll live forever, what does it matter?"

"If we don't reverse this curse, you won't have to ask."

Harwell left the table, giving Soryn a gentle pat on the shoulder before disappearing in the crowd at the counter waiting for coffee and food.

"What does the Order of the Rose have to do with all of this?" I asked.

"That's what I'm trying to figure out." Ben stared at the coin in his hand, brushing his thumb over the carved wooden circle. "The man in the archives, he was one of them."

"Yes. He was human." Soryn snarled.

"Not even a hint of remorse for the fact that a life was ended thanks to one of your kind?" he said.

"Stop glaring at Soryn. You can't blame her for all of this. Besides, I'm the only vampire here." I looked around, "Well. I'm the only vampire at this table. So, if you're gonna be mean, just be mean to me, okay."

"No, Brittany. You're just a silly girl who got caught up in something way above her head."

My throat burned, a mixture of hunger and holding back tears. Harwell came back with another cup of coffee, a basket of chocolate croissants, and a band-aid. "The barista wasn't too happy that she didn't get to bring you your coffee." We all turned to see her giving a wave to Ben.

"You sure no how to charm the ladies, don't you Ben?" I huffed.

He pulled at his necklace, "It's spelled to make me seem more appealing to vamps."

"You should get your money back." Both Harwell and Soryn chuckled as I memorized the look of the pendant. The strange smell I had come to associate with him was definitely coming from that.

A round of boisterous applause filled the cafe as a man took the stage, his all black attire marking him as a usual customer and allowing him to blend in to the dark smoky atmosphere. The gentle music that had thrummed through the air stopped as the vampire on drums started a low but rapid beat.

"Is there somewhere else we could go," Harwell asked, "I watched a man die today, the last thing I want to do is add to the horror with frat boy slam poetry."

"Okay." Soryn took charge, "Everyone go home for the night and we can meet up tomorrow and figure out our next steps."

All three of us spoke at once, the common complaint being that of the four of us, only one was indestructible at the moment. The ruckus from our table pulled the attention that should have been on the performer. The cafe was silent as everyone glowered.

"Sorry." I squeaked, skin crawling with all eyes on us as we gathered our things and weaved through the crowd and out the door.

We were almost half way down the trail that led back to campus when a high pitch voice flagged us down. A bright smile spread across Ashlie's face as she waved, her quick steps almost a sprint as we closed the distance between us.

"Hey!"

"Hi." I said, more than a little awkwardly.

A long pause held in the air as steady as the sunset peeking through the trees behind her.

"So, um… do you mind if I walk with you back to campus?"

"Weren't you just coming from that way?" Soryn hadn't stopped walking and was already several lamps ahead of us, both Jaxson and Ben close behind her. The strange feeling from the cafe had followed us onto the path and none of us were keen on staying put.

"Keith left a note on my white board to meet him at the Never Bean." A sliver of guilt seemed to wrap around her words as she stared past me.

Soryn laughed from up ahead, "He's probably just tied up somewhere."

"Soryn." I chided, catching up to the others just as a sharp rustling cut through the trees to my left. A chill shot through the air as we all stopped to look into the ever darkening woods.

"I'm not even going to lie, I'm getting a little freaked out here. I think there's an animal or something out there." She inched closer to Harwell and Ben, but Soryn planted herself in between.

"Yeah, maybe it would be safer if we all walked together. Besides, Keith isn't at the cafe. We just came from there." I hung back for a second while Jaxson, Soryn, and Ashlie followed the path.

I whispered to Ben, "Do the vampires usually mess with students?"

"That's the whole point of the blood drive. They get what they need, and the people of Sedgemoore are none the wiser thinking they've done this great service."

I grabbed the thermos from my bag. "You mean the blood drive that Soryn emptied out for me?"

The wind whipped around us, sending the smell of Bens' necklace swirling through the air. The sound came again, but quickly faded further into the trees. Whatever had been watching from the woods had found something else to pique its interest.

"They'll do another one soon. They always do. Let's get Ashlie back to her dorm." Ben said as we both made quick work of catching up to the others.

The dorms were loud, music trilled through the open night air. NSYNC collided with No Doubt as we ascended the step toward the glass door where a large brown WELCOME mat had been placed.

Everyone else walked through the doorway before I inched forward. I passed through. A thrill went through me for a split second before a sinking feeling pulled at my stomach, "Soryn. Knowing what we know now, do you think its safe to leave that there?"

She didn't have a chance to speak before the RA started in on us, "Hey! Gentlemen. You need to go back to your — Oh, Professor Harwell. Sorry, I thought you were a student."

"No worries. I was just making sure these three made it home safe." He took a chair beside the RA, "What uh— what extra precautions did the Dean put in place?"

"Precautions?" She asked, "None. Why? Did something happen on campus?"

He stood, "No. Just the fire alarm. I didn't know if he would be checking the others out."

I chimed in, "We're gonna walk Ashlie to her dorm. We'll be back in just a few minutes."

The second floor of the building was even more chaotic with girls rushing across the hallways and open doors leaving conversations and music thrumming through the tight corridor. I took a swig from my thermos, a pang of guilt clenching at my throat.

"I'm here." Ashlie waited in front of the closed door. "Thanks."

Keith's choppy handwriting was scrawled across the dry erase board. *Britt's dead to me. Meet me at the Never Bean.*

She was half way in the room before I felt the push back at the entrance. It looked like the rooms were still safe.

"You can co…"

I cut her off, "When did he leave you this note?"

"Brittany, I promise, we haven't done anything. I mean, not like, since you two were together or whatever."

"Yeah, sure, that's great." I pointed to the words on the board. "When did you get this?" Soryn bit at her lip, eyebrows furrowed as she realized what I was asking.

"I don't know. Maybe a few hours ago? I didn't notice it until after the fire alarm earlier."

Soryn stayed silent as we made our way down the busy stairwell, anger rolling off of her in heavy waves.

"I…"

She flashed me a cold stare and I shut my mouth.

The night air stirred around us as we met back up with Dr. Harwell.

"Where's Ben?" I asked.

"He said something about having to check back in and left."

"Good." Soryn finally broke her silence, "The last thing we need is another human around."

"Why? What's going on?" Harwell's fingers brushed her arm, a familiar gesture that she quickly pulled away from.

"Apparently, Renard isn't the only one siring new vampires."

———— ◆•◆ ————

The three of us stared into the well.

"Are you sure he was dead?" The panic was clear in my voice as we stared down into the deep dark pit. "Maybe he just came to and crawled out."

"I have been around enough dead people to know when they are in fact dead."

"Maybe he wrote the note before and Ashlie just didn't notice."

Jaxson stood, arms crossed, staring into the abyss, a look of apprehension on his bearded face while the dull blue spirit beside him mirrored his pose. "So let me get this straight," He worried at his jaw before pointing down the well, "We're hoping that your boyfriend…"

"Ex-boyfriend," both Soryn and I replied.

"Ex-boyfriend is down there?" He continued, "And if he isn't down there, that would be bad."

Soryn let out a slow breath. Small bits of rock scattered down the stone circle as the two of them moved closer. He placed his jacket over her shoulders when a visible shudder took hold of her and she sniffled from the cold.

Even the fallen leaves were silent. The air charged with unspoken anticipation as ghosts gathered toward the stone tomb where more that a few of their own bodies most likely rested.

"What now?" I asked.

She gestured toward the pitch black hole, "Now, you swim."

My displeasure at the suggestion came out as a sharp snarl. Jaxson grabbed Soryn by the shoulders, pulling her behind him in one swift move.

"Would you like to go instead?" She shoved past him.

He stared at her, helplessly, "She growled. At you!"

"You get told to jump down a death well and tell me if you don't want to growl at a few people." I balked before turning to Soryn, "Can't the ghosts just tell us if he's still down there?"

"They will do no more than nod and we can't trust them, anyway."

Jaxson backed away from the well, "Ghosts?"

We nodded.

"Vampires and ghosts." He shook his head before raking both hands through his hair in confused frustration, his voice held a tremor that bordered on hysterical. "Next thing I know you'll be telling me werewolves are real."

I laughed as Soryn gave me a sidelong glance, "Remind me to tell you about Paris."

"Werewolves are real?" Jaxson asked though she didn't answer.

A groan bounced off the muck coated walls as I began to lower myself down with nothing more than a rope tightened around my waist. The wind had begun to blow on the ground above, whirling through the rocky walls and spinning the smell of moss and death. It created a low moaning echo that pierced through my skin and set my every nerve on edge. With each layer of rock I descended, another wave of fear rolled through my mind of what might await me at the bottom of the well. As I looked up, the source of those horrors stared down at me with bright green eyes. Below me, several ripples broke the mirrored surface of the water, the source still too far to make out even with my enhanced sight.

I steadied one hand on the cold wall as the other gripped at the splintered rope. "Soryn, I don't think I can do this." Something splashed beneath me. The rope pulled at my waist as I twisted away from the sound, the rapid movement sending my body swinging. I splayed my arms and legs out against the aging wall, pushing against the stone with all my might and willing myself not to fall into the water below.

"Brittany, what's happening down there?" Worry laced Soryn's voice, "Are you…"

A shower of crushed rock began to fall as my foot went through the already ancient well. My nails dug long gouges into the stones that held to the wall as the others continued to fall around me. My skin crawled as an eerie blue light grew from the water below casting a frightening glow on the bones that the rocks had jostled loose from their murky grave.

Terror ripped through my lungs as something within me snapped. I clawed at the stone wall, forcing my body upward as the crumbling well threatened to pull me back under, the moon cast her warm light down beckoning me to the safety above.

A rushing in my ears like the sound of a million wings pushed through the electrified air and made it impossible to hear if Soryn or Jaxson called to me. A small hope began to radiate from my chest as the circle of light began to grow. I was close to the top. Another few feet and I would taste fresh air. The sound of rocks colliding was building as the entire well began to collapse under the strain.

"Brittany!" Soryn reached down for the rope that still held me at the waist. "Come on." Her voice was cut off as a large stone dislodged from the opening where she was leaning over the abyss. My heart fell as her body did the same. The rope gave a sharp drop before stopping just as abruptly.

Jaxson's voice was strained as he shouted from above, "Soryn!"

My hands gripped around her wrist as her feet kicked out at the darkness. "Don't you dare drop me, girl!"

Jaxson groaned loudly as he pulled at the rope, all the while I inhaled the smell of sweet iron mixed with death.

Soryn had a choke hold on me as I pulled her in, both of us clinging to the other as we made our painfully slow ascent.

With one final grunt, Jaxson pulled us over the crumbled side of the well, all three of our bodies crashing into the hard ground before scrambling further away from the death pit.

Heavy breathing was the only sound that filled the air for a long time as we all laid there. The specters that had been floating around had long since disappeared by the time Soryn finally broke the silence. "Was he down there?"

Shame wrapped itself around my throat in an icy grip. "I didn't get far enough to see."

She huffed before standing and grabbing my hands. "Come on, we need to find another way." She started off toward the woods.

"What?" Jaxson was up and stalking toward her. "Soryn, you both almost just died down there! Can you give everyone a second to breathe?"

"I'm fine and she can't die. Now let's go."

I stared at her in disbelief. "What is wrong with you?"

She stopped, Jaxson barely stopping himself from running into her. Her hands peeked around his arms as she gripped him, moving his body aside to glare straight through me. "What is wrong with me?" She took slow but deliberate steps toward me as she spoke, a palpable vitriol in her voice, "Over five centuries I have walked this earth and in all of those years I have sired one vampire. One!" Her footsteps quickened, the crunch of the leaves under her punctuating her words as she stalked toward me, "You have been this way for less than a fortnight and already you have damned another!"

"I didn't kill him, Soryn! Or did you forget that part?" Anger bounced through me, hitting every raw nerve I had just worked so hard to calm.

"You should have killed him! That I could stomach. But letting him taste your blood— that I can not forgive."

"I already told you, I didn't give him any of my blood."

"Then how is he leaving love notes around campus?"

"We don't know that was him."

"Exactly. Which is why you are going back down there to make sure his body is rotting right where it belongs."

"I'm not going to be doing that." She had a formidable aura and, despite the height difference, I fought the urge to back away as she invaded my space.

"I have spent too much of this afterlife caring for others for you to go and ruin everything."

"Says the woman who started the well full of bodies." I pushed again when a sliver of guilt met her eyes. "The woman who cared so much about money that she got herself cursed and killed an entire family all for a stupid dowry."

She was still for only a beat. Jaxson stood off to the side, staring at anything but our argument.

"You are right. I cared so much for that dowry that I gave up all the pleasures of being human." Jaxson gave a surprised huff as she grabbed his hand and pulled him closer to her. "Can you drive that thing out front?"

"The car?" He asked.

"Yes, the car."

He nodded.

"Well..." She tossed me a grin though her eyes were full of a sorrow she was trying so desperately to hide, "let's leave Brittany to it then." Soryn kept a tight hold on him as they moved across the yard toward the house.

"Where are you going!" I yelled, "We have a serious problem here!"

Her face was stern as she pivoted, her green eyes piercing into my soul. "You made the problem. You fix the problem." Without another word, she turned and left. The sound of the engine roaring to life echoed through the empty night air as they drove away.

Just as the sound began to fade, a laugh barreled through the darkness sending chills up my spine before the world fell silent again.

"Keith?" Only the sound of the sharp wailing wind answered.

Chapter Thirty-Three
SORYN

The cobblestone road gave a welcome respite to the events of the night as Jaxson led the way to his home. "It's just up here." He pointed toward a dark shop window several buildings away. Music flowed through the night air. Being here reminded me of how it was just before I slept. If I closed my eyes, I could almost hear hoof beats on the bumpy stone beneath me, the sound of revelry sent a lovely pulse through my veins. Renard and I walked these streets what felt like only a fortnight ago. My skin tingled at the memory of him placing his hand in mine.

"She does it again." He whispered in my ear, "That devilish woman tries to outshine my flower." His eyes went to the full moon above us before he inched closer to me, no more than a breath away from my lips, "Say the word and I will pull her from the sky and put you in her place."

"You could do such a thing?" I smiled, walking further along the old road, the lanterns casting puddles of light that washed my skirts in a yellow glow.

"No." He grabbed my hand, twisting me back to him. Whispers flowed to my ears as others looked on. He pulled me in even closer, his lips brushing mine.

"I could not." He held my hands to his lips and kissed one, "I would not share you with the world." He kissed the other. "You are mine." He pulled at my waist. "And I would have you know only my love as long as that light shines." He claimed my lips, his touch filled with a fire and passion that I had come to know and expect from him.

I tried to stay in the memory, wanting so badly to have that night be true. Wanting with every ounce of my being to stand there in front of the man that I loved and have him truly love me back.

Warmth coated my hand, "Soryn?"

Fingers brushed my cheek as I opened my eyes to see Jaxson. His brows were pulled down in concern as he squeezed my hand. "What can I do?"

A flutter made my insides seem to float, light as the melody that had grown in the air. My throat tightened as his eyes gazed into mine. A breeze carried my hair in gentle tendrils around my face and my heart dipped when his fingers barely grazed my skin as he tucked that hair behind my ear, his hand never leaving my face.

Heat flooded through my veins sending every nerve screaming but not with as much exuberance as my heart. She raged at me. *Remember.* Remember what this took from you before.

A burst of music came from across the way as a set of glass doors opened onto the street. A group of young people poured out, their laughter a welcome sound to block out the rushing of blood that pounded in my ears.

"What is there?" I asked.

Jaxson didn't move, just cleared his throat before speaking, "That's The Library." A hint of defeat hung on his words but when I turned back to him, his eyes were bright, his stature tall and no malice held there. If he held anger at my rejection, it wasn't shown on his face. His lovely face. I found myself wondering what his dark beard felt like. Was it coarse like horse hair that would scratch at my skin or was is soft like a warm blanket. I squeezed my hands into fists to keep from reaching out.

"Do you think the book could be there?" I crossed the cobblestones quickly with Jaxson on my heels.

"Not that kind of library." He chuckled.

"Then what kind…" A heavy hand landed on my shoulder.

The deep voice boomed to my right. "I.D."

"Soryn." I picked up his hand with two fingers and dropped it away from me.

"What?" The tall man in black glowered down at me.

Jaxson chimed in, "Hey man. She's good." He pulled a white card from his wallet. "Here."

They continued to talk, the quiet exchange boring me. Neither spared a glance as I continued on into the dark building.

Much like the skating rink place that Brittany had taken me to on our first night together, this place was dark, except for several colored lines that glowed in bright shades of green, blue, and pink. The music came from a stage, the singers voice flowed through the ocean of bodies that waved and crested through the space. My eyes went to the walls, where row upon row of books awaited.

My fingers itched to trace each spine and hope rose in my chest as I shot forward. That hope quickly fell into a deep chasm. My nails held streaks of color under them from scratching at the wall.

"I'm sorry. I was trying to tell you—" Jaxson yelled over the swell of music and voices.

"What is with this times fascination with fake books? What is this?" I gestured around.

"It's a bar room…tavern." He proceeded to give a horrible pantomime of dancing and drinking. Though I tried, the laugh that bubbled up my chest couldn't be hidden. My eyes searched for and found the only hope to salvage this night. If I would not find the book here, I would claim something else that this curse had taken from me.

"Give me a drink."

The man behind the bar stared down at his shirt bunched up in my hand. He slowly shoved it away. "I think it might be time to cut you off."

Jaxson hovered at my side, "Hey, Dom."

"Jaxson!" They did the strange thing where they slapped at each others hand. "I heard you were at the university now. That's killer man."

"Yeah, it's something." He shook his head, "Can I just get two beers."

The man glanced toward me as I leaned forward, challenging him to say no. "You sure she's good?"

Jaxson answered, "She's fine. Just a little…" Another server placed a row of small glasses down and I quickly drank the clear liquid. I hissed as the trail of liquor spread fire down my throat and landed with a heavy thud into my warming belly. A torrent of coughs ripped through me as I stared, wide eyed, at the two of them.

After a long beat, Jaxson answered, "She's not from around here." He smiled, "Just the two beers for me and put the shot on my bill as well."

"You should not pay him for that pig swill." I stared at the man named Dom. "From what witch did you claim this poison?"

At that, Jaxson laughed, waving to the confused-looking man.

Bodies bumped into ours as the music climbed and voices chanted in strange unison before the song changed and the shaking continued.

"Let's go find somewhere to sit."

I nodded, my throat still on fire from the drink.

We started for a row of dark alcoves with the words "The Stacks" painted in faded white letters overhead.

A burst of red coated Jaxson's cheeks, "Actually, maybe we should find somewhere else."

The floor was beginning to sway like a boat on water. A beautiful woman passed us, her hair surrounded by butterflies, her skin glistening in rhythm with the lights that flashed around the space. She smiled as she offered a platter of glass tubes with brightly colored liquid. I grabbed one and downed it as Jaxson shook his head at the server. The floral taste soothed my nerves. The glass tinked on the tray as I took the platter from the girl and moved toward a dark booth.

The group of men there eyed me with hopeful stares as I approached the seating area.

"Hey baby." One that reminded me far too much of Keith gave a dark smile as he slithered toward the edge of his seat, leaning on the square wooden table that held him in. "You looking for some company."

"I'm looking for an empty table." I downed another of the tubes, this one tasting like citrus. I stared at the men. "And it seems I've found one. You all just need to leave first."

The slimy one licked his lips before leaning back, splaying his hands wide on the back of the seats. "I've got an empty seat for you right here."

"I'm sure it is." I traced his frame with only my eyes, disgust painted on my face and my every word, "Quite empty. Much like that large thing on top of your shoulders."

A flash of rage coated his face as his friends laughed. "You think you're something special. There's only one thing girls like you are good for, anyway."

This was the reason the wells were full. Brittany could look down on me all she wanted. She could hate me, curse me, despise me. But in all my years on this earth, there was only one kind of life I would take. I stared at the man with a Cheshire grin. "If only our paths had crossed another time."

A haughty laugh escaped him as Jaxson approached, his hand hovering at my back, "Let's go find another seat."

"Naw, man." They all scooted out of the booth, "All yours. For now." He gave another slimly smile before disappearing into the dancing crowd.

I snarled at him before sitting down with my tray full of sweet drinks.

"You know him?"

"I've known many creatures like him." The fire spread in my mind as I took another tube and brought it to my mouth.

"Soryn, I know that tonight was — intense, but you need to slow down or you're gonna make yourself sick." He placed a hand on mine before I swatted it away. "We don't know who might be here." He whispered, looking wearily around the room.

"It's too loud and the lights are too bright."

"That's what happens when you drink too much too quick."

"No." I passed him one of the pretty colored tubes, only leaving one more on the tray. "I mean for vampires. It's too loud and bright to hunt in here." Whether it was true, I needed one night of truly being human and I didn't need Jaxson being my conscience through it.

"Please, join me. Let me have this night. With the ways things are going with the search, I may have no other like it."

He took the drink with a sad smile.

My heart pounded as the colors of the room swirled. The lovely barmaid had brought several drinks and Jaxson had told me much about his life before the night was over. His laugh had my belly fluttering as we talked about everything.

"That's why I fell in love with history." He said. The word love making my cheeks flush as his thumb brushed over my hand again. I had already lost count of how many touches we had traded. Most without thought, but as the night faded, the distance between us faded with it.

"So, should we go try to find Brittany?" He asked.

The hazy lights continued to pulse through the bar as I thought of the right answer. I knew the right thing was to have not left her there. My only solace from guilt being that she could not die. My skin pricked as a punch of shame filled me — her body couldn't die but that didn't mean she couldn't be hurt. The thought left an aching bubble in my chest as I swallowed the guilt down with another drink.

"You have yet to ask for a dance."

He chewed at his lip, a gentle and thoughtful gesture before meeting my eyes. "Would you care to dance?"

"I would."

The music was fast as we made sloppy movements with our feet.

My cheek rested against his as I got close enough for him to hear me, "I have a reason to be bad at this kind of dancing. What could possibly be your excuse for trying to crush my feet."

He laughed, the vibrations of it sending delightful shocks through me. "I never had a reason to try it before."

"Dancing?"

He nodded as the music changed again, this time a slower ballad. His hands went out to mimic the stance of the others that didn't leave the dance floor. I leaned into him, relishing the feel of dancing again. The mans voice crooned through the crowd. A deep breath brought a smile to my face followed by another as I imagined breathing in the words of the song.

"You shine so bright when you smile." Jaxson's words were a whisper, almost lost in the music that weaved its way through the air around us.

"Like the moon?" My stomach tightened and I couldn't hide the sorrow in those words.

He hooked his finger under my chin, "The moon doesn't shine. It only reflects." He brushed my cheek, "How could you ever follow when even your name means Sun."

My chest tightened in a vise like grip as his eyes bore into mine. The feeling warred with the lightness overtaking my legs, my knees wanting so badly to falter under me.

"I'm sorry, I shouldn't have…"

My lips swallowed his words for only a moment before my heart sank as he gently pulled away. "We shouldn't do this now. You're drunk and I…"

An anger consumed me as a familiar voice came from my left, "Soryn." Brittany's voice was on edge but still held a hint of mirth as she weaved in beside us. "I don't mean to interrupt.."

"You are not interrupting anything." The drinks from the night all seemed to war against me at once. My stomach turned with a heavy flop. "I just need a moment."

"Let's get you some fresh air." Jaxson's hand went to my back.

"I am quite fine without your shadow lurking over me." I brushed his hand away and made for the back exit. Their words blended together as Brittany closed in on him her voice angry and accusing.

A wall of cold air and cigarette smoke hit my face. I breathed it all in deeply. Bad choice. The coughing fit sent the insides of my stomach journeying upward. My feet moved awkwardly toward a row of dark bushes making it there just in time for the drinks of the night to finish their journey.

Hands closed around my hips, holding me steady as my body heaved into the foliage in front of me. "I hope this isn't one of

Brittany's favorites," I moaned, bending over to wipe whatever was left about my mouth on the bottom edge of the short black dress. The hands on my hips tightened as I straightened myself to stand.

"Let's just take it off then before we ruin it even more." A hand slid along the edge of the dress as my fingers clenched. My spine stacked upright as a jolt of awareness shot through me. The words that caused it sending a lance of rage through my soul.

A loud thud came just before the strange hands released me. My anger continued to swell as I swirled around, the earth swirling too just before Brittany caught me. As my blurry vision struggled to focus, a string of sounds filled my ears. Flesh hitting flesh in a deafening thwack.

My heart gave a sickening plummet as the two men in front of me struggled with each other and a fist connected with Jaxson's cheek. Just one punch was all that I saw land on his handsome face before the disgusting excuse for humanity was pinned by the throat against the stone wall of the building and cries for forgiveness fell from the broken man's mouth.

"If you ever touch another woman without their permission, you had better be looking over your shoulder." Jaxson leaned forward as the color began to drain from the mans face as he whispered his last threat, whatever words he said lost to the crowd. The animals eyes went wide as one final punch collided with his stomach. He collapsed as Jaxson loosened his grip from his neck.

Jaxson turned, reaching out a hand, but stopping short of touching me. "Are you alright?" His breathing was heavy as a trickle of blood fell from his lip and into his beard.

"I'm fine." I grabbed for Brittany's hand. She was becoming more and more accustomed to the darkness. It was obvious to see as her expression softened and her eyes looked from Jaxson to me. "Let's go. Now."

Jaxson's home was cozy and dark. It matched him perfectly and the smell of him coated the bed that Brittany and I sat on. The smell of dark tea and books swirled in a comforting warmth as he brought in two steaming mugs in one hand and a stack of clothes in the other.

"Are we safe here?" Brittany asked.

He dropped the clothes on a chair before bringing us the mugs, "As far as I know."

Both sets of eyes tracked me as I placed my mug on the side table and walked to the chair to eye the strange clothes. "Where is your water closet?" I tugged at the dress, wanting to be rid of it as soon as possible.

Jaxson moved toward the door, making sure to give me space to move around him. "I'll show you." We walked in silence down a short hallway. The dark brown walls were covered with newspaper clippings and relics of time.

"It takes a bit to get hot," he twisted at the glass handles before water began to flow from the pipe in the wall.

"I have one of those now, too." I said, not sure of what else to say as we stared at each other. The ease of the evening with him was long gone, replaced by an invisible wall that refused to budge.

He nodded and awkwardly shuffled around me in the small space. The evidence of the fight still colored his face.

"Look who has blood on them now."

"We probably shouldn't make this our thing."

The dried blood did a fair amount of smearing as I wiped a wet towel on his face. I fought to keep the lightheaded feeling from pulling me down as I took my time cleaning the wound that he got for protecting me. I laughed at the thought.

"I know you can handle yourself." His voice was low, "I know that if you wanted to, you could destroy anything in your way."

"Then why do you insist on constantly getting in my way."

My skin was on fire where he traced a hand up my arm. He took a deep breath before dropping it again.

I smiled before shoving him through the doorway. I locked the door and waited a long moment.

Renard's face flashed in my mind as the shower steam began to rise.

"I would have you know only my love."

He was right. No matter how much my heart was starting to beat for another, It would stop. Renard and I deserved each other, but Jaxson– he deserved so much more.

Scalding hot water met my skin as I stepped in the shower, willing every touch from the night to disappear from my body.

Almost every touch.

Chapter Thirty-Four
BRITTANY

The window from Jaxson's bedroom looked out on the long cobblestone street. My eyes should have been heavy from a night of staring out it and searching for answers. Answers to questions like; Is the Order going to kill us? Where could the spell book possibly be? Should I tell Soryn what I overheard Jaxson say? Would that change her mind about siring another vampire if we can change back?

Ben had broken my spiral when he made his way to the apartment only a few hours before sunrise. The search for any sign of Keith exhausting him beyond words. He said as much before passing out on Jaxson's couch. If Keith was out there, he didn't show his face. I had searched the entire town in the time between Soryn storming off and the laughter in the woods. Checking the well again wasn't an option and when one of the ghosts started following me everywhere with a sour face, I got the feeling I needed to leave.

Ben hadn't gotten any further in searching for information about who killed that man in the archive or why they had been bold enough to do it in front of Jaxson.

Both guys had been up for an hour by the time a pained groan came from the mountain of blankets on Jaxson's small bed. I couldn't help but give a sheepish grin as I mentally recounted their conversation— whispering about books and charms and the mystery of women.

"What's that smell?" Soryn twisted, kicking at the comforter surrounding her.

"That smell, my friend, is courting." I smiled despite the pungent aroma that filled the cozy green bedroom.

"What?" She moaned, grabbing the sides of her head as she stared at me through sleepy eyes.

"Bacon." I said, "It's bacon. The guys are making breakfast." She rolled to the side, head down as she made her way to the door. Her hands tugged at the baggy gym shorts that, despite her curves, were swallowing her.

Eggs, bacon, pancakes and coffee were laid out on the small table. I made myself comfortable on the large leather couch as Soryn made a B-Line for the food. She crouched in the chair, reminding me of a caveman as she grabbed a cup of coffee and shoved bacon in her mouth.

"Hungry?" Jaxson asked just before another pained moan rumbled out of her. "Hungover maybe?"

She mumbled something even I couldn't understand before dropping her head to the table with a hollow thud.

"I wasn't sure how you liked it." Ben handed me a coffee, a familiar sweet smell rising with the steam. My fangs shot out as his brow shot up.

"Thank you."

"No problem." For a split second, he smiled before clearing his throat and pacing the room. "So, I couldn't get much from my contact yesterday but I'm fairly certain that neither them or Mr. Dorsetty know that I'm helping you. For now, we have to keep up the act that you still think I'm some jerk trying to take your families shop."

"You're a jerk. Got it." I smiled as he went on.

Jaxson asked, "Why do you think everyone is fighting to get Brittany's curse? Especially this Order of Rosewood that we think Ben is a part of.

"My curse," Soryn groaned.

Ben groaned.

He continued, "Soryn's curse. Then they're obviously looking for the book but what would they get from that."

Ben spoke, "Especially if their goal is to eradicate vampires?"

My fingers tightened around my drink. Eradicate was something you did to pests or animals that went rabid. I still felt human. That hadn't changed. Soryn was a human. "Is that what you planned to do, Ben?"

He didn't look at me, "I'm not a part of The Order, but I have been considering that." A little panic met his eyes, "The book! Why they would want the book, not eradicating." He gripped tufts of his dark hair in both hands and paced for a moment before continuing on, "Look, a lot of what I've done for Mr. Dorsetty has been watching people— making sure that his assets are safe. In that time, I've learned a lot about him. Before Clarette made you sleep, Renard thought he had found a way to not only take the curse but to sire other true immortals with it as well. My guess is that The Order discover his plan, and they're still trying to keep that from happening."

"That sounds reasonable," Jaxson said.

Soryn tilted her head to the side to stare at Ben, " I know a hunter when I see one."

"You're not as perceptive as you think." The two refused to break eye contact as they continued their stare before Soryn finally put a palm to her aching head again.

"Alright, well now that that is out of the way—" Jaxson went to the table and placed two small white tablets in Soryn's hand. "Take those. It's not going to stop the jackhammer in your head, but it will help." He leaned on the wall behind her, being careful not to bump her chair as he did, "Can the spell be done without the book? The two of you made it work, right?"

"It is not so simple." Soryn pulled herself up to speak, "Brittany had the scroll. It's linked to the book and is the first part of the spell. Both need blood for their magic to work."

Jaxson leaned on the back of the couch, "Why isn't the scroll part of the book?"

"You would have to ask the one who made it."

"Could you make another one if you know the spell?" Ben asked.

"Are you offering up part of your flesh for the cause, because I would gladly…"

"What, Soryn? Go ahead and tell me what you would do. Nothing you haven't done to countless people before, am I right?" Ben's words fell heavy in the small room. "No wonder Clarette trapped you."

A hiss escaped Soryn's lips but it was Jaxson who moved. "Enough, Ben. No one but Clarette knows why she did what she did. We need to be working together. Someone is out there killing people to get at this book. Now whether it's Renard Dorsetty or some one else…"

"Like The Order." I added. It spoke volumes that Soryn had told Jaxson about Clarette and what she had done.

Jaxson nodded as he took Soryn's now empty glass to the kitchen to fill it back up. "Right. Well, whoever it is, we are all on their radar now. It doesn't do us any good to be fighting each other."

I stared between the both before speaking again, "He's just trying to help. Ben is the closest thing to Renard and The Order that we have right now, so please—" My words hung in the air for what felt like an eternity.

By the time Soryn begrudgingly spoke again, both Ben and Jaxson were exchanging furious looks. "I thought they both loved me. I loved them so much."

Soryn gave a slight shake to her head, before regretting the quick movement.

Jaxson shifted in the space behind her, his eyes filled with pain as he looked her over. His hand reached out for only a moment before he drew it back to himself.

My heart broke at the sight. After hearing what Jaxson had whispered to the creep last night and everything I heard him and Ben talk about this morning, it hurt my heart to know that she would take back the curse and miss out on someone who might actually love her. "If Renard found a way to take the curse from you as a vampire, does that mean that you would be able to be a human forever? Well, obviously not forever, that's the whole problem, but could you maybe not have to go back to this?" I gestured to myself.

Soryn gave me a sad smile, "I know that book by heart. If there was a way, I would have found it by now."

"Could Clarette have found a way?" I thought of the journal. After so many nights of scouring through the fading pages, there were still many that I couldn't understand. Maybe she had found the key to changing everything for Soryn.

Soryn's eyes narrowed on Ben as he lowered himself to the cushion beside me.

"Soryn?"

"Like I have already told you before, only those touched by the curse can read from the book. When Renard and I found it, only I could see what it held within it."

Jaxson finally sat, though still within arms reach of Soryn, "What would happen if we just burned the book when we find it." He grimaced, "I hate that those words just came out of my mouth."

Soryn shifted her body toward him, "I have been burned, staked, drowned, and beheaded. If the book did that to me, imagine what it must have done to protect itself." She put away the last piece of bacon before continuing, "Besides, I have tried." She brushed little bits of food from the over-sized D.A.R.E shirt and stood a bit too quickly. Jaxson grabbed her by the elbow, helping her while she swayed in place.

"Water closet, now." She mumbled out before bolting down the hall. Jaxson followed but after the loud slam of the bathroom door, he came back to join us in the living room.

"She's not gonna be up for any kind of searching for at least a couple of hours." The couch shifted as Jaxson planted himself down on the other side of me and raked his hands through his hair. His gaze stayed on the ceiling. My eyes went to Ben.

Blue eyes met my own. "I should go check in. See if I can find anything else out."

My hands ran down the length of my pants, my finger getting caught and ripping an even bigger hole in them. They were still dirty and torn from the well fiasco. My shirt, though it fared better, smelled like dirt and mold. "And I am going to run by the house and grab some new clothes for me and Soryn." I turned to Jaxson as I stood, "Will the two of you be alright? I'll be back as quick as I can."

Jaxson's face held a worried pinch until a bright glow took over, "I just got this." He held up a brand new DVD of The Mummy, still in the plastic wrap.

"I meant will the two of you be safe, not will you be entertained?"

"We'll be both." He smiled.

"Okay." I chuckled, "Tell Soryn I'll be back soon."

The hallway was dark. The stairs that led from Jaxson's apartment above the music store down to the street was a nice added buffer to keep them safe. "Ben, no matter what Soryn said in there, I believe you. If you say that you're not a hunter, then I want to trust you."

Ben stopped on the top step to look around the space, "Why? I'm the jerk trying to ruin your life, remember." A gentle smirk pulled at the corner of his mouth.

"True, but I think there's more to it." I didn't dare move any closer for fear I might spook him and send him back to being on the defensive. "There's a reason why you're choosing now to turn on Mr. Dorsetty." He shifted slightly, but stayed locked on me, "You don't have to tell me anything right now, but when you're ready— I'm ready to listen."

He stared at the thick wooden door that led back into the apartment. The door that separated my friend from the dangers that were trying to pull her back under. I just couldn't make myself believe that he could be one of those dangers.

"Be careful, Brittany. I might not think you're a monster anymore, but there are others out there who may need more convincing." He worried at his necklace as he continued to stare at the door.

"Soryn isn't a threat, Ben. I'm the only vampire here, remember."

"Vampires aren't the only thing to be scared of, especially in this town."

My unsettled nerves seemed to jump beneath my skin. Everything felt itchy as he continued to stare at me in the close space. "I'll make sure I'm fast then."

Ben planted his foot back on the landing, closing some of the distance he had created between us. "Do you want me to go with you?"

"No. I can't die. Remember."

"That doesn't mean you can't be scared." He gave an inward laugh before rubbing at a spot on his neck. "Besides, your boyfriend might be out there looking for you."

"Ex-boyfriend."

"What's scarier than an ex-boyfriend?"

A genuine laugh trilled out of me, "Well I'm still pretty new to this whole monster thing, so I'll have to get back to you on that."

He gave a gentle nod, the smile that had spread on his face now falling back to his usual stern stare.

"Brittany…"

I gave him a pat on the arm as I walked by, pulling my hat down low and my glasses on.

"See you in a bit, Ben."

<hr />

The sky was beautifully overcast as I stepped on to the sidewalk. *Unbreak My Heart* played through the air in short bursts as shoppers walked in and out of the music shop. Morning smells circulated the downtown street as the weekend crowd hurried along, most likely trying to make their purchases before the clouds broke their hold on the rain. My mind wandered to At Day's End. On a normal weekend, I would be there, greeting customers, shuffling through boxes, and dreaming of ancient worlds.

I found myself wishing we had more time before the blood moon. Maybe then I would have time to explore them.

The thought was gone as soon as it came as I approached the tree line and huffed a sigh. It was the fastest way back to the house. I curled my nose at the large tree trunks that created a wooden maze. I didn't love the idea of becoming a crash test dummy, but speed was the name of the game today. There was no way to know if someone was out there waiting for me, and I wasn't about to slow down to find out.

The Toms were busy painting the outside when I approached the house. "Hey guys."

"Hey Brittany!" They both said in unison. The house was beautiful. Despite their skeezy behavior at the University, they did have some skills when it came to renovation. And now that the house was up to date, they needed to get out of here. Until we knew what was happening, it was too dangerous to have too many people around.

Cloud white paint dripped down my hands as I took both paint brushes from the men. "You're all done." Focusing my energy on the two of them, I bore into their eyes. They stilled and absorbed my every word. "You were doing charity work for some of the elderly around town which took you away from the University. From now on, you have absolute respect for your work and the people that you work around. Pack up all of your stuff and leave. As soon as you hit town, you will forget that you've ever seen me, Soryn, or this house. Do you understand?"

"Yes."

The colorless eyes of the ghost girl peered at me through the upstairs window. "Could you be more creepy?"

The Toms were already to work gathering all of their supplies when I opened the front door. "Ah!" I punched out into the air, as a swish of blue glow pulled itself back into the form of the apparition. "What is your problem?"

The stairs no longer creaked as I walked to my room. The gentle creaks and groans that I had come to expect from the house were gone and in their place was a deafening silence.

The room was covered in clothes by the time I had packed two bags. Each overflowing with things that we would both need.

Although the time at Jaxson's might be temporary, there was no telling where we might have to go from here, since here was no longer safe. Whatever spell had kept this place from the world while Soryn slept was gone, and at least one person out there knew about it.

The small indigo journal felt warm in my hands. I had read its pages from cover to cover. Whatever Soryn had done to make Clarette turn on her, it wasn't in these pages. At least, not that I could find. The notes, though several seemed to be in Latin or some other language that was beyond my knowledge, seemed to bounce between absolute adoration of Soryn and complete loathing.

A blue glow pulsed around me, casting my silhouette across the freshly painted wall.

"What do you want now?"

The girl stood at the threshold, her dress swirling with some phantom breeze. Electricity seemed to spark in the air around her as she raised her arm to the window. Vibrations took hold of the glass as the anger in her face built to a terrifying rage.

"Go back!" Her words were a petrifying moan like the snapping of a tree limb in a hurricane. The window shattered outward sending shards of glass into the backyard.

Everything fell silent as she began to flicker and fade, her white eyes free of all their rage seemed to plead just before she faded completely from view.

My feet refused to budge as I stared out the broken window at the crumbling well.

It didn't take long before a neat pile of stones rested beside the gapping hole to the well. A layer of stones was wedged tight, their decent blocking the passage down to the watery muck below. With shoulders shrugged up to my ears, I slowly swiveled my head behind me as the hairs on my arms stood on end. Several ghosts had gathered in the spacious back yard, their wispy forms just barely visible in the daylight. None of them seemed to have the same energy radiating off of them as the girl had had in my bedroom, but all looked more than annoyed at the fact that I had broken their resting place. "Sorry guys, but repairs are gonna have to wait because I literately just fired my handy men."

A tug of guilt seemed to pull me back toward the well for one final look. A stray sun ray cut through the clouds as the day brightened into early afternoon, and with it a gentle flicker of light caught my eye. The places where I had clawed my way back up were free of the moss and muck coating that had hidden the stones underneath them and several layers down, something glinted again in the sunlight. My skin crawled at the thought of clawing my way back out of that hole.

———◆•◆———

The jagged rocks tugged at my already tattered clothing as I pushed myself flat against the ground that surrounded the opening of the crumbling well. As I lay there staring down I willed my arms to be long enough to not have to go spelunking again. There was no way I was reaching the thing that was lodged between the stones. At least not from here. It looked to be a small tube threaded with a chain, the two stones on either side of it, held it precariously in place.

It was most likely a relic from one of the bodies now permanently trapped down below.

"I would have guessed that even vamps used closets." Ben's voice held a laugh.

More rocks cascaded down as I twisted on the ground. An awkward laugh escaped me as he leaned over where I had been fishing for the small chain. "What?"

He took my hand, pulling me to him with one quick motion. "You're supposed to be getting clothes and heading back."

"And I am." I looked down at my clothes, even more filthy now with chunks of grass and earth clinging to them. I made quick work of dusting them off before walking back toward the house. I gestured for him to follow. "Let me grab mine and Soryn's bags and we can head back. Did you get anything from your contacts?"

Ben didn't move— instead he stood at the edge of the well, peering down into the darkness. "So this is where the old boyfriends go, huh."

"Only if they really deserve it."

"What if they have really nice cars?"

My neck prickled as an uncomfortable twisting worked at my insides. The words tried to stick in my throat as I croaked them out. "Why do you say things like that?" I tugged at my hat, trying my best to avoid Ben's gaze.

His footsteps were quiet as he approached.

"Because you won't be this way forever, Brittany. You won't be stuck like this forever and I find myself enjoying your company."

"You enjoy a vampire's company."

"Would you please stop doing that?"

"What, Ben? It's the truth, isn't it?"

"No. It's not. You're not one of them. You don't kill people just to…"

"But I have!"

"No, I know. It's just…" His hands clasped over the bridge of his nose before he pulled them across his temples, his frustration clearly rising, "You, Brittany Cordain— the woman that I've spoken to on the phone for years; the one that argued about the efficacy of selling artifacts to private collectors; the Brittany who spoke of her Grandma with such adoration and gave up so much to make sure that someone else's dream wasn't crushed." He inched closer before coming to a full stop again, not seeming to know what to do with his hands or feet.

"That woman is in there. We're going to find Soryn's spell book and you're gonna to be able to get your life back."

What if I didn't want it back? The thought left my stomach in knots. For that to happen, Soryn would have to die. That couldn't happen.

Even so I asked, "Have you ever thought of what it would be like to have all the time in the world? The places that you could explore, the things that you could discover?"

Ben's voice held a heaviness to it that gripped on to each word, "You know," his eyes bore into mine "when I lost my family, Mr. Dorsetty asked me a similar question." His glare softened before his eyes broke from mine, "I told him no."

He walked past me and into the house. The bags I had packed for myself and Soryn were sitting ready at the bottom of the stairs and he quickly hoisted both over his shoulders and headed to his car without another word.

"You said that a vampire killed them. Was it Dorsetty?"

"A vampire didn't deal the killing blow, but yeah, he had a heavy hand in what happened to them." He tossed both bags in before slamming the car door. "As soon as you let one of those leeches sink their teeth in you, you might as well be dead anyway."

Just when I had started to feel sorry for him again. I started toward the tree line that headed toward town.

"Brittany. What are you doing? We can drive there."

"No need to blow your cover, right? We still need everyone watching to think that you're a jerk."

"The windows are tinted. No one is going to know that your in there." He opened the passenger door and gestured for me to get in. "Please."

"I like the fresh air. Thanks."

After hitting my fourth tree on my way back downtown, I was starting to question my decision. Of course he couldn't actually like me. At least not yet. Not while I was like this.

Bark pulled at my hair as I leaned against a large oak and looked up into the canopy. Shafts of sunlight peeked through and made the puddles on the forest floor glimmer. Everything was so beautiful through my new eyes. Ben might not like me like this, but I was slowly realizing that I just might.

Chapter Thirty-Five

SORYN

"Yet again, I must tell you that mummies are not real."

"But werewolves are?"

"Yes."

"How can you be so sure?"

"Because I once had a thrilling…"

Jaxson put his hands up, "I mean about mummies. How can you be sure that mummies aren't real?"

"Because I have never seen one."

"Well, I've never seen a werewolf but apparently they're real."

The red letters on my borrowed shirt scrunched as I crossed my arms over my chest. "You are quite insufferable."

The boyish grin that crested over his face made my stomach flutter. He grabbed the tiny gray rectangle and the movie box continued its play. "Does your book look all fancy like this one?"

"It is nothing so extravagant."

Jaxson moved to the tiny kitchen, the beeping coming from the room signaling the completion of our second bag of popped corn.

"That's Hollywood for you." He made his way back to the couch before handing me the hot bag. "Most of the props they use aren't historically accurate."

He was up again in an instant. He grabbed my shoulders making several fluffy pieces of corn to fall in my lap. "Props!" He was up and pacing back and forth with an excited jump to his step. "Props!" His hands closed around mine as my treat fell to the floor, the crunching sound filling the air as he continued to say the word.

"Why are you yelling at me?" The pounding that had only recently subsided started to wrap at the base of my skull again.

"Oh, I'm sorry. I got carried away but—" he gently helped me to the couch before kneeling with a crunch in front of me. "The theatre department at the University. When we have things donated we sort through it all and anything we don't want or need goes to them for props or costumes or whatever they use them for."

I squinted at him through my hands.

"If its not logged in the History Department it may just be there."

A rush of adrenaline set my body alight, pushing the pounding in my head aside. Jaxson's excitement was contagious as I jumped on the couch. He grabbed be out of the air and spun and my cheeks flushed as he lowered me back down slowly.

A deep worry shadowed his face. "I'm sorry. Are you going to be sick again?"

My mouth wouldn't move as he looked down into my eyes. I could feel his own heart beat raging against my own.

Unstake My Heart

I couldn't keep him. No matter how my heart beat in my chest right now; No matter how his bright disposition made my soul soar; No matter how much I wanted to fall for this beautiful man; he would die. And I would be left to mourn him for all eternity.

Forcing myself away from his arms, I steadied myself and walked to the water closet in silence. My face was dripping with cold water when familiar voices joined in Jaxson's excitement.

A knock shook me from my reflection, "Hey Soryn, can I come in. I'm tired of smelling like a moldy foot."

Jaxson and Ben were busy talking away when I came back in the living room, pausing only a moment to grab the daisy covered bag that rested on the floor. It would be nice to have some clothes that fit. The bedroom felt oddly empty as I rummaged through the clothing. The long black skirt and burgundy shirt where a much better fit. My eyes trailed to where the baggy clothes Jaxson had given me to wear rested in a pile on the floor.

The door flung open and Brittany came in wrapped in nothing but a towel, her long blond hair dripping. Through the doorway, I could see Jaxson, his head buried in the fridge, while Ben's eyes were locked on her. I gave him a reproachful glare before closing the door behind her.

"What has gotten in to you?" I purred, not being able to hold back the bit of pride that I felt at her actions.

"Nothing, I just — I'm getting used to all this, I guess."

"On that note, did Jaxson tell you about the players?"

She tilted her head and shrugged. "Players?"

"The props, Brittany. And the costumes. You know. Players."

"The Theatre Department." She laughed. "Yeah, he told me." She pulled the towel tighter as she sat on the bed. "And lucky us, we have a friend that can get us in."

"Yay for us." The door handle was cold in my hand. If I was going to have to endure another day of Ashlie, I was going to need something else for my head.

"Hey Soryn, could you do me a favor?"

"What?"

"Could you go grab my clothes for me?" She pulled up on her towel and pouted her lips like a child. "I was so focused on other things that I forgot to grab them.

I couldn't help but laugh as I opened the door wide, "Bennie boy could you please bring me that bag?"

"Soryn!"

"Soryn!" Ashlie's voice, though not as bothersome as it once was still made me want to cram my ears with candle wax.

"You haven't received any more notes from Keith have you?" The chatter of the dorm dwellers was incessant as we made our way through the paper strewn hallway. Fliers touting different events hung from boards. My eyes wandered over every dry erase board looking for signs of Keith but I could find none.

"No. I haven't." She linked her arm in mine as we continued toward the stairs. "Is Brittany mad at me?"

My nose turned up as we descended. If the fates were merciful, they would have taken me right then. It quickly became obvious that they were not as Ashlie continued to ramble on.

"Do you have the keys?" I asked.

She bit her lip, rubbing at her arms as we continued toward the lobby, "About that. I could get in a lot of trouble if I just let you all in.

"We have Jax — Professor Harwell to escort us."

She raised an eyebrow before elbowing my arm, then scratched with two fingers at the air around her head. "Professor Harwell, isn't the best person to be escorting you around."

"What are you doing with your hands? That's strange even for you. Stop."

"Okay."

"What do you mean?"

She smiled–the thrill of a secret between us sparkling in her eyes, "You didn't hear it from me but I heard the real reason he left Sedgemoore was because he was stealing some of the artifacts from the history department and selling them on the black market. His uncle is friends with the new Dean though and that's why he got a job here."

A large group was gathered in the lobby around a movie box. The group was giggling as they sang in unison. We continued toward the door.

"What is this black market?"

Laughter rang out through the room while a barrage of clapping continued with more singing. Although, in truth, I would have described it as rhythmic yelling.

"I love friends!" Ashlie's exclaimed with an eager smile planted on her face.

A smirk bloomed on my face, "Yes." I patted Ashlie's hand. "You know who knows of friends? Brittany."

She gave a confused shrug before we finally made our way out into the fresh air. "You mean she watches them?"

"She is very close with them. And the ones she is close to love her dearly." I leaned in close, "They might even do anything for her."

My body went rigid as Ashlie let out a high-pitched squeal. "No way." She whispered fervidly in my face, "There is no way. Do you think she would introduce me?"

"To Brittany?"

"No." She shoved gently at my arm before linking it again. "I get it. And I promise, Keith is out of the picture. For good. Brittany is my friend and I wouldn't want to hurt her like that."

"Very good. And the keys."

She batted her eyelashes, "I know exactly where they're kept."

Her steps quickened as we journeyed across campus to meet the others outside the theater.

Brittany's face shown with confusion as Ashlie wrapped her arms around her neck. "I'm so glad we get to hang out. I can show you where everything is." Ashlie didn't let go of Brittany as she ushered us inside. The sound of piano music floated through the open space. I remembered learning to play in Edinburgh. It had been another thing to pass the ever turning years. Just one more thing that I would master and move on from.

A smile curled at my lips as a sharp note rang through the air followed by dissonant chords struck out of anger and punctuated by strings of curses. The others stared wide eyed toward the music while a warmth spread through my chest.

"That's painful." Ben said.

"That's passion." I replied before a cold feeling pulled at my insides like a skipping stone that sank at the end of its flight.

"So what are we looking for?" Ashlie smiled as she turned the keys to open the auditorium and backstage to us. "Halloween costumes?" She turned and pointed a finger at each of us, "but if you get caught in them, you stole them. Got it?"

"We're just looking for a book that we may have donated to the theatre group by mistake." Jaxson kept his distance as Ashlie flipped on the backstage lights.

We weaved through wooden planks holding up the walls of the set, to get to the storage room at the far corner.

"So I think a lot of them are in here in the prop room but some are out there on stage for the play." She turned, facing us with a dramatic curtsy, "I'm Lucy."

"Lucy?" Brittany asked.

"You know, Lucy. We're doing Dracula."

There was a shift in the entire group as all three of my compatriots started to laugh.

The prop room was covered floor to ceiling with shelves. Each one packed tight and overflowing with items of all sorts.

"We'll lock up when were done. Thanks Ash," Brittany said.

"Um, I don't mind hanging out for a bit. I don't have any plans or anything." She pulled her to the side, "And just so you know, Keith and I are so not a thing. He shouldn't have done that to you." Her brows were drawn in an attempt at deep concern.

"Great. I don't think you'll see him anytime soon but if you do," She leaned in close, a darkness swirling in her voice, "You should stay far away from him."

Ashlie stumbled into a metal can filled with wooden swords, the sound echoing through the room. "Okay, well, um — anyway, don't make a mess." She left, flashing a bright smile at Ben as she went.

"What was that about?" I asked as Brittany rummaged through a giant box full of what looked like facial hair.

"I can't exactly tell her–Hey, you know my ex that you tried to steal from me? Well my friend killed him and he might actually be a bloodsucking fiend so you should really grab some holy water and run for the hills. Can I?"

"That's a myth. Holy water doesn't do anything."

"What?"

"It's just really annoying getting splashed while you're trying to eat."

Jaxson's voice came from the back of the long room. "There are a ton of boxes that I recognize back here."

Ben walked passed us, "Some of the crates are still nailed shut."

"Where are you going?" Brittany asked.

"I'm going to find something to pry them open."

Boxes were piled high between us and Jaxson, making maneuvering toward him cumbersome. A bust with a broken nose stared at us from a high self as we made our way around a shelf completely covered in dismembered body parts.

"Ew." Brittany moaned as I picked up a severed arm.

"This is mine now." I smiled with my treasure as we rounded the corner and Jaxson came into sight.

"These are all marked for the history department." He gestured toward a few opened ones that were pulled away from the back wall. "Those might have been used for the set. We can go check after were done here."

Brittany asked, "Why aren't these even opened?" She picked at the labels attached to the boxes, "What if there was something of historical importance in here and you just chucked it out?"

"I couldn't tell you. I've never seen these." He gripped his fingers on the edge of the wood, the nails screamed their displeasure. He grimaced as his apologetic eyes met mine.

Brittany shuffled her feet back and forth for a moment before clearing her throat. "Maybe I should go look out on the stage."

"Yes." I replied, "Let's go."

"No. I'll go." She glanced to the side, "Jaxson won't know what he's looking at if he finds it."

"Y-ouch." He replied.

"You know what I mean."

Jaxson's eyes trailed down where I cradled my newly found prize in my arms. "You wanna lend me a hand." He smiled before turning back to the box he was fighting to open.

"You remind me of the mummy man right now." A blush rose to his cheeks as he tipped his head upward. "If he was completely insufferable."

"There she is." His shoulders squared as he went back to prying apart boxes with an even more fervent gusto.

Brittany's hand grasped my shoulder as we ventured back toward the door. "Why are you being so mean to him? Last night it kinda looked like you were ready to take a bite out of him." I barely opened my mouth before she threw up her hands, "I already know what you're about to say, but even this morning you both were acting like all you wanted to do was…"

"It doesn't matter." A darkness coated my words and seeped into my nerves. "We have to find a way to fix this mess. And when we do, he will go on with his mortal life just fine without me."

"Soryn, maybe…"

"Maybe we should get back to work. Yeah?"

The double doors creaked open behind us as Ben came back with several heavy looking tools. "Come, hunter," I took the tools and handed them to Brittany, "Let's go see if these show people are using my book to pretty up their silly little stage play."

The screeching of nails filled the auditorium adding to the horrible feeling in the pit of my stomach.

The room they had built on stage was made to look like a Victorian sitting room. The painted floor, with its speckles and faux cracks, looked like aging marble. I couldn't help but bend down to touch the illusion, my mind balking when the feeling under my fingertips didn't match what my eyes saw.

"How many people have you killed?" Ben's voice was quiet but firm. Resting against the railing that led to a raised space, he crossed his arms and stared at me. A hatred seethed under the surface there. This was the first time I had been alone with our friend from the order.

"How many vampires have you killed?" No malice painted my words as I took the small set of stairs; focus set on a bookshelf resting on the far corner of the raised platform.

"Two." He answered, though I could hear the faintest of regret on his tongue.

My fingers brushed the spines of the books. Though these were at last real, none were mine. Ben watched my every step back down, as if he waited for me to pounce.

"You are aware that at the present I am not a vampire, yes?"

His arms fell as he crossed to the bookshelf opposite my own. From far sides of the stage, we shuffled through the books placed along the space with only the knocking of tome on wood and rustling of flipped pages to fill the silence.

"Two seems like such a quaint number for a hunter of your…" I paused, "disposition."

"I don't enjoy taking life of any kind, but I will do whatever it takes to keep innocent lives safe."

More books moved as we continued. A sort of realignment took hold of the tension not unlike that held between warriors on two sides of an ancient battle; both realizing how much blood had been spilled. Maybe there was hope for him once the curse was restored.

"I know that she killed a man at the rink."

The hairs on my arms stood. The ease I was starting to feel quickly shifted and need to fulfill the promise I had made snapped back into place. A protective lightning bolt fired in my chest, sending shock waves of energy pulsing through me.

"I may not possess immortality, but know this and hear the truth in my words. If you harm her in any way, there is no power, no weapon, no person on the earth who would spare you from the nightmares I would reign upon your fragile mind and body."

"I'm not fragile."

"One hundred and eighty-three."

"What?"

"You asked how many I have killed. One hundred and eighty-three lives have been snuffed out by my hand. And of those souls, very few did not deserve the end that they were given. And trust me when I say, none of them thought they were fragile. And I took pleasure in showing them how mistaken they were."

Ben's body held a torrent of warring emotions as he gave an unwavering stare—the energy in the room built to a ringing in my ears as neither of us broke from our silent stand off.

"I would listen to her if I were you." A voice grumbled down from the darkness high above the rows of red velvet seats. The creaking of footsteps on metal wrapped the open space adding to the feeling of unease that had held us. The garbled voice was deep and strained. It bubbled as if its owner were choking on blood, an image that would have once set a smile on my face, now sent a shiver down my spine. My mind fought to control the shaking that overtook me and showed on my every limb.

"My, my, Soryn. It must be really something for you to feel the warmth seep from your skin like that." The laugh that dripped from the inky ceiling carved a pit in my stomach.

Ben was the first to answer, "Who are you?"

Did it snarl at him? "Hmm." It croaked. "Ben." The name sounded like a curse from its mouth.

"Hey, guys," Brittany's bright but defeated voice chimed from backstage just as Ben rushed to find the stairs that would lead up to where the disembodied voice had come from. His footsteps were still clanking upward when a torrent of foul air swept around me and sharp points dug into my shoulders.

"I may not be allowed to kill you, but I will make sure you and everyone else that did this to me suffers."

My stomach warred with the adrenaline speeding through my veins as I choked back the bile that rose at the putrid smell pouring from the monsters mouth.

"Are you guys having better luck out here?" Jaxson's voice trailed off as the piercing in my skin released.

My head spun as I swirled, looking out over an empty stage around me. Jaxson's hands were urgent as he searched my face for any damage before bringing me to sit on the floral settee at the center of the stage. "What's going on? Are you hurt?"

My heart gave a shuddering beat as a light snapped on in the darkness above. Ben's face was cast in an eerie glow as he searched the space where the mystery fiend had first appeared. "Someone was here." I whispered, an unfamiliar tone of fright seeping into my words. "Who was it?" Britney asked.

Ben answered with two words. "Heads up." Three pairs of eyes raised to follow an object as it flew through the air and landed on the stage with a rasping slide. The plastic and chain were splattered in a dried ruddy dark brown with only a small line clear from where it had scraped across the stage, revealing its original bright yellow.

Chapter Thirty-Six
BRITTANY

The air outside the auditorium was tainted with the same stench that had coated Keith's necklace. There would be no denying it. I had done what Soryn had warned me about. She had every right to hate me for it.

"I'm sorry". Only the muffled sound of Ben and Jaxson's worrying came as Soryn grabbed my arm, pulling us further behind.

"Your apology is not needed."

Shame collided with my insides as I rubbed at my elbows, unsure of what to do with my guilty hands.

Soryn huffed again. "You misunderstand." She kept us in step, but several feet behind the men as she continued. "Curses are a fickle thing and often change over time. The one we bear started with blood taken from one that was unwilling to part with it." Her eyes glared into the dark campus around us. "I believe that Keith took from you, and for that, the curse enacted its own retribution."

"And that's bad how?"

"Because now instead of seeking your heart, he will hunt it."

A nervous laugh coated my words. "I guess it's a good thing I can't die then, right?" Soryn's footsteps stopped. Disbelief and anger painted on her face as she turned it towards mine. "Have you not been listening? There are fates far worse than death. And a wicked man will use each of them to quiet the demons that he blames on you."

A scream wretched through the sky.

I didn't give even a glance back as I left the others behind—my body slicing through the night air. Without an ounce of doubt, I knew that scream was meant for my ears. The smell trailed through the campus like a putrid map, leading me straight to the source of the scream. A dark corner of the quad now encased in a deathly quiet.

An aching disbelief raised like a wall around me just before another scream tore through the silence. This time, the scream was my own. My mouth gaped wide as the shudder-some cry ripped through me and bloody tears poured from my face. My eyes burned as I looked on a familiar bench. Slumped as if she had dozed off after a long day of classes was an unmoving body. A bright red smear coated the plaque beside her, the still wet sheen making the name engraved there sparkle like some kind of sick gift tag. Ashlie's head was rolled to the side, to rest on the back of the bench. She stared off with unblinking eyes, trapped in a hollow mask of death.

"This book," Ben asked—the first words any of us had spoken in what felt like hours. "Soryn already knows everything that's in it, right?"

I nodded, "She's had centuries to memorize it, so yeah, I'm pretty sure."

He fiddled with the token around his neck, his leg perched back against the wall of Jaxson's office. Everyone had thought it best to lie low as quickly as we could before the chaos of a murder ripped through the campus. And this one couldn't be covered up like before. This was done with purpose. It was meant to be found — by me.

"Maybe she— I don't know—can think of someway to..."

"Don't you think that if she had it all those years, she would have found a way to break the curse if there was one?" I spat out.

"Britt, I'm just trying to..." He raked his fingers through his hair before crossing the short distance between us. He sat down beside me— the cushions on the small couch sunk slightly under his weight. His hand hovered in the space between us for a moment before he pulled it back, tucking in his coat pocket. "I just want to help. That's all."

My eyes burned into Ben's, his words stoking the anger that was already swirling in my gut. "You want to help? Why are you even here? Ashlie was murdered. An innocent life was taken and we're just sitting here." My voice cracked as I raised my volume to fill the small office. "Isn't it The Order's job to keep people safe from people like..."

"You?" He finished my rant.

My feet gave a steady thud on the well-worn carpet as I paced. There was so much I needed to say, but none of the words seemed to fit what I was feeling.

"I didn't like her, but she didn't deserve to die. And not like that." I could feel the blood on my cheeks before I even realized I had begun to cry. My hand curled around the bright red drop. I stared, thinking of all the blood that would have to be scrubbed from the bench. Scrubbed from my family's name. The bloody tear seemed to pulse under my gaze. My mind whirled as I wondered who's blood leaked from my eyes. Was this Ashlie's, too?

I screamed in anger as I wiped the rest from my face.

Ben wrapped his arms around me as I shoved at his chest. His body flew across the room and slammed into the wall. Several frames slammed to the ground with him.

"I don't need you to babysit me."

"I'm not babysitting you." He moaned, pulling himself from the floor.

"Well I can't die, so why else are you here? Are you just waiting for more juicy gossip to take back to whoever you're really working for. Is that it Ben? Who knows, maybe Soryn's right? Maybe you are a hunter."

He dusted himself off; his face which should have been full of anger held so much more, "Brittany, please…"

The anger I had searched for in his eyes finally started to come to the surface as he stared at the broken frames peppering the floor. "You know, if you really want answers about The Order, maybe you should…"

The door swung open, saving both of us from whatever lie was about to come from his mouth. Soryn and Jaxson hurried in the room, eyes going straight for the pile of broken glass and frames littering the office floor.

"If you didn't like my decorating, you could have just told me." Jaxson joked, trying and failing to break the wall of unease that was standing tall between us.

"You know me, always trying to change things that can't be changed." I said before a long silence filled the room.

"Could you both give us a minute?" Soryn's voice was calm but assertive.

"Need I remind you that there is a blood thirsty vampire out there." Ben said.

"Then maybe you should go do your job, hunter. That is your job, right? Killing the blood thirsty things." I glared straight into his eyes, daring him to back down.

His jacket whipped around him as he started to leave. "You know, if I was part of The Order, I probably would do a much better job of killing those things before they hurt the people I cared about." His eyes swept the room before landing on Jaxson. "I'm going to find him." He left quickly, slamming the door in his wake.

A strange silence fell over the room.

"Fetch the boy. The last thing we need is The Order blaming us if one of theirs go missing."

Jaxson laughed. A quick gesture before tamping it back down and giving us a chaste nod. "Please be safe while I'm gone." Jaxson brushed Soryn's arm, a veiled longing painted across the planes of his face and hers.

The door gave a click behind him and his footstep echoed down the long hallway.

"He's a strange one." Soryn smiled before hoisting herself up on his very messy and paper-strewn desk.

Ashlie's face was seared into my vision; her scream seemed to echo through the silence. No matter how long I lived, nothing would wipe either from my memory. The thought of an eternity knowing what happened to her, and that I was responsible– How could anyone live with that. When I looked to Soryn, she had one of Jaxson's pictures in her hand, a grin on her face.

"Tell me the truth. If you could stay human, like if the curse didn't turn you to ash or whatever, would you do it? For him?"

The smile fell from her face as she rummaged through the papers absentmindedly.

"Soryn." I moved to sit beside her, leaving several papers floating to the ground in my wake. "Maybe, I deserve to be this way."

A numbness settled over me as I spoke the words out loud for the first time. I had killed at least four people since I had been cursed. I may not have dealt the killing blow to Keith or Ashlie, but they were gone because of me.

"My punishment is yet to be fulfilled." She patted my leg. "Besides, how could I live a mortal life knowing what you had lost for it."

"But that's the thing. You're asking me to do the same."

Her brows furrowed as she worked her jaw back and forth. She looked everywhere in the room but at me— her eyes finally landing on one of the photos on the ground. "The things I did. I do not deserve whatever Jaxson may be able to give me."

"Love." The tears I had just sworn not to shed were trying very hard to make a liar out of me. "He loves you, Soryn. You don't deserve to be punished for a wicked family and dowry that was probably spent ages ago."

Her eyes sparkled as she brought a hand to my cheek. It was the most human gesture I had seen from her. Her smile was tight as tears glistened in her bright green eyes. "No, my darling girl. Like usual, you are wrong." She sniffled, "The dowry you speak of was so much more than coin. I have done many terrible things in my life, but I have sworn it all to protect my family. The night that you took my curse, I broke that promise."

She held my hand and squeezed as all the pieces snapped into place. Why she came to America. Why she followed the Cordain's so closely, and why she was fighting so hard to turn me back.

"Soryn, are you like my really, really, really great grandmother?" The sparkle of a tear dissipated before she pursed her lips. She gave a deep sigh while patting my cheek.

"No, I never had children."

"Then how?" I gasped, "Your dowry was..."

"My little sister. She was to go with me to serve in my new husbands house." Her tears refused to fall as she went on. "I thought that if I ran she would be spared from his wickedness. He took her anyway, as payment for my betrayal." A deep heartache twisted in my stomach. "Is he?" I couldn't form the words and instead just pointed to my chest.

"No, my sweet girl. His entire bloodline was wiped from history." A smile touched her eyes. "My darling sister was there that night and broke me from my hunger and rage. I swore then, to never leave her again. I followed and protected her in shadow as she found love, and I was fortunate enough to make sure she lived a long, beautiful life with her beloved." Her hand was soft against my face. "You are the newest branch of that great love, and I will not see her line end." She lowered herself from the desk, pulling me with her.

I sniffled, "So, can I call you Auntie Soryn?"

"Only if you wish for eternal pain and suffering." She smiled and patted my cheek but harder this time before bending to sort through the mess I had made.

"I am happy to have known what love felt like." Her fingers closed around one of the photos, "That will have to be enough for me."

Her face contorted as she squinted her eyes, staring hard at the picture now inches from her face. The soft expression that had just graced her face contorted to one of deep confusion.

"Is it one of those magic eye things?" I asked as she pulled the picture back and forth from her face. "You have to cross your eyes to make it out."

"I know this man."

"Well I would hope so, especially since you slept in his shirt last night." I chuckled, moving to see what she was staring at.

A picture of Jaxson with several other men smiled up at me. It looked to be a graduation celebration. Jaxson Harwell smiled toward the camera, his youthful face free of his signature dark beard. "He looks so happy."

"Not him." Soryn's voice was low as confusion hung on her words. She pointed at the man with an arm around Harwell's shoulder. "Him. That's the man that came to me on the night I was made to slumber."

"The man from The Order?"

She nodded.

"That's not possible. He would have to be..." My mouth fell open as a set of footsteps began to clip clop in the distance. I stared in disbelief as Soryn lowered herself to the couch. "Do you think Jaxson knows?"

"I think that, once again, my heart has proved to be untrustworthy."

The steps had closed in on the door as the sound of Soryn's heart beat loudly in the room. A pained gasp covered the sound as the door opened and Renard stood blocking out all light from the outside.

"Hello, love."

The heavy bust that was resting on the shelf was in my hand for only a second before a white streak soared through the air. This time, he was quick, his hand was raised in a fist and showered the ground in a crumbled stone.

"We need to talk."

Chapter Thirty-Seven
SORYN

"Will there ever be a night that passes that you do not outshine the moon?" Renard was a picture of allure as he stood in what was once our home, one hand tucked in his pocket while the other gently grazed against the line of his jaw.

The last time I had been in this room with him, his hands had hugged my waist as he twirled me through the sea of onlookers. The music had thrummed a beautiful melody as I stared into his eyes though the memory had somehow shifted in my mind. His handsome face was just as it was now, his voice a deep thrum that sent a shiver down my spine, but the rest...was different. The chatter of party goers seemed more angry than in awe. The rough patches where candle wax had spilled on the floor seemed cumbersome as the women who trailed through it gave disheartened sighs over their ruined skirts.

His face darkened as he stepped closer, pulling me in to that last dance again. A twirl before he placed a finger under my chin. My skin rebelled at his touch. Once upon a time, his embrace had felt like my home. I thought that being with him was what true love was like. The kind of love my dear Varushka had. Now I knew better.

"Renard, I am sorry." I took a step back, unsure why the apology fell from my lips.

"All is well, my love." He closed the space, the feel of his presence on me more like an animal hunting prey than a lover. Maybe in his mind, they were the same. The thought sent a chill that shook my entire body. "We will settle all this messy business," he grabbed my hand, kissing it before pulling me back in. "And then we will go back to the way things were."

A throat cleared behind him and he let out a sigh before turning to Brittany. "And you, dear child, will go back to your shop and your life."

A quick flash of a smile rose and fell on her face. She leaned against the banister and took a long draw of her mug. "That's great and all, but why exactly did we need to leave Ben and Jaxson behind to have this weird…" She waved her free hand around in the air, "whatever this is?"

He tugged at the bottom of his perfectly tailored suit. I liked this style of clothing on him much more that the trappings of the past. I found my mind wandering to what Jaxson would look like in the same clothes. The picture in my mind was a stunning.

Renard stepped closer again, misreading whatever look may have befallen my face as meant for him.

Brittany cleared her throat again, this time sounding like a dying goat. She crossed the space, and a chill ran through my arm as she linked it through her own. Despite the cold that came from her closeness, my heart seemed to radiate warmth.

Unstake My Heart

"So Uncle Ren, can I call you Uncle Ren?" The look of disgust on Renard's face said he did not approve. Brittany's smile only grew as she pulled me toward the couch, "Well, Uncle Ren, I'm not sure if you know this, but there is a psycho vampire out there trying to kill the people that are important to me. Maybe, instead of pulling us aside for secret meetings, you could do something about that." We plopped onto the couch with Renard at our backs. A spark of pride glowed deep within me. She was no longer the scared girl I had met in the basement of her family's shop. Now she was a brave woman.

Renard moved silently, lowering himself to a seat nestled just to the side of the couch. His hard face softened before he spoke. "And I'm sure you hold so much guilt inside for that. But you mustn't blame yourself for the horrors the one you sired has brought upon this town." A twitch at the corner of his mouth caught my eye before he continued. "But that is part of why I needed us to be alone. The gentlemen you have both been seen with," his knuckles whitened on the arms of the chair before he tugged at the sleeves of his jacket, "It seems they are not who they appear to be."

"Yes." I thought of the picture in Jaxson's office. "That seems to be true more often than not."

His brow ticked up, "Yes. Brittany, how well do you know your Ben?"

"He's not my Ben." She scoffed, though I could hear the hesitation in her voice.

"No. You're right. He belongs to me." He crossed his leg and stared into the flame. He always had a delightful flare for the dramatic, but right now, it wore on my patience. He was using it to toy with someone I cared for.

"He doesn't belong to anyone?"

His face softened again as he turned to look into my eyes. "No, darling, of course not. I only mean that he still owes a service to me." He turned his gaze to Brittany, "I protected him. I shielded him from prying eyes and took him in after his family's tragedy."

"What are you..." Brittany's eyes narrowed on him as he parceled out his story bit by agonizing bit.

"It's not my place but, I have kept Ben close since he," He breathed out and continued, "since he murdered his parents."

Brittany was on her feet in an instant, "You're a liar."

"I'm sure this must be difficult, but I can assure you, it is the truth. His father worked for me, and unfortunately, a deal for a very important piece went south and he was badly hurt." Renard's hands reached for mine, "I am truly sorry my love. I know we promised not to sire but the elder Sommers would have died." He stood, placing his hand on the mantle before turning back to stare into my eyes. "I couldn't have known that he would go home and destroy his young family. Poor Ben killed his father after he saw him attack his mother. He didn't know that she wouldn't stay dead and barely escaped her frenzied hunger when she too, turned."

"Kinda sounds like you got them killed." Brittany glared through Renard's cool visage.

"Brittany." I snipped out. The words in my jumbled mind were starting to form the same opinion but I knew Renard. The last thing I wanted was for her to make an enemy of him.

He smiled. The wide grin left an uneasy turn in the pit of my stomach. "Well, Ms. Cordain, the police thought otherwise. If not for me, poor Ben would be rotting in a jail cell to this day."

"Soryn, these years without you have been torturous." He leaned forward, reaching for my hands. "But there is a way that we never need to be parted again. I found a way to make that happen before The Order took you from me." He stood and pulled me up with him.

"What does that have to do with..." Renard cut her off before Brittany could finish.

"The book. It can bind us together, forever." He stroked my cheek. "You have no need to fear eternity any longer." His lips hovered over mine as my heart pounded a warring beat of hope and fear. "I just need you to give me the book."

Brittany stared at Renard, annoyance painted on her face, "Are you kidding me right now?"

"We've been trying to find it." Anger seeped through my words. "Do you think that I would have been suffering through all of this without cause?" I grabbed Brittany's hand. "We have been searching this entire town over for any sign of it."

He stared at our clasped hands, "It seems like you have been having quiet the time searching for it. I just want to make sure the allure of humanity isn't clouding your search."

"You suggest that I would leave her like this? That I would let the only family I had left become some accursed thing — that I would curse her with my eternity."

"Now's not the time." Brittany said, I held my hand up to her words as a realization collided into my body.

"You thought I would abandon her. Just as I was abandoned by the one that cursed me?"

"I did what I had to do to make sure you were inclined to find the book." His eyes pleaded, "Please forgive me. All I did was to ensure that we could be together."

"You sent that vampire in the library, didn't you? But what about the hunter? How could..." He stayed silent as another piece clicked into place, "The Order. Ben said you were working with The Order."

"Ben thinks a great many things that I want him to. And there are more than enough vampires in our beautiful town to keep an eye on the things I care about."

"Will you let the boy go? Release him from whatever debt you think he may owe you." I asked.

"Ben has done a wonderful job keeping you safe, but I think we can relieve him of that duty now that I am here."

"Renard, that is not what I …"

Brittany's voice was low and fierce as she slowly stood. "You will not hurt him."

Renard laughed, "Hurt him. No, my girl, I would no sooner hurt him than I would any other employee." He smiled again, relishing the reaction his words were inciting. "Soryn, I know how much you feared being alone."

"Could you stop that!" Brittany's eyes were locked on Renard. No. Not on Renard, but something to his right. "I am so sick of this ghost!"

"Stan?"

"No. The chick. Ever since the well, she's been super mad. She pops up out of nowhere just to taunt me."

"She?" Renard asked.

"Yeah, that one." She pointed to the blank space between his chair and the fireplace.

Renard's voice was smooth as he stood and moved to where I had wandered to the window. "Soryn. I need you to come stay with me. Let me help you find the book. Let me protect you until the blood moon."

"I am fine here."

"Yeah. She's fine here. With me." Brittany said, crossing her arms as she closed the distance to plant herself between Renard and myself.

A twitch worked at Renard's jawline. "I'm sorry to say this, especially if it hurts you Brittany, but how can you be so sure of that? There is a young vampire out there, probably scared out of his mind and overpowered by the thirst for blood. He blames you. You should have been more careful, but instead you sired a monster and put everyone in danger."

My heart sank as fast as Brittany's face did.

"No. Whatever Brittany may have done, Keith's actions are of his own making." I stroked Renard's jaw out of habit. A feeling of guilt curled in my gut as I pulled my hand back slowly. "Brittany has controlled her self just as you did after I sired you. We are the worst parts of ourselves when we change, but we are inevitably ourselves."

A flash of something dark shadowed his face.

"If only that were true, my love."

Brittany said, "Well, as soon as you find Keith, let us know and we'll keep looking for that book." Her focus shifted away from us again as she spoke to the air. "Leave me alone for five minutes, alright?"

"Please come with me," Renard begged before he pulled me around my friend and crashed against me. His smell was intoxicating, reminding me of the years we spent in each other's arms. Confusion fogged my brain as his cold, hard lips moved against mine. My hands met his chest as the kiss ended and a spark shimmered in his eyes. "Is that a yes?"

"I will continue to search with Brittany." I kissed his cold cheek. "I will be safe."

A tense smile covered his face. "At least let me find better lodgings for you."

"I think the boys did a great job fixing up the place."

"Fine." He said, "But know this. I will not sleep soundly with the knowledge that you are putting yourself in harms way."

"That's alright, love. I've slept enough for the both of us for a while." I smiled at my jest, but Renard gave a terse nod before kissing my hands.

His footsteps were hard against the worn floor as he jerked open the door and slammed it closed behind him.

Brittany was up and out the door before I knew it.

I whispered into the room, not knowing which spirit would hear my plea. "Whoever you are, please leave her alone. She has been through so much already." A familiar smell of charcoal and paper filled the room.

Chapter Thirty-Eight
BRITTANY

"Hold up. We've got something to get straight."

Renard turned back to me, the gravel beneath his shoes rasping under his quick movement.

"Something we agree on." He pointed his finger toward me, "You may trace your lineage back to some long bygone version of her but know this, you are so far removed that any family bond you share is only in ink. There is no blood shared between you and whatever hope you had of keeping her magic will be squandered. I will share her curse, girl. And you will become another fallen leaf on her tree."

A smile crawled at the corners of his mouth and pulled at something deep inside of me. Rage twisted into burning courage as I stared straight into his hollow eyes. There was no love for Soryn in them. He was angry about losing something he deemed his. If she had taught me anything, it was that we belonged only to ourselves.

"If you think that I'm scared of you, you're dead wrong. And I will make damn sure that Soryn knows what kind of thing you actually are."

"Are you sure you want to do that? To rob someone you care for of love and happiness. Doesn't she deserve to be happy?"

"I've seen her happy, and you weren't anywhere around."

His smile fell, distorting his face into a mask of disgust and rage. "Soryn has had lovers before. And they have all been nothing more than a game to her. She will always return to me."

"Not if I have anything to do with it."

"Are you so sure you have me read correctly, girl?" He smiled again. "Because you do seem to have a habit of reading people wrong. Did poor Keith even stand a chance? And then there's my Ben."

"He's not your Ben." I repeated.

"He's been with me for years and you have turned his fate in a matter of weeks. Is anyone truly safe from you, Brittany? And just remember this — you may not fear me now, but you will not be immortal forever. Soryn will not leave that curse upon you, and very, very soon you will not be my problem."

My eyes locked with his in silent battle. "Do you think Soryn would ever forgive you if you hurt her family? Are you so insane to think she would stay with you if you hurt me?"

He played with the cuffs of his sleeve as he smiled over my head. "I have done things in this life that even Soryn could not fathom. What can I say? I will do anything for love. Anything." The hint of a foul smell twisted on the wind as he went on. "I've seen what you do to the one's you care about. Are you sure you want to put poor Ben in danger?"

"Is that a threat?"

He turned his back, walking into the darkness to where his car waited. "Merely an observation. People do seem to end up dead when you're around."

◆•◆

"How are classes still happening right now?"

"It suits no one to mourn in private when there is money to be made from the dead."

Several students passed by sporting shirts with Ashlie's face on it. It must have been a picture from her upcoming show. The bench where I had found her less than a week ago was covered in flowers, stuffed animals and candles. There was a group huddled on blankets by a tree telling stories of how amazing she was. A loud cry went out from the group.

A wave of disgust rolled through me as we hurried away from their theatrics.

"Have you talked to Jaxson about the photo yet?"

"No."

"No?"

"Why aren't..."

"Have you talked with Ben yet?"

"Touche." I stared up into the bright sky letting the harsh light that filtered through my dark shades sting my eyes. I squinted hard, and looked down to my feet. I hadn't seen Ben since we had fought in Jaxson's office. We had been laying low, sticking to Soryn's house while Renard continued his daily onslaught of begging Soryn to come away with him.

The University felt alive despite the events of the last week.

Orange and brown leaves dripped from bobbing branches as the wind played with the ones that fell in gentle bursts. The fluttering of leaves left a subtle whisper in the air that mixed well with the Halloween decor that filled windows and announcement boards. The board outside the auditorium already had a large poster of Ashlie. Just below, there was a change of cast for Dracula, the part of Lucy already filled by someone else.

Despite deaths workings, the world kept moving forward.

"Soryn?"

"Yes?"

"What happens if we don't find the book? I know you didn't want to talk about it, but I think it might be time to consider—" My head felt foggy as I waited for the words to come. They didn't. Instead, my hand grabbed at hers and she gave mine a gentle squeeze.

"Then you find someone else that deserves this curse as soon as you can. Hopefully, if your years as a vampire are few, you will still live out a good life."

"Without you."

She patted my hand. "You were never supposed to know me."

As we approached the auditorium doors, several students stood there passing out programs. I opened the folded paper to see more pictures of Ashlie smiling up at me.

The theater seats were packed and there wasn't a dry eye in the house.

The lights began to flicker and the already low voices hushed. For the next half hour, we sat through stories and slam poetry that, if I was honest, only had a light smattering of Ashlie related content.

As the lights went up, the Dean of the university took center stage. My eyes went big as I elbowed Soryn and pointed to the spot where she and Jaxson had sat the night of Ashlie's murder. There on the couch, just behind where the Dean stood, was the fake severed arm that Soryn had left behind.

Her startled laugh was like thunder in the midst of the immense quiet right before the Deans speech. If the sound of bodies twisting in seats wasn't unnerving enough, the eyes that bore into the two of us certainly was.

Panic and word vomit were the only things at my disposal as I looked down at the group of guys in the row ahead of us and shrugged, "She's the kind of girl that laughs at a funeral."

All but one of them turned back with the rest of the crowd while one nodded, "I love Bare Naked Ladies."

"Who doesn't?" Soryn's head turned slowly toward me, a look of utter confusion as she pointed to the man.

"I'll explain it later."

Several police officers were in attendance and were staring the two of us down while the Dean spoke. "Thank you to everyone who spoke today. Ashlie was a shining light in this school and she will be dearly missed."

I leaned forward, focusing on the voice addressing the crowd. I had heard it before.

"In light of this tragic passing, the university has decided that all Halloween festivities that were set to take place on campus are to be canceled." A sharp chatter was weaving through the space from group to group as he went on, "This includes all fraternity, sorority, or house parties of any kind." The chatter built as his voice rose, "The Sedgemoore police will be patrolling heavily around the campus as well. This is for your safety until the responsible person is apprehended."

My ears twitched at the familiarity of her voice. I had heard it before. On the other end of the call that Ben took in the shop and again when I had followed him in the admin building.

"I think Ben's contact is the Dean, and she is definitely a vampire." I whispered to Soryn.

"How do you…"

I put my hand to her shoulder as another voice trickled to my ear. A laugh, coarse and out of place and only loud enough for my ears to hear.

My eyes darted to every dark space. The overpowering smell of cucumber melon, Burberry, and everyday body odor filled my nostrils but even without his stench, I knew he was somewhere lurking. The pull of a large crowd too much of a draw for him.

The auditorium emptied slowly. By the time everyone was gone, so was everything that pointed to Keith being there.

"We have to end him before you are mortal again." Soryn walked down the sloped aisle to stand on stage.

"I'm with you on that one." I shook my head as she reached for the severed arm, swinging it over her shoulder as she walked back to me.

The sky outside was still bright, barely passed noon when we re-emerged into the quad. "When you tried to end it, when you were ready to go, I mean — why didn't you find someone who deserved it?"

"Because the only monsters that deserved it more than myself would have seen it as a gift and used it to make others suffer. I could not embrace death knowing that I had damned innocent lives."

"You've never taken innocent lives?" My head hung down as I whispered the question, a knot forming in the pit of my gut.

"I have tasted much innocent blood."

"That doesn't exactly…"

"Only when I first turned did I waste innocent lives. And even then, the lives trapped there were already being punished through no fault of their own."

"What about me? I killed that guy at the Rink."

She was silent.

It wasn't lost on me that she was asking me to do just that if we failed. "Maybe I'll just stay a vamp forever." I said, punctuating my words with an awkward laugh when Soryn paused her steps to stare at me. "Joking." I smiled. "Besides, the last thing I want is to see you go poof."

"I'm getting more opposed to that idea as well."

Angry students milled about the yellowing grass and tense conversations erupted around us. "This is so unfair." "…already learned her lines." "… not like it's really gonna happen again." "… already bought the beer." "…costume was so hot."

The cloud of conversations circled around the same theme. The dead girl was so rude for ruining their fun. A much different attitude from the performance several of them had just put on in that theater.

"Some of these monsters certainly seem deserving."

Soryn eyed them, "Ignorance breeds evil men and death makes a mockery of the mind. Give them time, and if they are willing, they will grieve their words. If they aren't willing, then they would be deserving of our hatred though they would be passed the point of caring." She looked into the group and shook her head, a sadness hung over her that I couldn't even begin to fathom.

The car ride back to the house was calm, like a blanket had settled over the car, blocking out the busy streets and voices that boomed from outside.

The comforting calm was immediately broken as my foot slammed on the brake. Several police cruisers were waiting in the drive way with their lights flashing.

"What's going on?" Soryn peeked over my headrest to see the scene in front of us while a police officer waved us forward.

"You don't have any outstanding warrants that I don't know about, right?"

"I'm fairly certain that there is a village in Spain that may still have a mark on my head, but I doubt that's what this is about."

"I was actually kid…"

She cut me off, her voice dripping with excitement, "Oh. Oh. There was also this one merchant further up the coast that caused a bit of mayhem, and I will admit their artist rendering of me was stunning." She smiled.

"No, Soryn. I very much doubt they are here for that."

She shrugged.

With the car in park, we both walked around to the front where two officers waited.

"Hi. Can we help you?"

"Brittany Cordain?" The officer spoke with a clipped edge to his voice. Either he was scared of the house or he knew to be scared of us. Either way, he was trying very hard to hide it.

"Yes?"

He reached for me, "You are under arrest for the murder of Ashlie Marcher. You have the right…"

Soryn was quick to grab the officers arm. "You have the right to take your grubby little hands off of her before I take away your right to keep them?"

The other officer grabbed her hands so quickly that they must have suspected what Soryn would do. "Soryn Floaire. You are under arrest for threatening an officer of the peace."

"You want a piece, I'll give you a piece."

"Soryn! Chill out." He held my hands out to the officer. "We haven't done anything wrong. It will be alright. We've got this." He finished reading us our rights as we were placed in separate cars.

It was an unnecessarily long ride to the police station as the officer seemed to take the longest way possible. I had long since lost sight of Soryn's car when he pulled into a dark garage. The officer in the front seat turned but noticeably avoided eye contact. He knew exactly what I was.

"Who are you?" I demanded.

"You are going to be escorted to another vehicle."

"Where is Soryn?"

"Soryn is being booked right now."

"Like hell she is!" I kicked at the door. The crack of hard plastic was the only satisfaction I was given. The car was reinforced. "What is this?"

"He wanted me to tell you that she will be alright. She will burn so brightly that the fires of hell will seem a reprieve from anyone who would think to harm her."

I stopped mid-kick at the words. Those were the same ones I heard Jaxson hiss in the mans ear at the bar.

"There are people there to keep her safe. She has to be seen getting booked, but she will be safe."

The officer opened my door and walked me to another car only this time my seat was far less cozy. He kept his eyes down as he spoke, "I'm really sorry about this but —" He popped open the trunk and gestured inside.

"You know I could rip you apart and throw you in there instead, right?"

"Yes ma'am. I am fully aware of what you are capable of." He looked up, "I've also been told that you are one of the good ones. The ones we help."

"The ones we help?" I mouthed the words over and over again as I lay with knees to my chest in the small cramped trunk with nothing but a Surge can rolling around to keep me company.

The car continued on for what felt like forever but was more likely somewhere around fifteen minutes. When the car finally slowed, a familiar voice spoke to the driver.

"Is she alright?"

"Yes, sir. She should be in lock up by now."

A deep breath proceeded his heavy words, "Get back as quick as you can. I don't want eyes off of her."

I could hear a slight shuffling of feet. The officer was nervous.

"And hey, make it believable."

Gravel crunched beneath heavy feet as someone approached the trunk. Jaxson's voice was on edge when he spoke. "Hey Brittany, it's me. I'm going to open the trunk. Cover your eyes if you don't have your glasses on."

The trunk gave a click and light slowly poured into the small space.

"You know, you could have just bailed me out like a normal person. The jail break was a little unnecessary."

Jaxson's face pulled up in a gentle smile. "Unfortunately, murder charges are a bit tricky to walk away from."

He held out a hand to help me out. The all black car pulled away as he ushered me a short distance into the back of the gas station just down the road from At Day's End.

The dimly lit room was covered in row upon row of cardboard boxes, their contents spilling out onto shelves. A mixture of sickly sweet and onion smell flooded my nostrils.

"Do you often have secret meetings in the back room of gas stations?"

Another voice answered, "We do when the owner is an old friend." The man shook my hand before placing an icy red drink in it. "I hear these are your favorite."

His eyes were deep in color and kindness. He brushed the dark brown hair away from his wide circle wire-rimmed glasses. He cleaned the lenses on the bottom of his red plaid shirt. I could smell the blood mixed with the cherry frosted drink and my stomach gave a lurch of betrayal as I set it on a box of Funyuns.

"May I then? It smells too delicious to go to waste." He placed his glasses back before reaching for the drink. "I haven't tried it like this before." He smiled before taking a large gulp, grimacing when the taste hit his tongue. "And I don't believe I will try it again." He laughed showing off the sharp points in his red-coated mouth before he licked them clean.

Jaxson worked at a spot on his temple. "We don't have a lot of time." He checked his watch, "They are going to find out she's gone any minute now if they haven't already. I would like to get to Soryn before things get too out of hand."

"Soryn can handle herself."

"I didn't say she couldn't, but that doesn't mean she has to be alone."

"We need to give it time for Renard to see her there." The plaid vampire patted Jaxson on the shoulder, a soft move that reminded me of my mom. "I get it. We'll be as quick as we can."

It was then that it hit me. "I've seen you before. Soryn saw you before."

He said, "I'm sure this is the first time you and I are meeting."

"But I've seen you. In the picture in Jaxson's office."

He looked at Jaxson, "You put a picture of me in your office?"

"That's what professors do. They put up degrees and pictures of graduations and stuff like that."

"What's going on!" My head spun with all the explanations and scenarios my brain was cooking up. "Who are you?"

"My name is Nathanial Harken, head of the Order of Rosewood." He bowed his head, "And I am at your service."

Chapter Thirty-Nine
SORYN

"You're going to have a very bad time when my friend stops being so nice." I smiled at the thoughts of what she could do to them. She wouldn't, of course, but it was fun to think about it.

"Don't worry, your friend said to make sure you are nice and comfortable during your stay with us." The man's smile held no warmth in it as he shoved me in a cell.

"Where is she?" The other cages were empty.

"Could we have a moment please?"

"Mr. Dorsetty." the officer, took a step back, closing the cell behind him. Iron bars separated me from the two men. "I wasn't aware you would be here."

"It's alright, Glen."

"I'm sorry, Sir, but she's not allowed to have any visitors." He leaned in closer to Renard. "She assaulted a police officer."

Renard laughed, "Wouldn't be the first time." He turned to me. "Remember Barcelona?"

"I have tried very hard not to remember Barcelona."

His hand brushed past the bars to stroke through my hair.

"Sir, you can't touch the prisoner."

Renard turned to the man. The officers feet shifted back and forth uncomfortably as he stared straight into Renard's eyes. "I am breaking no rules and you are happy to go do some paperwork while I speak with Miss Floaire."

"I'm happy to give you some time alone, Sir."

The door closed with a sharp thud behind him.

"You couldn't have maybe compelled him to let me out of here?"

He leaned on the bars. "Times are different now, Soryn. I could have had him let you out, but then there's all the paperwork and computer files to destroy. Honestly, it's much easier this way."

"Where is Brittany?"

He looked around. "I'd fully expected her to be here. In fact, when I heard that they were bringing her in for killing that girl."

"You know she didn't kill her. Keith did."

"Yes. Keith. Well, responsibility for those we sire is a lesson that we all must learn sometime."

An alarm went off right before a rush of police came barreling through the door.

"Mr. Dorsetty, we're going to have to get you somewhere safe."

"What's going on?"

"The officer that brought in the Cordain woman was found unconscious in the garage. We're on full lock-down, Sir. No one in or out."

My joy was so great I could have floated through the roof. "That's my girl."

A mixture of emotions were splattered on the faces staring at me through the bars. Renard's face however, was unreadable.

"I'll be back as soon as I can." He left without another word.

As the hours slogged by, I became more and more annoyed. There were one hundred and fifty tiles on the ceiling, twenty-two bars on my cage, one dirty toilet in the corner, and zero Brittany coming to my rescue.

The alarms had long since gone silent but neither Renard nor the police officers had come back. The sound of rain began to trickle into my cell as I stared up at the brown spotted ceiling and shrugged. I had lived in worse. My eyes locked on the silver metal toilet as a horrible aroma wafted through leaving stagnant air lingering around me.

I tried to shut out the smell by pressing my hands to my face but it did little to block out the offending odor.

"If they don't let me out of here soon, I'm going to die of suffocation." I whispered, not expecting an answer. One came anyway.

"Tsk. Tsk, Soryn. If you die, how will Brittany ever survive." The raspy croak was even worse than before. A bolt of bone chilling fear shot through me sending all of my nerves at attention. To the right of the bars, stood Keith. His skin was a pale green pallor that would have matched the color of his eyes if not for the shocks of bright red that rimmed them. Only one side of his face pulled upward as he smiled down at me, showing a partial row of his brown stained teeth. The shirt he wore was almost clean and out of place on his dying frame. He had left the black shirt unbuttoned and there were several shallow scratches on his exposed chest where spots of darker green and brown muck painted him in a gory mess.

I fought back the urge to yell out or be sick.

"I really should thank you, you know." He trailed his fingers along the bars as he paced in front of my cell, "If you and your little friend hadn't killed me when you did, Brittany's blood would have been out of my system."

"Brittany never meant for you to turn."

"Oh, I'm sure she would have loved to keep me if I let her." He glared into the cell with a tilt of his head. "You know, when your boyfriend, not the professor but the rich one, when he paid me to get closer to her I never realized that she had such a wild side. I was truly shocked and," he breathed in deeply, "pleasantly surprised. I almost missed out though. I nearly bolted when he explained what I needed to do in that basement but hey, money is money right and college is expensive."

"Renard hired you to wake me."

He snapped his fingers and pointed at me, the gesture pulling a nail from his hand. "You know," He flicked the nail toward me as I pushed another wave of sickness down. "All he had to do was give me what I wanted and things could have turned out better for him." He smiled at whatever joke he was telling in his head. His smile was a grotesque mockery of happiness as he slid his hands under his shirt to his back exposing even more of his rotting flesh.

My heart gave a thunderous pound in my chest as the air seemed to be sucked out of the room. Even Keith's putrid smell was blocked out by the sight of him holding the one thing that could save Brittany. The leather that bound it was as pristine as the day I had last seen it. A fluttering pounded inside of me as he flipped through the cream-colored pages full of markings, spells, and stories of each woman the curse had touched. "What I don't get, is why there is so much fuss over a book."

"How did you find that?"

He tapped the book on the bars as he rambled, ignoring my question. "Have you ever woken up at the bottom of a well and started salivating over the rotting body beside you? No? Just me then?"

He waited but I couldn't take my eyes off of the book.

"Interesting." He followed my gaze and continued to tap. "Well, let me tell you something, it's not the best Friday night I've ever had. But you know, when you're sucking the flesh off some dead guys arm, you really put things into perspective and find yourself." He snaked his hand across the bars leaving a trail of something that looked like pond scum dripping everywhere he touched. "I found a lot of things before I pulled myself out of that place. Including a very angry ghost chick and this." He flipped through the pages before snapping it closed again.

"Give it to me, now."

"You see, that's not going to be how this works. We both have something the other needs. You have a way to read this and fix whatever is happening to me and I…" He played with the shirt again, pulling at the collar with a smug face, "I have Ben."

Hurried voices started filtering into the cell. Something was happening outside. "The two of you did this to me and the two of you are going to fix it. Or I'll make sure both Ben and Professor Harwell pay for it."

"I'm going to kill you. And this time, I'll make sure that it sticks."

I could see the anger in him build as he looked toward me. The voices on the other side of the door were building as they closed in on us. A cracking sound escaped Keith's mouth before he finally gave me a terrifying scowl and left.

Four police officers came in, each one of the cops covering their nose or waving their hands to disperse the smell. Immediately, I could tell those that had smelled death in their years, the recognition of it written on their face while the other two stared between me and the toilet with wide horrified eyes.

"We've been instructed to move you to another facility." The officer looked around the large empty space, hand on hip, before locking eyes with me.

"Where is Brittany?" I asked.

No one answered as they unlocked the door and escorted me out.

The officer holding my elbow addressed the two wide eyes men, "You two hold back. Do a sweep of the cells real quick and then meet us outside."

They both glared at her and then me before nodding.

"Enjoy." I said with a smile.

As soon as the door shut, the officer at my elbow picked up speed, shuffling me through the building until we emerged outside. "Get in." She held open the passenger door to an all black car.

"I am not leaving this place without my companion."

"We're taking you to her."

The driver reached around my waist grabbing for a strap and clicking it. "Safety first." She smiled and turned the key. The belt began to move across the ceiling, locking me in place with a hiss. "What witchcraft is this?"

The car lurched forward.

I puffed out a breath hoping that wherever Keith may be, he wasn't following.

Chapter Forty
BRITTANY

"Wait. How come you didn't have to ride in the trunk?"

"They put you in a trunk?" Soryn slammed the car door and glared at the old woman.

"Hey, I didn't drive her. Take it up with the boss." The woman had barely finished her last word before her wheels were kicking up a puff of dust as she pulled away from the gas station. Holding the back door of the place ajar, I signaled for Soryn to hurry inside.

"Brittany, we don't really have time to rob a merchant right now. We have big problems." Her words trailed off as she entered, her body frozen as she stared at the two men waiting inside.

Nathanial spoke first, "No need to rob anything. I know the owner."

"I remember you." Her voice was strong but I could see where she was slowly inching back toward the door, her hand placed firmly in mine. "You look much more — undead, than the last time we met."

"And you look much more — un-undead." He grinned, "Funny how much can change over the years."

"Even funnier when you slept through all of them."

"I am sorry for what happened to you and your friend."

"For what The Order of Rosewood did." She squeezed my hand, "glad to see that you are no longer a part of that charade, however," Her eyes finally moved to stare down Jaxson who hadn't taken his eyes off her since she walked in. "It seems that age has made you no better at choosing your company."

"Soryn," I leaned down to whisper in her ear, "Nathaniel is the head of The Order of Rosewood." Her eyes snapped to mine, "and Jaxson works with him."

She slowly turned her head back to them. "I stand by what I said."

"Please, Soryn, you have to believe that I'm…" Jaxson's plea was cut short.

"A dull minded shabaroon."

"No, I'm…"

"A mooncalf of a man."

"Soryn, you don't have to…"

"I stand by what I said!"

The room was quiet as eyes bounced from person to person. Soryn's chest huffed up and down, the anger boiling in her becoming more and more clear.

Jaxson turned to Nathaniel, "I don't even know what she said."

"Ask your little Jeeves man." She sneered at him.

Nathaniel patted Jaxson on the shoulder before whispering in his ear that it might be best for him to go watch out front. He nodded and left.

"Well, I'm sure you are wondering why…"

Soryn held her hand in the air for Nathaniel to stop and turned to me. "We have very big problems. Keith has the book and Ben."

"What? How do you know that?"

"Keith came to me when they had me locked in jail. He showed me the book and demanded for us to fix whatever malady ails him or he will kill Ben."

"Is there a way to un-make him a vampire?"

She grimaced, turning her nose up as she spoke, "I don't believe that he is a vampire. Something is very wrong. I believe that he took your blood and I believe that because of that, the fates have cursed him to walk the earth as a ghoul."

"A ghoul?" Nathaniel asked. "I didn't think ghouls were real."

"Well your little trickster friend out there didn't know werewolves were real either." She turned, hands on hips as she chided him. "You know, for a band of monster hunters you are very ignorant of what's out there."

The cardboard box I lowered myself to only gave slightly. My head spun as I tried to focus on their conversation. Instead, all I could think of was what might be happening to Ben.

"We are monster hunters, Soryn, but not all creatures that walk the earth are monsters."

"Can we focus please!" An all consuming panic enveloped me. "Are you sure that he has him?"

"I'm certain he was wearing the shirt Ben had on the night you found Ashlie."

The room seemed to shift under my feet as a wave of overwhelming fear and nausea churned within me. "He's had him for almost a week?" I could hear the tears in my voice as I spoke, "We have to get him back." The though of what Ben had already been through made my stomach turn. And now, he had been taken by someone who would surly take pleasure in causing him pain. My vision was a hazy red as I blinked back tears.

Silence.

Nathaniel spoke first, "We will get him back. Ben and I have a mutual friend that cares very much for his well being."

"The Dean." I replied.

"Yes. An old family friend. Another one of Renard's victims who just happened to stay a few steps ahead of him. Both she and Ben have been doing their best to take him down from the inside. She called me a few days ago when she hadn't heard from him." Nathanial looked to me, "I am sorry, Brittany. I know you have come to care a great deal for him."

"Don't say sorry like he's already dead!" My foot slammed onto the sticky laminate floor as I threw my misplaced rage his way.

Soryn's hand was in mine before I took another step. "Why would you help us?" She asked Nathanial.

He placed a hand on my shoulder, "Because that is what we do. We help the good ones live in peace and we make sure the bad ones get exactly what's coming to them."

Soryn gave him a sharp stare, "The Order needs a new slogan."

He chuckled, "It's much better than the old one— *if it's not human, kill it.*"

"Do you think he's alright?" I said, barely above a whisper.

Soryn answered, "Believe me when I say that Keith is one of the most daft creatures I have ever encountered but he is also desperate. He came to me while I was surrounded by guards and brought the book with him."

"Not that daft." I said, "He knew you would be there." I stood while the rest of the pieces fell into place. "He may be an idiot, but who ever is pulling his strings isn't."

Soryn rolled her long black sleeves while her brow pinched in thought. "Keith said that Renard was paying him to get close to you. He wanted you to wake me. However, I think its safe to say the puppet has cut his strings. Or at least he's pretending to."

"Why is Renard so convinced he can share the curse?" I asked.

"He loves me. He will do whatever it takes to truly spend eternity together." She rubbed her arms as she spoke.

A mournful sigh came from Nathaniel. "We tried to tell you before. Renard is not who you think he is."

"He was by my side for over one hundred years. I think I knew him fairly well."

"That is something his wife would say."

"We did not marry."

"You did not marry, but he did." His face was solemn while he spoke soft and low, "Renard Dorsetty was married but his new bride was murdered. She was found on the night Renard should have died on the battlefield."

"He would have told me." Soryn spoke to the air as movement shifted by the door. Jaxson had come back and was sitting on edge as he listened to the story.

"The reports we had built on him were gruesome. For years after, he killed seemingly without cause. It took us six months to realize he was killing anyone that resembled you."

Jaxson finally spoke, "He tried to kill you. When you were," he swallowed, "beheaded in Barcelona. That was him. That's when he realized that you were truly immortal."

"And he just told you this over a pint at the tavern I suppose?" She joked, her calm facade refusing to unravel.

I couldn't speak. I knew Soryn's heart was crumbling inside her chest but she stood tall.

Nathaniel continued, "We just suspected much of it until you disappeared and Renard went quiet for a long time. We knew he would try to claim your curse what we didn't know until recently was how many vampires he had sired to make sure he would keep control of the town while you slept.

I had had enough. "We are less than a week from the blood moon, we know who has the book, and I can't be killed. So let's end this."

Soryn grabbed a giant bag of 3D Doritos shoving several in her mouth before cracking open a warm soda and downing it. "Let's do this."

Both of us marched toward the door. The sound of Soryn's steady beating heart a cry to action as we walked into the bright light of day.

"Hey!" Both Nathaniel and Jaxson called. "We need a plan."

"Kill our exes. That's the plan," I said with more bravado than when I had accepted my second place award and my fifth-grade spelling bee.

"Alright. So where are you going?" Jaxson asked.

I turned to Soryn, "Do you…"

"I thought that maybe you…"

"Uh-uh."

"Ok, well maybe we should…"

"Figure that out first?"

"Yeah."

She rocked back on her heels, "It felt really…"

"I know right. Like I was about to go all Lost Boys on someone."

We walked back toward the store and Soryn gave me a firm nudge. "I have no idea what you're saying but I agree with how you're saying it."

"If the two of you are done with the macho man thing," Jaxson crossed his arms, and leaned against the open door, "I may have an idea of how to get Ben and the book back."

Nathaniel stared out from the darkness as he went on, "Soryn. How do you feel about house parties?"

Chapter Forty-One

SORYN

At Days End was a flurry of anticipation as the night of the Blood Moon and the All Hallows Eve Party were at hand. Brittany had been tip tapping on her electric typewriter constantly for days. The sound was enough to make one wish for the grave — again. My heart dipped at the thought.

A cacophony of pings, dings, and doors openings flooded out from her computer as my head ached for silence.

"There are so many people saying that they are going to be there. With the Dean canceling everything, it's like everyone was just waiting for someone to be brave enough to plan something." She jotted down several names before continuing with her pecking like a hungry hen at the keys. "There are a couple other parties that people are talking about, but I think we can still get a decent enough turnout to get Keith's attention."

"If his draw to you isn't driving his every move yet, a chance to make another spectacle surly will be."

Brittany was restless, her fingers tapped an uneven rhythm on the glass counter.

"Everything will be fine." I stopped there, unable to find any words to comfort her anxious drumming. I hoped everything would be fine. I wished on every star above that our plan would be successful; but I knew, somewhere deep in my soul, if I still possessed such a thing, that neither one of us would ever be the same.

Her hands shook as she pulled a small blue book from her bag and extended it to me. "I'm so sorry I didn't give you this sooner. At first, I was afraid that you would use it to hurt me but after getting to know you and getting to know her, I didn't want this journal to hurt you."

A painful tightening threatened to tear at my throat as I fought to hold back the emotions that the all too familiar handwriting brought to the surface. "How did you…"

"Grandma Winnie gave it to me on the night we changed." Brittany held on to my arms, the cold of her touch rebelling against the warmth that shone from her eyes. "Soryn, I feel like I need to warn you about…"

"I'm going to go check the basement for more decorations." She didn't say anything as I took Clarette's journal and descended into the dark space. My foot hung on the bottom step. Renard's face seemed so dull as I stared at his aging portrait. Clarette had been a truly exceptional artist and it had brought so much joy to buy her paints and canvases to explore with. I only wish now that she had had a better subject. Her image gently swirled in my memory. Lovely. The smiling face and warm glow she gave to everyone was infections. Brittany reminded me much of her. My heart wished more than anything for her family line to be somewhere far away, with paintings and charcoal sketches plastering the walls of their homes in beauty. A coldness wrapped around me like submerging into an ice laden pond. My fingers gripped the journal before plucking the dagger from the desk. I plunged the gold blade into the latch in the painting with a bit more force than needed and opened my tomb.

The carvings on the floor were still deep without footfalls or the wear of time to disturb them. I had avoided this room since I awoke. The dark wood of the coffin was smooth. Even the places where grooves had been carved to match the floor were sanded. Whoever had made my tomb had been a skilled worker. A skilled artist.

The long skirt I wore made it difficult to hoist myself up and into the box. A calmness washed over me as soon as I laid my head on the dark green pillow and the smell of vanilla and cedar wood brushed like a phantom over my senses.

"*I can help you.*" The last words I had heard from my Clarette still seemed to echo through the chamber, finding their way to my ears despite the passage of time.

The indigo journal had begun to fade but the writings and charcoal drawings inside hadn't. I read through the pages, hoping beyond hope that what Renard had said was true. Perhaps Clarette did feel regret and fled. I had driven her to fear me. I had shown her death and destruction and blamed her for falling prey to that fear. Tears cooled my face as I traced the words she left behind.

My mind fumbled trying to puzzle through her words. Sketches of the spell book, along with directions for making glue and paper lined her final pages. Spells were scrawled along-side runes that matched the ones I could see from where I lay. The drawings were all hers alone, but I was certain of one thing. Someone had changed her words.

Unstake My Heart

Soryn has become something that I do not recognize. The evil that grips her immortal form had to be stopped. Now that she sleeps, I will leave this place. It will be upon our great family to hold her wickedness at bay.

On every page that spoke of my evil, the writing was not in her hand. Someone else had changed her words. I stared at the page that spoke of her escaping the Township of Cordain. It was written by a liars hand. She hadn't feared me and she hadn't been the one to betray me after all.

A burning sensation clung to my throat as I gripped the sides of the coffin to steady the spinning. She knew what Renard was. But how? How could she have seen through his deceit in a matter of years when I had been with him for so long?

My heart had betrayed me but my blood never would. My blood. Clarette was my blood and my family and if I wasn't such a stubborn ass, I would have seen it so much sooner.

Her quick scrolling script became heavy as her writings in the journal came to an end though her words seemed to lighten. Where most passages spoke of evil, her true hand was apparent in her love of art.

Renard's portrait is one that holds my heart. There is only one other like it. Unmoving as an oak will I be in my hope to bring knowledge to those who may have let their passions rest. Perhaps I shall even create a semblance of where it all started and from there even the deepest of roots could be severed.

My eyes darted over the words again. Could it be? Hidden in a love letter to her craft, she had left a message. Something just for me. Even the deepest of roots could be severed. I had gifted her those very words over the course of our friendship. Once when she had feared being trapped by a wicked man. Once when he had carved his claim in the bark of a tree. And again when I had laughed as both the tree and his life went up in flames.

I fumbled my way to the edge of the coffin, it teetered like a boat in a storm. I pulled my hand back inside just before the entire box crashed to the ground.

"Soryn!" Brittany was fast. Her face peered into mine as she held the lid aloft. "What are you doing?" She shook her head in disbelief.

"I know what happened." I hugged her, squeezing so tight that if she had needed breath, her face would no doubt have been a beautiful shade of blue. "That ghoul doesn't have the book." I laughed, unable to suppress my joy.

"But you said he showed it to you."

"Yes. He showed me a book made by a very skillful hand, but not my book."

"Wait, uh, why is that a good thing Soryn?"

"Because, if he doesn't have the real book, then I know exactly where it is."

"I don't follow."

Her eyes darted back and forth searching for the ties that would connect what I said. Her blank expression showing that she could find none. I laughed again.

"The same person who made that book, carved these symbols, and painted that portrait." She had left me so many clues. "The journal, the spell on my home, and the biggest of all, the tree in the portrait." A twisting began to close in on my chest. "She had planned everything. She knew what Renard was up to. She saved me from the curse my heart had fallen to." My heart broke all over again. I had thought her a traitor. I had chosen my love for Renard over the one person who had truly loved me enough to save me. And because of that, Clarette had kept me in the dark. Because of that, I knew exactly where she had actually gone all those years ago and why Keith had found the book in the well.

I swallowed down the knot in my throat, "Tell me about the ghost that has been tormenting you."

Brittany's head straightened as her eyes locked with mine. Her hand came to her mouth in a gentle gasp and held there as she spoke, every word confirming what I had already known. Clarette had given up everything to stop Renard and save me.

———————◆•◆———————

Dark windows greeted us as we approached the Cordain's family home.

Brittany cleared her throat as she stared at the front door, "Are you sure it's in there?"

"Our family has done a fair job of keeping inventory of all antiques and artifacts in their possession. The painting that we seek was listed as one the family kept." My heart sank as I thought of Clarette, weaving her plan all alone.

"Jaxson will you go in with her?"

"I do not need to be chaperoned." I huffed back.

"Please. It would make me feel a lot better knowing that if either of them are in there waiting for you, you at least have a hunter with you." My face went red with Brittany's plea.

Jaxson's head popped around from the passenger seat. "Let's go."

I huffed and puffed. I knew why Brittany wouldn't go in. Just in case everything went wrong, she wanted to make sure her family was safe. Even from her. Knowing that didn't make it any easier.

"Come on liar. Let's go rob an old lady."

Jaxson let out an airy chuckle before taking my hand. My head screamed at my heart to pull away. My heart was an idiot. I glared at him but let the warmth of his skin seeped into mine as we knocked on the door.

I heard footsteps on the stairs. Brittany had sunk down and out of view in the car as Winnie opened the newly replaced door. "Soryn! Sweet girl, how are you?" She pulled me into a hug and I breathed her in. The smelled of ointment fought to overpower the hint of caramel that clung to her.

"Hi, Winnie."

"How many time do I need to tell you to call me Grandma Winnie?"

That wasn't going to happen. Jaxson bit his lip, holding back a laugh.

She looked around behind us. "Were's my little honey bear?"

"She's back at the dorm studying."

"She's so smart. Just like her grandma." She smiled, "And who is this handsome man you've brought with you?"

"He's my…he's a friend." I dropped his hand.

"Jaxson Harwell, ma'am."

"Winnie, I was wondering if I could look at some of the paintings you've collected? I'm doing a paper for art history and I think one of them would be perfect for it." I smiled, hoping the old woman's love of company would override her quick wit.

"Come in. I'll fix you both some tea while you find which one you're looking for."

Jaxson's hand rested on my back for only a second before he pulled it back and shoved it in his pocket.

"I saw one of this beautiful oak tree with carvings in it. It looked like it was probably from the late 1700s."

The shaky clink of glasses and slow shuffling of slippered feet carried into the foyer where we waited for her answer.

"I believe that one is down the hall in the study." She said. "Go ahead, darling. I will be there as fast as my old legs will let me."

The dark brown bookshelves and aging spines on tomes were a familiar sight. I had already searched through this entire library in hopes of finding my book but Jaxson went straight for the shelves, several sporting frames of Brittany and her mom. A bright pink blanket was tossed over the back of a large cozy looking arm chair. The book Brittany had been reading months ago before all of this had happened was still sitting over the puffy arm, waiting for her to come back to it. I was going to make sure she did.

"I never wanted to lie to you." Jaxson's words were soft as he grazed the shelf.

Mine were sharp, "I've already looked through all of those. Besides, were looking for a painting of an oak tree." The wall of paintings seemed to pulse as I inched closer, studying each framed piece of art.

"I know we're going to find a way to fix all of this, and there's going to be time for us to talk everything over after. I just want you to know that, I'm not going anywhere."

"You do realize that there are only two possible endings for this. Either Brittany and I change back, or she is cursed with eternity while I turn to dust." I turned back to the painting wall, "So you can break your heart over a pile of ash, or spend the rest of your mortal life pining over an immortal as you whither away. Either way, there is no happy ending with me. Ever."

"I would rather spend a few glorious days in the Sun than live my whole life not knowing anything but darkness." His fingers traced my arm sending a delicious warmth through my whole body.

"There is only darkness where I am concerned." My heart was shattering in my chest. This man had lied to me. Just as Renard had lied to me. "And I'm not so sure you deserve the light."

"You're right." His face was drawn. I knew the words I had spoken were lies as soon as they left my lips and yet he believed them. "I've not been perfect, Soryn. My whole life I've followed The Order. I've done what I've been told. I've taken lives and followed orders that I shouldn't have but believe me when I say, there is nothing that I regret so much as following the order to lie to you. If I had a lifetime to say sorry for what I've done to you and your trust in me, there wouldn't be a day where I didn't try to make it up to you."

My heart broke all over again, though this time the pain ached in a different way. I mourned the future where I could see him live up to his words. The pain in my chest was growing steadily more urgent as neither of us seemed to be able to move. I had to break the silence. "I hear flowers and chocolate work pretty well."

He small pull at the corner of his mouth hinted at the smile he was trying so hard keep to himself. "Not coffee and croissants?"

"I guess it depends on how sorry you are." I couldn't help but let out a small laugh when he pursed his lips and began to nod.

"I would give you everything, Soryn. Just to know that I made you smile— made you laugh, I would give up everything else."

"And I would never ask you to." The knot forming in my throat left a tremor in my words. I cleared it before moving back toward the wall, "but I will ask you to get back to work. We have a tree to find and you are being very distracting."

He didn't say another word as he walked to my side, his eyes glazed and a coy smile playing at his mouth. I looked him up and down before letting out an annoyed sigh, "You know you don't have to tower right next to me. It's a big wall. Go look over there."

His mouth twitched up with a grin, "Yeah, but if I go over there, who's going to search all the ones you can't reach."

I narrowed my eyes up at him, "What?"

"Can you even see all the way up here?"

"I can see perfectly fine from where I stand. Thank you."

"Oh, yeah." He smiled in earnest. My heart fluttered in my chest at the sight. "What's this?"

He pointed to a painting of a horse, high up on the wall.

"A painting."

He stared me down, "Of what?"

"Of you being a horses…" He picked me up, lifting me toward the painting as a flood of curses escaped me. His hands gripped my hips as he held me up in the air and I held his shoulders. As our eyes locked, I found myself wishing we could stay here, in this moment forever.

He lowered me slowly until my feet brushed the floor. My breath hitched as I spoke, "Like I was saying, horses…"

His lips collided with mine. A rush of adrenaline flooded my veins as the urgency to kiss him back overtook me. I couldn't keep him, but I could kiss him.

A gentle cough came from the doorway where Winnie stood with a tray of ornate tea cups and biscuits in hand. "I'll just leave these here." She gave me a wink before placing the clinking cups down on the desk. "I'm feeling a bit tired after all this excitement, anyway." She slowly hobbled her way to me before patting my hand gently, "Soryn, sweetie, just lock up when the two of you head out." She smiled, before curling her finger toward Jaxson. He bent down to her level.

She gave him several sharp pats to the cheek. "Be a gentleman."

"Yes, ma'am."

She smiled and started to leave, turning back in the doorway, she pointed toward the wall behind the antique desk where several of the paintings were covered in the familiar bursts of color. "It's that one over there, dear."

My heart pounded as I neared the dark wooden frame. Emerald leaves coated the once bare branches. A broken heart covered the initials that had been carved with paint into the bark. The symbols and swirls that matched them trailing out in the same medium. Each piece of Winnie was pulled away revealing another artists work.

"Was this tree important to you?"

"I hated this tree. I had it burned to the ground." I smiled, "Clarette had a suitor. He was rich and handsome and wicked. He carved their initials into this tree as a reminder to her."

"Did he hurt her?"

My eyes met his as I smirked, "No. He went missing before they could wed." I shrugged.

He turned his head slightly, his brow arching as a slow smile emerged. "I love that fire."

"There is something deeply wrong with you then." My heart skipped over itself at his use of words.

He shrugged and reached for the frame.

The desk was covered in notebooks with Brittany's messy scratching all over them. I stacked them neatly to the side before turning the painting over on the flat surface. A cold pulse came from the covered backing as I slid Jaxson's knife along the edge. The thick material curled like peeled fruit as it came away from the canvas and frame.

I couldn't believe it. There, stowed safely away behind one of her paintings was my book and sticking out from one of the pages, was a folded note, covered in Clarette's elegant writing.

Soryn,

My heart breaks to know that I have brought you to this dark place. My hope was to free you of the loneliness that haunts you and instead, I have given someone I thought would keep you safe, the greatest weapon against you. I found a way to share or end your curse. You saved me and it was my greatest wish to repay that kindness. I thought Renard was the answer, but I have learned too much to bind you to him. He is evil, Soryn. The Order of Rosewood has shown me that but I may have always known it. Just as you knew about Samuel.

The book has shown me how to keep you and your home safe until your return. Forgive me for placing you under the sleeping spell. If I was not able to wake you, then please hold tightly to whomever in our great family did.

The curse is in our bloodline. The crone didn't have to perish, nor do you. Our family has always held the curse and the key.

Forgive, Soryn and live.

With every bit of my love, Clarette

The book was just as I had remembered save for several pages of Clarette's drawings and instructions on how to break the curse. My heart leaped as I stared at Jaxson in disbelief.

"What does it say?" Jaxson's hopeful eyes bore into mine.

For the first time, I actually believed I might survive this. And as he looked at me, I realized that after centuries of guilt and sorrow, I wanted to. The frame clattered to the ground as I pulled him to me, relishing in the feeling that just maybe, this could all be real.

Chapter Forty-Two
BRITTANY

"So what happens if neither of them show up?" I said as I popped a battery in the last candelabra. The mantle was already overflowing with pumpkins and other Halloween decor, but it managed to just fit.

Jaxson tied off more decorations to the upstairs balcony before shouting down, "We know that Renard will be here. Nathanial has already confirmed it with his contacts." Soryn watched his every move as he leaned over the balcony and spoke, "He's not going to give you up that easily. I wouldn't either." He winked at her and a bright pink flush rose on her cheeks.

I arched a brow.

"Shut up." She puffed out.

"Who are you talking to?" I asked.

"Both of you, shut up." She was putting up a valiant effort to hide her smile. "Come on. Help me get the stuff from outside."

The vines and tall grass that had been cleared were starting to grow again, tickling my ankles as we walked toward the barn.

"We should see if the Tom's can come out and take care of all of this."

"Mm Hm." I could tell she was trying to avoid talking about what had happened between her and Jaxson. They had come out of Grandma Winnie's house with the book and looking more than a bit disheveled.

"Aren't you going to say anything?" She asked.

I kept silent and stared ahead toward the barn.

Her voice was loud as we entered the aging space. "There is nothing happening between Jaxson Harwell and I."

"If you say so."

She turned, full stop to glare at me with her hands on her hips. "I do say so."

"Okay."

"Okay?"

"Alright."

"Alright."

I grabbed a table that had been moved during the renovations while Soryn picked up the tools we needed and stormed ahead. We had made it half way back across the yard before I couldn't hold it back anymore.

"Hey, Soryn."

She paused but didn't turn. "What?"

"What was your favorite part about being a vampire?"

She glanced over her shoulder, her face pinched in thought, "I liked that people still feared me."

"Mm hm. I can see that." I waited, but she kept moving forward. "Don't you wanna know what mine is?"

She reached for the door. "Fine. What is your favorite part about being a vampire?"

In that moment, I donned a smile that could have put the Cheshire cat to shame. "I like being able to hear everything."

She shook her head and turned the knob before her eyes went wide and an even brighter flush coated her face and chest.

I whispered, "Everything." A raucous laugh tore through me as I walked around her, through the door, and face first into Clarette.

A yelp escaped my lips, but I managed to hold on to the table.

"Are you two alright?" A concerned Harwell was already several steps down the staircase by the time I refocused.

"Yeah." I gently placed the table on the ground before reaching for my friend, "She's here."

Clarette's face had transformed back into the beautiful but sad specter that had first greeted me on the night we changed.

Soryn's eyes sparkled as she spoke to her.

<hr />

Jaxson and I had moved around the house as quietly as possible, leaving Soryn to make her thank you's and goodbyes to the air. As she spoke, Clarette's blue hue had started to shift to a radiant yellow glow before she finally looked up at me and smiled. Her hand lingered on a long metal charm hanging from a chain around her neck. Her final look at me was full of purpose before she reached out to Soryn and disappeared into thin air.

Soryn's hand went to her cheek where Clarette had touched her. "She's gone." She looked at me. "Isn't she?"

I nodded, "But I think there is something she left behind."

<hr />

It had taken less time and effort than I had thought to retrieve it from the well. I couldn't take my eyes off of the slightly patinated necklace that hung at Soryn's chest. Another token from the well. Another note from Clarette. She had left crumbs everywhere in the hope that someone would find them and save Soryn.

"What is it?"

"It's something that I had made for her. She was never without it." Soryn opened the tube to reveal a thin pencil wrapped in paper.

"How is that not disintegrated?" I asked.

"I can only assume she placed some kind of protection on it, just as she did the book and my home." She smiled. "She was truly amazing." Familiar words were echoed on the small scroll.

The curse is in our bloodline. The crone didn't have to perish, nor do you. Our family has always held the curse and the key.

Forgive, Soryn and live.

The sound of car stereos began to thump in the distance.

"I miss regular carriages." Soryn said, staring out of the door as more costumed people pushed in passed her. The cars just kept coming. Piling around the long drive way, there would be little to no chance of the ones already here to leave for a long while unless it was on foot. Both of the front and back yards were full of what looked to be a good mixture of the university and surrounding town.

A group dressed like Spice Girls smiled and laughed as they teetered up the pathway to the house. Baby Spice gave me a hug, "Thank you so much for this!" Her words slurred slightly already, "I never thought you were into this kind of thing but here you are!" She said, obviously meaning it as a compliment and falling horribly short.

"Here I am."

She giggled. "And you're a vampire. So cute."

My body stilled for a moment before she pointed at my pointy teeth and costume.

"Oh, yeah. Well, enjoy the party."

The group chuckled to each other before entering the house.

Soryn glared after them. "You know, there is a very good chance that someone will die tonight. There is no harm in pushing fates hand." She shrugged giving an innocent face that suited her Evelyn costume well.

"That's not necessary."

"No. What's not necessary was their attitude — and your costume." She eyed me up and down, "Really, Brittany, you could have come up with something a bit less…"

"Obvious?"

"Yes. Also, you could have just used your own teeth."

I gave a wide smile around the pearly white fake fangs.

"Fine." We made our way inside as she let out a loud groan.

"I thought you threw parties all the time back in your day."

"Yes. I threw parties. This is not a party." She circled her hands around, "This is a frantic pit of chaos." She pointed to me, "You should talk to the 'A-owl' about who they send your messages to." She huffed and pushed aside a group of guys mixing drinks in the kitchen. She pinched her nose, "I don't think these have showered in a fortnight." Several of them laughed loudly before moving deeper into the party with cups in hand.

I couldn't help but laugh. "AOL, not A-owl. And, I definitely didn't message all of these people." I looked around the party recognizing many faces but only a handful of the ones that I had actually invited.

Several brightly colored papers had been tossed in the trashcan. I handed the crumpled paper to Soryn, "Someone made party fliers."

Another rush of people came pouring in. The doors to the house stood wide open as laughter filtered in from both the front and backyards.

She crumpled the paper again and tossed it into the surging crowd. "In that case, I am sure Keith has learned about our celebration."

I nodded as a foreboding feeling curled in my chest. Using a big crowd was a sure-fire way to lure him in, but this felt excessive — and dangerous.

My eyes scanned the throng of bodies for the millionth time. An itching grew in my fangs. The hunger I had been able to almost master in the past few months was starting to claw at me. Hopefully, he made himself known sooner rather than later.

Soryn whispered. Even then, it was hard to hear her over the fog of voices and music that circled the large space. The sound of drinks being downed and refilled made my throat ache.

"I need to go outside." I said. She nodded reading the look on my face.

Despite the open sky, the backyard was a buffet of smells and beating hearts. None of which were the one beating heart that I needed to hear the most. My eyes burned as I searched the unmasked faces wandering in the back yard for his.

"We'll find him. Keith wouldn't kill him yet. He still needs him."

I nodded as a conversation piqued my interest between songs.

"You promised me." I knew that croaking voice anywhere.

I leaned into Soryn, "He's here."

I lost the voice as the music began to thrum through the open air again and the people bobbing back and forth around the yard shouted to be heard. But there was no denying he was here.

"I'll go tell Jaxson." She squeezed my arm, "Be careful."

I hugged her and ran. The voice sounded like it had come from somewhere behind the barn, so I went in the opposite direction.

The voices and smells of the party quickly faded behind me as I bobbed and weaved between the trees. I wasn't sure where I was headed yet, but I was running like hell to get there.

The white washed bricks of town square blurred into view as I clipped another tree. I stopped and waited. Keith wouldn't be stupid enough to bring both the book and Ben to the party. We knew that. He was somewhere hidden from me. As I waited for the person I trusted most in this world to confront the ghoul, I could only hope that somewhere in the town of Sedgemoore, Ben's heart still beat.

It felt like an eternity had passed when something flashed at my side. The tree I had hit blocked any clear view but the burst of leaves and shaking of branches meant one thing. When it happened three more times, I knew. I looked back toward the way I had come as the smell of a storm rushed past me.

The little black square in my pocket felt heavy as I pulled it out. The pager that was supposed to give me directions to where Keith was hiding Ben. Instead, I used it to send a warning to my friends. My heart broke as I thought of him somewhere all alone and beaten.

I whispered an apology into the night air as another burst of wind tore through the trees several yards to my right. There was a war headed straight for Soryn and I was half a town away waiting for information that would no longer be coming.

"I'm sorry, Ben. Please hold on a little longer."

Chapter Forty-Three
SORYN

"He's here." I said, shutting the door to the upstairs bedroom behind me.

"That was fast." Jaxson's Rick O'Connell costume suited him well, most of the items coming from his own wardrobe. "And Brittany?"

"She's ready and waiting."

He brushed his hand along my cheek, "Are you ready?"

I stared at the over sized book in my hands. The weight of it so much heavier than any other tome. Every death that should have fell upon me flashed in my mind. I thought of Renard, who at this very moment, was readying himself to share my curse for all eternity. A smile pulled at my lips at the thought of his face when he found out that after decades of making a fool out of me, I would return in kind.

"In centuries of being a vampire, I have never been more ready to revel in the site of blood."

He pulled at the tan leather straps that curled around his back — the costume perfectly hiding his hunter gear in plain sight. "Let's go save Ben."

The party downstairs was raucous. Jaxson hung his head with a forced half smile as several students from the university shouted their hellos and insisted on him doing something called keg stand.

"College parties are weird." I smiled.

"Weirder than tracking down a ghoul, destroying an evil psychopath and helping my girlfriend do a Freaky Friday swap with her super great grand niece?"

"I'm not your girlfriend." I eyed him.

He smiled, the brightness of it adding a glint to his eyes. "Of course not." He leaned down to get closer.

I stepped away, "Renard might be here."

His face went serious again. "You're right. Sorry."

Ghosts, reapers, and pop stars bounced about the room with a trance like mirth as the music and voices continued to swell. A large body in one of the many white ghost masks bumped into me, spilling the contents of his red cup all over my shirt, the red drink reeked of strong liquor and stained the white material.

He laughed as he pawed at the spilled drink, feigning an attempt to wipe it away. "Oh, my bad. It's just," His eyes trailed over me. "white shirts, you know.

Jaxson surged forward before I threw out an arm to hold him back.

I chewed on my lip as I leaned forward, going on my toes to make sure I was close enough for him to hear me. "If you lay your hands on anyone else here tonight, I will personally make it my mission to see that you know exactly what it feels like to have an animal claw at your flesh." I leaned in close enough to hear as his breath hitched behind his mask. "And even as you scream, they will not stop until every last bit of you has been devoured."

He froze as I pulled the mask from his face and shoved it at his chest. "Enjoy the party."

He still hadn't moved as we continued our journey to the yard.

A sea of red cups and costumes flooded the space. "We need to hurry and find Keith."

"You found me."

I spun to where the voice had hissed in my ear. Although there were more bodies than I could count, none seemed to be the source of the voice. We continued to push through toward the barn where several large vessels had been set up to dispense even more drinks.

"Getting closer." The voice hissed again.

"Where did all of these people even come from?" My annoyance was bubbling over into anger as a group of girls began singing at the top of their lungs on the far side of the yard.

"Step into my office." Keith's death rattle slipped into my ear again sending a shiver of nausea through me. The barn loomed just ahead of us, and we cautiously stepped inside.

"Didn't you like my fliers?" Deep in the dark corner of the barn, something shuffled toward us.

"I was not aware that you were invited?" I scoffed at Keith. Or what was left of him? His skin was an even sicklier shade of pond sludge.

Rotting blood trickled through his teeth as he spoke, "Oh really, Soryn. Like you didn't set up this big surprise party just for me. Whatever."

Jaxson moved beside me.

Keith tossed him a smug look. "You know, you really should be careful who you trust."

His dead, bloodshot eyes slowly trailed back to me, "Your precious little professor isn't really as innocent in all this as you think."

My hands fluttered about my chest. "What ever could you mean?"

Keith smiled, "He's not even a professor."

Jaxson glared at Keith, shaking his head, "No, you can't believe him, Soryn. He's a liar."

He nudged me in the shoulder, "He's probably just trying to get back at me for failing him."

"I deserved an A on that...." He took a rattling breath, "That's not what I'm talking about. He's a hunter."

"Okay, I'm not against hunting. Everyone needs a hobby." I shrugged, taking pleasure in the vein that was throbbing at the sallow skin of his temple. "Maybe after we help you get over all of this," I waved my hands toward him, "the two of you could go hunting together."

He struggled for a moment to calm his erratic breathing. "He's a vampire hunter you stupid..."

"Watch your next words." I hissed, "If you want our help, you're going to have to play nice."

"Like you played nice with me?"

"This suffering was of your own making. We didn't make you help Renard. We didn't make you take Brittany's blood. And the whole killing you and tossing you down the well thing, well, that was completely because of your lack of manners, which I don't know your upbringing so I won't bring your parents into this, but, you probably could have been raised better." I shrugged, "But, hey, what do I know." I gave a coy smile as more of the inky substance poured from his gaping mouth.

Jaxson began to search around the space as I went on. "Look. We all want something. You want to be a real boy again and we want Ben back."

He snarled before pulling the book from beneath his shirt and tossing it at my feet. "If you even think of trying something, I'll know. I'm not stupid."

"Questionable, but alright."

He snarled again. "You think you're so much better than me, don't you? Like I'm beneath you because you think you're so hot."

I picked up the book and brushed over the hand etched cover. The necklace resting under my shirt seemed to warm on my skin as I hugged the book to my chest. A beautiful forgery.

Jaxson stayed silent as he continued to case the barn, Keith not sparing him a glance. His hatred was focused entirely on me. "Well, we can't all be as handsome as you."

He smiled a wicked smile, "Well, if you like the way I look then you're in luck."

"What is that supposed to mean?"

"Where's my girl?" Keith asked.

"Inside waiting for us. Where is Ben?"

"You know if we're going to make this work we really can't lie to each other." He picked at the skin falling away from his nails, "Alright. Fine. I'll tell you where Ben is once you've worked your magic and given me the book back."

"We need the book, though."

"So does my new friend." He glared, "You should be grateful. He's doing all of this for you. Although, why he wants to impress you so bad is totally beyond me." He scoffed and more black speckles fell on his dingy green chest. He turned to Jaxson before moving at lightening speed, closing his hand around his throat and holding him aloft against a beam. The whole barn seemed to shake as several layers of dust rained down from the rafters. "Love. Am I right?"

"Alright! Let him go. I'll help you, I promise I'll help you." The small tube of blood Brittany had given was cold in my hand as I pulled it from my pocket and flipped pages in the empty book. An old Romanian lullaby fell from my lips as I whispered it to the blood before handing it to Keith along with the book.

He downed it greedily before tossing the empty vessel aside. He closed his eyes as a shiver ran through his whole body. The skin on his chest began to lose its green hue as he locked eyes with me, the bloodshot in them barely visible though the color had yet to return.

"Are you happy now?"

He smiled before moving toward the open barn doors.

"Wait! Aren't you going to tell us where you have been keeping Ben?"

He smiled. "You think I'd come to a party without my wingman?" He nodded toward several bales of rotting hay piled in a back corner. "By the way, you had better hope Brittany didn't get too far." He smiled, "Just in case Ben needs the same treatment." He laughed, the crackle in his voice still present but fading, "It would be a shame if he died and you didn't have your little book."

He was gone before we began casting handfuls of rotting hay aside. A beep beep sounded. Jaxson pulled the little black pager from his pocket, squinting to make out the little writing box in the darkness.

My heart dipped in horror as my fingers closed around an icy cold hand. "Ben!"

There was no movement as I continued to uncover him. His exposed chest was covered in cuts and bruises. His head flopped as I took hold of his shoulders and shook him. Brittany's name barely above a whisper, fell from his cracked and broken lips.

I hugged his neck, "You're alive." When I pulled away, I could see where the color had begun to fade from his eyes, his skin taking on a sickly hue.

"No—no—no. Ben. Did he make you drink his blood?" I twisted his body back and forth looking for a bite mark that I was certain wouldn't be there.

He nodded before breathing out, his body going lax again in my arms.

"We need to cover him back up." Jaxson's voice held an urgency as he began to push the pile back over him.

"Stop it!" I put my ear to his face and a weak stream of air cooled my cheek. "He's still alive. Tell Brittany to come back and she can get him to safety."

He pulled me up before pushing frantically on the pager sending out another flow of beeps. "Soryn, listen." He tucked the device back in his pocket before resting his hands on either side of my face, the panic in his own sending my heartbeat racing. "Brittany is already on her way here." He held my hand as we ran to the barn doors. "But we need to leave, now."

Jaxson surveyed the party with a focused tilt to his chin. His hand curled around my hip to pull me in closer as his other hand rested on the weapon at his holster.

It was as if a cloud had descended around the space. The loud conversations and boisterous music had all but faded as every last soul stood in frozen apprehension.

"Hello darling." Renard's voice was calm as it moved like a breeze through the still bodies. "Are you ready now?" He held out his hand as Jaxson held me tighter.

"What did you do?" I asked, looking out at all the people we had lured here with false promises of revelry.

"They aren't hurt. Nor will any harm come to them." He moved through the crowd with confidence, eyes locked on mine with devilish charm. He turned to Keith who was still salivating over his slowly renewing appearance. "The book."

Keith beamed and handed over the fake book and Renard flipped it in his hands before reaching out again. "Let's find somewhere a bit more quiet to start our eternity."

I leaned further into Jaxson as he held tighter to me. Renard laughed.

"Soryn, you're human mind is playing with you. You do not have feelings for this mortal. I have stood by you through the passages of time. We can put things right." He held out his hand. "You will be by my side for all time."

He moved with such speed it made my stomach turn and my head spin. The warmth of Jaxson's hand quickly faded as Renard ripped me from his arm. The leaves flew by with a rasping flutter that drowned out all other sounds, including Jaxson's frantic shouts for me. My legs and arms were tired from kicking and punching any bit of him that I could reach. My lungs ached from the barbs I called into the night air. The small clearing where we finally landed was covered in flowers and crumbling brick. Candle light flickered over the orange and brown leaves that had fallen over what had once been a small home.

"Renard, take me back right now."

"Why darling? So you can go back and pretend with that hunter?" He stalked closer, the candle light deepening the sharp lines of his face. "Why would you want something so fleeting when the two of us are so close to having forever?"

"No one should live forever, Renard." I held firm as he inched closer to tower over me.

"I know, my love," He stroked my cheek and his familiar smell brought memories of moonlit walks and fiery embraces. He had been my everything for so long, the thing that pulled me from my never ending battle with death and back into the world. How could all of that have been a lie? Did he really hold such hatred for me when his eyes lit up as they stared into mine? Had they held the same light when he looked into hers?

"Is that what you called her?"

"Who?"

"Your wife." I glared daggers at him.

His face fell as a dark shadow of hatred passed over it. The glint was back in his eyes as he rubbed my arms. The feel of his cold skin on mine sent the hair on the back of my neck on end. The candlelight flickered as the clouds above swallowed the moon.

"There is no one before you." He flashed his false smile at me as he lied again.

"I have tried to picture her so many times since I learned about her existence. Her beautiful face is young and swollen with tears at the thought of her new husband dying in battle. I've imagined the horror she must have felt to have him come back to her as something else. Was she frightened? Is that why you killed her?"

"My life before you was no life at all." He ground out.

"I am sorry, Renard. I am so very sorry that I left you there. My anger with death was so great that I thought denying her you when you were so close to her was just. But you can't escape from what you have done."

"I do not wish to escape." He walked away behind a low wall and reemerged with two glasses and a bottle of wine. "The pain that I caused before I came to you haunts me. I chose to be a monster before, but I choose a life with you now. I am perfectly content with the way things turned out." The glass clinked against the bottle as he poured the dark red wine. "It's your favorite. I had it brought from Italy for when you awoke. I've been saving it for two hundred years just for this moment."

My nose curled at the thought, "You realize that will taste worse than that merchant in Madrid."

He laughed. A sound that was rich with memories and warmed the spot that had held it for so long.

"We will make so many more beautiful memories. Just the two of us again. Exploring the world and turning it to our will."

"And Brittany? What happens to her?" I watched the red liquid swirl leaving a red smudge around the edge where it touched. "Will she be trapped as she is?"

"She will go back to as she was." Renard took a drink, "It's all here in the book."

My hand went to the chain that hung at my chest. "How did you figure it out?"

"The book. I was going to tell you the good news at the party that night but then you disappeared." He brushed his hand through my hair.

I gently plucked the book from his hand, flipping through the blank pages. "How did you read it though?"

The corners of his mouth pulled down in sorrow. "Clarette and I worked so hard to make things perfect for you. Poor thing was so frightened when the hunters trapped you. She was grief stricken when she realized they had tricked her into harming you. I never saw her again after that night."

My feet moved toward him instinctively, years of being together left an aching in my heart. "Why didn't you tell me that both of you were trying to break my curse?"

He leaned in and brushed his fingers along my arm sending a chill through me, "You have suffered for someone else's wrong doing for centuries. The last thing I wanted to do was hurt you more by giving you hope and then dashing it away."

The glass had begun to feel awkward in my hand as I stood there. The smell was dark and woodsy as I brought the wine to my lips and took a hesitant sip. It was delicious but not like what I remembered.

"Do you like it?"

"It's much better than I would have expected." The air in the clearing felt heavy as the candle lights flickered.

"Are you going to try it?"

He tipped his glass up and smelled it, "I have nothing to mix with it. Yet." He gave a shy smile, so unlike the confident man I had loved. His eyes held on to the moons glow as he stared into my eyes. Without a second thought, I held my hand out offering him what he needed to join me.

He smiled as he flicked the ring on his left thumb over my wrist. The little blade concealed in the band was still sharp as the day I had bought it for him. Warm blood trickled into his glass and down my hand.

"Do you remember when I gave you that?"

He downed the glass quickly. "How could I possibly forget?"

"Hmmm." My whole body felt like I was standing in a large vat of warm honey. A melody that I never thought I would hear again played on the wind as the smell of vanilla and cedar wood swirled in the air. The light from the rosy moon played off of the wine glass as Renard plucked it from my hand.

"Alright, my darling. It's time."

The book made a satisfying thud as I tossed it to the ground. "Can you hear the music?" I took his hands and wrapped them around my waist. My feet moved back and forth in a hazy daze.

"My love, we need to…"

"Varushka and I used to dance to this song."

Renard sighed as he continued to dance, spinning me around the crumbling walls where someone had once lived. He smiled before dipping and pulling me back slowly. "You know, I quite like you like this." He glanced up before setting me back to my feet and placing the book back in my hands. "Now. Let's get started on forever, shall we?"

Voices yelled from a distance, the voices sounded like waving fog horns far out at sea. The pages of the book fluttered back and forth in the growing breeze. I traced the lines on the cover with my finger, drops of red from my still bleeding wrist smudged and blended with the dark brown material. "She was just so talented."

"Who darling?"

"My Clarette."

"She truly was. I just wish she could have seen you so happy. You don't have to be alone anymore, Soryn. I'm all that you will ever need."

It felt as though something was scratching at a dark corner in my mind.

"I don't need you." The fog in my brain was still turning in a dense gossamer glow.

"Of course you do, love." He took the bottle of wine and tipped it up to my lips, the sharp earthy liquid left a warm sensation radiating through me as I smiled at him. He leaned closer, his breath on my ear as he whispered, "Finally the moon has realized her folly and hidden herself away so that you can shine."

A flicker of something pulled at my mind before Renard's lips met mine. I drank him in, like so many nights before. He was my life, my love. And we would spend eternity together. I would never be alone again.

Chapter Forty-Four
BRITTANY

A barrage of screams crashed into me like a wall of sound as I broke free of the tree line. The cars were packed like sardine cans as people bunched up inside, doors holding shut but only a few engines running. The ones that's lights were on were stuck like the rest, unable to budge from the tightly blocked drive way. I held my place behind a large tree trunk and took in the scene in front of me. Several men and women stalked around the closed vehicles, a menacing hunger rolling off of them as they peered in the closed windows.

An earsplitting cascade of shrieks came from a red roll-top convertible. The Spice Girls were being jostled around inside by a large vamp. His arms bulged as he shook the car like a vending machine that had taken his money and his snacks. More screams came from inside. At least for now, the vampires in the driveway seemed content with teasing their dinner.

My movements were light as I maneuvered around the fence and into the back yard. A dark black robed body lay crumpled on the ground, its limbs twisted at strange angles like it had been tossed from a height. My eyes went straight for the roof line of the house to confirm what I had already suspected. Several vampires were perched there like a pack of beautiful but deadly gargoyles. Screams rang out from inside the house. It seemed that everyone who didn't drink their meals was either laying still in the yard or trapped inside. The baristas from the cafe were here as well, the shrieks from inside the house grew to a terrifying pitch as they tapped with long nails on the windows.

A loud grunt came from the direction of the barn and I slowly crept as far away from the house as I could. A branch snapped beneath my foot as I finally made it within running distance of the barn. I stilled. My body froze as I squatted down beside an old oak. I had never won at hide and go seek as a kid. No matter where I hid, my friends would always find me. I remembered the feeling of my heart racing and the blood rushing in my ears as I tucked myself away in a closet or under a bush. There was nothing but silence where I sat hunched in the woods.

Until there wasn't. Footsteps began to hit my ears like alarm bells.

I took a small slice of hope in the fact that my heart wasn't pounding in panic for them to hear. My mind seemed to clear in an instant. I stared at my hands before looking down toward where my heart rested in my chest. My unbreakable hands. My unstakable heart.

"No!"

My fingers curled around the branch that had given me away. The broken middle now a jagged bunch of wooden spikes. The footsteps coming toward me were joined by wicked laughter as I stepped out of the protection of the trees.

"Brittany." The tall thin framed woman that stalked toward me held a malice in her eyes that on any other day would have sent me into hiding. Today was not any other day.

"Mr. Dorsetty said that you would be here soon. He wanted us to make sure you felt right at home." The grass crunched as she paced in front of me like a cat about to pounce.

The bark scratched at my skin as I held it tighter.

"You see, I just have one little problem with that." I said as a courage that I had never felt before built like a tidal wave within me.

Laughter echoed behind her followed by three sharp thuds as the baristas surged forward from their place of torment. The sound of screaming inside the house had silenced. All eyes were on me.

"And what might your little problem be exactly?"

"This is my home, and you weren't invited!" My hand shot out as the jagged branch flew through the air. Time seemed to slow as it barreled toward her. My heart swelled. I was doing it. I was going to fight to save everyone that I loved and these undead creeps weren't about to stand in my way. My mood quickly dimmed as the branch soared right passed her head and embedded itself into the barn wall.

Everything was quiet as I stared eye to eye with the vamp I had just failed to stake. My feet shuffled back and forth, "That was just a warning shot." I lied, surprised that any trace of bravado clung to my words. "So if you and your friends know what's good for you, you'll leave right now."

It was as if the night was holding its breath; waiting for whoever would make the first move. Laughter erupted from the vamps eliciting more screams from the people inside the house. I moved quick, the laugh barreling out of the woman in front of me in a forceful grunt as I slammed into her small frame. Her body slid across the ground as I clung to her shoulders. finally stopping its momentum just before the already broken well. She struggled to get up as I slammed my fists into any area of her that I could reach. A crunching sound filled the air as I felt her chest cave in under my fist. Her eyes were wide as she gasped over and over again like a hooked fish. A visceral moan flooded from her mouth as I jammed a piece of the broken well into her already bloodied chest before shoving her over. The stones that had been wedged together were knocked loose from her dead weight and sent up a rancid cloud of debris and putrid air.

"Who's next?" This time my voice did shake.

The three girls from the cafe charged at me. Their sharp nails sliced into the skin at my neck and chest. Stars popped in my vision before the world came in to focus again. The stars were shining above and the red moon seemed to pulse as I slowly sat up from the ground. A flurry of gasps and whispers rang out. I bolted forward, grabbing an old rusted pitchfork and breaking it over my knee. The metal prongs made a satisfying whoosh before they hit their mark. My feet pounded on the ground as I ran forward, stabbing another vamp in the shoulder with the broken pole before pouncing on another. My fingers dug into skin as I yanked at the frosted tipped hair of a large guy, a chunk coming away as he launched me in the air and through a window.

Another round of shrieks went out as I rolled to a stop, glass shards cutting deep into my side. A sickening squelch made me flinch away as I pulled a piece out and dropped it to the floor. Rage filled my soul as I marched toward the kitchen, the petrified party goers parting as I stormed through. My hands shook as I opened the fridge, pulled forward the case of untouched nonalcoholic beer, and grabbed a pack of blood that I had nestled in between the cans. Dark menacing eyes peered in through every window as I ripped the plastic with my fangs, the cold blood soothing my wounds and strengthening me as it oozed its way through my broken body. A surge of energy pulsed out just before I let out a satisfied sigh and burst back out the window and straight into another burly looking vamp. Limbs flew as several of them descended on me. A sharp pain shot through my chest as I looked down to see a wooden stake, the sharp point coming through the space where my heart was. Bloody tears ran from my eyes as I ran backwards, pulling the large vamp with me until my body slammed against the side of the house and he slammed into me. He fell to the ground with a thump, the stake now firmly stuck in his own chest.

The screams from the house had turned to a strange battle chant as everyone inside began to cheer for me. I couldn't help but wonder if this was what it felt like fighting in the coliseum. The biggest difference being, it was easy to fight when you knew you couldn't be killed. Though, getting stabbed was no less painful. The cheers continued as I fought my way through two more vamps. By the time I could slow, I had lost count of how many times a normal vamp would have died. I was truly unstoppable.

"Brittany!" Keith stood at the entrance to the barn with a beaten and bloodied Ben at his feet. I rushed him, "Ah ah ah." He held a long knife to the top of his head, "Wouldn't it be a shame if you got the reputation for turning all of your boyfriends into undead freaks?"

"What have you done?"

He knelt down to grip Ben's chin in his hand. "We've just been having some fun — talking about honeys; downing some blood. You wouldn't understand. It's bro stuff."

"No. You can't do that to him." A panic clutched at my torn and bloodied chest. "Please don't kill him. Please. I'll do whatever you want just don't."

He barred his teeth with every word, the anger he felt leeching into every syllable he spoke. "You wanted me so bad, before, Brittany. You were so pathetic about it. You know how much Dorsetty had to pay me to act like I could stand to be around you?

All to get you into that stupid basement. I should have known then, but I thought, you know its good money. But when I found out what you really were, what I could be." He squeezed Ben's face before tossing his head hard to the ground. A muffled shout came from the barn.

"Now that this is what it should be," He presented his body like it was some kind of prize, "I'm really going to enjoy myself."

"So why don't you just give me Ben and go. You're better. Soryn made sure of it." I lied, "No reason to stick around."

"I suffered more than anyone has ever had to. That pain doesn't just go away." His rage was building again. "Everyone forgot about me. They just went on like nothing happened." He had begun to pace, "Oh but when Ashlie died, oh that was something. Everyone was so heartbroken."

"Stop it."

"I will. Once everyone understands what I had to go through. That's when I'll stop." He brought the knife down and into Ben's chest. A bloom of red coated his skin where the knife had pierced.

The world seemed to slow as I ran to him, pulling him into my arms as a puddle of blood collected on his chest before spilling over on to the ground. "Ben. Ben!" I shook him as his eyes opened, a haze beginning to overtake them.

"Ben. You have to tell me what to do." My whole body shook as I held his face, pleading for some kind of answer from him. "If I leave you like this — If you die before I bite you, you're going to be like him. There's no way back from that."

"What are you talking about?" Keith smiled as he looked down on his handy work.

"You stupid, arrogant prick! There is no cure for you. You stole what wasn't meant for you and you're being cursed for it. Soryn gave you some of my blood but once you use it up, that's it. You go right back to being as disgusting on the outside as you are on the inside." My voice came out dangerously low as I held Ben,

"Do you really think we would help you after everything that you have done? Keep rotting in hell, Keith."

Ben's hand rose to my face, and despite the blood trickling from the corners of his mouth, he smiled, "That's my girl." He tried to nod but the effort of it caused another tremor to shake his body. "Do it."

I didn't hesitate. Keith's angry scream blurred into the background as my fangs sunk into the skin on Ben's neck. His heart began slow to a stop until he stilled completely, the hand that had brushed my face fell lifeless to the cold ground.

When I looked up, Keith was gone.

I had barely made it onto the dirt and hay covered floor inside the barn when a wave of screams came again. This time, it came with the shattering of glass and the splitting of wood. The vampires were done with their game of taunting their prey. Whatever reason they had had to stay out was gone and with each new victim claimed, another patch of crimson dripped from their deadly fangs. I propped Ben under the window. His body was ice cold, his breathing still painfully absent. This was how it was supposed to work but to my eyes, he was dead. Completely.

"Ah-yiddle-hap-leez." Jaxson's hands were bound and hooked over a bolt in the wall. Several of the rotted boards by his legs were split and crumbling where he had kicked at them. Given another hour or so, he might have taken the wall down. I plucked him down and removed the bit of fabric tied around his mouth. His teeth dug into the ropes at his hands quickly undoing the knots.

"The Order is coming. I have to warn them."

"I can help."

"You have to help Soryn." He pulled the book and another small vile of blood from its hiding place at his back and placed them gently into my shaking hands. "Renard took her. Do whatever it takes, but please…" His voice cracked, "Please don't leave her trapped with him."

He hugged my shoulders.

"Good luck, Brittany." A deep sorrow strangled his words, but before I could offer any words of hope, Jaxson was gone.

The blood-red moon was at its highest point in the darkened sky as I settled myself near Ben.

Chapter Forty-Five
SORYN

The blood Renard had smeared across the open book had already started seeping into the pages behind it. I could feel my face fall as I stared at its ruined center. "Why would you do that?"

He hooked my chin with his finger, "It's time." He kept a tight grip on one half of the book, "Say the spell to take the curse back and when the curse touches your blood,– the blood you have just shared with me–I will change with it."

I chuckled in his face, "But you," I booped his nose, "are already a vampire, sir."

He gave a terse grin, "Yes, but when your Brittany took on the curse willingly, it fulfilled part of the spell. Your own blood has forgiven you. Now," he kissed my forehead and leaned in, his breath tickling my neck as he spoke, "you are free to join the one you love for eternity. All you have to do, is say the spell and we will be forever linked."

"You're funny, Jax…." My head spun, "Um, no." Confusion swept through me as a trickle of heat began to radiate from my heart. The blood moon was high among the stars.

Renard kissed me. I took a shaky step back, confusion plastered on my warming face, "Do you really love me?"

"It cuts my heart open to hear you ask that. I have done everything for you. I have stayed here, I have made this place somewhere where we could call home. I've watched over your family. Knowing all that, how could you question my love."

"It's just…"

"What more do I have to sacrifice to be worthy of you, Soryn?"

The moon darkened above me as a lovely familiar voice whispered to me through the wind. Her words lit a fire in my soul — a burning flame that I couldn't extinguish as the heat that had started in my chest continued to spread. The fog I had felt since I had drank the wine was fading. My blood called to me. It was time.

I touched his cheek and smiled.

"When love you find within the blood; Your mortal twine to them be severed. Absolve err from wicked bud; Join in eternity the clock untethered."

The world shifted around me as my knees gave way. The sounds and smells of the forest crashed into my senses as I struggled to take control. The burning that had only moments ago burst out of me, now crept back beneath my skin where it was quickly suffocated by an icy blanket of darkness. A sorrowful pang lurched in my gut as my tongue traced over the fangs that had been absent for months. The mortal part of me was gone. My arms tensed with rage and my jaw clenched as I stared down Renard. Whatever elixir or herb he had laced in my wine was gone as well.

I glared down at the empty glass he had taken from me, "How dare you?"

"How dare I?" His laugh was wicked as he began to circle me.

"You created me, Soryn. I've only used what you taught me over the centuries. You took a dying man and turned him into a monster."

"I was only trying to save you."

"You were only trying to save yourself!" The anger in his words shook the air around him. "Do you have any idea what its like to go to your wife who is supposed to honor and obey you and have her deny you entrance into your own home!" He smiled as he looked passed me, "My feet may not have been able to pass the threshold, but the blade I threw at her willful throat did."

"I'm going to rip you apart," I growled.

"To this day I regret that I didn't get to taste her blood, but I took great pleasure in tasting every woman that reminded me of you."

Renard didn't budge as I stalked toward him.

"And now, nothing is going to stop me from making sure that everyone you care about, chokes on their own blood. Starting with your Brittany."

A rustling in the leaves marked someones quick approach.

"Like you hurt Clarette." It wasn't a question anymore.

"She served her purpose just as The Order served theirs. Unfortunately, she was clever. Obviously not an inherited trait. When I threw her in your favorite well, I had no idea she had the book with her." He held it up in triumph. "Well, it all worked out though, didn't it." He glared at me, the full range of his hatred pouring from his evil eyes. "And now, I think it would be best if you took another long nap, my pet."

"No."

Whoever was approaching was going far too fast to be anyone coming to my aide. Brittany would be mortal now. Somewhere back at the house, she had opened the actual book, used our combined blood, and said the spell. A tightness wound through my

366

chest and I found myself missing the feel of needing to take a deep breath to calm it. I willed the chaos in my mind to still. This was for the best. The stake tucked into my skirt felt at home in my hand as I plucked it out and twirled it. I glared at the man that brought me to this point. "I think it's time to make amends for the pain you have caused."

His chest puffed out as I came closer while a smug look of defiance and victory was painted across his sharp features. "You can stake me all you want. We are in this together now. Do you truly think that you have no blame in all of this?"

I ignored his taunts and continued forward slowly. His pride kept him in place. "Oh, there is certainly blame to share." I pouted my lips at him, "Once upon a time, I robbed some poor worms their dinner. I think it's time I rectified that."

My legs pushed off the ground hard as I lunged forward, the nails I dug into his chest wiping the smug smile from his malicious face. His back hit the ground hard as I delved deeper, the sound of it like a spike driving through stone. The sound grated at my ears almost as much as his pained voice did.

"Soryn, please."

The tips of my nails punctured the edges of his heart. "Beg all you want, but you lost all hope of mercy the moment that you decided the rest of the world was beneath you." I leaned in closer, burying my claws further still. The pained groan he let out mixed with the sound of wind rushing through the trees. "You do not get to take pleasure in so much pain and then ask for absolution when death calls."

"You can't kill me." He let out a guttural yell before throwing me through the air. The stake was still gripped firmly in my clean hand as the other dripped with blood. He grabbed at his chest, his face contorted with malice. The smell of blood and dirt wafted through the air. Eyes on my prey, I dusted off the bits of rocks that dug into my hard skin before standing.

"Why are you pretending to be the hero? You have done more harm than most."

"I am no ones hero. There is no such thing. There are villains and there are those who have learned to take on the burden of their wickedness. I have vowed to keep mine from this world from now on."

"The world would have been better without you in it."

"I don't believe that anymore. For you however, I have my doubts."

"Are you going to put me to sleep?" He taunted, a smile pulling at his lips though rage still swirled in his eyes.

"You know, Clarette really meant for you to have this sooner." I tossed the book at his feet. "She is the reason you wanted me out of the house. Isn't she? You had us arrested because you saw Clarette and you knew you couldn't control me if I knew what you had done to her."

"I would love to stay and chat about how truly clever I am, but I think its best if we part ways until you have calmed down. It does no one good to give in to hysterics." He knelt, chest still dripping blood, to pick up the book.

"Even if that book were real, your plan never would have worked." I couldn't help but bounce a little at the confusion on his face as he unintentionally knelt before me. "You see, for you to share my curse, you would have to actually love me."

"Clarette told me all about the spell before she turned on me. She said you only had to love me. You were so desperate for anyone to accept you, that you believed me when I said I cared for you. "

"But that's the thing— once you know what real love feels like, you can't be fooled by a cheap knock off."

"What..."

That was the only word he had time to utter as I flung myself at him again and plunged the stake through his heart. He sputtered and clawed at the wooden weapon as I buried it even deeper into his chest. His eyes dripped blood as he laid spread out on the cold hard dirt.

"Oh, really, Renard." I stood, placing my foot on the end of the stake. "There's so need for hysterics." I pushed down, twisting my heel until all signs of life faded from his shriveled skin and he transformed into a pile of unrecognizable bone and muck.

"Mr. Dorsetty! You have to come back to the house. It's turning into a bloodbath." Keith burst through the trees, gouging divots in the earth as he came to an abrupt halt.

My pearly white fangs brushed against my lips. The smells of fighting, blood, and fear clung to him. "And you're just in time for another."

He shot one quick glance to the worm food at my feet before taking his leave back the way he came. "Oh, Keith." I knew my sing song call would make it to his ears and I counted to ten before I gave chase.

Chapter Forty-Six

BRITTANY

The cold was the first thing I noticed. It seeped into my skin and left my teeth chattering as I clung to Ben. Jaxson had gone long before I did the spell. I could no longer smell the blood that was being spilled just yards away from us as we stayed hidden. The window above us was too big of a risk so I stuck to squinting through a crack between two aging boards as bodies were pulled from the house one by one. Each as unmoving as the last.

"That's the last one!" One of the vamps yelled at the others. "Gregory, stay with the others until they come to." I could hear the sadistic glee in his voice, "They're gonna be hungry."

"You would think that with a party full of college kids, there would be more of them."

"Yeah. Any idea where the ghoul is."

"He ran off to cry to Dorsetty."

Another body dropped to the ground beside them. The backyard looked like a morbid sacrifice of scantily clad pop stars and slasher monsters. The cause of death more obvious on some than others but each sharing one specific wound. Two bloodied bite marks. The cries from those left in the house were deafening. They were calling for me. The victory chant that they had sung earlier was now a desperate plea.

"She already ran off and left you all here." The laughter continued, "She's long gone."

I was me again. Just me. I pulled Ben further into the shadows of the barn. Whatever little amount of stealth I may have had before was completely gone and I grunted out a pained breath while pulling him away from the window. A sob hitched in my chest as I realized the meaning of dead weight.

"I'm so sorry, Ben." I kissed his cold cheek before covering his body with a damp and musty smelling cloth. The cries for me continued as I walked across the dirt packed floor. I was mortal again, and I was probably going to die if this didn't work. Despite my fragile body, I held my head high as I left the dark safety of the barn.

I could hope that Ben would wake up. I could hope that Soryn was still out there somewhere. I could hope that Renard was dead. But hoping would only get you so far. And in that moment, I hoped that my one semester of theatre class in high school would take me far enough.

"Where did we leave off?" Heads whipped around to stare at me with wide eyes as I emerged from the barn. My hair was a jumble of matted locks and my dress had been ripped in several places leaving the cold wind to whip at my bare skin. The forced smirk on my face held firm as I readied myself for one of two scenarios; one, they still thought I was an unkillable enemy and ran like hell or two, they saw right through me and ripped me to shreds.

Several of them took shaky steps backwards as I slowly moved forward. Mostly because if I didn't move in some way, they would absolutely see how bad my body was shaking.

"Listen, we don't have any beef with you." A short man with baggy pants and a worn leather jacket dropped the woman that was dangling from his shoulder.

I swallowed the urge to throw up as her body flopped to the ground after rolling down the pile of other lifeless bodies. "Well, you've made an awful mess of my house and back yard so I do kind of have beef with you."

"Look, we're just doing what we were told."

"And now, I'm telling you to get out." The courage coursing through my veins was intoxicating as the look of fear locked on several hardened and pale faces. "Unless you want to end up like your friends over..." My foot slipped on an empty red cup. The view of the sky quickly replaced that of bodies and scared vamps. My heart pounded in my chest as the blood rushed in my ears. When I propped myself back up on my elbows, the bodies were the only part of that scene that were unchanged.

Instead, a herd of bloodthirsty vamps were inching toward me, licking fangs and clenching fists.

"I wouldn't if I were you. I've got powerful magic. Look what I did to your friends. To Keith!"

A strange buzzing sound began pouring out from the woods as they prowled forward.

"Not to ruin the fun, but she was an unstoppable killing machine not that long ago?" The voice came from one of the tall baristas. Now the only one since the other two were rotting somewhere in the yellow grass. "How do we know this isn't a trick or something?"

"That's right." I said, "Do you really want to risk it?" My butt ached as I pulled myself up and rubbed off the grass and dirt. I tried to snap finger guns at them, but a sticky goo coated my fingers where I had dusted my self off. The insides of the ghost face guy were spilling out onto the ground where I had had the misfortune to slip. My stomach tightened. Nope. This wasn't going to end well for me. My body convulsed as I vomited.

Somewhere in the woods, the strange buzzing had turned into a creaky scream that barreled toward us.

"She killed Dorsetty!" Keith's words were drown out by another wave of nausea that ripped through my empty stomach. I wiped my mouth with the back of my hand. All eyes were on me.

"Her?" One of them grabbed the back of my dress and held me there.

"No you idiot!" Keith yelled out as something slammed into the roof of the house.

"Me." The voice was powerful. It was deadly. It was unmistakably Soryn.

I bounced on my toes, "Ooh, you guys are in trouble now." I bent my head back to fake whisper to the vamp holding me. "If you were hoping for a happy ending, this ain't it."

Sharp gusts of wind streaked through the night air. Soryn shot me a smile and a wink before darting after each of them. It sounded like someone was smashing boulders in the woods as she made quick work of tracking down each and every one of them. I could hear a distant scream trailed by Soryn's laughter. She may have been killing but at least she was having fun doing it.

Keith's cold hand clamped on my shoulder. My entire body froze as I sent out a silent plea for her. The smell that assaulted my nose as I was pulled back would have made me puke if I hadn't already emptied everything in my stomach just seconds before.

In an instant, Soryn was there. Standing in front of me with a screaming Keith in her clawed hand, though the cold grip on me still remained.

"Let her go. You don't really want to hurt her. I know you do not."

Something growled in my ear though not the monster I had thought. He was locked in Soryn's grip.

My breath hitched, "Ben?"

"You smell amazing." He said as he nuzzled into my neck.

"I gotta say, you've smelled better." My voice shook with fear.

Keith laughed out, "See Brittany. You destroy everything that you touch. You can go ahead and kill me but you're going to have to live with what you've done."

Ben growled again before turning me to face him. His features were sharp and his skin held a gray pallor. He still looked to be close to deaths door as he rattled out his words. "I'll pay you back, I promise." My heart shuddered as his beautiful blue eyes slowly hooked up and narrowed on Soryn.

"Ben?"

He smiled before he took off, barreling straight toward her. She held Keith out at arms length and Ben snatched him up without hesitation. His arms flew wildly before parts of his target were strewn about the ground like Kieth confetti. As he looked back to me, he smiled showing off two sharp fangs. He wasn't like Keith after all. I ran to him but stopped short as I eyed the bloody bits of gore that trailed down his bare chest.

"Thank you." He said.

I nodded as he moved closer.

"Let's continue this afterward." Soryn collected us behind her. In front of her, several of the bodies in the pile had begun to stir. She pointed to the house, "Get them out of there and away as fast as you can." She grabbed Ben's arm. "Not you. You just woke. Without blood, you are a danger to them."

"I've got this. You help Soryn." I ran. My feet pounded on the stairs as I took them two at a time. The screaming that had come from upstairs had been replaced by a deathly silence as I approached my bedroom door. A cold chill skittered up my back as I entered. Darkness and body odor blanketed the space where at least two dozen fright stricken people huddled on my bed and floor.

"Let's get you all out of here."

"What the hell is going on?" Several murmurs joined in questioning as I struggled to get the group moving. A shout came from outside, knocking a few of them from their stupor. "Did any of you have the punch?"

Eyes wandered and heads shook as I tried to think of a way to explain what they were seeing. "Yeah, well someone laced the punch, so yeah, we just need to get all of you out of here before..."

"Do we look like idiots to you?" Two boys dressed like the guys from Bio-Dome shut and blocked the door.

"Kinda, yeah." I said.

Another voice boomed from downstairs and the sound of more things breaking rang out. Without warning, the house began to shake. Shouts and screams filled the large bedroom as I darted to the window and ripped off the blackout curtains and cardboard. Down below, the pile of bodies had vanished. Only a large dark stain marked where they had been. Scratching rasped at my ears just before a face popped into view. A freshly turned vampire scratched at the window before giving it a long drawn out sniff. Her eyes popped back open along with a wide grin. And then, she was gone. A pained cry leaving her as she was pulled back to the ground.

Several men and women were on her in an instant. She thrashed and screamed for only a moment before the one with a leather weapons halter forced something into her mouth and she calmed. Jaxson tipped the brim of an invisible hat at me, his bright familiar face a welcome sight.

"Calvary's here!" He shouted before darting toward another group fighting in the far corner of the yard.

The door swung wide and Nathaniel stepped in. "Good to see you still kicking."

"What can I say. I'm a survivor." I smiled just before hands burst through the window and gripped on to my arm. The rush of cold air and adrenaline made my skin sting as I fell. Nathaniel's reaching hands brushed my foot a second too late to grab me. Cold fangs bit into my neck as the air swirled around my body. I bit back but the arm I was trying to gnaw on was hard. My teeth ached from the strain.

Bolts of electric pain shot up my spine as we collided with the ground below. Spots burst in my vision while a fog of voices descended. The heavy weight that had clung to my body and neck was abruptly pulled back and replaced by gentle hands and urgent whispers.

Nathaniel's voice hovered in the background, shouting orders as the noise of fighting died down. "No. Get her back with the others. She may still be able to be helped."

"If you don't end her now, I will!" A black sky was starting to cloud at the edge of my vision as Soryn knelt beside me.

I grabbed for her hand. "No. No, she didn't mean it."

Ben's voice came from my left, "I don't care. I want her dead."

Jaxson's voice came from somewhere above, "Can you take it out?"

"Take it out? Take what out?" My vision continued to wane as I strained to lift my head. It felt like a bowling ball as I stared down at metal prongs poking out of my stomach like three morbid birthday candles. "Oh."

I could just make out the red streaks that crept their way down Soryns' face in a blur. The world went silent. I was going to die here and maybe that's what I deserved, but she didn't deserve a lifetime of guilt for it. "This isn't on you." My chest felt cold as I went on, "You are the best friend I could have ever asked for."

"I made a promise. Please, please don't leave me yet." The tears she had always tried to hold back fell in earnest as she pleaded. "My darling girl. You are supposed to live. I was supposed to be able to save you."

"Then save yourself, Soryn. Please. I'm not afraid of forever anymore." My shaking hands reached for her but my body refused to move.

"Brittany." Ben's voice was a low plea. "What are you talking about?"

"*Our family has always held the curse and the key.* The crone that cursed Soryn, she was family." She didn't forgive herself for what she did to you, and she burned because of it."

"And what if Clarette was wrong?" Soryn's sobs shook my body, sending tiny bolts of pain through my middle. The numbness that had been creeping through me quickly returned.

Clarette's words echoed in my head. Forgive, Soryn and live.

Soryn took my hand in hers as I tried to speak, my words coming out in crackling breaths. "I forgive you, Soryn. You just have to let go and forgive yourself. I choose this. Do the spell again."

"We barely reversed the spell this time. I wont risk it again. What if she was wrong. You deserve a mortal life. You will be fine. We can get you to a doctor. You must be fine."

My eyes watered and strained to bring her into focus as the taste of blood rose in the back of my throat. "Do you trust Clarette?"

"Please." Her words were barely a whisper as blood ran from her eyes. "I can't do this to you."

"Your not doing anything to me." I tried to smile, "We're doing this for both of us." I looked for Jaxson but my vision had already darkened so much that only Soryn's face remained. "I want this, for both of us."

Unstake My Heart

Jaxson's voice fell over me in a frantic whisper, "Soryn, she's bleeding out fast."

"Soryn, please." Ben's voice cracked as he pleaded with her, "I—I—" whatever words he was trying to say were caught in his throat.

Someone placed the book in Soryn's hands, the brown blur fading and swirling with a deep red. Both our blood ran over the pages as we spoke and I did my best to repeat her words;

"Ichor of the dead, shadowed by time and veils unsung,
Give to me the breath of life, purchased by kindred tongue
Twist what has been stolen to carve away the heart,
Until the moon bleeds malice born, and curse is rent apart.

When love you find within the blood,
Your immortal twine to them be severed.
Absolve err from wicked bud,
Join in eternity the clock untethered.

By blood sealed and bargain struck."

A pitch black fog swallowed the world around us.

Chapter Forty-Seven
SORYN

"Brittany." My voice was sharp as it echoed through an eternity of darkness. I reached out to find her hands searching for mine. "Brittany. My darling girl, are you alright?"

Her eyes were wide as she stood and stared into mine.

"I mean, five seconds ago I was bleeding out on the ground and now I'm not so, I guess— yeah, I'm alright."

"Where are we?" The darkness seemed to swirl as we spoke and light began to pierce through the nothingness that surrounded us. Brittany clung to my hand tighter as a voice cut through the rest of the darkness, it's gentle waves casting a warm glow that radiated through the space with every syllable it uttered.

You are where the curse was forged.

A lush green forest on the edge of a field of golden flowers began to break through the last bit of haze. Leaves swirled through a breeze that didn't seem to touch my skin. And just where the light of the sun hit the darkness of the forest, two figures stood.

"Is that…" Brittany muttered.

"I think…"

Silence followed, except it wasn't silence. An eternity of voices flowed through my mind, each one told its story of the curse.

The two figures joined hands, their stance mirroring mine and Brittany's and thought their lips stayed unmoving, I knew that the voices I heard next were theirs.

Though blood held your curse, your forgiveness held your fate.
You have done what centuries of our great line could not.
Go now, Soryn, and live a mortal life.

Warm streaks ran down my face as something within my chest seemed to be set free. My heartbeat fluttered back to life and a beautifully painful breath filled my lungs.

"You're really crying, Soryn." Brittany raised her arm, the traces of blood that had marked my sadness were wiped away with the help of the mortal tears that could not be stopped.

She gazed down at her arm and smiled, the sight of it the most beautiful thing I had ever seen in my centuries of life. Mortal tears flowed from her eyes as well.

"The curse— it's broken."

Brittany smiled at my words, but only for a moment. The happiness on her face slowly faded along with the warm light of the meadow.

Whispers began to hum in my ears as her legs buckled from under her. Her warm smile was taken over by rivulets of blood that sputtered from her gasping mouth.

"Soryn?" Pain clung to her words and shattered every bit of my beating heart. "I love you."

"No, my sweet girl. No— no— no— Stop! That can't be all!" My words came out in frantic pleas as the light began to fade back to darkness. "You must save her! I take it back! I will take the curse again! Just please, save her!"

The world around us continued to fade back to darkness.

She has made her choice just as you have made yours.

"What does that mean? No. No! This is not good enough!" My broken rage barreled through the void as the world we left— the world where she was dying a mortal death came back into view. "Stop! Please, don't take her from me, too!" A deep breath caught in my throat as Jaxson replaced the darkness, his face a mask of fear as he reached for me. My mortal heart beat heavily in my chest.

She was still dying. There was no curse to turn her. No curse to bring her back. She had helped destroy the thing I hated more than any evil on this earth; the only thing that could have given her back a mortal life.

But that was not what my darling girl wanted.

Chapter Forty-Eight
BRITTANY

Tendrils of darkness suffocated the red moon as Soryn's face blurred in and out of sight.

She has made her choice just as you have made yours.

The words continued to circle in my head as deaths frigid grip trailed up my veins and toward my heart. I had made my choice, but my voice was gone.

Soryn's words were cracked with sorrow as she spoke, "I love you as well, my darling girl and I know now what you would choose." Her voice seemed to echo in the dark sky around me as she gently called out for Ben.

I could feel bodies shuffling around me, each touch like a thousand needles piercing my skin, before his voice whispered low in my ear, "Come back to me."

Something warm and wet hit my lips as a swirling pulsed through my throat. A white hot pain consumed my stomach as I was twisted and the metal prongs torn from my broken body.

Tears streamed from my eyes as I rolled my head to the side. Though my vision blurred in and out from the pain coursing through me, my eyes caught the sight of a small pile of embers that pulsed on the small patch of scorched earth beside me.

The book was gone. I had already forgiven Soryn a long time ago. And now, after five hundred years, she had done what none of our ancestors who had kept the curse alive had been able to; she had forgiven herself.

A searing pain lanced through my neck as an onyx veil suffocated the air around me. I breathed in the pain knowing when I opened my eyes again, it would be forever.

EPILOGUE
A lifetime later
BRITTANY

The town had changed so much over the decades. Sedgemoore had become a sanctuary for the supernatural and those who loved them. Our black SUV pulled into my old parking spot of At Day's End. We had sold it twenty years ago. The new owners were a sweet couple who kept most of the odd knick knacks. Soryn and I had spent so many nights here since then, laughing in a booth and talking about all the adventures Ben and I had gone on or Jaxson's and Soryn's home renovations. I stared at the sign that hung above the door. Sanguine Sprinkles and Swirl.

Ben opened my door and smiled down at me, "Have I told you lately how absolutely stunning you are?"

"Not since this morning."

My fingers wrapped around his as he pulled me to his chest. "You're stunning and I love you."

I smiled as his lips met mine. "I love you too, Benny Boy."

A tightness pulled at my chest as a sad smile crept across Ben's face.

The bell chimed as we entered and a flurry of voices welcomed us. My hands reached for a little girl with ink black hair and emerald green eyes. Her chubby little cheeks glowed red as she nestled herself in my arms. "Why hello, sweet girl. Who are you?"

She giggled, "Auntie!"

"Oh. You must be my little Aine! But how can that be? You were only this big the last time I saw you." She rested on my hip as I made a show of measuring her with my hand. She eyed it knowing what would come next. As I tickled her, her giggles were a soft bell that rang through and lightened the weight of the somber room.

"Aunt Brittany." Claire's voice was horse with tears. Ben reached for me to give him the precious little bundle so Claire could wrap me fully in her arms. She was still the most beautiful thing I had ever seen. But when you come from so much love, it would be hard to be anything less.

"I like your choice of venue." She smelled of vanilla and cedar— just like her mom. I breathed her in slowly as she squeezed harder. A gentle sob caught in her throat.

The sun had just begun to fade through the darkened windows when we finally made our way back out. My eyes stared out across the buildings, both new and old that lined the streets that I would always call home. The top of a bright yellow building touted the words Tom and Thomas Restoration. Music whispered from phones as people past each other on the sidewalks. My chest swelled as I breathed deeply, taking in all the smells that coursed through the air of my once sleepy Sedgemoore. It had been awakened decades ago and life flowed through every part of it.

Unstake My Heart

The smell of a storm clung to the old and new bricks though no clouds hung over head.

The drive through town felt warm and welcoming. The tragedies it had endured did not dim its light and I waved to more than one vampire as we drove along the winding road, the trees zooming by in a blur.

Ben's hand rested on my thigh and my fingers intertwined with his as they had so many times over the decades.

"How are you holding on in there?" He asked.

I tapped on my temple, "I'm fine."

His eyes held mine for a second before going back to the road. "I mean in here." He placed my hand on my heart and covered it with his own.

"I'm going to see my best friend." I smiled. The gravel turned to packed earth as we pulled through the wrought iron arch. The dirt had already been packed down, the black clad mourners long since gone as we approached the bright white stone marker, the date on one side newly carved into its face. A tear rolled down my cheek as I looked at the picture set into the marble. Soryn and Jaxson smiled at each other over the most beautiful baby I had ever seen. I stared out over the familiar but age worn stones around us. My soul felt heavy as I read the names tucked around the grave. Winnie Cordain; Sarah Cordain and so many more whose great bloodline was watched over by my dear friend until she could watch over her own.

"I hope you can rest now, Soryn. Don't worry about your babies." I kissed my fingertips before touching the sun-warmed stone, "I've got them from here."

A soft note of cedar and vanilla whispered past my cheek and as I breathed it in, I smiled, knowing that my friend could finally rest.

AUTHOR'S NOTE

Thank you so much for reading *Unstake My Heart!* I truly hope the story and characters stay with you as they have with me. Leaving the world of Sedgemoore isn't easy and perhaps one day these characters will come to life again.

Until then, my next book will be diving back into the dystopian world of Coranta. So be sure to check out;

Dire Mistakes (Book 1)

Dire Consequences (Book 2)

Dire Fates (Book 3) Summer 2026

If you enjoyed *Unstake My Heart*, I would truly appreciate it if you would consider leaving a review on Amazon or Goodreads. Support from readers means so much and is monumentally important to authors.

If you would like to be in the loop about future books, events, ARCs, or signings, make sure to join my newsletter at SueJamesBooks.com.